Praise for ▼

'A rural story that has ... intrigue, a complex hero⌐ ... ⌐at's not to love?'

—Karl⌐ ⌐ Australian author, on
Clouds on the Horizon

'Encapsulates everything I love about the romance genre and so much more. A go-to author for rural romance for the head as well as the heart ...'

—Joanna Nell, bestselling Australian author

'Penelope Janu's fresh, bright, funny new twist on rural romance is an absolute delight. Her wit is as sharp as a knife. She is one of my absolute must-read authors.'

—Victoria Purman, bestselling author of
The Women's Pages, on *Up on Horseshoe Hill*

'Intriguing characters and a colourful setting: if you like romance and a little mystery, get ready to enjoy this novel.'

—Tricia Stringer, author of *Birds of a Feather*, on
On the Right Track

'Take a break from the news and spend time in Horseshoe Hill. Well written, interesting and filled with heart, *Starting from Scratch* is the perfect weekend read.'

—*Better Reading*

'Oh, how I do love reading a novel by Penelope Janu, it's always an absolute pleasure and I find them hard to put down. *Up on Horseshoe Hill* is no exception, I read until the early hours of the morning and picked it up again as soon as I was awake.'

—*Claire's Reads and Reviews*

'*Up on Horseshoe Hill* is a novel that I would recommend for animal lovers, for rural romance lovers and for those seeking an engaging read.'

—*Great Reads and Tea Leaves*

'Penelope Janu succeeds in delivering fans old and new an engrossing tale. *Up on Horseshoe Hill* is a novel that awakens our sense of hope that love can prevail, even when life deals you with a series of devastating setbacks to overcome.'

—*Mrs B's Book Reviews*

'*On the Right Track* by author Penelope Janu is on my unputdownable, fave reads category. There was humour, tension, chemistry amongst a backdrop of family drama that just keeps the pages turning.'

—*Talking Books Blog*

ABOUT PENELOPE JANU

Penelope Janu lives on the coast in northern Sydney with a distracting husband, a very large dog and, now they're fully grown, six delightful children who come and go. Penelope has a passion for creating stories that explore social and environmental issues, but her novels are fundamentally a celebration of Australian characters and communities. Her first novel, *In at the Deep End*, came out in 2017, followed by *On the Right Track*, *On the Same Page*, *Up on Horseshoe Hill* and *Starting from Scratch*, as well as a novella, *The Six Rules of Christmas*. Penelope enjoys riding horses, exploring the Australian countryside and dreaming up challenging hiking adventures. Nothing makes her happier as a writer than readers falling in love with her clever, complex and adventurous heroines and heroes. She loves to hear from readers, and can be contacted at www.penelopejanu.com.

Also by Penelope Janu

PENELOPE JANU

Clouds on the Horizon

First Published 2022
Second Australian Paperback Edition 2022
ISBN 9781867255932

CLOUDS ON THE HORIZON
© 2022 by Penelope Janu
Australian Copyright 2022
New Zealand Copyright 2022

Published by
HQ Fiction
An imprint of Harlequin Enterprises (Australia) Pty Limited (ABN 47 001 180 918),
a subsidiary of HarperCollins Publishers Australia Pty Limited (ABN 36 009 913 517)
Level 13, 201 Elizabeth St
SYDNEY NSW 2000
AUSTRALIA

A catalogue record for this book is available from the National Library of Australia
www.librariesaustralia.nla.gov.au

MIX
Paper | Supporting
responsible forestry
FSC® C001695

Printed and bound in Australia by McPherson's Printing Group

To Michaela and Max

CHAPTER
1

Stripes of silver hang in the air and rivers of water crisscross the track, but Camelot, black as the clouds, treads confidently over the uneven ground. Leaning forward in the saddle, I stroke his rain-soaked neck. I breathe in eucalyptus and the dampness of the earth.

My face is wet, as is the hair that's come loose from my plait. Between the tops of my knee-high boots and the leg flaps of my oilskin coat, my jodhpurs are sodden. I run a finger inside my collar and re-fasten a press stud, shivering as we skirt around the tree roots. Notwithstanding my gloves, pins and needles prickle my fingers as I clench and unclench my hands. When I push Camelot into a trot, my body warms, but the wind is cold on my cheeks.

Camelot, as happy as a platypus swimming in a stream, breaks into a canter at the top of the rise, and I laugh as I pull him back. 'Not today, boy.'

A rumble of thunder sounds in the distance as we pass Mr Riley's shearing shed and sheep pens. The water tank is shrouded in mist.

When Camelot shies, edging off the path and into the bush, I increase the pressure on my outside leg to bring him back to the track. He complies but tosses his head as I guide him towards the copse of gums and the narrow dirt road that leads to the churchyard and home. He shies again, skittering sideways. I steady him, patting his neck, when he takes a tentative step.

'What's the—'

A long dark shape lies across the track, blocking our path. I kick my feet free from the stirrups and slide to the ground, my heart thumping hard. I bring Camelot's reins over his head and loop them through my arm.

The man lies on his front with an arm thrown out to the side. One of his legs is bent at the knee and the other is straight. His pants are dark; his white shirt sticks to his skin. Kneeling at his side, I touch his shoulder. Even through the rain, my gloves and his shirt, I feel his body stiffen.

He spins and rolls onto his back.

'Oh!' I sit back on my heels.

He's in his late twenties, maybe early thirties. He has a straight nose and a strong jaw. Blood trickles from his temple to his ear. 'Hvem er du?' he whispers.

I lean over him. 'What?'

He's shivering so hard that his whole body trembles. His eyes flutter closed. 'Who are you?'

'Phoebe. Who are you?'

His eyes open again and he blinks as if trying to focus. 'Phoebe Cartwright.'

'How do you know that?'

He lifts an arm and drops it. He shakes his head. With a shuddering exhalation, he passes out.

I pull off my gloves and rest my fingertips against his neck, counting carefully through the fear that tightens my chest. His pulse is faint. Breathing laboured and shallow. Skin cold and pale. Sight, hearing, touch, taste and smell. It's my job to know about the senses, but this is beyond me.

When his eyes spring open, I jump. 'Telefon,' he mutters.

'There's no reception here.'

He's cleanly shaven. His thick, dark hair looks recently cut. He's wearing a business shirt and suit pants. His shoes are city shoes, leather with narrow eyelets and long thin laces. Why is he in the middle of nowhere, alone and icy cold?

How does he know my name?

I touch his cheek and he flinches. 'Who are you?'

He shakes his head. 'No.'

'You've bumped your head. You're freezing. Tell me your name.'

He utters a string of words I don't understand. Danish? Swedish? I *think* it's Scandinavian. Another shudder takes over his body. He stares at me and swallows. 'Get my phone.' He lifts his hand, but just like before it drops back to his side. 'Find it.' His voice disappears but I read his lips. 'Pocket.'

'We have to get out of the rain.' I look towards my home, a kilometre away. And then I look up at my horse. Now that the shape on the path has taken human form, Camelot is curious. When he lowers his head, only half the length of the rein separates us.

I turn to the man again. 'I don't suppose you can ride?'

'Motorsykkel?'

'A thoroughbred.' By the time I indicate Camelot behind me, the man's eyes have drifted closed again.

He shakes his head. 'No.'

'I don't think you could get onto him anyway. Can you stand? Can you walk?'

His eyes open and his brow creases, as if he's considering my questions. And then, as if in slow motion, he rolls onto his front. He moans as he comes up on his hands and knees. He's slender but his shoulders are broad. The muscles on his arms and chest are clearly outlined through his shirt. I'm average in height, but there's no way I could carry him. I don't think I could drag him either.

Mr Riley hasn't sheared in his shed for years, but he keeps winter hay, tools and other paraphernalia here. It's likely to be weather-proof and even if it isn't, it'll be safer than being outside. I put my hand on the man's shoulder.

'There's a shed twenty metres away. We can go there. Other-wise, I'll have to ride home and call an ambulance on the way.'

'Telefon.'

A bolt of lightning splits the sky and thunder breaks it open. 'That settles it.' Getting to my feet, I take hold of the man's arm with both hands and pull as hard as I can. 'You have to help. You have to stand.'

It takes a minute at least for the man to get off the ground. I pull his arm around my shoulders. Even stooped over, he's tall. When Camelot nudges my back with his nose, I stumble.

'Cut it out, boy.'

'Telefon,' the man whispers, as blood drips on his shirt. Another bolt of lightning, closer than the last.

'Why won't you tell me your name?'

'Nei.'

I don't know what he's up to or where he's from, but he's far too weak to cause trouble. I adjust his arm over my shoulder. 'Let's get out of the storm.'

When I take a step, the man stays rooted to the spot. He holds out a hand and Camelot sniffs it.

'Vakker hest.'

He speaks nicely enough, but I have no idea what his words mean. When he sways towards Camelot, I pull his arm more tightly around my shoulders.

'You have to walk.'

Leaning so heavily on me that I'm forced to brace my legs to stay upright, the man takes slow, leaden steps to the shed. Camelot, his footfalls soft on the rain-soaked track, walks patiently behind us.

The shed isn't locked, but the bolt is stiff and I can't work it while supporting the man. I balance him against a wall. 'I won't be long.'

A moment after I release him, his knees buckle. I shove my shoulder against his chest to support him as he slides to the ground and slumps against the wall, his head tipped onto his chest. Another flash of lightning illuminates the bolt, but even two-handed I can't pull it back, so I rifle through the grass and find a brick. I whack the curved end of the bolt until it slides clear of the barrel. I pull against the doors and they swing outwards. The shed smells of hay, wool and dust and it's even gloomier in here than it was outside. Camelot baulks at the doors, but after I double back and pat his rump firmly, he walks tentatively over the threshold. When I loop his rein through a sheep pen on the far side of the shed, he stares back with big black eyes.

By the time I return to the man, he's facing the wall, pressing both hands against it as he works his way up. He leans on me as we inch towards the shed, but when we get to the doors, he reaches out and grasps the frame. He looks inside. Sways.

'Nei.'

'Yes!'

When I push him through the doors, he staggers towards a stack of hay bales, dropping to his knees just before we get to it. The doors crash shut, plunging us into darkness.

A whimper works its way up my throat.

I swallow compulsively, stilling the memories, the old, relentless fears.

'It's not locked,' I say aloud, my voice thin and high.

My eyes adjust. The windowpanes are filthy but rain streaked. I can see the outlines of gum trees through the glass. Light filters through the six half-doors behind the shearing platform. Shearers would have pushed freshly shorn sheep through the doors to scramble down the ramps and quiver in the pens.

I can breathe.

Camelot's bit jangles. When he shifts a leg, his shoe scrapes the concrete. I make out a stirrup iron, glistening dully in the darkness. Another gust of wind rattles the doors on their hinges.

I can get out.

I step carefully to the doors and push them open, ignoring the gusts of icy wind and rain as I kick the half-brick under one of the doors, creating a wedge. By the time I get back to the man, he's flat on the concrete. Concussion? Hypothermia? Either way, he has to warm up. Dragging six bales of hay off the stack, I lay them out like a bed.

'Can you get up there?'

He doesn't have the strength to stand, but I yank until he kneels and, pushing and shoving, roll him onto the bales. He lies on his back, groans and loses consciousness again. My hair sticks to my face. Rain or sweat? When I feel for his pulse, even weaker than it was before, I see a card through the pocket of his shirt and slide it out. The cardboard is wet through but the words, black on white, are clear enough.

United Nations First Committee
(Disarmament and International Security)
Sindre Tørrissen

He doesn't have a title, but the string of initials next to his name suggests scientific qualifications. There's a UN email address and two telephone numbers.

'Sindre?'

His eyes briefly flicker open. 'Sinn.'

Whoever he is and wherever he's from, he won't warm up if he's wearing wet clothes. My fingers are stiff and clumsy as I pull his shirt free of his pants. After I fumble over the top two buttons of his shirt, I grasp the front panels to rip the remaining buttons through the holes.

'Sorry about that.' I undo his cuffs before rolling him onto his side to pull off the shirt, then push him onto his back again. Thunder rattles the roof and lightning brightens the shed. His chest is firm, his abdominal muscles clearly defined.

When I exhale, my breath is white. 'Your pants are wet too.'

I peel off his socks and tug at his shoes. I undo his belt buckle and button, and unzip his fly, exposing his underpants. 'I'm not looking. I promise. And those can stay on.'

I focus on the hay as I pull off his pants, dropping them onto the pile with his other wet clothes.

Opening the press studs of my oilskin, I shake off the worst of the moisture. I pull the man onto his side, spread the coat out behind him and, brushing off the hay that's stuck to his skin, roll him onto the coat. I draw the thick cotton lining around his body. The coat covers most of his legs and torso, but isn't wide enough to wrap around his chest, so I take off my sweater and smooth the wool, warm from my body, from his waist up to his neck. I gather the coat around his sides. A drip from his hair rolls down his cheek, joining a trail of blood trickling across his throat.

Taking off my T-shirt, I fold it in half and rub his hair, shivering when drips fall from the end of my plait and down my spine. He blinks.

'Du er vakker.'

'I can't understand you,' I say as I hastily pull my T-shirt back over my head. The fabric is damp. I shiver again and rub my arms. 'I'll see what else I can find.'

Camelot's saddle blanket is warm and mostly dry. I remove his saddle and rest it over a railing before wrapping the padded rectangle around the man's feet, tucking it under his heels to secure it. I frantically search the perimeter of the shed before finding a stack of hessian sacks on the shearing platform. They're clean and thick, rough against the insides of my arms when I pick them up. I shake them out and layer them on top of the man, then I free the cape of the oilskin from under his shoulders, lift his head and lay a folded sack beneath it, positioning it like a pillow.

He's trussed up like a mummy, but he'll be warmer. So why, all of a sudden, is he so frighteningly still? Shivering is the first stage of hypothermia. After that, the body preserves energy for the vital organs—the lungs, heart, brain and kidneys. I burrow through the sacks and coat and touch his side. His skin is as cold as marble. I search for the pulse at his throat but can't find it.

'Please don't—'

Feathery beats. One. Two. Three. Four.

I take a shaky breath. 'Thank you.'

I feel down his side again. He's dry now. Any heat he produces, he should keep.

When his head jerks towards me, I jump. He murmurs something unintelligible and I put my hand on his cheek. I push back his hair. 'Sinn?'

'Ja.'

'Are you Swedish?'

'Norge.'

'Norway?'

He swallows. 'Telefon.'

I pick up my phone from a hay bale and hold it out. 'I've already told you. No reception. That's why I have to ride home.'

He grasps my hand. 'Satellitt.'

'I think you have hypothermia. If you warm up too quickly or move around, you could go into cardiac arrest. I should get a signal around five minutes from here, and I'll call an ambulance. It'll take an hour for it to get here from the hospital, but Camelot and I will race home. I'll get my car and come back with blankets and something warm to drink. You can't move while I'm gone. Do you understand?'

'Satellitt.'

'There are no doctors in Warrandale, so the ambulance will be the quickest way for you to get help. I'll be back in thirty minutes, maybe less.'

I try to prise my fingers free, but he holds on. He opens his mouth and shuts it again. Besides 'telefon', I haven't understood much of what he's said since I brought him into the shed. I put my other hand over his.

'You have to let me go.'

He shakes his head. 'Nei.'

I pull my hand free. 'I'll be back as soon as I can. Don't move. Please.'

'I have ...' His brow furrows as he whispers the words. I bend closer to listen. 'I have a satellite phone.' His dark gaze focuses on my face. He swallows. 'I have reception.'

When he does speak in English, he barely has an accent.

I use the torch on my phone to find his clothes and lift them to the hay bales before feeling the weight and shape of his phone through his shirt. The phone is zipped in a pocket that must have sat at his hip. It's not chunky like the satellite phones I'm familiar with, but black and slender like a regular phone.

The hessian sacks lift as he raises his hand. 'Here.'

When I give him the phone, he holds it up. It glows, highlighting his features. His face is attractive. Exceptionally attractive.

He doesn't dial or do anything else. I don't know that he'd be capable of it. His hand drops heavily to his chest and he closes his eyes.

'De vil komme,' he whispers.

I roll his shirt into a ball and press it against the gash on his head. 'I don't understand.'

He mutters. 'They will come.'

I didn't hear anyone on the other end of the phone, so how does he know that they'll come? Who is 'they'?

When his eyes close, the phone slips from his fingers. I make sure my sweater covers his chest, wrap the oilskin up and over his sides again, and secure the hessian sacks. I press the edges of the cape around his ears and brush back his hair.

'I wish you'd stop moving around.' I lean a hip against the hay bales as I pick up his phone and push the buttons at the side.

'Phoebe.' He croaks my name. When I look down, it's straight into his eyes. A shudder passes through him. 'Leave it.'

I put the phone back on his chest. 'I can't get anything on the screen anyway.'

He frowns as if he's lost his train of thought. 'Go home.'

'Leave you here? After I've gone to all this trouble? You said they were coming. Will there be a doctor?'

'Forget this.'

Camelot's shoes scrape on the concrete when he pivots and faces the rear of the shed. I run to him, afraid he'll pull back, dislodge the pen and panic. I put my hand on his neck, quivering with tension. 'Easy, boy,' I say as I untie him. 'What's the matter?'

Rain pounds on the roof and the wind howls through the trees. But there's another sound as well. At first it's a whir. Then it's a roar. The incessant thump of helicopter blades directly above us.

I tighten my grip on the rein and lead Camelot, toey but compliant, to the hay. *They will come.* Who are they? Who is he?

'Sinn?'

He opens his mouth before closing it again.

'That is your name, isn't it? Sinn Tørrissen. You work for the UN.'

Silence.

'You know my name. Why can't I know yours?'

He shakes his head. 'No.'

The helicopter isn't overhead any more, but it's still very loud. Mr Riley grows corn and canola crops on cleared land to the west of the shed. A helicopter could easily land there.

I touch Sinn's arm. 'Has the helicopter come for you? Should I go outside and tell them that you're here?'

He's shivering again. He attempts to roll onto his side, but when I put a hand on his shoulder and gently push, he collapses onto his back. I lean over him, securing the hessian beneath his arms.

'You have to stay still.'

When another shiver passes through him, he clenches his teeth. They're even whiter than his face, and perfectly straight. I press the backs of my fingers to the skin at his neck. He swallows and shudders again. But I'm certain he's warmer than he was. I rewrap his feet with the saddle blanket.

'Do you come from Norway? That's what you said before.'

'Gå hjem.'

'I don't understand.'

His eyes are brighter than they were. 'Go home.'

The doors open wide and I jump. Squinting, I try to look past the broad shaft of light that spills into the shed. Camelot skitters, his reins rushing through my fingers. One of the men standing on the threshold is extremely broad-shouldered and dressed in city clothes. The other man has brutally short hair and is wearing grey fatigues. He has embroidered patches on his arms and a badge on his chest. When he shines the light into the shed again, I turn away and hold a hand above my eyes.

'Who are you?' My voice isn't as steady as I'd like it to be.

'Lower the torch.' A woman's voice. Dressed in black and carrying a bag, she says something else to the men before pushing past them and striding confidently towards me. Her hair is short and fiery red and her face is peppered with freckles. 'Sorry that took a while.'

I stand between her and Sinn. 'Who are you?'

'I'm not here.' She smiles and holds out her hand. 'Who are you?'

My hand lifts automatically. 'Phoebe.' We shake briefly. 'What do you mean—'

She jerks her head towards the men. 'Politics.'

Sinn's eyes are closed; he's deathly white.

'Are you a doctor?'

'I'll check him out and then we'll get him to one.'

I step aside but stay close to Sinn as she drops the bag at her feet and pulls out a stethoscope, blood pressure equipment and a lunch box–sized container that rattles as she puts it on the hay bales. She pulls on gloves and pushes aside the hessian to take Sinn's hand and feel for his pulse. When she addresses him, she tips her head to the side.

'This'll teach you to jump from a moving van.'

He grunts before looking from the woman to me. 'No names.'

'I got the directive,' she says, listening to Sinn's heart before pressing both hands down his arms, torso and legs. She moves the shirt from his head and touches the cut before lifting his eyelids and shining a torch into each of his eyes. She places a thermometer into his ear.

'He slips in and out of consciousness,' I tell her. His head is bleeding again so I press his shirt against the cut. 'He can walk and doesn't seem to be in too much pain, so I guess no broken bones. He was freezing. I took off his clothes to warm him. I think he's better than he was, but he could have concussion. You'll take him to hospital, won't you?'

'We'll do what needs to be done.' The woman squints at the thermometer. 'Thirty-five point six. Could be worse.'

The broad-shouldered man walks towards us, looking cautiously at Camelot as he skirts around him. 'Okay to butt in here?' he says in an American accent, smiling as he runs a hand through his dark blond hair. He'd be in his early thirties.

'Looks to be a superficial head wound,' the woman says, 'but I'll sort out a scan just in case.'

'I found him on the track,' I say. 'He wasn't making much sense.'

'Being cold and wet in freezing temperatures will do that to you,' she says. 'You did a great job with him.'

'Did he really jump from a van?'

She glances at the broad-shouldered man. 'Eight hours ago.'

The man, still keeping well clear of Camelot, stands at Sinn's head and squeezes his shoulder. 'Hey, buddy. You gave us a hell of a fright back there.'

Sinn swallows. 'They didn't see me.'

The man and woman wrap a large silver blanket around Sinn. By the time they've finished, his eyes are closed. His breathing is deep.

'Is he going to be okay?' I ask.

A sleeve of my sweater peeps out from the top of the blanket. The woman moves it aside to check the pulse at Sinn's neck before tucking it in again. She smiles reassuringly. 'All good. Exhausted, that's all.'

The man at the door calls out. 'Stretcher is on its way, lieutenant.'

As he brushes hay from my oilskin, the broad-shouldered man considers my T-shirt and jodhpurs.

'You must be cold yourself.'

I reach for my coat. 'Yes.'

He smiles. 'Thanks for your help. Really appreciate it, but ...'

'You weren't here, right?' I shrug into the coat and fasten all the press studs. 'I can't know your names and I get no explanation.'

He smiles apologetically. 'You got it.'

I lay the saddle blanket over Camelot's back before turning to the woman. 'You were addressed as lieutenant. Are you in the navy?'

The woman and man exchange looks. 'No comment,' she says.

'My sister Patience is in the navy. She wears the same camouflage as the sergeant over there.'

'Is that right?'

'Are you in charge?'

She grimaces as she glances first at Sinn, still asleep, and then at his colleague. 'Not the boss of these two, that's for sure.'

'Sinn's with the UN, isn't he?'

The other man attempts to hide a frown. 'Did he tell you that?'

When Sinn mumbles, I put my hand on his arm. His lashes, inky-black crescents on his cheeks, open for an instant before they drift closed. He probably has a family that cares about him. A wife or partner. What if he'd died so far from home? Repressing a shiver, I bunch my hands into fists and put them into my pockets. I stamp my feet, suddenly frozen.

'I offered to call for help, but he only wanted you. Why was that? Why so secretive? Why can't I talk? What is he hiding?'

The woman's face is expressionless as she peers closely at the bruise on Sinn's forehead. The hair at his temple is thickened with blood.

'Take it from me,' she says, 'you can trust him. He'll be grateful for your help.'

'What was he doing all the way out here? How did he know my name?'

The American's brows lift. 'What *is* your name?'

'Phoebe Cartwright.'

He whistles a breath. 'Is that right?'

'Have you heard of me too?'

'Can't really say.'

I pull Sinn's card from my pocket. 'Are you from the UN like him?'

The man plucks the card out of my hand. 'Where did you get this?'

'Besides his phone, it's all he had on him.'

'We'd really appreciate your cooperation with keeping a lid on this.' The man's smile is strained.

'Because you've finished here? I won't see you again?'

'Say nothing, Phoebe.' The man looks at Sinn, still asleep. 'When he's back on his feet, he'll be in touch.'

CHAPTER
2

My home was once a very small church, built on the outskirts of
the country town of Warrandale. Three liquidambar trees gather
in the middle of a circular driveway. Even in winter, when five-
pointed leaves carpet the ground, the trees hide the church from
the road. Two years ago, when the bank lent me more money, I
had local carpenters build an L-shaped extension at the rear of
the church: two small bedrooms, a kitchen and bathroom. The
addition has the same slate roof as the church. A verandah, added
on last year, overlooks three hectares of gardens, a paddock, two
stables and a yard. Crown land, dense with tall eucalypts, forms
a backdrop. Mr Riley's hundreds of hectares of farmland are just
across the road. As I sit at the table in the living room, com-
prising most of the original church, sunlight filters through the
stained glass windows, casting gold and pink smudges on the
floorboards.

Four days have passed since I found Sinn Tørrissen. *When he's
back on his feet, we'll be in touch.*

Sinn was conscious when the man in fatigues and another navy man lifted him onto the stretcher. After I'd saddled Camelot, we followed them out of the shed and I bolted the doors behind me. By the time I'd tightened Camelot's girth, put my foot in the stirrup and pulled myself into the saddle, the men had carried the stretcher through the gate. The helicopter squatted near the dam on the far side of the paddock.

I told Sinn I didn't like secrets.

Phoebe, Patience and Prim. Sisters with too many secrets.

When I googled Sinn, I found a reference to him and the UN committee listed on his card. There was only one image, taken two years ago. The man in the photo was dressed in a black Norwegian naval uniform and his cap was low over his eyes, but I'm certain it was Sinn. Why would he—

My heart skips a beat when the gravel on the driveway crunches under the wheels of a car. Tidying my hair, I walk to the window. Matilda, five years old with pigtails jumping, hops along the gravel to the path. I smile as I turn to my border collie Wickham, curled up in his bed in front of the heater. His tail thumps a beat against the zebra-striped cushion that matches his colouring.

'Brace yourself, boy.'

Matilda shouts, 'Phoebe! I'm here!' as I walk to the door. By the time I reach the porch, she's skipping through the garden towards the stables.

Jane, Matilda's mother, is in her mid-thirties and teaches yoga and pilates. Her leggings have see-through panels and are blue and white like her runners. 'Matilda is obsessed with Mintie,' she says as she zips her puffy jacket.

'I introduced them in her last session. She didn't touch him, but she came close.'

Matilda's arms are wrapped closely around her body as she peers at the horses. Mintie, a dappled grey Welsh Mountain pony with a forelock that falls almost to the end of his nose, shares a stable yard with Camelot. 'One horse, two horse.' Matilda nods as she counts.

'Excellent counting,' I say, 'and the horses are happy to see you. But would you like to come inside now?' I hold out an arm without touching her. 'It's very cold this morning.'

'She's had a good week,' Jane says quietly, as we follow Matilda, who's running up the path. 'I did as you suggested and bought the school clothes she's most likely to tolerate. I ordered the same styles in larger sizes as well.'

'Not having to get used to a uniform means she's got one less thing to worry about.'

Matilda doesn't process sensory information—touch, smell, sound, taste and sight—in the way that most people do. Her particular sensitivity is with touch. She's starting school next year, so I'm working with her family to get her used to behaviours like sitting on a carpeted floor with others around her, turning the pages of a book, cutting and pasting, and wearing different clothing than she's used to. Matilda is intelligent and friendly, but if she doesn't master these everyday things, she might be anxious and unhappy when she starts school, or she could fall behind in her schoolwork.

When I open the door, she runs past me and into the living area.

'Matilda!' Jane rolls her eyes. 'Sorry, Phoebe.'

I smile. 'Remember when she wouldn't let you out of her sight? I'll see you in an hour.'

I flick on lights and turn up the oil heater as Matilda sits on the floor a few metres away from Wickham. I often work outdoors with the children, or on the verandah, but in the colder months the church serves as my workspace as well as my living room. The ceilings are high and there's no insulation, so it's difficult to keep in the heat.

'Are you warm enough, Matilda?'

'Wickham is very warm.'

I laugh. 'Border collie dogs have very thick coats, don't they?'

Wickham's tail thumps steadily as he and Matilda stare at each other. I crouch on the floor between them and hold out a hand. 'Would you like to pat him, Matilda?'

She jumps to her feet and rubs her hands up and down her sparkly blue jeans. 'No! No touching!'

'I'd never make you do something you didn't choose to do. But look at Wickham's face. I think he *wants* you to pat him. Maybe you could sit down, and explain to him how you're feeling?'

She rubs her hands on her jeans again, but then she sits. 'I don't like it.'

'You don't like Wickham?'

'I like Wickham!'

'What don't you like, then?'

'I don't like his fuzzy hair.'

I nod. 'You don't like his fur. So you could say something like, "I think you're the best, cleverest and most handsome dog in the world, Wickham, but I don't want to touch your fur today."'

She grins. 'Yes.'

'Wickham might not understand exactly what you mean, but he'll know by your friendly voice that you like him. You can tell the girls in your ballet class how you're feeling in just the same way. "I want to be your friend, but I don't want you to put your arm around me, or hold my hand."'

When I turn to Wickham, he holds out a paw and I stroke his chest. 'I think your doll Elsa's hair is even longer than Wickham's fur.'

She touches her pigtail. 'I want *very* long hair like you.'

I smile. 'I'm happy you like my hair, Matilda. Now,' I point to the table and chairs, 'let's do some activities.'

'Not sticky glue!'

I shake my head. 'I have a special glue stick. Let's give that a go.'

Matilda finds it difficult to adapt to incoming sensations because she's hypersensitive, or oversensitive, to touch. She has a loving and supportive family, but when she grows up, avoiding things like public transport, shopping centres and crowded workspaces will limit what she can achieve. By practising these skills she'll gain confidence and her life will be fuller, notwithstanding her sensory preferences and aversions.

'Are you hungry, Matilda?' Even the sensation of food in her mouth can be difficult, so we sometimes eat together. 'I have soft bread and your favourite honey. We can have morning tea later on.'

'I don't like strawberry jam. It's got lumps.'

'I like crunchy food. I think I'll have an apple with crackers.'

By the time Jane collects Matilda, she's made a collage, eaten morning tea relatively calmly and washed her hands, and handed me carrots that I've fed to the horses.

'Homework?' Jane asks, as Matilda skips to the car.

'She did really well with the glue stick, so keep working on craft activities. Try gluing different-textured items, such as paper, fabric, buttons and leaves.'

'The tantrums at bath time are less extreme than they were. I let her select the towel that she wants like you suggested.'

'If articulating what she wants, rather than screaming, will be more successful for her, she'll do it more often.'

When Matilda reaches the car, I whistle for Wickham. In a flash he's by my side. 'Matilda!' I call. 'Wickham has come to say goodbye.'

A few months ago, Matilda would yell at the thought that Wickham might touch her. Now she tolerates him well. She presses her mouth against the palm of her hand and blows a kiss.

'I'm so proud of you, Matilda,' I say. 'What a lovely way to say goodbye to Wickham.'

Jane laughs. 'Can we try that with Great Uncle Ray?'

'Encourage Matilda to tell him that she doesn't want to hug him, but she'd be happy to greet him in a different way. Develop a special wave, or a compromise she's comfortable with.'

After Jane straps Matilda into her car seat and shuts the door, she turns back to me and hugs me tightly.

'Thank you, Phoebe.'

'She's doing really well.'

'I know, but …' Jane's eyes fill with tears. 'When people look at her like she's a spoilt brat—or worse—it breaks my heart.'

'Instead of judging, they should look at what Matilda's behaviour is telling them, and adapt to it accordingly. Children are often more accepting and flexible than adults.'

'You've made such a difference.'

'I love working with Matilda. I always look forward to seeing her.'

'You looked after your younger sisters, didn't you?'

'We looked out for each other.'

Jane glances at her daughter, sitting in her car seat and playing with her doll. 'I'm quite a few years older than you, but I remember when all of you holidayed in Warrandale.'

'It was good of Auntie Kate and Uncle Bob to put up with us.'

'You Cartwright girls were inseparable.'

I grimace. 'You must have thought we were odd.'

'We were fascinated by how close you were.' She smiles. 'And how pretty. Jeremiah followed you around like a puppy, remember that?'

I laugh. 'He's broken a lot of hearts since!'

As Jane's car turns out of the driveway, my next client arrives, and after that appointment I see three more children. It's almost five before Wickham and I walk towards the stables, via the grave-yard that came with the church. There are eight graves, four with upright sandstone headstones, two with headstones that've fallen on the ground, one with a timber cross, and one with a granite slab that lies lengthwise over the grave. A wrought iron fence surrounds the graves. Not long after I bought the church, Mike Williams, Warrandale's farrier and blacksmith, offered to repair and rehang the gate, but I told him I'd prefer to keep it off.

He laughed. 'You reckon the residents might want to leave?'

'No one likes to be shut in.'

The grave with the cross is one of the earliest. Originally it would have been painted white; now it's bleached white by the sun. The inscription, engraved on a small brass plate, is weatherworn and faint: *Anna Amelia Andrews. 22 December 1908 – 10 January 1909.*

I angle my arm to fit through the fence and pull out a weed. 'Hello, sweet baby,' I whisper.

The largest grave belongs to Warrandale's first vicar. His granite blanket is dark in the rain, but sparkles with quartz when the weather is fine.

The Reverend Samuel Brockman, husband of Mary Elizabeth Brockman and father of John, Robert and Alfred. 22 June 1881 – 2 November 1915.

I pull another weed from the vicar's grave. 'How's your flock doing today?'

By the time I reach the stables, the drops of rain are heavier. Mintie is anxious to follow me under cover, but Camelot seems keen to remind me he hasn't been out today. I'm doing my best to work around the horses when my phone, sitting on a barrel of feed, starts to ring.

I don't recognise the number. 'Phoebe Cartwright.'

'Sinn Tørrissen.' His voice is as deep as I remember it, but sharper, more assured.

'I'm allowed to know your name now?'

'We have to talk.'

The wind rattles the rafters and Camelot spooks, skittering away from the door and forcing me against the wall. I grasp his halter and push him back, clipping on a lead rope and tying him to the piece of string that hangs in the corner of the stable near the trough. Raindrops pelt on the roof.

'Phoebe?'

'I heard you.' Wickham jumps over the half-door and, tongue lolling, sits at my feet. 'Why do we have to talk?'

'Are you at home? I can be there in an hour.'

'How do you know where I live?'

'Can I come?'

When I laid him on the bales of hay and stripped off his clothes, his eyes were closed. His pulse was weak. His skin was white and cold. Do I want to see him again? Do I have a choice?

I run my fingers through the water trough to check the level. 'I'll be here.'

CHAPTER
3

After Sinn's call, I shower and change, then sit in front of the heater. Puzzles, books and cards form a messy semicircle around Wickham and me as I plan tomorrow's sessions. But when I re-read my notes, they barely make sense. What are the objectives? What are the outcomes? I close the notebook with a snap.

Headlights sweep into the driveway. An engine cuts out. A door slams. I can't see Sinn from here, but I hear his footsteps as he treads lightly up the stairs to the porch. Three seconds of silence. His knuckles rap on the ironbark door.

Running my fingers through my hair, I walk across the living room. Last month I turned twenty-eight, but I've always looked young for my age. I should have pulled my hair back into a bun or a braid or—

After Mum had the stroke, my sisters and I would catch a bus to the hospital's repatriation unit, and I'd kneel with my back to Mum so she could brush my hair. Even Patience, who was always so active, would sit still and watch. Mum couldn't braid my hair any more, but she'd tell me what styles she liked best. Sometimes, when she'd forgotten I was going on thirteen and too old to wear plaits, she'd ask for them.

At the door, I wipe my hands down my pale blue jeans. The wool of my socks is cream and fluffy like a newly shorn sheep. I reposition the V-neck of my faded pink sweater, push back my shoulders and open the door.

Even in the shed, I was acutely aware of his physical appearance. Long legs, flat stomach, broad shoulders, strong jaw and high cheekbones. There are new things as well. He has good skin. His mouth is well shaped. His eyes are grey. He's wearing black jeans, a thin steel-coloured sweater and a white-collared shirt. His boots are the kind of boots that visitors wear for a weekend in the country.

'Sinn.'

He holds out his hand. 'Phoebe.'

The press of his palm is cold against mine. But not icy cold or dangerously cold or frighteningly cold.

I nod stiffly as I step back against the wall. 'Come in.'

He looks around as we walk into the living area, too long and narrow to furnish conventionally. I should probably create specific 'spaces' for work, dining and reading. As it is, I rely on eclectic furniture from secondhand stores. An old-fashioned chintz-patterned couch sits under one of the stained glass windows, armchairs either side of it. The dining table and chairs are near the kitchen. The oil heater is up that end too.

When Wickham looks up from his bed and wags his tail, Sinn crouches and scratches under his chin. He smiles, a flash of white teeth. 'Not a guard dog?'

'He's inclined to like just about everybody.'

Sinn glances at the heater before pulling his jumper over his head and draping it over the arm of the couch. He folds up his sleeves, creating creases that stop short of his elbows. The skin below his neck is tanned. He tucks in his shirt where it's loose at his hip.

The hip where he hides his satellite phone. The phone that summoned a helicopter.

I've been anticipating his arrival. So why is my breathing so fast? I close my eyes in an attempt to think calmly and rationally, to slow my racing heartbeat. But all I can see is an image of him lying cold and unconscious, wet and alone. My chest constricts and an ache works its way through my lungs to my throat. When I draw a breath, the sound that escapes is a squeak.

It's no wonder that Wickham sits on my feet, looking up in concern. I run a hand over his head before I half-walk, half-run to the kitchen. When I open the door to the verandah, a blast of damp air stings my face.

'Do you want to stretch your legs, Wickham?' I force out the words.

He looks up at me questioningly.

'Go, boy, check on the horses.'

He disappears in a blur of black and white, but I continue to stare, pretending there's something to see as I push back inexplicable tears.

Hearing Sinn behind me, I stiffen. Hiccough. Feel one fat, foolish tear and then another roll down my cheek. I swipe an arm across my face.

He leans over my shoulder to pull the door closed. 'Phoebe?' he says. 'Are you all right?'

In my dreams, I've walked through a brightly lit shed wheeling a drip. I've patched a hole in the sky, hung shirts out to dry, smoothed stark linen sheets on a hay bale bed. I've dreamt he was on a track with his hand encased in ice and I couldn't get a needle through his skin. I put my hands to my throat to keep down a sob.

'Phoebe?'

When I spin around, my hands, curled into fists, brush against his chest. He catches them to steady me. He frowns as he searches my face.

Are his eyes grey? Or blue? Greyish blue. Blueish grey. Dark and light. Light and dark.

When I tug at my hands, he releases them instantly. I walk back to the living room, plucking tissues from the box that I keep on the sideboard for the children.

'Why are you upset?' he asks.

'Why were you out in the storm? Who were those people?'

'I was delayed. When Nathan Gillespie, the American, lost my signal, he got others involved.'

'Why wouldn't you let me call for help?'

'It wasn't necessary.'

'Even though you could have died. What family do you have? Do you have a partner?'

'Parents.' He shrugs. 'A brother, aunts, uncles, cousins. No partner.'

'Did you tell your family what happened?'

'No.'

'I couldn't find your pulse.' I link my hands, unlink them. 'It scared me.'

He pulls his collar aside. 'I have a pulse now.'

'Let me see.' The words, and my hand, hang in the air between us.

He frowns. He opens his mouth and shuts it. He stiffly nods.

His skin warms my fingertips. *One. Two. Three. Four.* 'You were bleeding.'

'A graze.' His jaw is tight.

'Were you concussed?'

'No.' He looks straight ahead. 'Anything else?'

I drag my eyes from his mouth and drop my hand. But then, ignoring the tension in his body, I grasp his hand. His fingers are long; his nails are short and neatly clipped. When I place my fingers on his wrist, his pulse beats strongly. I count again. The numbers mean nothing, but I can't let go.

'Phoebe?' My name sounds different on his lips. 'We have to talk.'

I lift my face. 'What about?'

He mutters something under his breath. And then he pulls back. He blinks and curses. He strides across the room and stands at the window, his hands thrust deep into his pockets.

Did I offend him? I kneel and collect my materials, still in front of the heater. When I put them on the table, the cards spill out of their box and I sort them back into order. I line up the edges of the workbooks and stack them. I reassemble the puzzles, smooth down my sweater and square my shoulders.

He has a crease between his brows. Does he think I might touch him again? Or cry? Should I tell him I don't cry?

I don't cry often.

The backs of my thighs press hard against the table. His frown deepens. His gaze travels over my face. 'Phoebe? Can we talk?'

One of my feet is on top of the other because my toes are cold. When I wrap my arms around my middle, he looks towards the kitchen. He has a long stride but a graceful one. Once he's closed the door, he faces me again. His expression is even grimmer than it was. He glances at my mouth.

'Are you all right?'

It's the second time he's asked me that. I lift my chin. 'Even before I found you, you knew my name. Tell me why.'

'Can we sit?'

I don't want to sit with him on the couch, so I lift the square-backed redwood chair from its spot at the head of the dining table. He steps forward.

'I can manage, thank you.'

He waits for me to sit first. The cushions on the couch sag under his weight, so we're much the same height.

'I knew your name,' he says. 'I also know about your family. Can I confirm details?'

'Why do you ...' I sit straighter. 'Go on.'

'Your sister Patience is twenty-six and an officer in the navy. Primrose is twenty-three and studying veterinary science. You were born in Dubbo and lived there until, six years ago, you moved to Warrandale. You're a paediatric occupational therapist.'

'Why would you want to know all that?'

'I'll explain later.'

I cross my arms. 'Where do you live?'

He hesitates. 'I'm based in Norway.'

'What do you do?'

'I'm a naval officer.'

Posture. Confidence. Physique. 'This is a long way from the sea.'

'I'm on secondment to a UN committee.'

'That's what was on your card, but your role wasn't specified. What do you do there?'

'The committee's focus is transnational security—ammunition and drug trading, money laundering, people smuggling.' The grandfather clock strikes seven times. 'There are associated committees and sub-committees. Members are from Europe, Asia, the Middle East, North and South America.'

'Right.'

'In the navy, I'm a commander.'

'Are you in charge of a ship?'

'Not generally.' The hint of a smile. 'My expertise is ocean currents, meteorology, climate variations.' He shrugs. 'Radars, global positioning systems, satellites.'

'Why did you go on secondment?'

'The committee needed a European from a military background.' He stretches out his legs. 'I trained in military intelligence. I have expertise in IT and weaponry. I expressed an interest.'

'What's your role?'

'Criminal activities cross borders. They can be tracked through information and other systems. Most of the time, I sit at a desk.'

'You weren't doing that when I found you.'

He hesitates. 'I have an investigative role, not a policing one. I was following a lead.'

'You still haven't explained why you're here.'

'What do you know of horseracing?'

I sit further back in my chair. 'I own an ex-racehorse.'

'What do you know of betting syndicates?'

'Nothing.'

'That's untrue, Phoebe.'

'If that's your view, why ask the question?'

'Answer it.'

'That night you were sick. You didn't want me to know who you were, or that you knew of me. Why was that?'

'I saw your father yesterday. You hadn't told him you'd found me.'

'What do you want from him?'

'Information on a racing syndicate. Were you aware of your father's association with one?'

I cross my legs at the ankles. Uncross them. 'I knew he did some work for a syndicate.'

'He managed a syndicate set up by Martin Roxburgh. Do you know him?'

'He owns a thoroughbred stud and training facility in Denman.' Sinn's gaze goes to my hands, pressed between my knees. 'I have nothing to do with Martin. I have little to do with my father. My sisters have less.'

'Why is that?'

I jump to my feet. 'I have an early start tomorrow.'

'It's Saturday.'

'I see clients in the morning.'

'Your father was a well-regarded mathematician and academic. Why would he take on management tasks for a racing syndicate?'

'He doesn't do it any more, does he?'

'It was wound up years ago. I asked why he did the work.'

'He needed the money.' I clear my throat. 'Did you get any sense out of him?'

'Very little.'

'If he has done something wrong, I don't know anything about it.'

'Why assume he's done something wrong?'

'Your questions—you talked about illegal activities.'

'You lived with him until six years ago. Your sisters lived there too.'

'Patience left at nineteen. Prim and I left after Prim had finished school.'

'The professor resigned from the university over fifteen years ago.'

'When my mother had a stroke.'

'How did he support the family?'

'Savings.'

'He had none. And when your mother returned to New Zealand, she took all her money.'

'She needed it!' I lower my voice. 'Her sister and brother-in-law, they care for her there. They run the dairy farm she grew up on. She has another sister close by. She's happy.'

He nods. 'How often do you see—'

'You said the committee doesn't have a policing role.'

'We investigate and advise,' he says. 'National police forces and INTERPOL deal with enforcement.'

'You sound like a police officer.'

'I don't want you to be involved.'

'I'm not!'

'Convince me of that.'

The clock strikes the quarter hour. 'After he left the university …' I attempt to speak slowly and clearly, like I don't feel sick and my heart isn't racing. 'I knew my father worked for a syndicate, he did the accounting work, book work, things like that, but he didn't like to talk about it.'

'I've been told he had assistance with his work.'

I stand and, spinning on my heel, walk through the living room to the front door. Cursing quietly, he has no option but to follow. When I whistle into the glow thrown by the porch light, I imagine Wickham, bounding down the back steps and racing past the graveyard. Within seconds he's on the porch and running circles. As I step over the threshold, he sits and lifts a paw.

'Get your towel, boy. Towel.'

He doesn't hesitate, jumping onto the bench and tugging the towel free from a hook on the wall. When he brings it to me, I rub it over his legs, stomach and tail. By the time I straighten, Sinn is spiking his fingers through his hair, pushing it back.

'Your father is unwell,' he says.

'Physically and mentally.' I walk down the steps to the garden. 'I'm surprised he opened the door to you. He's paranoid, he has dementia.'

When he holds out his hand, I take it. We shake briefly—a fleeting press of palms. A rumble of thunder sounds in the distance. High thick clouds hide the moon and stars.

'When can I see you again?' he asks.

'I don't see why you'd need to.'

'When?'

'Do you have far to drive?'

'I'm renting a house in Denman. It's an hour away.'

'You'd better get back before it rains.'

'It won't.'

'How do you know?'

He stands close to my side as he points to the clouds, pale against the darkness of the sky. My body warms. I dampen down the tingling in the pit of my stomach.

'Cumulus and stratus,' he says. 'No precipitation. The storm has passed.'

His arm touches mine, just for a moment. Did he move or did I? I want to get rid of him yet I want to keep him close.

'Phoebe?' he says. 'When?'

He knew about Patience and Prim. He knew about my father. If I hadn't found him on the track, assuming he'd lived, he would have come searching. I know men like him. I know how they operate. He would have bided his time, gathered information and worked out vulnerabilities. Tears burn the backs of my eyes.

'I don't want to see you again.'

CHAPTER
4

A golden sun glows over the treetops as, at six in the morning, I walk to the stables. My boots are wet from the grass, but there's no sign of yesterday's puddles. As Sinn predicted, the storm petered out.

He was right about other things too.

I take off Camelot's night rugs and run my hand over his pitch-black coat as he walks into the stable yard. When the gate to the paddock squeaks on its hinges, he looks at it suspiciously. 'Nothing can hurt you here,' I reassure him, patting his rump as he passes.

And nothing can hurt me here.

Even before Mum was settled in New Zealand, Dad had run out of money and the bills were piling up. Patience and Prim could wear my old school shoes and uniforms, but that left little for me. I'd noticed that Dad was spending more and more time at the computer. He was gambling online. He said he did it on our behalf. To support us.

Only it didn't. Whatever he won, he lost again. Until he'd lost so much there was no chance he could ever recover it. Prim, who we tried to protect from the worst of it, sometimes let things slip. The school social worker began to take notice. Going to live with Mum was out of the question. There was a chance that Auntie Kate and Uncle Bob would have let us live with them in Warrandale, but they were even older than Dad, and they wouldn't have wanted to cross him. Our fear of being separated by the government was greater than our dislike of our father. We had friends and were settled at school. Patience and I were adept at hiding the truth. Prim got better at it.

Camelot, his coat shining brightly in the sunlight, trots through the paddock to the trees at the boundary. He turns abruptly before facing the stables again and cantering helter-skelter towards me. His tail, long and thick, flies behind him like a flag. Twenty metres before he reaches the gate to the yard, he slows to a trot. He hangs his head over the fence—nostrils flared, flanks heaving and dark eyes bright. I rub between his ears.

'You like to stretch your legs in the mornings, don't you, boy. After you've cooled down, I'll rug you again and find you some breakfast.'

I would have been sixteen when Dad accepted a position with the Roxburgh syndicate. Managing the syndicate gave him an income, stopped him gambling on his own account and, as he refused to claim a pension, kept us clothed and fed. Two years later, Dad's health deteriorated further, and he forced Patience to help with his work. I was midway through my final school exams, and it was only after I'd finished that she told me about it. She'd always been gifted with numbers; it was one of the few things our father respected.

After I let Camelot into the yard, he follows me to the feed room and snoops around the buckets. When I pick up his saddle to move it out of the way, he pricks his ears.

I look to the scatter of clouds. 'I'll take you out later if the weather stays dry.'

It's legal to bet on horses, and syndicates are legal too. But Dad was secretive about what he did, telling anyone who asked that he had work with an auditing firm. Was the syndicate dodgy? Is that why Sinn asked those questions? If Dad has done something wrong, could Patience be in trouble too?

As soon as I'm back from the horses, I make a mug of hot chocolate and pick up my phone. The communications recruit who answers my call eventually finds my sister.

'Lieutenant Cartwright.'

Patience might be on a ship a few hundred kilometres off the south coast of Tasmania, but her voice is perfectly clear. For the first time since I saw Sinn last night, I manage a smile.

'Hey, Patience. It's Phoebe.'

'What's the matter?' she says. 'Are you okay? How about Prim and Mum?'

'We're all fine. Are you?'

'Everything is good,' she says breezily. 'Going great.'

'Patience,' I say firmly. 'Tell me what's wrong.'

'Phoebe!'

'Well?'

'You're a witch, Phoebe. I swear it.'

'So, talk to me.'

'There's someone I work with,' she says. 'He's hassling me, but I don't want you to worry. I can handle it.'

'What's he doing?'

'He flirts with junior officers. I'm doing my best to ignore him without pissing him off too much.'

'Can't you lodge a complaint?'

'Nothing serious is happening. And his role and mine … it makes it hard. But if it doesn't stop soon, I'll report him.'

Sinn's sweater is neatly folded where I left it last night. I pull it towards me. The label says 'Laget i Norge'. Made in Norway? The wool is finely woven, light and soft.

'Are you sure you're okay?'

'I can handle him. Really. So tell me what's happening there. Why did you call?'

A few minutes ago, I was desperate to speak to Patience. But now … I push Sinn's sweater out of reach. 'I don't want to worry you with something else.'

'Talk to me.'

'It's just … I think someone is looking into what Dad did in managing the Roxburgh syndicate. I told them—'

'What? Who?'

'His name is Sinn Tørrissen and he has something to do with a UN committee. It looks into transnational issues, like money laundering, people smuggling, drugs and guns.'

'Why would he care about the syndicate?'

'It seems it might be relevant to whatever it is he's investigating. He didn't say so, but I think something dodgy went on.'

Silence.

'Patience? Are you there?'

'If it was something illegal …' Her voice is suddenly thin. 'I helped Dad with the books. Do they know I was involved? What does Dad say?'

'He said nothing to Sinn. I haven't had the chance to talk to him yet, but I thought you should know, just in case.'

'You said drugs and guns, didn't you? I was eighteen when I finished that work. If something was wrong, and anyone found out—'

'How could they find out? Dad's unreliable, and I'm not going to talk.'

'I helped him for two years.'

'He made you do it. You can't be responsible. I'll sort it out.'

I hear a murmur of voices. Patience's words are clearer than the others. 'My sister, sir. Yes, sir. Sorry, sir. Immediately, sir. Phoebe?' she says. 'I have to go.'

'Who was that?'

The line drops out.

It was Patience who had to change most after Mum had the stroke. Before that, even at ten years old, she'd argue about the environment, equal rights and whatever else caught her attention. It wasn't in her nature to be shy or back down. She would never have deferred to my father, or done something she didn't think was right.

She only did that for Prim and me.

On Thursdays I have an outpatient clinic at Dubbo hospital, and usually drive to my father's house at lunchtime. Three bags of groceries sit by my feet as I press the bell for the third time. It's programmed to ring quietly, but I'm sure he would have heard it.

'Dad! Are you there?'

The blinds in the front rooms—his bedroom, and the bedroom I shared with Patience and Prim—are closed. I unlock the door, collect the bags and let myself in.

The carpet smells musty. A cobweb, thick with dust, hangs like a rag from the cornice in the living room. Even though the linen cupboard door hasn't locked in years, my heart rate quickens as I pass.

The kitchen is at the end of the hallway. I tap lightly on the door. 'Dad?'

Chair legs scrape on the linoleum. 'Who is it?'

I turn the handle. 'Phoebe.'

My father, tall and gaunt with thinning white hair, places both hands on the table and pushes himself upright. Without looking at me, he shuffles to his study, a long, narrow space off the kitchen that once would have been a verandah. He won't let me clean the windows in the study, so they're almost as filthy as the one above the sink. He sits in the armchair next to the desk, piled high with books and papers.

'Why are you here?'

I place the bags on the floor. 'I always come on Thursdays. It's my day at the hospital.'

'That didn't answer my question.' He winces as he stretches out a leg.

'Have you had lunch? Should I make you something?'

He reaches for a book and flicks through the pages. He picks up a pen and puts it down again.

'Dad? Would you like a toasted sandwich?'

'What time is it?'

'After twelve.'

'Very well.'

Prim believes our father was born a bastard, but Patience and I have a better recollection of the stories our aunt used to tell us. Almost sixty years ago, he was one of the few thousand men conscripted to war in Vietnam. He was a university student, reserved but prodigiously clever, when he left the country, and a very different man when he returned. He became a successful but reclusive academic, living on his own until he met Mum. His background, and the way he failed to cope after Mum had the stroke, could never be an excuse for how he treated us, but maybe his injuries, or untreated post-traumatic shock, made him something he should never have become.

Patches of the kitchen linoleum are worn through to the floorboards and the roof leaks, but there's no point sending tradesmen here when Dad won't let them in. I spend twenty minutes washing a sink full of dishes and wiping down the benches. I unpack the groceries, placing them carefully in the pantry and fridge with barely a sound. I make him a sandwich: chicken, tomato and cheese.

He watches as I weave my way through the papers around his desk. 'Is the district nurse still coming on Tuesdays and Fridays? I've transferred another payment to Meals on Wheels.'

'I don't need sustenance, or a nurse.'

'What about the ulcer on your leg? It'll get worse if it's not dressed.'

'I don't want them here. Tell them to keep away.'

After placing the sandwich and tea on the desk, I perch on the edge of a chair. 'You'd be less likely to fall if you used your stick or a walking frame.'

He glares over the rim of his cup. 'Don't lecture me. This is my house. I'll do as I like.'

I link my hands together. 'Sinn Tørrissen. He came to see me. He told me he'd seen you too.'

Dad's hands are generally steady, but they shake as he lifts the sandwich. 'What did he say?'

'He wanted information. He talked about the Roxburgh syndicate. You know about it, don't you? How did it work?'

'I followed instructions.'

'He said you managed it.'

'An agent placed the bets. I did the accounts and other paperwork.'

'Patience helped though, didn't she? What did you tell Tørrissen?'

'He had no right to come. Knocking and knocking.' His sandwich still in one hand, my father puts his hands over his ears. 'If he leaves me alone, he can have them.'

'Have what?'

'I kept them all.'

'What did you keep? Are you hiding something?'

He pushes the plate away. 'You deal with him. I won't talk to him. I won't let him in.'

'I don't know what he wants. I don't know what information you have.'

'I didn't want the work. Patience didn't want it.'

'So why drag her into it?'

'It paid my debts.' His eyes are clearer now. His voice is stronger. 'I printed it out, all of it, it's in the records.' He pushes papers around his desk, stacking them before spreading them out again. 'They told me to destroy everything. They thought I was crazy. But they needed me.'

'Who told you? Who needed you?'

'I don't know who they were.'

'How could you not—'

'Send him away!' When he throws out his arm, the plate flies from the desk and crashes to the floor. His hands on his ears, he rocks backwards and forwards. 'Stop it! Stop it!'

I drop to my knees and grasp the plate. I pick up what's left of the sandwich. 'Don't shout.' My voice breaks.

'Send him away!'

'Who do you mean? Sinn Tørrissen? Why is he interested in the syndicate?'

When he refuses to answer, I carry the plate to the sink and stare through the grime to the garden. A jacaranda tree takes up most

of the space. In spring and early summer, the branches are covered
in a mass of purple flowers. When my sisters were little, they'd run
around the tree, holding out their dresses in the hope of catching
blossoms.

'If he comes again, you mustn't tell him about Patience.'

'He doesn't care about Patience.' When my father gets to his feet
and walks towards me, I reach for his arm but he shies away. He
points to the floor, jabbing his finger. 'The records are under the
house. I don't want that man here. I don't want his questions. Give
him the records.'

'What's in them?'

'Take them! Take them now!'

'No!' When he flinches, I lower my voice. 'I have to get back
to work, and later it'll be dark.' I cross my arms. 'I'll collect them
tomorrow.'

His eyes dart around the room. He returns to the desk and shifts
the papers again. 'I don't want him here.'

'If he comes back—' I do my best to speak calmly, '—keep
Patience out of it. Once I've looked through the records, I'll talk to
her. She'll know what to do.'

'Listen to me!' My father slices the air with a hand. 'He doesn't
care about Patience!'

'What do you mean? How do you know that?'

'Tørrissen knows I had help.' As his face flushes red, the shrapnel
scars on his skull glow white. 'He thinks it was you. He thinks it
was you who helped me.'

U

The community nurse is re-dressing Dad's leg when I arrive at his
house on Friday morning. I put the meals I've cooked into his fridge
before taking the back steps to the garden. Filtered light finds a way
through the lattice under the verandah, but I walk cautiously, the

torch held in both hands, to the storage room. The single ceiling globe burnt out years ago, but the plastic containers stacked just inside the door are easy enough to find. Swallowing hard to keep down waves of nausea, I balance the torch on a brick and carry the boxes to the garden before going back for the torch. When I'm in the garden again, I stand under the bare winter branches of the jacaranda tree and put my hands on my knees. Ten deep breaths. My head clears.

I can get out.

The sun is going down by the time I take the boxes from my car. There are eleven ring binders, all meticulously indexed. One binder contains details about the syndicate, and how it was set up. Another binder contains emails, where Dad has answered questions about things like contributions and taxes. The only name I recognise besides Dad's is Martin Roxburgh's. A third binder records payments made into Dad's account, the last one dated only a few weeks after Patience left home. The remaining eight binders contain pages of spreadsheets, which seem to be consistent with the accounting I understood Dad and Patience did for the syndicate. There are neat handwritten notes and calculations on some of the pages. Some of the writing is Dad's, but most of it is my sister's.

When my phone rings on Friday night, I fumble for it, answering before I look at the screen. 'Yes. Yes?'

'It's Sinn Tørrissen.'

'Oh.'

'Did I wake you?'

'No. I … What time is it?'

'Nine.'

I yawn. 'Oh.'

'I'll call in the morning.'

The narrow strap of my pyjama top falls from my shoulder and I pull it up. 'Why did you call? I told you I had nothing to say.'

'I have more questions. We need to make a time.'

A shiver passes through me; goosebumps pepper my arms. The timber bedhead is cold against my back. I pull up the doona to cover my legs.

'Next Wednesday week, I can see you then. Could you come at five?'

'If that's my only option.'

'In the meantime, please stay away from my father. He's in the early stages of dementia. Even without that, he's easily confused. He set up the syndicate, and then he did the bookwork. That was all. He only did what was asked of him.'

'Besides your father, is anyone aware that we've met?'

'I haven't told anyone.'

'Don't. I'll see you Wednesday week.'

There's no caller ID on his number. He can call me, but I can't call him.

CHAPTER
5

Sinn is due in an hour. But Benjamin, my three-thirty appointment, hasn't arrived yet. Sitting in front of the heater, I finish the last of my cheese sandwich and glass of milk, warm my hands and get to my feet. Wickham jumps from his bed, wagging his tail excitedly.

'C'mon, boy. Let's bring the horses in.'

Clouds skitter across the sky as I shrug into my coat. Camelot, eyes expectant, trots to the gate and peers over it. I hold out my hand to catch raindrops and show them to him. He nuzzles my palm.

I laugh. 'You never give up, do you?'

When I clip a rope to his halter to lead him into the stable yard, Mintie follows closely. I leave their stable doors open so they can wander in and out. Mintie nudges me in the side and I wrap an arm around his neck.

'I'll come back soon.'

I'm at the gate when Benjamin, eleven years old with big brown eyes and curly black hair, runs down the path.

'Phoebe!' he shouts. 'Thanks for letting me brush the horses first.'

I push damp hair behind my ears. 'Good try, Benjamin. But we'll be brushing the horses at the end of the session like we always do.'

'Sorry we're late!' Benjamin's dad, Terry, an electrician ex-rugby player originally from Tonga, has a bear's physique and a generous smile. He waves from the top of the driveway. 'Back in a while.'

'See you then,' I shout, as I herd Benjamin up the path. He stops at the graves, tipping his head to the side as he reads one of the headstones that lie on the ground.

'William Robert Tilley. 7 March 1897 to 7 March 1913.' He wraps his hands around the spikes on the fence, gripping them tightly. 'Dead on your birthday. That sucks.'

The sandstone is weathered, but the words are clear in the wet. 'Always and forever in our hearts,' I say. 'Rest in peace, our beloved son and brother.'

'That *really* sucks.'

When Wickham comes charging up the path, Benjamin drops to his knees and hugs him.

'Now you're both wet.' I laugh. 'Come on, Benjamin. You two can share a towel.'

Half an hour later, Benjamin, his elbow on the table and his chin in his hand, puffs out his cheeks and blows a raspberry. 'This is so *dumb*,' he says, squeezing open a peg with his index finger and thumb and lining it up with the other pegs around the rim of the container.

'You're doing really well, but try to alternate the fingers you use to grip the pegs.'

He picks up four blue pegs with his middle finger and thumb, and five red pegs with his fourth finger and thumb. He frowns with effort when he uses his little finger and thumb to pick up the white pegs.

'I did it!' He smiles as he holds up his hand for a high five.

'You're a peg whiz.'

'Pegs suck.'

'They're useful for strengthening the small muscles in your fingers. They improve your fine motor strength.'

'I can swing a crowbar all right.'

'When do you do that?'

'Gran lets me whack cane toads when I stay with her in Cairns.'

I grimace. 'Isn't there a kinder way to get rid of toads?'

'Like what?' He grins again. 'Chuck pegs at them?'

'If you pick up a crowbar, you use your whole hand.' I tap the tips of my fingers with my thumb. 'Fine motor coordination is mostly about the fingers. Can you take the pegs off now, please? Use your other hand.'

He slumps in his chair. 'Pegs suck.'

'Next time you hunt toads, document it in your journal. The peg and other exercises we do will help with your writing.'

He points to a tub of therapy putty. 'I could chuck that at toads as well.'

I laugh as I open the lid and hand over a bright green wad of putty. 'I've buried beads in this. How about you find them by pinching the putty between your fingertips?'

'Beads suck.' He looks longingly outside. 'Can I brush Camelot after I brush Mintie?'

'I'll consider it. *After* you've finished your activities.'

When I hear the crunch of wheels on the driveway, I push back my chair and look through the narrow window. The rain has stopped. A four-wheel drive pulls up and the driver's door opens. Sinn steps out, stands next to the car and looks at his phone.

'Who's that?' Benjamin asks.

'His appointment is after yours.'

'You seeing giant kids now? How come he can drive?'

Sinn is wearing a sweater like the one he left behind the last time he was here. Being from Norway, he probably has a cupboard full of them. When I give him back his sweater, should I ask about mine? I laid it on his chest to keep him warm.

I blow on my hands, suddenly cold.

I'll buy myself a brand new sweater. I'll forget about the hay bales in the shed. I'll forget about him.

When Sinn looks up I turn away sharply, even though there's no way he could see me or know what I'm thinking. I do my best not to glance back at him too often until finally, ten minutes later, Terry pulls off the road. He clambers from the cabin of his ute and pumps Sinn's hand like they've been friends for years.

Benjamin slumps in his chair again. 'Dad's early. That sucks.'

'We'll finish your handwriting practice and then we'll go to the horses. I'll let your dad know we're running late—he won't mind waiting because you're working so hard.' I encourage Benjamin to sit straighter in the chair as I turn the page of his exercise book. When he picks up his pencil, I reposition his fingers and remind him of the pencil grip. 'Bend your fingers at the first knuckle. That's great.'

'I got six goals at footy last week,' he says, as he forms the letters.

'Running, jumping and kicking. Your big movement skills, your gross motor skills, they're exceptional.'

He raises his thumb. 'You got that right, Phoebe.'

'Loosen your grip on the pencil a little. Excellent. You hardly need to press down at all.'

'Scotty reckons I'm the oldest kid ever to write with a pencil.'

'Distract him. Tell him about your cane toad annihilation plan.'

'What plan?'

'Chucking pegs.'

When Benjamin and I walk down the verandah steps, Mintie, standing in the stable yard, nickers a greeting. I clip a lead rope to his halter, take off his rug and walk him into the garden as Camelot watches. Benjamin forages in the grooming bucket for a brush.

'Reintroduce yourself before you start,' I remind him.

Terry's laugh is loud and long as he leads Sinn past the graveyard towards the horses. When Mintie presses his nose against my stomach, I rub between his ears and tidy his long silver forelock, smoothing it down until it sits between his eyes like a fringe. Benjamin pats Mintie's neck.

'Good horse. Don't kick me.'

Sinn's jeans are black and so are his shoes. Even dry and in daylight, his hair is darkest brown. When he squats to pat Wickham, his fringe falls over his forehead. He sweeps it back.

'Did you do good for Phoebe, little fella?' Terry asks. 'How was the writing?'

'Phoebe said it was ace. That's how I got to escape.' Benjamin looks curiously at Sinn. 'Your car's the new Landcruiser, right? How many cylinders?'

'Eight.'

I hand Benjamin the currycomb, an oval-shaped brush with short rubber bristles. 'Mintie's waiting for you.'

Benjamin pushes his hand through the strap and holds his fingers around the edge of the brush before running it down Mintie's neck and working his way across Mintie's sides towards his rump.

'That's really good, Benjamin. You can swap hands and do the other side now. Don't forget, squeeze the tips of your fingers around the brush, hold for five and then relax.'

'My fingers kill when I do that.'

'Remember when you could only brush Mintie's neck before you had to rest? Not only are your fingers stronger every week, but Mintie benefits too. Win, win.'

Doing purposeful, functional tasks or real-life activities has been shown to be more effective in treatments than simulated exercises, because they engage the brain. Children like Benjamin respond to these activities much more positively too.

'Phoebe?' Benjamin opens and shuts his fingers. 'When can I start on Camelot?'

I loop Mintie's rope around a fence post before I take Benjamin into the stable yard. He's equal parts terrified and impressed by Camelot, who stands quietly as Benjamin climbs onto a crate. I hand him a comb with widely spaced teeth.

'Put all four fingers and your thumb on the spine. That's right. Comb through his mane with long strokes, right to the ends. Loosen your grip and count to five, and then start again.'

'Can I sit on him?'

I laugh. 'No way!'

Sinn and Terry shake hands before Terry walks to the fence. 'We've kept Phoebe's friend waiting long enough,' he says to Benjamin. 'C'mon, little fella, let's get you home to your mum.'

Benjamin grumbles as he steps down from the crate, but laughs as he and his father throw imaginary balls on their way to the path.

I'm adjusting Camelot's rug when Sinn unties Mintie, strokes his neck firmly and leads him through the gate. He lifts Mintie's rug from the railing.

'You want this on?'

'Yes, please.' It was pouring with rain when I helped Sinn to his feet in the storm. When he held out his hand to Camelot, he wasn't afraid. He said—

I stand on my toes and look over Camelot's back. 'What does "vakker" mean?'

'It means beautiful.' He hesitates. 'Why?'

'The morning I found you, that's what you said to Camelot.' Should I tell him he said it to me too—after I took off my T-shirt so I could dry his hair?

He throws the rug over Mintie's back and buckles it at his chest, before threading the straps through his back legs and clipping them up. He frees the pony's tail.

'Do you ride?' I ask.

When he scratches under Mintie's forelock, Mintie butts him in the stomach with his nose. Sinn smiles. 'Not since I grew out of ponies.'

A breeze lifts the cape of my coat and it flaps around my ears. I straighten it before bunching my hands and shoving them into my sleeves.

'Are you cold?' Sinn asks. 'Should we go inside?'

I'm wearing jeans, a T-shirt, a sweater and boots. My coat covers me from my neck to my calves. He doesn't have a coat. I must be warmer than him.

'Do you mind if I see to the horses first? It'll be dark soon.'

He waits in Camelot's stable, leaning against the wall with his arms crossed, as I fill Mintie's hay net and check his water. Lugging another hay net, I open Camelot's door. When the wind gusts through the gap, rattling the iron roof, Camelot's head snaps up. His nostrils flare.

Sinn straightens as I close the door behind me.

I grasp Camelot's halter and speak against his muzzle. 'It's only the wind, boy.' He settles as I hang the hay net from a joist. A kookaburra laughs and others join in, their calls cut short when rain drums on the roof.

'Phoebe?' Sinn raises his voice. 'Can we go to the house?'

The shadows around us are almost as dark as Camelot. 'We can talk here.'

Sinn walks slowly but deliberately across the stable. Up close, I see the tightness in his jaw.

'Why are you putting this off?' he asks.

I undo the top button of my coat. 'I have no idea what you want.' Outside the stable, a trickle of water flows over the gutter. When it lands on the concrete, a watery arc flies into the air.

'I want to get this out of the way,' he says.

I look over the stable door to the sky of threatening clouds. 'Go ahead, then.'

'I've been told you worked with your father. Did you?'

'Who told you that?'

'That's irrelevant.'

'Why are you so interested in the syndicate?'

'We want to find out how it operated.'

'Why?'

He looks outside. And then back at me. 'Will you help if I answer?'

Camelot stamps a foot as he pulls at leafy stalks. 'I'll consider it, yes.'

'This is confidential.'

'I didn't tell anybody about the helicopter, or how I found you. Why would I tell them this?'

He crosses his arms, emphasising the breadth of his shoulders. 'The original members of the Roxburgh syndicate were paid a proportion of profits in line with the investments they'd made. A later investor, a new member, put millions through the same syndicate. Distributions were, presumably, paid into bank accounts he had access to. We want to identify the later investor. He's our target.'

'What was my father's role?'

'He set up the syndicate. He handled the accounts and paid distributions to the original syndicate members. He did the same for the later investor. Beyond that, we don't know.'

His expression is difficult to read. When I drag my gaze away and walk to Camelot, Sinn stands at his head. Unlike Nathan, the man who came in the helicopter, he's not afraid of my big black horse. I doubt he's afraid of very much at all.

'Dad used to complain about the work; he thought it was beneath him.' I smooth Camelot's mane. 'He was paid a wage, nothing more.'

'We're aware of that.'

I kick aside straw as I turn. When I look up, it's straight into his eyes. 'What does all this mean?'

'We suspect our target laundered money through the syndicate. The money was raised through armaments trading: rocket launchers, machine guns, heavy firearms. We need a connection between the money paid in and the money taken out.'

'So you can identify who it was who did the laundering?'

'Yes.' He strokes Camelot's neck. 'Some munitions traders are directly involved in insurgencies and conflicts, others supply the goods. Either way, innocent people, mostly women and children, lose their lives.'

'I don't think ... I can't see my father tied up in anything like that.'

'Or you?'

'I didn't know anything about it!' Camelot skitters and I lower my voice. 'Dad did the bookwork, that's all I know.'

Sinn walks to the half-door and places his hands on the top. He looks up at the gutter. The droplets on his sweater glisten silver.

'You don't always tell the truth, Phoebe.'

I lift my chin. 'I'm not lying about this.'

'I agree.'

'Oh.'

'Oh?' His smile is fleeting. 'What we want from your father is information. He communicated with the original syndicate members, mostly through their business managers, by email. He paid out earnings via bank transfers. He likely communicated with our suspect, or his agents, in the same way. Eventually, we'll trace a lot of this. But that takes time.'

'If I hadn't seen the navy helicopter, I wouldn't know as much as I do, would I?'

'No.' His voice is clipped.

'You wanted to hide why you were here. Why?'

'I didn't want to warn your father I was coming.' Even in the dimness, I see the crease in his brow. 'You were an unknown.'

Mintie looks through the wire-topped timber wall that separates his stable from Camelot's. When I put my hand to the wire, he pushes his mouth against it, hopeful for a treat.

'I have something I think you'll be interested in. When I talked to my father last week, he told me he was instructed to destroy files relating to the syndicate.'

'By whom? Did he do as they asked?'

'He didn't tell me who'd asked him, and he appears to have destroyed the electronic files, but he also had hard copies. There are spreadsheets that relate to the accounts, and there are emails.'

'Where are they?' he asks.

The hills in the distance are a black silhouette. 'Arms dealing, all those things you talked about, they're horrifying. If Dad's records might help, I'll give them to you.'

'Are they at your father's house? We can go there.'

I walk to the stable door and rest my hands where he rested his. 'I'll bring them to you. Next week.'

'Why wait?'

The rain has eased to a shower, a flutter of windswept drops. I feel them on my hair as I reach for the bolt on the other side of the door. My thumb catches on the casing of the bracket. 'Ow.' The skin is scratched, not broken; I rub it on my jeans.

'Phoebe?' His voice is gruff. 'Can't we get this out of the way?'

I spin around. 'No!'

'Give me a reason.'

'Where do you live? What's your email address? Your phone number? I *did* have a card, but that was taken away.'

Jaw tight, he takes a slender wallet from his pocket and pulls out a card. When our fingers touch, a flash of heat moves up my arm.

'You didn't ask for ID last time I was here,' he says.

'I should have,' I say, as I put the card in my pocket. 'I don't know anything about you.'

When he lowers his head, his hair touches mine. 'On December eighteen, I will be thirty-one. I own a house near the coast in Bergen. My brother is Leif. I'm renting a house in Denman.'

Within a few shaky breaths, our hands are clasped between us. His hold is light. It would be easy to pull away when he guides my hand to the side of his neck, but my fingertips search for his pulse.

The first time I touched him, I searched frantically. The second time, I reassured myself that he was well. This time, it's different.

I can't see the shade of his eyes. But I know the shape of his lips. I know the timbre in his voice and the warmth of his touch. His scent is pine and something else.

He searches my eyes. 'Is it fast?'

I count to twenty. 'Yes.'

He runs a finger down the side of my face. When I shiver, he sighs, placing his hands on the tops of my arms. My fingers slide from his neck to his chest. Now I feel his heartbeats.

'Phoebe?'

He takes my hand and lines up our wrists. Pulse against pulse. An ache, strong and sweet, flows through my body.

'You'll call me,' he whispers. 'Yes?'

A tingling awareness flows through my veins. Do I want to kiss him? Does he want …

He wants the documents.

I've agreed to do what he wants me to do.

I know how this works. How could I ever have forgotten?

An icy chill seeps down my spine. *Do as you are told.*

I wrench my hand away and take a jerky step back. I shake my head. 'No.'

He lifts a hand and drops it, then peers into my face. 'Phoebe?' He frowns. 'I didn't—'

'Forget it!'

When I open the stable door and walk into the rain, he follows, closing the door behind us. He runs to catch up and opens the gate to the garden.

'When will I see you?'

'Sometime next week.' I put my hand in my pocket and feel for his card. 'I'll email to let you know when.'

I run over the grass and take the steps to the verandah two at a time before, heart thumping hard, I sit on the bench and kick off my boots. Wickham, tail swishing like a helicopter blade, runs past me and down the steps. When he sits at Sinn's feet and lifts a paw, Sinn crouches and strokes between his ears, rubs under his chin, scratches his chest.

The ground is sodden. The rain is steady. The westerly wind blows over the hills and into the valley.

Sinn has no coat. His shoes will be wet.

'Wickham!' I shout. 'Come!'

When Sinn opens the door of his car and slides behind the wheel, the interior is flooded with light. The headlights cast watery beams across the gravel.

Wickham bounces up the verandah steps and shakes, showering a circle of droplets onto the decking. I take a towel off the hook and drape it around him, sink to my knees and rub. We both watch the car as it turns onto the road. The taillights flicker around the bend and disappear from sight.

Sinn might be attracted to me. He might be using me.

Either way, it doesn't really matter.

I've learnt my lessons well.

CHAPTER

6

Before I step into the kitchen, I put my hand inside the door to turn on the light. Wickham, his fur especially curly, runs past me and sits at the fridge.

'Won't be long, boy.'

After I turn on the laundry light, I throw Wickham's towel into the sink, before turning on the two frosted glass wall lights in the living room. The lamps in the bedrooms have low wattage globes. One, two, three. Finally, I switch on the light that hangs over the dining table and its mismatched chairs.

Benjamin's workbook is at one end of the table and Sinn's sweater is neatly folded at the other. My vision blurs as I pull out a chair, sit and rest my chin on my hand. I look around my house, carefully lit to keep darkness at bay.

Do as you are told.

Dad became hypersensitive to sound as a result of a head wound he sustained in Vietnam. He often worked from home and met Mum, another mathematician, when they edited a journal together. Even though she was thirty-five to his fifty, they were intellectual equals, had both grown up in regional areas, and respected each other's privacy. When I was fourteen, Auntie Kate explained the arrangement they'd entered into. Mum wanted a career, a stable home and children. Dad agreed he would tolerate tears and childhood noise, so long as Mum was responsible for running the household.

And maybe that would have worked out satisfactorily, if Mum had stayed well enough to protect us.

Dad was so angry after she had the stroke. Fortunately, he didn't blame her. But he did blame the medical profession, the healthcare system and, by extension, the government. As Mum had suffered hypertension since she fell pregnant with me, he also blamed his children.

Mum's older sister Debra came to live with us after Mum got sick, but when it became clear that Mum would be moving back to New Zealand, Dad sent Debra away, informing her it was about time he and his children managed on their own. As soon as she left, I pestered Dad in the same way Debra had, telling him Patience needed school shoes and Prim should go to the speech pathologist about her stutter.

Mum had only just left the country when he locked me in the dark. For years, I blamed myself for how it had happened.

Patience and Prim were asleep. Dad was in his study. It was the night before the Christmas concert at school. I couldn't practise my flute in the room I shared with my sisters, and I couldn't practise in the living room because it had a common wall with the study. The linen cupboard was about a metre and a half squared, its three shelf-lined walls stacked with pillows, blankets and towels, and I decided to practise in there. The latch was a simple bar and hook but set high on the outside of the door, so I climbed on a chair to release it, before sitting on the floor of the cupboard with my legs crossed. I left the door ajar so there was enough light from the hallway to read the music. My book of carols was propped up on a shelf.

I hadn't yet finished my scales when Dad appeared at the door, so I couldn't have been playing for long.

'I told you not to practise at night,' he said.

'I didn't think you'd hear.'

He didn't reply, just shut the door.

The click of the latch.

Footsteps on the floorboards.

Silence.

I didn't call out too loudly for my sisters because, back then, I was more afraid of my father hearing me than I was of the dark. I'm not sure how much time went by, but there was still light coming under the door when I pulled bedding onto the floor, carefully placed my flute on a shelf, curled up and went to sleep. I reasoned that Dad would let me out eventually, because he'd want me to get Prim ready for school.

When I woke, it was impossible to see my hands in front of my face. I was disoriented. I yanked more pillows and blankets from the shelves as I tried to get my bearings. I shivered with cold even though it was summer. The walls closed in. I yelled until I was hoarse and banged on the door with my fists. When the flute fell on the floor, I picked it up and climbed the shelves. At first, I tapped the flute against the place I thought the latch must be, but I couldn't dislodge it. I braced myself against the shelf and hit harder.

Harder and harder and harder and harder.

Eventually I fell.

I was smothered in blankets.

I suppose I passed out, because by the time I came to, the door was unlatched. I had bruises and scrapes on my arms and legs. My fingers were sore and I'd cut my thumb. I washed my hands and put on a plaster.

After we'd dressed for school, my sisters and I sat at the kitchen table. I pushed corn flakes around my bowl because my throat felt too dry to swallow. Patience, sitting next to me, ate WeetBix and read a non-fiction book about dolphins. Prim was on the opposite side of the table. She was only eight. I hadn't done her hair yet; dark brown tendrils curled around her face.

I'd hidden the flute under my bed, so Dad must have gone searching for it. When he laid it in the middle of the table, silent tears streamed down my face. The flute had been Mum's. I didn't want to see it but I couldn't look away. The blowhole was dented and the keys and plugs were twisted and broken. Patience moved her chair in close. Prim looked from me to the flute and back to me. 'It was an accident!' she said, even though she had no idea what had happened.

'Phoebe disobeyed me and this is the result,' our father said. 'Let this be a lesson to you. *Do as you are told.*'

That night, when I insisted on sleeping with the light on, Patience made me tell her what had happened. And the next time Dad went out, she marched to the garden shed, her ponytail swinging, and found a hammer. She stood on a chair and bashed the latch until it was irretrievably broken. I was terrified we'd be punished, but Dad acted like nothing had happened. He didn't say a word.

Perhaps he didn't have to.

I'd already learnt my lesson.

Scooping Sinn's sweater off the table, I walk determinedly to the spare room and put it in one of the boxes with my father's documents.

Sinn is secretive. He has his own agenda. He's the kind of man I
don't need in my life.

Hi Patience,

*Dad kept copies of documents (including spreadsheets) that relate to
the work he did for the Roxburgh syndicate. Sinn Tørrissen has good
reasons for wanting to see them (and he tells me he'll be able to trace
them eventually). Call me when you can and I'll fill you in.*

Love, Phoebe

Tall narrow poplars line the strip of bitumen that leads to Mandy Flanagan's house, a weatherboard cottage painted blue and white. I climb over the horse gear in the front porch, knock and then open the door.

'Mandy! Are you there?'

When there's no answer, I follow a concrete path lined with box hedges towards the stable block and yards. Many of the Welsh Mountain mares—greys and blacks with small compact bodies, widely spaced eyes and delicate faces—graze behind post and rail fences. But a number of ponies, their forelocks the same shades as their coats, peek over the doors of the stables. Captain Wentworth, Mandy's stallion, is stabled at the front of the block and has his own yard. He's as black as Camelot with a thick long mane.

'Hello, Captain,' I say, brushing aside his mane and rubbing his neck. 'Where's your cabin girl?'

I hear Mandy's laugh before she emerges from a stall on the other side of the aisle. She's fit and tall, looking much younger than sixty in her dark brown jodhpurs and tall black boots. She lowers the handles of a wheelbarrow filled with straw and manure.

'What excellent timing,' she says, pushing her curly hair from her face before blowing a kiss. 'You can put the kettle on.'

'Can I give you a hand?'

'And dirty your yellow dungarees?' She smiles as she lifts the barrow again. 'I'm almost done. A pot of English Breakfast would really hit the spot.'

The eat-in kitchen at the far end of the stable block is twice the size of the kitchen in Mandy's house and has a cobbled brick floor, exposed beams and a recycled hardwood table. I take chocolate biscuits and milk out of the fridge and rummage for mugs.

Ten minutes later, Mandy appears and washes her hands at the sink.

'Lovely,' she says, sitting opposite me at the table and pouring a mug of tea.

'How many ponies are you stabling?'

'Way too many, considering their coats.'

'Mintie's is twice as thick as Camelot's, but it doesn't seem fair to leave him outside when I bring Camelot in.'

She smiles. 'Mintie's a lucky fellow.'

Mintie's pedigree name is Daleford Minted Silver, and he'd been Mandy's second stallion until he fell in his horse float on the way to the Easter Show. The injury ended his stud career and as it was no longer safe for him to be ridden, rehoming was difficult. I offered to take him on.

'He's an angel with my children. He deserves to be spoilt.'

'Are you still seeing clients six days a week? And writing up reports and balancing your books on Sundays? It's unsustainable, Phoebe.'

'The kids are great. The paperwork is a pain.'

'You're left with no time for anything else.' She raises her brows. 'Which brings me to—'

I hold up a hand. 'No, Mandy, there isn't anyone.'

'You could do with some support.'

'Can I remind you that you've never paired up?'

'I have all that I need right here.' She takes another biscuit before pushing the packet across the table. 'Which is not to say I didn't try other ways of doing things.' She counts on her fingers. 'In my twenties, I lived with men. In my thirties, I lived with women. Polyamory was invigorating in my forties, but,' she winks, 'for better or worse, it wasn't for me.'

When I stir my hot chocolate, the froth gathers around the inside of the mug. I scrape it with my spoon. 'I've had boyfriends, but no one I've wanted to commit to.'

'And now you're in the friend zone with them.' She grimaces. 'Bar one, I suppose.'

'I'm well over Robbie Roxburgh. And the others … I didn't want to hurt them by promising them something I couldn't deliver on.'

Mandy reaches across the table and grips my arm. 'They're not all like your father, Phoebe. Or Robbie, for that matter. There are good men out there. Kind and caring men. Tell me you know that.'

I force a smile. 'I know that.'

She raises her brows. 'Reassure me on the theory.' Mandy is a psychologist. I saw her professionally in my final year of school.

I sip my chocolate. 'My father abused me—not often physically, but verbally.'

'Go on.'

'Abuse and neglect leave invisible scars.'

And not so invisible ones. Last night, I didn't sleep well. But if my house hadn't been lit up like a Christmas tree, I wouldn't have slept at all.

'Phoebe?' Mandy says. 'What are you thinking?'

'If I have to see or think about my father too often, things get worse. But I know how much I can tolerate. It's important to keep my distance.'

'From him, certainly, but not from others.'

'I guess.'

'He doesn't care about anyone. Not even you.'

'He's eighty and unwell. He needs assistance.'

'He's never going to change. You've suffered enough.'

'As have Patience and Prim.'

'You did an amazing job shielding them.'

When Mandy passes the biscuits again, I take two. 'Prim is happy. Sometimes I worry about Patience.'

'She looks like a gazelle, but she's a lioness.'

'She *was* a lioness. Now I'm not so sure.'

'She'll find her way. Just like you will.'

'I was hoping I already had.'

Mandy tips her head to the side. 'Do you want the friend or the psychologist?'

I shrug. 'The friend with expertise.'

'Quit running.'

'What?'

'You would have heard of the fight or flight response to a threat? They both have their place, but you have a tendency to take the latter course. That's not surprising given your background, but I'd hate to think you were suppressing your true nature. You're tough, Phoebe. Tough as old boots.'

I laugh. 'I'm happy to hear that.'

'I wish I could have done more when you were young.'

I fill her mug from the pot. 'Since I didn't ask for help until I was almost done with school, you did remarkably well.'

'Do you have to maintain contact with your father?'

'He's deteriorating mentally. Anyway ...' I wipe a finger around the inside of my mug. 'If I neglect him, doesn't that make me like him?'

'Certainly not!'

There are only three biscuits left by the time we walk down the path to my car. Mandy opens the door and leans on the frame.

'Thanks for the tea,' she says.

'I love coming here.'

She smiles. 'Children, ponies, hot chocolate ... there's no hope for you at all. How's your mum, by the way?'

'Really well.' I glance at my watch. 'But I'd better get home. She worries if I'm late to call on Sundays.'

I've only just opened my laptop when the Zoom call comes through. I'm sitting at the living room table. Wickham, lying on his bed, wags his tail.

'There she is,' Mum says, pointing at her screen. Mum is in her mid sixties but her skin is still smooth. Her hair, once as fair as Patience's, now has streaks of white. Patience and I share her blue-green eyes.

'Hey, Mum. It's nice to see you.'

'And you, my darling.'

'It's Phoebe, Mum.' At the start of every year, I send new pictures of my sisters and me, and Debra hangs them up in Mum's room.

'You all look so alike. How are your sisters?'

'Patience and Prim are well. Prim's hair is dark though. Remember?'

Aunt Debra pops into view and whispers something in Mum's ear.

'What have you been up to?' Mum asks. 'I want to know all about your week.'

Mum survived a minor cardiac arrest, but a medical procedure she had afterwards dislodged a clot. It travelled up an artery to her brain, causing irreparable brain damage. Although she has some paralysis, her physical abilities are remarkably good. Her memory is not.

I tell Mum stories about my clients, Wickham and the horses, and my sisters. 'Patience is on her ship in the Southern Ocean between Tasmania and Antarctica. Prim is still in the Northern Territory. She won't be back until the end of the year.'

'The Northern Territory? Have I been there?'

'I'm not sure, Mum. Prim has a research job as part of her postgraduate studies. It's a project about pain management in cattle and sheep. She'll be working as a vet the year after next.'

'A research position? Clever girl.'

I adjust the screen. 'Tell me about your week. Are you still feeding the orphaned calves?'

'I've been very busy, my darling.' She turns to Debra. 'I have been busy, haven't I?'

Debra is a few years older than Mum, and has lived on the farm her whole life. 'She's very busy, Phoebe, and not only with the calving. There's been a lot of work in getting the vegetable patch ready for spring. And Carol has had problems with her knees. Your cousins are busy with families of their own. They've been so grateful to Barbara for helping Carol with the household chores. Those two, they laugh so much. Isn't that so, Barbara? You and Carol cook so many stews and cakes, we hardly know what to do with them.'

Mum smiles at the screen. 'I love to cook.'

'When Prim is back from the Territory, we hope to get over there again. Maybe June next year?'

'You're welcome any time, Phoebe,' Debra says, 'but we understand, Barbara included, that you've got your own lives to live. She's perfectly happy here with us and we love having her.'

My smile is unsteady. 'Yes, we're all very lucky.'

Raucous galahs perch in the paperbark trees. When Wickham puts his head in my lap, I smooth out his ears and stroke his long fur.

Debra moves closer to the screen. 'Are you all right, love? Are the other girls well and happy?'

'Of course.' I clear my throat. 'You know I keep an eye on them.'

CHAPTER

8

I'm standing on the back verandah on Monday afternoon when my phone buzzes in my pocket. I swipe the screen in relief.

'Patience!'

'Is everything okay? I only got back into range this morning. What did Dad say?'

The ends of my ponytail blow over my shoulder and into my face. 'He made copies of emails and accounts and spreadsheets. He wants nothing to do with them and told me to take them away.'

'What are you going to do with them?' There's a catch in her voice.

'I have to do what's right, so I'll give them to Sinn. I wanted to warn you first.'

'I looked him up. You know where he's from, right? You know what the UN Committee on Disarmament and International Security does?'

'Sinn said the syndicate was okay originally, but then someone else joined—it was infiltrated. And after that happened, some of the money coming into it was from proceeds of crime, money to be laundered.'

'Who infiltrated it?' Her voice rises with her words. 'Phoebe? Who?'

A black and orange ladybird skitters up my instep and perches on the toe of my boot. I lift her with a finger and sit her on the shoe rack.

Ladybird, ladybird, fly away home,
Your house is on fire and your children are gone.

'I have no idea, but he calls them his target. He said the money coming in could have been from armaments trading.'

'What?'

'You only did what Dad told you, Patience. We all did.'

'It's … it's …'

My knees wobble and I sit on the bench. 'Patience,' I say quietly, 'you're scaring me. What's going on?'

'Dad had to explain how the syndicate operated so I could do the calculations and make the payments. The early members invested tens of thousands of dollars, a couple of them a hundred thousand.'

'Martin Roxburgh was one of them, wasn't he? Sinn calls it the Roxburgh syndicate.'

'The others had accountants and managers. I had no idea who engaged them.'

'What happened to the money?'

'It was paid to a Hong Kong company that placed bets on races in Asia and the Middle East. Profits came back to Australia and the syndicate members were given shares in proportion to what they put in.'

'Dad sent the money to Hong Kong. He did the accounting and made the payments. And that was okay?'

'I guess so. And the syndicate made money. Not a fortune, but a reasonable return for the investment. But I only got involved when Dad's pay went up, and things got more complicated.'

When a blast of wind whistles up the hill, I press the phone closer to my ear. 'What changed?'

'Another entity, a new member, put money into the syndicate,' she says, 'but the original syndicate members weren't allowed to know anything about that. Dad said it was none of their business. He was paranoid that they shouldn't find out.'

'Did Martin Roxburgh know about the new member?'

'I have no idea, but there was a lot more work, which is why Dad needed my help. We paid the disbursements into a lot of accounts— they changed all the time, every week, every month.'

'More money than previously? How much?'

'Enough that I counted and recounted the zeros. I had to make sure I had them right. There were hundreds of thousands a week, millions a year.'

'You think that's the money that was laundered?'

'Tørrissen will be tracing it.'

'It's not like you knew where the money came from.'

'Even so, when people find out about this, I could be in trouble, serious trouble.'

'You didn't set it up. You didn't know.'

'I was eighteen. And I knew things didn't add up. The original members didn't know about the later member and they never got to see all the distributions that were made. It was like we had two sets of accounts. If Dad did something illegal, so did I.'

'You were sixteen when you started. Dad was abusive. You were coerced. The navy would recognise that.'

Silence.

'Patience?'

'The navy needs to be convinced you can cope in a crisis. If they knew my background, the way we grew up, they'd never have taken me on.'

'You graduated with honours at university, and you topped your classes in training. In seven years, you've never put a foot wrong.'

'I didn't declare I'd had counselling or seen a psychologist. I lied on my application, and afterwards.'

'If we give the documents to Sinn, we're cooperating. We're not covering up or making things worse.' I struggle to sound more confident than I feel.

'Yes,' she says. 'We can't hide anything. If it comes out that I was involved, so be it.'

'Sinn thinks it was me who was involved.'

'What! Why?'

'Someone told him Dad had help. As I'm the eldest, I guess they assumed it was me.'

'You have to tell him it wasn't!'

'Why?' I search for the ladybird but can't find her anywhere. 'If I have to, I'll explain I had no choice. We had to help our father whether we wanted to or not.'

'No, Phoebe. I won't let you—'

'People around here, people who know me, they'll understand.'

'You can't—'

'I already have. And that's good, Patience, because there's something else. You've written on some of the pages, notes and calculations. I have no idea what the numbers mean, but Dad has done similar things.'

'They were …' She sighs so loudly that I hear it. 'Dad did the initial calculations, but I refined them—for all the accounts.'

I shut my eyes. 'You did what you were told.'

'But—'

'Sinn already suspects money was laundered through the syndicate, so that won't be news to him.' When I walk down the steps, two pairs of eyes look up expectantly. 'I'll give him Dad's records, but only on my terms. I want to be included, to be told what's going on.'

'What's the point of that?'

'If I know what he's up to …' When I open the gate to the yard and latch it behind me, Mintie pushes past Camelot and snuffles in my pocket. 'I can protect you.'

Just before I climb into bed, I send an email.

> *Sinn,*
>
> *I'm working at Dubbo hospital on Thursday and can come to you afterwards. Five o'clock? Please send the address.*
>
> *Phoebe.*

> *6 Hunter Lane, Denman—the house is adjacent to Roxburgh Racing Estate.*

CHAPTER

9

I arrive in Denman early, so stop at a café to buy a hot chocolate. The town is much larger than Warrandale but almost as quaint, with tree-lined streets and terraced shops. A sandstone church glows golden in the wintery sunshine, and footpaths bustle with kids fresh out of school. Painted timber houses with smart winter gardens and neatly fenced paddocks line the road that leads back onto the highway.

Roxburgh Estate is ten kilometres out of Denman. I keep my eyes on the road as I drive past the security gates—black wrought iron between tall white pillars. Twenty years ago, Martin Roxburgh purchased hundreds of hectares of land and a homestead. He doubled the size of the house and built a stable block, yards, a training track, equine swimming pools, a sales arena and vet facilities. Six years ago, when I was dating Martin's son Robbie, land was cleared for a second house. Robbie will be living there by now.

I see glimpses of the river as I turn off Hunter Lane to a driveway lined with pine trees. Twenty metres on, the chimneys of Sinn's rental house appear, and then the house itself. It's a single-storeyed brick with sandstone foundations—old but very well maintained. A Moreton Bay fig with fleshy green leaves separates the house from the parking area.

As I park next to Sinn's car, Nathan crosses the verandah that extends the length of the house. The last time I saw him, he was walking through the rain to the helicopter. Smoothing down his dark blond hair and smiling broadly, he jumps from the verandah to the grass.

My boots have low heels, but they sink into the gravel as I step out of the car and brush down my dark blue dress. My hair is loose; I tidy it behind my ears.

'Phoebe Cartwright, knight in shining armour,' Nathan says, holding out his hand.

I smile as we shake. 'Nathan Gillespie, right?'

'Nate. Only my mom calls me Nathan. Fantastic to see you again. Wasn't that a storm and a half?' He looks at his watch. 'Did we change the time?'

'I was running early. Sorry.'

'Sheesh.' He yawns, then rubs his eyes and shakes his head.

'Did I wake you?'

He points to the verandah. 'See that day bed?' He rolls his shoulders. 'Working Euro time zones is a killer. Sinn pushes through.' He grins. 'I nap after lunch.'

'That sounds like a sensible idea.'

He stands next to me as I open the boot, nodding slowly when he sees the boxes. 'How about you leave these to me? Sinn was in the yard when I passed out. Walk around the house and you're sure to meet up.'

The 'yard' is at least half a hectare of European gardens: azaleas, standard roses, gardenias and camellias. Manicured box hedges surround a fountain, and a sandstone path leads to a tiled rectangular pool. Sinn is crouching in the middle of a sweep of lawn near the post and rail boundary fence.

'What are you up to?'

He's much too far away to have heard me, but he picks up whatever is at his feet, straightens and turns. Our eyes meet as he walks towards me—head high and stride long.

His sweatshirt is blue like his jeans. He holds out his hand. 'Phoebe.'

'Sinn.' I deliberately stiffen my fingers as we shake. 'I brought Dad's records.'

'You're early.'

'My last client cancelled.'

He looks over my shoulder. 'You saw Nate?'

'He's taking the boxes inside.' Our eyes meet again. 'I won't keep you long.'

'Now that you know where I live?' He smiles. 'I'll take you through the house.'

It's only as I follow him across the decked area that extends from one side of the pool that I focus on the box in his hands. 'What is that?'

We walk up the steps to the back verandah. 'A rain gauge.'

'I have a glass tube at home.'

He stops by the door and shows me the rectangular box, crammed with plastic and metal components. 'These are used in automated weather stations.'

'How do they work?'

'Before I install it, this will be enclosed, but ...' He indicates two tiny brass containers. 'When these fill with water, they tip.

It generates an electronic pulse that's recorded by a counter. The gauge measures the amount of rainfall, and the rate at which it falls.'

I bend over the device. 'They're like miniature buckets.'

'It's called a tipping bucket rain gauge.' He smiles again.

An answering smile tugs at my mouth. 'The buckets can't hold much rain.'

'Zero point two millimetres of precipitation.'

I look over the railing to the lawn. 'What were you doing over there?'

He points to the roof. 'The gauge should be twice as far away as the tallest obstruction, and thirty centimetres off the ground. I was looking for a place to put it.'

Stepping further away, I survey the garden carefully, as if it's my job to find the best place for the gauge. Over the fence from the lawn is a paddock, presumably part of the Roxburgh property. A group of mares, rugged against the cold, gather under a pep-percorn tree with low-hanging branches. When a woman wearing an Akubra walks towards the horses, they turn towards her. She whistles.

'There are no rainclouds today,' I say.

'There will be tomorrow.'

'How do you know?'

'Satellite images.'

Satellites. Radars. Ammunition. 'Yes.' I link my hands. 'Of course.'

'Are you cold?' He opens the door. 'Come, Phoebe.'

I wipe my feet on the doormat before following him through a kitchen and living area—sleek, modern and clearly a new addition—to the hallway with rooms either side that leads to the front of the house.

'It's a nice place. How long will you be here?'

The hair at the nape of Sinn's neck kinks at his collar. When he turns his head, I see him in profile. It's not only in Warrandale that I find him attractive.

'Until we're done.'

Nate sticks his head out of a doorway near the end of the hallway. 'Hey again, Phoebe.'

Now that I'm here, why am I tempted to run? Flight. Or fight. Mandy warned me I favoured the former. She also said I'm tough as old boots.

Sinn stands back to let me through. This seems to be the formal lounge, but most of the furniture has been pushed against one wall. There are two desks side by side, multiple laptops and screens, a printer and other office equipment. Nate has already taken the folders out of the boxes and piled them on an antique dining table.

'Can I get you something?' he asks. 'Coffee? Tea?'

'I had a hot chocolate on the way, thanks.' I hang my bag on the arm of a chair before I walk between the men and divide the folders, separating them into piles. 'One of the folders details payments made to Dad for doing the work.' I glance towards Sinn. 'For the past seven years, he's been forced to rely on a pension. You already knew he had no savings.'

'I didn't—'

'Yes, you did.' I indicate another pile. 'These folders are the spreadsheets that account for what money came into and out of the syndicate, before and after your target came along.' I open the folder on the top. 'This is Dad's writing and,' I find a page at the back, 'this is mine.' I resist the urge to cross my fingers.

'Thank you,' Nate says.

'The other folders contain details on how the syndicate was set up, and emails.'

'We'll work through them,' he says.

I turn to Sinn. 'You know my father has dementia. Even before that, I don't think he had the capacity to be adversely affected by anything he did wrong, but I have my sisters to consider. I don't want them hurt.'

He picks up a folder and flicks through it. 'I don't believe you or they will be,' he says.

'If someone laundered money through the Roxburgh syndicate, that's illegal. It's also why you're interested in the documents.'

He hesitates. 'Yes.'

'It was tens of millions of dollars, wasn't it? From what I can see, my father, while keeping things quiet from the original syndicate members, worked for this other entity, presumably your target, as well. He got paid separately for it.'

Sinn's eyes narrow. 'Potentially.'

Nate whistles. 'You been doing some reading, Phoebe?'

When I point to the documents, my hand isn't as steady as I'd like it to be. 'If I can understand some of the figures, you won't have a problem.'

'You didn't know this before?' Sinn asks.

'When I helped my father?' My skin warms, but I lift my chin. 'He might have known what was going on, that it wasn't right, but I had no idea what it signified.' The window looks onto the More- ton Bay tree. As I focus on the closest branch, I do my best to speak evenly. 'When Dad was too unwell to look at the screen, or type, he'd read out numbers and I'd write them down, copy them into the spreadsheets, things like that. Sometimes he needed help with sending out the accounts and transferring money. I did that too. But that didn't mean I knew it was illegal.'

Nate, grimacing, sits on the table and swings his legs. 'You're worried about the implications of what your father might've done. That's because mud sticks, right?'

'Yes. Which is why I want to know what you're investigating, what you might find out.' I look from Nate to Sinn. 'I want to be involved.'

Sinn's eyes close. When he opens them again, his expression is grim. He looks over my head. 'Nate? Can you get me an espresso?'

'You need a shot after all, Phoebe?' Nate asks, lightly touching my arm. 'I do cappuccino, latte, whatever you want.'

I try to smile back. 'I'm fine, really.'

Nate's footsteps quieten as he walks from the floorboards to the carpet in the hallway. The door to the kitchen clicks shut.

Sinn paces to the window and back again. 'Our work is confidential, sensitive.'

'I can be useful.'

'You can't.'

'So I should stand back? Leave everything to you?'

He's about to reply when his phone rings. He takes it from his pocket and glances at the screen before going to the far side of the room. At first he speaks in monosyllables. Then, 'I have them, yes.' After he disconnects, he faces me again.

I rest a hand on a folder. 'Will they be useful?'

'They might be worthless.' He smiles stiffly. 'Unlike you, we haven't yet read them.'

'I've helped already by bringing the records. I could do more.'

'You can't—'

'I can! And it's not just about protecting my sisters. You told me about the guns, the ammunitions traders, how innocent people are killed. If my father has done anything contributing to that, I want to—'

'You're not responsible.'

'I still feel guilty!'

He scans my face, then holds out his hand and drops it to his side. He has faint lines of tiredness at the sides of his eyes. Instead of setting up his rain gauge, he could have slept on a day bed.

Or hay bales.

'Trust me,' he says.

I shake my head. 'I don't do that.'

'I'll brief you when this is over.'

Two young lorikeets, purple, red, yellow and green, perch on the railing. Heads tilted to the side, they peer through the window. Do Nate and Sinn feed them? To survive in the wild, they'll have to fend for themselves.

'I saw Martin Roxburgh's name in the emails. He was a member of the syndicate, wasn't he? Do you think he was involved in the illegal activities as well?'

Sinn's frown deepens. 'He was a member of the syndicate, yes.'

'You won't want him to know that you're onto him, will you?'

'You shouldn't have read the emails, Phoebe.'

'Why not? My father's name's all over them.'

'He did the accounts.' Every time he looks towards the documents, his jaw tightens. 'Give me a chance to look at them.'

'I won't change my mind.'

'Nor will I.'

'I'll talk to Martin. I'll tell him you're suspicious of him.'

His head snaps up. 'What?'

'I know him. He likes me … or he did. If you won't let me help you, I'll tell him his name is in the emails, lots of them.'

'Are you threatening me, Phoebe?'

'Someone told you that I helped my father.'

'Yes.'

I look around the room. 'You've got this house, your computers, a brand new car. You must have a good reason for living in the country.'

'Yes.'

'Wealthy people with interests in racing live in this district. People like Martin Roxburgh, and probably others in the syndicate. You want to be in the thick of things, don't you?'

'The syndicate is one line of inquiry. We have multiple.'

'Will the people here cooperate?'

'No legitimate business wants to be associated with criminal activity. It's in their interests to do so.'

'Like I did.'

'You know more than you should.' He steps closer—so close I see flecks of blue in his eyes. 'This is my work, Phoebe. I don't want you involved in it.'

When I step back, I notice the boxes, lined up neatly under the table. At the bottom of the closest box is Sinn's dark grey sweater. I bend and take it out.

'I forgot to give you this.'

When I hand it to him, his arms stay stiff by his sides.

'Sinn? It's yours. Take it.'

His eyes seem darker. The shadows? The shade of the sweater? Because he was up all night? His eyes slip to my mouth.

'What?' I whisper.

His hands cover mine as he looks towards the folders. 'I'll read them. Then we talk.'

My words come out in a rush. 'I won't say anything to Martin Roxburgh until then.'

He runs his thumb over my wrist. 'I don't like to be threatened.'

The wool of the sweater is soft. The touch of his hands, though cool, heats my blood. His chest lifts and falls. We're so close that our toes almost touch.

'We'll talk, like you said.'

He closes his eyes for a moment. 'Tomorrow morning,' he says, 'don't ride your horse.'

'Why not?'

He lifts a lock of hair from my shoulder. 'There'll be a storm. Lightning.'

'If I wasn't out in the last storm, I wouldn't have found you.'

My hair slides through his fingers. When his thumb glides up my throat to my ear, my breath expels in a rush.

'Sinn?'

'This is unfair,' he says.

I'd like to stand on my toes, put my hands onto his shoulders and find the pulse at his throat. The temptation to kiss his mouth is—

The door at the end of the hallway opens. Nate whistles.

When I take a step backwards, Sinn releases my hands.

Nate is halfway down the hallway, an espresso cup and saucer in each hand, as I reach the front door. I open it wide and stand on the threshold, foraging in my bag for my keys.

'You going already?' Nate says.

My face is warm. 'I'll see you soon.'

'I'll look forward to that.'

I can't hear what Sinn says, but his tone is abrupt. Nate glances at me and winces before walking back into the room.

The lorikeets are still on the railing. A matching pair. I want to protect my sister. If Dad has done something wrong, I'd like to do what I can to put things right. However …

The lift in Sinn's lip when he smiles. The touch of his hand.

His secrecy. His arrogance.

I need to guard against them.

CHAPTER

10

On Friday morning, I jump out of bed well before my alarm goes off. I told Sinn I'd give him time to read Dad's records, but more than a week has passed and I haven't heard a word. Did he think I'd give up on being involved? If I don't hear from him today, I'll chase him up.

Camelot is already in the yard and nickers a greeting, keen to go out notwithstanding the darkening sky. Crossing the road to Mr Riley's property, Wickham trotting happily at our heels, we ride through the paddocks to the shearing shed. Camelot champs at the bit when we reach the lane that leads to the fire trails.

'Only thirty minutes.'

Within an hour, the drizzle has turned to a downpour, but Camelot is safely in his stable again, and Wickham is curled up in his bed in front of the heater. Dropping my wet clothes into a heap on the bathroom floor, I step into the shower, but have barely rinsed my hair when the doorbell rings. Reaching for a towel and wrapping it securely around my body, I slip into my ugg boots.

'Who is it?' I call.

'Jeremiah.'

Jeremiah's teeth were always startlingly white, but since his braces came off years ago, they've also been perfectly straight. Even in uniform, with his wavy black hair and boyish smile, he looks younger than his twenty-seven years.

'It's pissing down out there,' he says, stamping his boots.

'You'd better come in, then.'

When he wraps his arms around me, something hanging from his belt digs into my hip.

'Ow!' I step back and point to the kitchen. 'I'll dry my hair and get dressed. Can you put the kettle on? Heat the milk?'

He laughs as he loops his thumbs through his waistband. 'I'm on duty.'

'Your handcuffs and badge are a giveaway. And you've ironed your shirt.'

He looks me up and down. 'Can't focus on policing with you half dressed.'

'As if you'd even notice?' I push him towards the kitchen. 'My first client is due in half an hour. I'd better hurry up.'

By the time I walk into the kitchen, Jeremiah is sitting on a stool and flicking through a pocket-sized notebook. He's made himself a cup of tea and there's a mug of hot chocolate on the bench next to it.

'Thank you.' I reach for bread. 'Toast?'

'I'm good, thanks.' He takes a pencil from his pocket. 'Answer a couple of questions for me?'

'Yes, Constable Jones.'

He rolls his eyes. 'Honour the badge, Phoebe.'

I sober. 'Always.'

He turns a page of his notebook. 'Mr Riley reckons someone's living in his shearing shed. You ride up that way, don't you? You seen anything untoward?'

I put two slices of bread in the toaster. 'I'm up there all the time. I haven't seen anyone.'

'Neither has anybody else. But Mr Riley thinks someone's broken in and moved stuff around. He's blaming itinerant workers, the fruit pickers. He's planning to sell and is worried they'll put off a buyer. He's getting doddery, not as switched on as he was, but my sergeant said we've got to do the right thing, ask a few questions and get back to him.'

'It might have been me,' I say, waving my hand vaguely. 'A little while ago there was a thunderstorm when I was out, and I took Camelot into the shed. I suppose we were there for an hour or so.' I frown. 'I'm sure I closed the doors when I left.'

'The doors aren't the problem.' He looks at his notebook. 'Did you happen to move the hay bales around?'

I wish Sinn were here, watching me stick up for him. 'Yes—I wanted somewhere to sit. And I took sacks from the shearing platform and spread them on the hay bales. I should have put everything back. But I only went there once. I didn't take anything.'

He laughs as he flips the notebook shut and picks up his mug. 'Stop looking so guilty, Phoebe. Case closed. I'll give Mr Riley a call on the way back to the station. He won't mind you going in there.' He lifts his brows. 'So long as you don't move in and—'

A clap of thunder sounds overhead.

The lights flicker and die.

My breath catches in my throat as I spin on the stool.

And then, as I see the paddocks and the stables through the windows, my heart rate gradually slows.

I can get out.

Jeremiah stands and pushes past me. 'You're on town power, right? Where's your electricity box?'

The lights turn on again.

'Oh!' My mug is on its side in a puddle of hot chocolate. 'Did I do that?'

'I sure as hell didn't,' Jeremiah says, squeezing out a sponge and mopping up the mess.

'It wasn't even dark.'

He smiles sympathetically. 'Triggers.'

When my sisters and I came to Warrandale in the holidays, we stayed with Dad's sister and her husband. The year I'd turned fourteen, a group of local children, including Jeremiah, invited us to join them at the camping ground for a sleepover. I wasn't keen, but Patience and Prim were giddy with excitement, meaning I had to go too. Uncle Bob reassured me that the camping ground lights would be left on all night, and he'd pitch our two-man tent between a lamppost and the toilet block. Jeremiah's mother lived just over the fence and his older brother, who was eighteen, had promised to keep an eye on us. It was the last week of the break and we were due to go back to Dad in two days' time.

By eight o'clock, Patience and Prim were tucked up in their sleeping bags and I was squashed between them. I reached for the torch that Artie Jones, Auntie Kate and Uncle Bob's next-door neighbour had lent me. Guaranteed twenty-four hour battery life.

The day had been fine. We'd eaten dinner under a full moon and thousands of stars. There would have been *some* light, but when one of the kids flicked the mains switch and turned off the power, darkness was all I could see.

And smell and hear and taste and feel. In my eyes, nose and ears. In my mouth. When I held out my hands, I touched it. I imagined breathing it in: thick, dense and black as bitumen.

When I woke up, the lights were on and the tent flap was open. My sisters and Jeremiah were shoulder to shoulder and leaning over me. Jeremiah had a phone in his hand.

'I'll call Mum.'

'No!' Patience slapped the phone out of his hand. 'If your mum tells Dad why Phoebe was scared, he won't let us come back. Phoebe knows what to do.'

Sitting up shakily, I rested my forehead on my knees. I took deep breaths. In through the nose, out through the mouth. Patience delved into my sleeping bag and located the torch, turning it on before picking up my hand and wrapping my fingers around it. Prim yawned as she lay down next to me, taking my other hand and holding it securely.

'When Phoebe gets scared of the dark, she can't breathe,' she explained to Jeremiah. 'That's why she goes to sleep and we can't wake her up until she has a rest.'

Patience put her hands to Jeremiah's ear and whispered, 'It's also called having a panic attack and passing out.'

I didn't see Jeremiah again until the next school holidays. When someone suggested we spend another night in the camping ground, he refused to be a part of it. Years later, when we were at university, we dated. He stayed over a number of times but our relationship didn't last long. Soon enough, we were back to being friends.

I hug him at the door. 'Thanks, Jeremiah.'

'What for?'

'Lots of things.' When I see he's waiting for more, I shrug. 'It was nice of you to follow up on Mr Riley's complaint.'

He pats the notebook in the pocket at his chest. 'All sorted now.'
He grins. 'Though Mr Riley will be disappointed. He had his heart
set on an arrest.'

∪

Jeremiah has only just left when Saxon, pixie faced and six years
old, charges up the steps.

'Phoebe!' He holds out his arms as he runs across the porch.

'Hello, Saxon.' I take a step to the side, avoiding his hug, before
crouching down low and holding out my hand. 'I'm very excited to
see you too. Do you think we could shake hands like we practised
last week?'

Saxon, who has hyposensitivity and learning difficulties, takes
hold of my hand with both of his, before running his fingers up
and down my arm.

'I'm very proud of you, Saxon, shaking my hand like that. But
now it's time to let me go. I have to say hello to your mum.' When I
prise open Saxon's fingers, he drops to his knees and runs his hands
over my boots.

'Hey, Phoebe.' Kelly is twenty-three, with lightly freckled skin
and closely cropped dark hair. She smiles tiredly.

'Come in. How was the week?'

'We've had worse.' She bends down to tuck Saxon's singlet and
shirt into his school pants. 'I thought you might call to cancel after
last time. How's Wickham?'

'He's had worse too. Saxon ruffled his fur, that's all.'

'He pulled out a chunk.'

'It was my fault. I shouldn't have looked away.'

'Poor dog.'

'When Wickham yelped, Saxon was upset. He'll be more careful
today.'

'His teacher said thanks for the email.'

'We agreed there's a lot we can do to make things easier for Saxon and the class. It's warm inside. Do you want to stay? Or have you got something to do in town?'

She looks longingly towards the car. 'He's such a handful. It's not fair to leave you all on your own.'

'Saxon and I have such a lot to do, and I'm sure you can find something else to keep you occupied.' I smile. 'Go get a coffee.' I take Saxon's hands and pull him to his feet. 'Give Mummy a hug, Saxon. Then we'll get to work.'

After I shut the door, Saxon, under-reactive to sensory input and also sensory seeking, runs ahead of me and does a full-body dive onto the couch. He grasps the cushions, repeatedly opening and shutting his hands.

'Saxon?' I put a hand on his elbow. 'I have activities we can do on the verandah. We haven't played find the dinosaur before. Put the cushion down, sweetheart. Let's go play some games.'

When I hold out my hands, he takes them. 'Where's your dog?' he asks.

'I told Wickham to stay at the stables until we'd finished here.'

I've filled three sensory bins—the red one with sand, the blue one with rice and the green one with water—and put small plastic dinosaurs in each. Saxon has a set period to burrow into each bin and find the toys, before moving on to the next one. The thrill of the hunt heightens his excitement, but also regulates what he's doing.

'Stegosaurus! Pterodactyl! Brontosaurus!'

After the game, he stands on a step and we wash our hands in the sink in the laundry. 'That was great work, Saxon. Thank you very much for moving from bin to bin when I asked you to. You followed the directions very well. And it was great you found Tyrannosaurus Rex. I haven't seen him in a while.'

When I turn off the tap, he reaches for it. 'I want more!'

'Our hands are already clean, Saxon. Now it's time to do another activity. Do you remember what we did in the garden last week?'

We're at the top of the steps when Saxon spots the wheelbarrow and runs to it. He picks up the handles and follows me around as I collect twigs and bark from beneath the trees. Everyday 'heavy work' like this—pushing a trolley, climbing a fence or play equipment, or lifting and carrying groceries—can assist with body awareness and also improve regulation. Even better, Saxon doesn't see it as work at all.

Wickham puts his front paws and nose between the railings of the fence whenever we pass.

'When can we get him?' Saxon asks.

'After we've done one more thing.' I show Saxon three ice-cream containers. One contains soft rubber balls, another thick rubber bands, and the third has little pouches filled with rice. 'Which one would you like to put in your pocket?'

'Balls!'

When he picks up a handful of balls, I carefully remove all but one. 'You have a pocket in the front of your school pants, don't you? Put it in there. Good boy. I'm going to call Wickham now. When he sits in front of us, you can pat him. But if you feel like pulling his ears or tugging his fur, I want you to squeeze the ball instead. Can you give that a try?'

He puts his hand in his pocket and grins. 'The ball is in here.'

'I'm so happy you remembered that, Saxon.' I whistle. 'Wickham! Come!'

Wickham leaps over the fence, wagging his tail cautiously as he climbs the steps to the verandah, but sitting obediently as Saxon strokes his back.

'He's enjoying that very much, Saxon. See the way he's looking at you? That's his way of thanking you for being so gentle.' I guide Saxon's hand away from Wickham's head. 'Remember what to do if you feel the need to touch harder?'

Saxon puts his hand in his pocket, visibly relaxing when he takes out the ball and squeezes. 'I can squish the ball.'

'You've learnt that already? Well done! I'm so proud of you. And when your hands are gentle again, Wickham would love to be patted.'

Saxon jumps down the porch steps to Kelly at the end of the session. 'I'm going to school!'

'That's right.' Kelly smiles. 'So how about you say goodbye to Phoebe?'

When he runs towards me, I bend down and hold out my hand. 'I'm happy that you're looking forward to going to school, Saxon. Can we shake hands?'

He shakes my hand up and down with both of his. 'Mrs Dempsy is my teacher.'

'How are you going to surprise her today? Do you remember what we talked about? What are you going to do?'

'Shake her hand!'

I laugh. 'You're such a clever boy.' I stand and turn him so he's in front of me. 'Can you show Mummy what you can do when you *want* to touch something, like the glue pot in the classroom, even though Mrs Dempsy doesn't want you to?'

He purses his lips. 'Annabelle screams when I touch her hair.'

'Jeremy doesn't want you to poke his sandwich either, does he? But if you feel like doing that, or the other things, what can you do instead?'

He grins as he takes the ball from his pocket, squeezing it with both hands. 'I can do this!'

Kelly looks at me questioningly as Saxon runs to the car. 'What's that all about?'

'It's a distraction—a safe and socially acceptable way for Saxon to stimulate his senses. Would you mind giving it a try this week?'

She gives me a thumbs up. 'Anything to save Annabelle's plaits.' As she straps Saxon into the car seat, she looks over her shoulder. 'I'll see you at the fete. Terry's put you in charge of the baby animal stall, hasn't he?'

'Chicks and ducklings, goats and a pony. Gus will lend us two orphaned lambs as well. Do you think people will pay to feed them their bottles?'

'The town kids will go crazy for it.'

'Are you in charge of the audio again?'

She rolls her eyes. 'After last year's disasters with the microphones, I hoped I'd be dumped, but Terry's found someone to do the set up. He's coming early to connect the computer to the speakers and other gear, and I'll take over from there. Terry said he roped him in when he saw him here.'

I rub my arms. 'What's his name?'

'Sinn something?'

Lottie's eyes are wide, her woolly white face intent, as she sucks at the teat of the bottle. I kneel in the straw, loop an arm around her hind legs and bring her towards me.

'If you're not careful, Lottie, you'll swallow the teat.'

We're in the far corner of the pavilion, a giant shed that's open on the long sides but closed-in on the short ones. By nine o'clock, the space will be filled with two lines of stalls. The goat kids are due any time, as are the chicks and ducklings. A miniature pony, easier to keep in a confined space than Mintie would be, should be here by ten.

I undo the press studs of my oilskin and pull up my socks before sitting and crossing my legs. As I lean against a bale of straw, a shadow appears over Lottie.

'Phoebe.'

'Sinn.'

Kelly told me that he would be here. And I saw him thirty minutes ago, carrying boxes of equipment to the portable stage that overlooks the playing field. So why does my heart skip a beat? He's wearing elastic-sided riding boots, obviously new but not out of place. His jeans are navy. As is his sweater. His eyes are dark and so is his hair. My heart skips another beat. Two beats. Maybe three.

Lottie's short fluffy tail spins like a propeller. The other lamb, Lucy, is a few weeks old like Lottie, but half as big again. She lies sleepily on her side, the wool around her mouth still damp with milk.

'Have you read my father's documents?' I ask.

'Yes.'

When Lottie tugs at the bottle, I pull her even closer. 'Don't worry, sweetheart. I won't take it away.' I look up at Sinn. 'Would you like to sit down?'

He hesitates before climbing over the low picket fence and sitting on the bale of straw. He stretches his legs to the side to leave room for Lottie.

'Do you remember the shed? Lying on the hay bales?'

He hesitates. 'Some of it.'

I took off your clothes. As warmth moves up my neck, I lift the bottle higher so Lottie can get to the last of the milk. When she loses her grip on the teat, she frantically searches and trips over my leg. She lands in my lap.

I laugh. 'Lottie!'

Sinn takes the bottle from my hand as Lottie clambers upright. When he offers it to her, she lifts her face and grasps the teat, trapping me between the lamb and his legs. My shoulder presses against his knees.

Picking up a handful of straw, I dab the milk that dribbles down Lottie's chin. 'Thank you.'

'Kjære.' There's a smile in his voice.

'What does that mean?' When I look up, our eyes meet.

'Sweetheart.'

I tear my gaze away. *Think of something else.* Beneath the lamb's woolly body, her ribs are thin and delicate.

'The lambs need regular bottles.'

'What happened to their mothers?'

'Lucy's mother died the week after she gave birth. Lottie's mother rejected her.'

'Why does that happen?'

'It's called mismothering,' I say quietly. 'A ewe with twin lambs might reject one of them because she has too much to cope with. Or a maiden ewe, one that hasn't lambed before, might not manage for other reasons. Gus helped Lottie's mother during the birth because she was in distress. Afterwards, Lottie couldn't stand without help. Her mother might have thought she wasn't strong enough to survive.'

'She is well now?'

'In the hours after a lamb is born, it's important for them to suckle and get colostrum, the early milk, because it builds up their antibodies and strengthens their immunity. Gus tried to help Lottie and her mother with that, but it didn't seem to work out that well. Lottie got sick the day after she was born. She had antibiotics and was vaccinated, but by then her mother had given up. Gus took over, but she's still very small.'

'What do you feed the lambs? For how long?'

When I look up to assess how interested he really is, his brows lift. 'The milk is a special formula,' I tell him. 'It's a natural alternative to ewe's milk and the lambs have it as often as possible, small amounts so their tummies don't get too full.'

'How long are they fed like this?'

'By ten to twelve weeks they'll be eating grass and ready to be weaned.'

His forearm brushes my shoulder when he changes the angle of the bottle. 'You stay here all day?'

My V-neck sweater is pale pink and new, like his boots. I fold the panels of my coat across my front.

'Yes, but we can talk after Lottie has finished.'

As I shift position, my ponytail pulls. He inches his leg back to free it. 'What do you want to talk about?'

'The Roxburgh syndicate.'

I ignore his mumbled curse, putting a finger in the side of Lottie's mouth to release her grip on the bottle. She searches for the teat, but when I turn her around, she walks on shaky legs to Lucy and, as if suddenly realising her tummy feels too heavy for her legs to support her, she crumples to the straw. She rolls onto her side and her eyes flutter closed.

I smile. 'Have a good sleep, baby.'

Sinn gets to his feet abruptly. And as I stand and stretch out my shoulders, he looks everywhere but at me. When I hold out my hand, he stares at me blankly.

'Can I have the bottle, please?' I prompt.

As I store the bottle in the crate, a truck backs into the pavilion, its reverse alarms beeping. Terry rushes around and tells the install-ers where the stalls should go. Most of the vendors will sell local produce: fruit and vegetables, honey, jams, marmalades and relishes, and homemade cakes and slices. The indefatigable Hendrika Boos, from the Country Women's Association, is in charge of the craft stalls. She's dressed in a version of traditional Dutch clothing—a fully gathered skirt and brightly coloured apron with a short velvet jacket.

'Good morning, Sindre!' she shouts from the far side of the pavilion.

'How do you know Hendrika?' I ask.

'Terry introduced us.'

'Why did she call you by your full name?'

He hesitates. 'She doesn't approve of contractions.'

'Your stall, Phoebe!' Hendrika shouts again. 'It is the click bait!'

'I hope so!'

Sinn looks confused. 'What does she mean?'

'This stall doesn't make much money from sales because we have to be careful about who we sell the animals too, but it's one of the most popular. Hendrika is like a marshal, directing the children's parents to the other stalls when they're on their way to this one—and when they're on their way back.'

'You do this every year?'

'Yes. The profits from the July fete go to the Rural Fire Service, and December's fundraising contributes to the Christmas committee activities. But there are other benefits too—Terry and Hendrika make sure everyone gets involved, so newcomers get to meet the locals.'

He looks from my eyes to my mouth to the lambs, and then back to my eyes. 'The syndicate, Phoebe,' he says. 'I don't want you tied up in my work.'

I kick my boots free of straw before looking at him again. 'You said the folders might be useful or worthless. What did you conclude?'

He smiles stiffly. 'The former.'

'Terry asked you to help with the audio when you were at my house.'

'Yes.'

'Did you agree because you were worried you mightn't have the information you wanted from me yet? Did you think I might still be able to be useful?'

'That was a possibility, yes.'

'Now I've served my purpose, you don't think I'm useful any more. Why did you even come out here today?'

When he mutters something in Norwegian, I turn my back, making sure the lambs' water dish is full and the lamp that'll keep the chicks and ducks warm is switched on. By the time I face him again, he's standing with crossed arms on the other side of the fence.

'Come outside.'

The fence is low, but as I step over it, my coat catches. I stumble. 'Oh!'

He takes my arms at the elbows then releases one of them to pull my coat free.

'Thank you.' My voice is a croak.

His hand slides down my forearm to my hand. We both look down as he threads his fingers through mine. I tighten my grip. As if I'm afraid that I'll lose him.

The pavilion is a kaleidoscope of sights and sounds and scents. A bright winter's day. Wet grass, fresh straw. Chatter and laughter. Metal poles on concrete. Coffee and pretzels, bacon and eggs.

His thumb brushes the back of my hand. Touch. Why is it different with him? When he pulls, I follow him outside and we stand behind the solid timber wall at the end of the pavilion. Hundreds of hectares dotted with gum trees stretch into the distance. Out here, we're alone, the thrum of the pavilion behind us.

He lifts our hands and rests them between us. 'You asked why I came?' When he cups my face with his other hand, his fingers are cool on my neck. He lifts my chin higher with his thumb. 'Why do you think?'

'I—' I swallow. 'To feed the lamb?'

His eyes shut for a moment. When they open, they're not exactly happy, but not as serious either. 'Try again,' he says abruptly.

There's only a step between us. A breath. A heartbeat. A pulse.

Standing on my toes, I wind my arms around his neck. My fingers find his hair where it kinks at the nape of his neck.

He growls as his arms slip inside my coat and wind around my waist. Chest, abdomen, hips and legs. He lowers his head. I breathe against his mouth. The warmth builds quickly, from my toes to my thighs, my breasts to the top of my head.

His lips are firm. Small kisses. Longer ones. Top lip, bottom lip. He flicks the side of my mouth with the tip of his tongue. His arms tighten, his hands slipping into the back pockets of my jeans and lifting me higher.

He pulls back a fraction, talks against my mouth. 'Du er vakker, Phoebe.'

Vakker. Beautiful.

I find his lips again. My tongue circles his. I want to know all of his mouth. All of him. The pulse at his jaw thrums against my wrist. His heartbeat on my breast is hard and fast like mine.

His hands slip out of my pockets and trail up my body. His eyes are bright. 'This, Phoebe.' His lips are on my mouth. They trail kisses to my neck. 'I want this. You.'

My hands slide from his shoulders to his chest. When I feel for his nipples through the wool, his breath catches. I kiss him again. I bunch the fabric of his sweater in my hands.

'I want to help.'

When he licks a line across the top of my lip, my breath expels in a rush. He kisses me again, slow, wet and sweet. I touch his face, the dips beneath his cheekbones, his angular jaw. With a fingertip, I trace a line around the rim of his ear. I touch the pulse at his temple and feel his smile on my lips.

'Am I breathing?'

'Yes,' I whisper.

He presses tiny kisses from my mouth to my throat. 'You asked what I remembered of that day. I remembered you.' He pulls the neck of my sweater to one side and traces my bra strap with a finger. 'And this.'

The sky is baby blue, his eyes are blue-grey. His hair is over his brow. The morning of the storm, he was cold and unwell. But now he's warm and strong. I don't know him. He doesn't know me. Yet …

I stand on my toes again, kissing his mouth much more carefully than he kisses mine. I search for the contours, the shapes and the textures. His kiss lightens to match my pace, but his heart isn't in it. Soon enough, he's back to searching deeply.

I have to breathe through him.

'Kjære.'

As the wanting builds, his hands sweep down my sides. I wish he'd touch my breasts, ease the ache between my thighs. I wish—

When a microphone emits a series of long high squeals and Kelly's voice stutters over the loudspeaker, Sinn lifts his head.

'Fuck.'

His arms loosen a little, but his eyes stay on my mouth. A few seconds pass. A minute? We kiss again, a tangle of tongues. I tug at his T-shirt, pulling it free of his jeans and burrowing under his sweater to find a path to his skin. I flatten my hands over his abdominal muscles. My fingers glide over the ridges of muscle and bone to his sternum and—

He grasps my hands through the sweater. 'Phoebe, listen.' His breaths are all over the place. 'Listen, sweetheart.'

I take an unsteady breath. Someone is shouting my name. 'Oh.'

He studies my face. He runs a thumb across my bottom lip and back. He looks over my shoulder. Hesitates. He dips his head and kisses my mouth again—slowly and thoroughly. Possessively.

'Phoebe!' Terry calls out, much closer now, laughter in his voice. 'You almost done out here? I've got Mike on the phone. The goats are on their way. And Hendrika's made you hot chocolate and put it under the heat lamp.'

The microphone squeaks again. Kelly's voice rings out. 'Testing, testing. One, two, three.'

I free my hands from Sinn's clothes. 'Let me go.'

His arms drop to his sides. Terry, his phone to his ear, walks around the corner and back to the pavilion.

'You knew he was there, didn't you?'

Sinn tucks in his T-shirt and holds out his hand. 'Take it.'

I shake my head and cross my arms. 'No!'

He opens his mouth and shuts it. Snaps. 'Why not?'

'I want to help you. I want to know what happened with the syndicate.'

His jaw is firm. 'You. My work. They don't mix.'

'Is that why you kissed me? To concoct an excuse to exclude me.'

'Concoct?'

'Make up, fabricate.'

'You kissed me back.'

It shouldn't matter. It was only a kiss. But …

Tears sting my eyes. 'You did it to convince me to butt out.'

'That's not true.'

'I have to get the goats.'

'Phoebe, don't—'

I'm blinking furiously, my eyes on the ground, all the way to the pavilion. Lucy is awake, looking curiously at the volunteers as they erect the stall adjacent to her pen, but Lottie is still asleep. I lift my coat carefully before stepping over the pickets. Taking uneven little steps, half walking, half running, Lucy crosses the pen. She leans against my leg and looks up.

Sinn, on the other side of the pickets, squares his shoulders. 'I'll be at the audio.'

I nod stiffly. 'I'll come to you after work on Thursday. Until then, I won't say anything.'

His eyes narrow. 'About what?'

'We talked about this before. Martin Roxburgh might have something to hide.'

'I've already spoken with him.'

'Since I gave you Dad's records?'

'No.'

'Was it Martin who told you that I helped my father?'

'Leave this, Phoebe.' He rubs his temple. 'The syndicate, it's only part of what we're looking at.'

'If you don't let me help, I'll talk to Martin. I'll warn him you've got new information that might implicate him.'

He runs a finger up and over a picket. 'This is the second time you've threatened me.'

'I can help you.'

'I don't agree.'

'You must think Martin has something to hide, or you wouldn't be scared that I'd talk to him.'

He leans over the fence. 'What scares me,' he says, 'is you sabotaging six months of work.'

'I haven't seen him in years, but he'll listen to me. I'm sure he will.'

'For fuck's—'

'I'm not stupid! I won't do anything you don't want me to. But Martin knows about my father. Maybe he'll let something slip. Maybe he thinks I know more than I do.'

'You know nothing. He might know less.'

'Or not.'

'It's too risky.'

A gust of wind shoots through the pavilion, ruffling my hair. I pull up my collar and put my hands in my pockets.

'My father kept things to himself like you do. He punished us when we spoke up.'

'Don't compare me to him.'

'You do things to suit yourself.' When Lottie wakes, coming up on her knees and struggling to stand, I kneel on the straw and lift her.

'That is also unfair.'

'Mud sticks, just like Nate said.'

Hendrika, who took the blame for Patience when she 'liberated' hundreds of battery hens, walks from stall to stall with a clipboard under her arm. Mike, who Prim followed around like a puppy, limps towards me, a goat kid in his arms.

'We have friends here, people who care about us and have been kind. I want them to know I did what I could to fix things. And, if my father is implicated, I have to protect my sisters.'

Sinn walks away before striding back again. 'I don't want you to be involved.'

'I'll see you on Thursday. By that time, maybe you'll have thought up something useful I can do.'

'Give me your hand.' His eyes are cold.

When I stand, my heart thumping crazily, he grasps my hand and opens my fingers. He pulls up the sleeve of his sweater and turns his arm, exposing his wrist, then guides my fingers to his pulse. His heartbeats echo mine. They warm me. They frighten me.

'Touching like this,' he says, 'is personal. If you get involved with my work, the personal is over. We can't do this any more.'

'Right.'

'Phoebe?' His voice is sharp. 'Confirm you understand.'

I return his steely gaze. 'Me. Your work. They don't mix.'

CHAPTER

12

On Sunday morning, the grass, white and thick with frost, crunches under the soles of my boots. When I whistle, Wickham leaps onto the front seat of my car before bouncing into the back and looking expectantly between the seats. I'm wearing gloves, but rub my hands together before I take the wheel. 'Mike will be happy to see you, too.'

By the time I reach the outskirts of Warrandale, the mist has lifted. Even so, I have to keep the wipers on to clear moisture from the windscreen. Does mist count as rain? Could it tip the tiny brass bucket in Sinn's fancy rain gauge? I grip the wheel so tightly my fingers ache. That kiss …

There's no point pretending it didn't happen when I relived it all through the night. *Me. Your work. They don't mix.* And that shouldn't matter to me. Because soon he'll go back to Norway, to his ships, radars and satellites. A man like him has no place here.

I drive past the Warrandale community centre, pavilion and playing field. Two neat rows of shops and offices, many a century old, march down the hill to the roundabout. Mike's house, a Federation cottage only half the size of his shed, is on a large block of land at the bottom of the slope. As soon as I turn into the parking area and open my door, Wickham leaps over my lap and onto the gravel. We skirt milky brown puddles as we walk to the shed.

Mike leans over the workbench, his shock of white hair sticking out at wild angles. He looks up, a hammer in midair, as Wickham, tail wagging madly, runs towards him. When Mike smiles, wrinkles crease his face.

'How's my favourite dog, then?'

'Hi, Mike.'

'I thought you'd get a sleep-in, Phoebe. You left the fete after I did.'

'I've come to help with the lambs. Sorry to send them home with you.'

'It's not like they'd fit in your car. Gus's neighbour will collect them at midday.' He looks at his watch. 'You okay for the ten o'clock feed?'

'Thanks for doing the six.'

'Like I wasn't up already?'

I walk to the workbench, littered with different-sized sheets of metal. 'What are you making?'

'A letterbox.' He grins. 'One of those "bespoke" ones. The rich blokes down in Denman get some artist to do a design, and I take over from there.' He waves a piece of paper marked with 3D drawings. 'They reckon this is a work of art.' He shakes his head. 'Don't make sense to me, but I'm not paid to ask questions.'

I smile. 'Do you like making letterboxes?'

'I'd prefer to be shoeing a horse, but this is money for jam.' He winks. 'The cash will come in useful for the war memorial restoration. Speaking of which, your graves could do with sprucing up. The vicar died in World War One, didn't he? With the council matching the town contributions, he could get a new headstone out of this.'

'He hasn't complained about the current one. And his name is on the memorial in the park; I think he's happy with that.'

Wickham, still sitting at Mike's feet, lifts a paw and Mike holds out his hands. 'I get it, mate. You're not allowed to jump up, but an old bloke like me can't be squatting.'

I laugh. 'Wickham. Up.'

When Wickham puts his paws on Mike's chest, Mike rubs his hands over his fur, ruffling it before stroking it smooth again. 'All I did was find him a good home,' Mike says, 'but I reckon he's grateful.'

I moved to Warrandale not long after Robbie and I broke up. Soon afterwards, Mandy Flanagan, wearing her psychologist hat, declared I needed some company. She contacted Mike, who talked to his farmer friends. The dog they found was young, clever, handsome and sociable, but had no interest in the job he was raised to do—just like Jane Austen's Wickham.

I smile. 'We're both grateful.'

Wickham licks Mike's neck. 'You smell like a bunch of roses,' Mike complains.

'I don't like to send my children home smelling of dog.'

'Don't reckon it'd do them any harm.'

I laugh. 'I'll let you get back to your letterbox. Do you mind if I leave Wickham with you? He'd prefer to be here than with the sheep.'

'He can keep me company, no problem.'

'Are the lambs in the yard?'

'Figured they'd like the fresh air. Lottie is only pocket sized, but she's full of beans. Don't seem fair her mum left her behind.'

Lucy, lying on the ground, looks up as I climb over the railings. Lottie bleats loudly, rises clumsily to her feet and runs through the puddles. When she presses her shoulder against my leg, I stroke her woolly head.

'It wasn't your fault you got left behind, little lamb.'

Mandy used to tell me that, even though I'd been unable to depend on my father as a child—an important criterion for developing healthy relationships in adulthood—she didn't think I had too many abandonment issues. My mother had loved me. She still does. I was not only close to my sisters, but Auntie Kate, Uncle Bob and my New Zealand family. And even though I rarely confided in my friends at school and university about my home life, our bonds were strong and genuine. After Robbie Roxburgh and I broke up, Mandy reassured me it was Robbie, not me, who was the problem. She'd remind me about coping strategies. *Have fun with your friends. Find a job you love. Live in a community where you feel you belong.*

I was at university and working part time at the hospital when Robbie and I met. He'd been sitting in the Emergency waiting area, his arm strapped to his side after a fall at a polo match. It was a painful fracture, but as I approached with an elderly patient, he gritted his teeth and pushed chairs out of the way so we could pass. When I thanked him, he leant in close and read my name. 'My absolute pleasure, Phoebe.'

Robbie was confident and good-looking, with tousled light brown hair. A few years older than me, he'd grown up in Sydney and attended an expensive private school before living on campus at a city university. Martin, Robbie's father, had spent years commuting between his harbourside house and his stud. When he divorced for the third time, he decided to live in Denman permanently. Robbie joined his father and worked in property development after he'd finished post-grad studies in management in the US.

Prim was still at school when Robbie and I started dating, so we only saw each other occasionally. Initially, I thought Robbie and I had little in common. Polo, racing, parties and Instagram followers meant nothing much to me. But Robbie, carefree and attentive, persevered. Martin and I always got on well. I was aware that he knew my father, but we never spoke about him. Now I wonder ...

Was there a reason for that? Because Martin and my father were involved with the syndicate? Or whatever it was hiding? Martin didn't act like a criminal. He gave me advice on the business aspects of setting up my own practice, and even though I knew little of racing, we'd talk about horses. I'd cared for and ridden friends' horses when I was a teenager, but had never owned one of my own.

Until Camelot.

Martin had bought him for one of his clients at the yearling sales and, as his looks were as impressive as his bloodline, he'd cost a fortune. When he raced as a three-year-old, he showed potential, but was placid by nature and never in a hurry to finish first past the post. As a result, he was gelded as a four-year-old and sent to Roxburgh Estate to be sold. He was worth far more than the amount I paid for him, but the owner wanted him to have a good home.

My independence compared to the other women Robbie had dated was likely a novelty at first, but it rattled him when, after we'd been going out for almost two years, I started looking for a property to buy in Warrandale. Auntie Kate, following Uncle Bob's death, had moved to a retirement house on the coast so she could be closer to her friend. When she'd sold her cottage in Warrandale, she'd given Patience, Prim and me what she called a nest egg, insisting we should have it at a time when it could do us most good. Prim paid her university fees up-front. Patience's money is probably still in the bank. I used mine for a deposit on the church. That worried Robbie, particularly as Martin had applied to the council to build a second house at Roxburgh Estate.

Robbie told me he'd gone out with other women in the hope it would make me care for him more. He complained that I wouldn't choose an engagement ring, and had borrowed from the bank, not him, when I'd bought the church. He said he was sick of competing with my family, home and career.

And when I wouldn't take him back after he cheated, he said I was 'way too old' to be afraid of the dark.

I'd liked Robbie. A lot. His accusations had hurt. I hadn't guarded my heart as much as I'd needed to. I'd been naïve to trust him and his circle of friends.

I lean through the railings and pick a few blades of grass. When I offer it to Lottie, she turns her head away.

'Sometimes it's good to try new things,' I tell her. An image of Sinn, sitting on the bale of straw, leaning over my shoulder and feeding Lottie her bottle, comes into my mind. 'On the other hand, it's important to learn from your mistakes.'

CHAPTER
13

The sun sinks below the horizon as I turn into the driveway of Sinn's house. My last hospital appointment ran over time, and a colleague waylaid me in the carpark, so it's already after six. I park alongside Sinn's black four-wheel drive, in the same spot I parked last time. A narrow strip of cloud, long and charcoal-grey, draws an uneven line above the treetops.

The sensor lights activate as I approach the front door, highlighting the path and verandah. Vibrant striped cushions are scattered on the day bed. I knock lightly, and then cross my fingers. *Please, Nate. Get to the door first.*

Sinn opens the door, his hair a little messy. Not sleepy messy, but messy like he's run his fingers through it. He's wearing one of his dark V-neck sweaters with jeans.

'Phoebe.' He frowns. 'You're late.'

'Sorry.'

His scowl deepens when I hold out my hand, but he shakes it. He doesn't appear to be flustered, or thinking about the kiss.

His work and me don't mix.

As Sinn stands back to let me in, Nate walks out of the room they use as an office and joins us in the hallway. He's not as tall as Sinn, but his shoulders are massive.

'Hey there, Phoebe,' he says, smiling broadly as we shake hands. 'Good to meet up again.' He glances at Sinn. 'I'm hanging out for a break, buddy. How about we chat in the kitchen?'

The hallway is shadowed, but lights from the kitchen create stripes along the floorboards. I walk quickly, pausing as I step through the door. The kitchen bench is wide and white, with two black stools either side. I unbutton the toggles of my hip-length coat, the same colour as my navy dress, and lay it over the closest stool.

When Sinn moves to the far side of the bench and takes cups and saucers from a cupboard, Nate follows him into the kitchen.

'Nice outfit, Phoebe.' He grins. 'What'll you have?'

'Um ... water is fine.' I smooth down my dress. My tights are red, my boots long and black.

'Still or sparkling?'

'Still, please.'

As I sit, he pours a glass of water from the filter tap and pushes it towards me. 'What else do you want?'

'What are you having?'

He suppresses a yawn. 'Another late meeting, so it'll be coffee for us, but ...' The pantry is in the corner of the kitchen and he opens the door. 'In addition to everything else, the agent who stocked the cupboards gave us a shelf of herbal teas.'

'I'm happy with water.'

Sinn, picking up a cup and saucer, replaces it with a mug. 'You drink sjokolade, yes?'

'What?'

'Chocolate. To drink.'

'Oh. Yes. I'll have that if it's not too much trouble.'

Nate smiles. 'No trouble at all, so long as you tell me how to make it.'

Sinn places cocoa, sugar and a carton of milk on the bench, points to a large stainless coffee machine and gives instructions to Nate. When his phone buzzes, he looks at it briefly. He glances at Nate. 'Tor.' He turns to me. 'Excuse me.'

As Sinn closes the door behind him, Nate holds up the mug. 'I didn't catch what he said,' he whispers conspiringly. 'How do I make it?'

I join him in the kitchen. 'I'll put in the chocolate, and you can heat the milk. It tends to boil over in the microwave, so I do it in a saucepan.'

'What century is this again?' He's laughing as he fills a metal jug with milk and angles it under a nozzle in the coffee machine. He points out the settings. 'You want low, medium or high heat for the milk? Froth throughout, or just on the top?'

I smile. 'This is like a café. I'd like very hot milk please, and plenty of froth. Do you have marshmallows?'

He points to the pantry. 'Go take a look.'

There are no marshmallows, but Nate locates chocolate sprinkles on a high shelf behind the flour and spoons a generous quantity over the top of the other ingredients.

'Thanks, Nate.'

He bows. 'I can add sjokolade to my repertoire of drinks.'

I'm laughing when Sinn, no hint of a smile, opens the door. 'Ready to start?'

Nate pulls out the stool next to his. 'Take a seat. Your coffee's getting cold.'

Sinn and I skirt around each other as I return to my side of the bench. He drinks his espresso as I scoop up melted chocolate.

Nate blows across the top of his cup. 'Sinn tells me you want to join our little team.'

'It won't be a team,' Sinn says sharply.

'You've made that clear,' I say.

'Go ahead, Phoebe.' Nate smiles encouragingly. 'Tell us what you can bring to the table.'

I take a deep breath. 'There was only ever one syndicate, but it was like my father kept two sets of accounts: one for the original members, and one for those members and the new investor—your target. After the new investor came along, the syndicate was used to launder money, presumably money from armaments trading, and the money was paid into a lot of different bank accounts.'

Nate holds up his hands. 'Whoa, there.' He swivels on his stool to face Sinn. 'How much is she supposed to know?'

'Less. Than. She. Does.' Sinn articulates each word.

I scoop up froth with my spoon. 'Martin Roxburgh was the driving force behind the original syndicate, and his name comes up in emails that relate to the second set of accounts.'

'Your father managed the syndicate,' Nate says. 'He must have allowed the new investor in, but we don't know what Martin's involvement was.'

'I liked Martin when I saw him socially. I'm not suggesting he's done anything wrong, but if he has, then I might be able to encourage him to help you.'

Sinn pushes his empty cup away. 'He's already cooperated. Like other members, he's answered our questions about the syndicate.'

'Have you asked him about the new investor?'

'No,' Sinn says.

'Why not? When he's the one most likely to have known about him?'

Nate holds up his hands again. 'We don't *think* the others knew. Maybe they just weren't named in the emails. Whatever the case, none of them are volunteering information.'

'Can't you force them to tell you what they know?'

'Getting information voluntarily is less likely to alarm our target,' Sinn says.

'Anyone with a connection to money laundering risks reputational damage,' Nate says, 'so we encourage people to speak to us off the record. For them to do that, they've got to be convinced we won't reveal sources.'

'And those associated with our target, even remotely, could have got an incentive, a kickback,' Sinn says. 'Money could have been deposited in their bank account from an anonymous source. A diamond might have been given. A ski trip to Aspen.'

It's warm in the room, but my hands are cold. I wrap them around my mug. 'The recipient would be afraid the kickback would be revealed if they spoke up?'

'You got it,' Nate says.

'But if you found out that someone did get an incentive, and you didn't report them, doesn't that mean they'd get away with it?'

'Karma.' Nate shrugs. 'They'll pay their dues some day, but for now …'

'You look at the bigger picture. Armaments trading takes innocent lives.'

'Thousands annually,' Nate says.

'So …' The sprinkles have melted and sunk to the bottom of the mug. As I stir, the chocolate rises to the top. 'There are plenty of reasons why people *won't* talk to you. How are you planning to change their minds?'

'Softly, softly,' Nate says. 'We mix with them socially, get to know them better, hopefully get leads on contacts and old conversations. It's not unusual for racing and gambling to be associated with organised crime. But we're from the UN. We're the good guys. What's not to like?' He winks. 'Most people try to be helpful. And those with something to hide like to give the appearance of helping.'

'They keep their own secrets,' Sinn says, 'and give other people's secrets away.'

'Do you know who the target is?'

'We have a fair idea,' Nate says, 'but links that'll hold up in court are hard to find.'

'Which is why you need more information.'

Nate, suddenly serious, places his hands flat on the bench. 'Besides keeping quiet about what you know, how do you think you can help with that?'

'Martin Roxburgh might know more than he's letting on.' I stir my chocolate, creating a whirlpool. 'But you're afraid of frightening him away, otherwise you'd have asked him why his name is in the emails. And, like you said before, you want people to voluntarily tell you what they know. That way, you can control things and your target won't know what's happening.'

Nate elbows Sinn. 'She's not bad.'

'Shut up, Nate.'

'You asked how I could help.' I stir my chocolate again. 'If I'd done something wrong like Martin might have done, I'd be concerned if I saw you with the daughter of someone who knew all about the syndicate.'

'Go on,' Nate says.

'If Martin thinks I know more than I do, and he thinks you're getting information out of me, he might ...'

'What?' Sinn says.

'I don't know! He might slip up or—'

'If he runs, he's of no use.'

'Unless ...' Nate raps his fingernails on the bench. 'We don't want to lose him in case he has information, or can lead us to someone who does, but—' he glances at Sinn, '—we've got nothing out of him so far but slaps on the back and canapés. Making him uneasy, throwing him off balance by having Phoebe around, that could work.'

'I don't want her around.'

'Roxburgh has invited you to a house party next month. You're going, right?'

'To meet his associates.'

'Are spouses and partners invited?'

Sinn's eyes narrow. 'I'm going with you.'

Nate grins as he looks from me to Sinn. 'You and Phoebe. You're not a bad proposition.'

When I drop my spoon into my mug, droplets of chocolate splash onto the bench. 'Is the house party at Roxburgh Estate? I could go too, couldn't I? Sinn could pretend I was his girlfriend.'

'No, Phoebe,' Sinn says.

I avoid his gaze as I go to the sink for the cloth. But as I wipe up the chocolate, our eyes meet. I raise my chin. '*Yes*, Sinn.'

His chair scrapes the floorboards as he stands, but I focus on the cloth, moving on from where I was seated to other, perfectly clean, regions of the bench.

Nate pulls up his sleeve and looks at his watch. 'We've got a call soon. Can we take a rain check? Maybe meet again next week?'

'We can settle the arrangements then.' I push my glass and mug towards him. 'Thank you for the hot chocolate.'

'Phoebe,' Sinn says, 'don't—'

'What?' I pick up my coat and hold it in front of me. 'You know why I want to do this. You know it's important to me.'

'That doesn't mean—'

'I didn't tell anyone about the navy helicopter, did I? And you spoke to my father before I did. I haven't said anything to Martin. I'll do what I'm told. And I won't do anything stupid either—like jump from a van in the middle of the night and freeze half to death.'

'That's irrelevant.' His phone vibrates on the bench but, lips firm, he keeps his eyes on me.

'You'd better take your call.'

He glances at the phone. 'Give me two minutes,' he says, before walking to the doors at the back of the house. 'Tor.' The verandah lights up when he flicks a switch. 'Hva er i veien?'

The gardens and paddocks are in darkness. Stars hide behind the clouds, as does the moon. I can't see the swimming pool or rain gauge. The thoroughbred mares won't be at the peppercorn tree— they'll be back in the yards at Roxburgh Estate. The yards are at the rear of the house.

Martin Roxburgh's house.

And the house he built for Robbie. Should I tell Sinn I know him? I *knew* him. Would he care?

Please, Robbie. Don't be at the house party.

As Sinn opens the sliding doors, a gust of icy air blasts into the room. 'I'll walk Phoebe to her car,' Nate says.

Sinn puts the phone against his chest. 'Wait for me.'

Nate stands back after opening the door to the hallway, but I check he's turned on the lights before I precede him.

'The sitting room is on the left,' he says from behind me. 'I'll light the fire, and you can put your feet up.'

I shake my head and shrug into my coat, checking my pocket for keys. 'It'll be after eight by the time I get home. My dog will be waiting. I have to stable the horses.'

Nate grimaces as he looks towards the kitchen. 'Sinn said to wait. He won't be long.'

'I have to go.' As soon as I step onto the verandah, the sensor lights turn on.

'It was his cousin; that's why he picked up.'

I walk down the steps to the path. 'He can talk to whoever he likes.'

'Tor's wife Golden is pregnant with twins. They're not due until next year, but Tor hasn't slept since he found out.'

'Is his wife unwell?' I stop on the path. 'Are the babies all right? Please, Nate, go back inside. Tell Sinn to take as long as he likes. I'll call him tomorrow.'

'Golden tells me she's fine, the babies are fine.'

'Then what's—'

Nate lifts a hand and holds it above his head. 'Tor's got three inches on me, and Golden—' he indicates my shoulder height, '—is tiny, about up to here. He's petrified that something will go wrong.'

Wind rustles through the leaves of the fig tree. 'You and Sinn are so far away from your families.'

'We come and go, the same as your sisters do.'

'Prim will come back soon. One day, I hope Patience will come back too.'

He smiles. 'Tor and Golden live a few hours out of Sydney, and Sinn has another cousin who spends a lot of time here. Have you heard of Per Amundsen? He's married to Harriet Scott.'

'The environmentalist with the ship?'

'Per is Norwegian Navy.'

'I've seen pictures of him and Harriet.' I blink. 'He's like Sinn, isn't he? Intense, serious.'

'Compared to Per, Sinn is a laugh a minute.' He grins. 'It's Tor who has charm, but take it from me, the others warm up when you get to know them.'

Sinn's four-wheel drive obscures my car completely. I increase my pace, overtaking Nate, and stand on the brick edging that separates the path from the parking area. I blow on my hands before putting them into my pockets.

'Sinn will let me do this, won't he?' I ask. 'Find out what happened with the syndicate?'

'Maybe.'

'Why is he so opposed to it?'

'For starters, he wasn't happy with what happened in Warrandale. You finding him like that.'

'I was upset about it at first, but ... now I'm okay.'

'We knew you'd worked with your father. We had reason to distrust you. Since then, he's changed his mind.'

'Another reason to let me help.'

'In our last assignment, Sinn was flexible in getting where we needed to go.' He tips his head to the side. 'So what's his problem with you, Phoebe? You got any insights?'

'He's arrogant. I can't be the only person he doesn't get along with.'

'At the very least, people respect him. They admire him.' He lowers his voice. 'I'm thinking you haven't googled him?'

'I checked out the UN committee he said he was associated with. I found a picture of him in uniform.'

He looks over his shoulder before turning back to me. 'Eighteen months ago,' he says, 'an explosion in the engine room of a Norwegian naval ship blew a hole in its side. Four men were killed in the blast, others were injured.'

'I read about it.'

'The captain thought the ship could be saved. Sinn was second-in-command and he disagreed. He said if they didn't get the crew into rescue boats, they'd be lost with the ship. Against orders, Sinn loaded the boats, sending them out as the ship began to roll. He piloted the last boat to leave.'

'Was everyone okay? Was Sinn?'

'Except for the mutiny allegations, yes.'

'What?'

'He was court martialled. The trial took weeks, but at the end of it he was not only exonerated, he was decorated. Even so, he needed a break. And that,' Nate's brows lift, 'is what brought him to—'

A curse. A footstep. A scatter of drops from the tea tree shrubs. 'You finished?' Sinn asks.

Nate jumps higher than I do, but he recovers more quickly. 'Night, Phoebe,' he says, squeezing my arm. 'Hope to see you again real soon.' He brushes past Sinn and walks to the steps, taking them in pairs. The door slams shut.

My heart is thumping double time. And I'm no closer to my car, hidden on the other side of Sinn's, than I was five minutes ago.

'Nate did nothing wrong, he was just trying to explain—he doesn't know why we argue.'

Sinn crosses his arms. 'Why do we argue?'

'We wouldn't if you'd let me do what I want.'

'You can't fix what your father did.' He's standing further back than Nate was and I can't see his expression. But I can imagine the crease between his brows. *They respect him. They admire him.*

'Please, Sinn.' Even bunched in my pockets, the tips of my fingers are numb. My heart is suddenly heavy.

He steps closer, his mouth set and grim. 'If I agree, you do *exactly* as I say. No more threats.'

'I promise I—'

The lights go out. Darkness descends.

I hold out a hand and look for a gap, a sliver, a fracture of light.

Nothing.

Fear claws its way up my throat.

The air is deep and thick and damp. I'm cold. Bitterly cold. I step back and—

The ground disappears.

'Oh!'

'Phoebe!'

I stagger. Something breaks my fall—Sinn's car against my back.

My heart races. My breaths are fast and loud. But now I can think. The timer expired and turned off the lights. When did I leave the house? Five minutes ago? Ten?

My father at the door. 'I said ten minutes! Turn out the light!'

Prim's whimper. 'No, Dad. It makes Phoebe cry.'

'Turn out the light!'

Sinn is talking but I can't make out his words. Deep breaths. Even breaths. In. Out. In. Out. His car is behind me, so the tree must be in front of me. Beyond the tree is the house. Beyond the house is the garden. I'm not trapped.

I can get out.

My keys are in my pocket. My car is on the other side of Sinn's. When I open the door, the ceiling light will shine. When I turn on the engine, the dash will light up. When I activate the headlights, silver arcs will spill onto the ground. I'm not trapped.

I can get out.

Sinn's fingers dig into my arms above the elbows. 'Phoebe,' he says. 'What is it? What happened?'

'The lights—' My voice is a croak.

He keeps hold of one arm as he shines his phone in my face. 'What the fuck?'

As I wrench free, my elbow hits the car's side mirror. 'Ow!'

He holds out his hand. 'Let me—'

'No!' I back further away. 'Just—' I put my hands on my knees and suck in breaths. 'I'm tired. I haven't eaten. That's all. I'm fine.'

I focus on the light from Sinn's phone as I take one shaky step at a time. My car lights up when I open the door. The passenger seat is crowded with boxes and bags—puzzles, books and toys. I throw my coat in the back and sit behind the wheel, fumbling as I fasten the seatbelt. Holding the key in two hands, I push it into the ignition.

'Sinn!' Nate shouts from the house. The spotlight behind the cars glows brightly once more. 'They're on the line!'

'You'd better go,' I say.

'You shouldn't drive.'

'I should.' I nod stiffly. 'I'll be fine.' When I finally look up, it's into his eyes.

He crouches. Puts a hand on the wheel. 'Phoebe, what is it?'

'Nothing. It's— I'm fine.'

'Come into the house.' He speaks quietly and calmly. Reassuringly, as if to a child. 'I'll make sjokolade like it is in Norway. I'll drive you home.'

'No.' I shake my head. 'I'll pull over if I need to.' I switch on the headlights and release the handbrake. 'When will I hear from you?'

Never taking his eyes from my face, he stands and steps back. 'I'm going to Brussels,' he says stiffly. 'Nate will call.'

CHAPTER
14

Mintie can't be ridden because of the injury to his leg, but a few times a month, riding Camelot, I lead him onto Mr Riley's land. He trots intermittently to keep pace with Camelot's walk, and canters when Camelot trots. We don't go too far or too fast, so Wickham comes with us. When he's not running in front of the horses, he makes his own path, rummaging in the scrub and following scents. If we encounter sheep or cattle on neighbouring land, he comes back to heel, as if to signal that they're beyond his brief.

Mr Riley's old truck is parked in the lane, near the sheep pens and shed. When Wickham, tongue lolling, darts over the fence to drink from an old enamelled bath, I walk the horses through the gate to the lane to wait in the shade of the gums.

'Phoebe!' Mr Riley appears from the back of the shed, bracing his bandy legs as he leans on a crowbar. 'You got a minute?'

I change Mintie's rope to my other hand, nudging Camelot with my heel to bring him around. 'What's the problem?'

He puts his hand to his ear. 'Speak up!' Mr Riley's hearing has been poor for years, but he won't wear a hearing aid.

I raise my voice. 'How can I help?'

'The agent tells me if I want to sell this land to one of them hobby farmers, I've got to clean it up,' he shouts. 'I was planning on taking these tools to the shed, but I can't even open the door.'

As I slide from Camelot's back and loosely tie the horses to a post, Mr Riley walks back to the shed. He watches as I wrestle with the bolt, but I don't have the strength to pull it across.

'Looks like I'll have to break it,' Mr Riley says. 'Trouble is,' he holds the crowbar in front of him, 'I've got a bung shoulder and can't lift this high enough.'

'There might be another way.' I kick through the grass and find a half-brick—possibly the one I used on the day I found Sinn. After turning it with my boot to make sure it's free of spiders, I pick it up and bash the end of the bolt. On the third hit, the bolt shoots through the barrel.

Mr Riley pushes against the doors, scraping them over the concrete threshold when they stick. He grins. 'Good work.'

The hay bales, lying six by two where I dragged them, are greenish gold. The hessian sacks are a toffee-coloured heap on the ground.

'Bloody squatters,' Mr Riley says.

I touch his arm. 'Didn't Jeremiah tell you it was Camelot and me who came here? I should have put everything back. Do you want me to do that now?'

'No point,' he says, 'when them squatters might come back.'

'But I don't think there are any squatters.'

'Not since I bolted the doors.'

When Wickham appears, I signal, sending him back to the horses. 'Mike keeps recycled parts in his foundry, Mr Riley. I'm

sure he'd help you to fit a bolt that didn't jam. He could probably
fix the hinges as well.'

'Next you'll be telling me to get a padlock, which'd be putting
even more good money after bad.' He scratches his ear. 'Bolt cut-
ters, Phoebe, that's what them squatters would use. When I sell, the
new owner can sort them out.'

I pick up the sacks, fold them in half and lay them on the hay.
'You don't mind selling?'

'If I get the right price, it'll free me up to buy the property
between my sons, which is closer to my other farm. They'll run
their land with mine and increase their herds, and I'll get more time
to see to my crops.'

It's barely eight o'clock, not much later in the morning than when
I was here weeks ago, but the shed looks very different. Notwithstanding decades of grime, sunlight floods through the windows.
There's not the darkness of the storm. Or the darkness of last
night.

I *thought* my fear of the dark was under control. There'll always
be triggers, but last night's flashback to childhood was unsettling. I
was fourteen when the streetlight outside our bedroom went out.
Prim gave me her old nightlight in the shape of a panda, but Dad
found it and took it away. After a week of broken sleep, Patience
dragged me to the local council after school. She marched inside
the town hall building and told the receptionist that the broken
streetlight was an issue of public safety, explaining our father was
so *ancient* that he could fall on the footpath and *die*, so they had to
come and fix it.

That incident, and what happened in the camping ground a
few months later, prompted me to see the school social worker.
After reassuring me that privacy laws meant she wouldn't talk to

my father, she referred me to Irina, the psychologist I saw before Mandy.

Nyctophobia. Fear of the dark.

Irina was in her thirties. She had a broad smile, a strong Russian accent and wild brown hair tied back with coloured scarves. I'd watch her mouth, bright with red lipstick, as she enunciated phrases that were new to me. Exposure therapy. Sometimes she'd shut the blinds, hold my hand and gradually dim the lights, an actual exposure to what I feared. More commonly, she'd encourage me to visualise my fear. I'd close my eyes and imagine the lights had gone out.

I learnt to reduce the panic and anxiety that I felt in the dark. If I'd been game to tell her what had triggered the panic—my father locking me in the cupboard overnight—she might have been able to do more. But I didn't trust privacy laws enough to do that. I told her I'd inadvertently locked myself in.

'For how long?' she asked.

'Not that long,' I lied.

'It was night time?'

'Yes.'

Irina taught me other things too. Cognitive therapy. I learnt to identify the types of terrors and fears I experienced when I was anxious. Smothering blankets. Fathomless wells. And replace them with positive or realistic thoughts.

I'm not shut in.

I can get out.

Sitting in the bright little room at the back of Irina's house, I could easily believe what she told me: being in the dark doesn't always lead to negative consequences. At home with my father, it was more difficult to rationalise my fears.

'Achoo!' When I sneeze repeatedly through the dust, Wickham's bark rings out.

Mr Riley, sorting through rusty tools on the shearing platform, looks up.

'The horses are outside, Mr Riley. I'd better head back.'

He tips back his hat. 'If I find a buyer, Phoebe, I reckon I could put in a good word for you. Let them know you help out around the place in exchange for bringing your horses on the land.'

'And that would be the truth, wouldn't it? Because I tell you about broken fences and feral cats and—'

'Course you do,' he says. 'But that don't mean I've got to tell the buyer.'

I smile. 'Would you like some help before you sell, Mr Riley?'

'Reckon I do, and thanks for offering. My grandson Tom said he'd give me a hand, but you know these young fellas, not too reliable. I'll give you a call in a week or so.'

Wickham waits at the door, running circles around me as I walk into the sunshine. Camelot flicks his tail across his rump and stamps his foot. Mintie, standing at his side, looks startlingly white to his black.

White and black. Dark and light. *Exercises to control your breathing.* I'll look for the fact sheets Irina gave me, and practise relaxation strategies. She was confident I didn't need medication to curb my anxiety because I didn't have anxiety about other things. Even so, she warned me to stay away from drugs and alcohol.

My fear of the dark was under control. But ever since I found Sinn …

I swing into the saddle before crossing my fingers over Camelot's rein. 'Things will improve when he's gone.'

CHAPTER
15

On Friday morning, over a week since I was in Denman, I receive a text.

Hey, Phoebe. Can I see you later today? Nate.

I don't finish until 4 but after that is fine. If I don't answer the door, I'll be at the stables.

Benjamin sometimes has a lunchtime booking, to save him from missing football training or mountain bike practice after school. He's still brushing Mintie when Jane arrives with Matilda.

'Won't be too long!' I call.

'We're early,' Jane says. 'Is it okay if we watch?'

When I wave, Jane takes Matilda's hand and they walk across the garden, but they're twenty metres away when Matilda spots Wickham, lying in the shade of a bottlebrush tree.

'No! I don't want him!'

I whistle to Wickham. 'Here, boy.'

As he bolts across the grass towards me, he runs past Matilda.

'No!' she screams.

'Bloody hell,' Benjamin says, 'that little kid's got a massive set of lungs.'

'Watch your language,' I say, hiding a smile as I push Camelot back from the fence and tie him to a ring near his stable. 'After you've finished that exercise, Benjamin, do you think you could do me a favour?'

He winces as he clings onto the brush. '… eight, nine, ten.' Wedging the brush between his knees, he stretches out his fingers to give the muscles a break. 'Another one?'

I laugh. 'Holding on to the brush helps you to improve your fine motor skills. It's not a favour.'

'Even though you're killing me?'

When Wickham ducks through the fence, I stroke his ears before sending him to the stable. 'So how about that favour?'

Benjamin grins. 'Depends what it is.'

'If I can get her down here, it would be really good for Matilda to see how well you're doing with Mintie. Would you mind?'

'Peer pressure, right? Do I get paid?'

'I'll give you a bag of manure for your dad's veggie patch. Digging is good for hand strength too.'

As Jane fetches a picnic blanket from her boot, I explain to Matilda that I'd like to sit with her and her mum. Jane spreads the blanket out a few metres away from the fence. She waves to Benjamin.

'Aren't you in the local AFL team? Matilda's dad used to play in Sydney—he coaches at your club when he can. His name is Lachlan.'

'Lachlan Shaw? Who played for the Swans? You're joking, right?'

Matilda sits next to Jane on the blanket. 'Do you remember Benjamin?' she asks her daughter. 'We've seen him at the oval with Daddy.'

Matilda shakes her head. 'I don't like the ball when it's wet.'

'Next year,' I say, 'Benjamin will be in Year 6 at your school, and you'll be in Kindergarten.'

'Benjamin does activities with Phoebe like you do,' Jane says, 'so he can have more fun at school.'

'Yeah.' Benjamin rolls his eyes. 'Writing is really fun.'

I hold back a laugh. 'Could you tell Matilda how you brush Mintie, please, Benjamin?'

Benjamin takes the currycomb from the bucket. 'This one is to get Mintie's hair out when he's moulting, and this one ...' He pulls out a brush with thick soft bristles. 'This is the one for his belly.' He bends down low as he brushes Mintie's stomach and between his front legs before rummaging again and pulling out a wide-toothed comb. 'This is for Mintie's mane, tail and forelock.' When he pulls the comb through his own thick hair and it covers his eyes, Matilda laughs out loud.

Jane peppers Benjamin with questions, and Matilda listens closely. After a while she stands, so she can see Benjamin and Mintie more easily.

'Would you like to go to the fence now?' I ask. 'You don't have to touch Mintie, but you'll get a much better view.'

I climb over the fence and stand at Mintie's head as Benjamin combs through the pony's long silver tail with his hand.

'Separate your fingers as wide as you can, Benjamin. Stretch them out, count to ten and release. That's great.'

He swings Mintie's tail back and forth. 'Looking good now, mate.'

Jane laughs. 'You could be a hairdresser.'

When Benjamin picks up the ends of Mintie's tail and pushes them through the fence, Jane and I are just as surprised as Matilda. 'You wanna have a turn now?' he says.

Jane and I exchange glances, waiting for Matilda to scream, but besides blinking hard, she holds her ground. As Benjamin waits, she reaches out a hand and, with just her fingertips, strokes Mintie's tail. She pulls her hand back quickly, but doesn't step away.

'Mintie doesn't kick or nothing,' Benjamin says confidently. 'Want to give it another shot?'

This time Matilda opens her fingers like Benjamin did, and runs them through the strands.

'It's like Elsa's hair,' she whispers.

'The girl from the *Frozen* movie?' Benjamin says. 'My brother reckons she's hot.'

'Talking of Elsa,' I say to Benjamin, 'could you show Matilda what you did with Mintie's forelock last week? Do it as tightly as you can.'

He grins. 'No worries.'

Matilda's eyes widen as I turn Mintie towards the fence, and Benjamin separates his forelock into three. Biting his lip in concentration, he plaits all the way from Mintie's ears to the end of his nose.

'Great work, Benjamin.' When we high five, Matilda steps back, but a few moments later, returns to the fence. 'What do you think, Matilda?'

She smiles shyly. 'It's like Elsa,' she whispers.

When Terry arrives to collect Benjamin and take him back to school, Jane and Matilda go into the house. Benjamin does cartwheels over the grass as I tell his father how helpful he's been. Terry pulls his shirt down over his rounded stomach and tucks it into his shorts. He's unusually straight-faced.

'Remember last year, Phoebe? Benjamin was the class clown—in trouble left, right and centre. His mum and I lost a lot of sleep over that. This year? He's a different boy.'

'Bright children like Benjamin tend to hide their difficulties. That can make it hard for a teacher to work out what's going on.'

'Sure, he's good at footy, but that isn't enough. Not when you gotta write legible to get a job, and use a computer to do your banking. I know he complains, but every night he catches balls on his fingertips like you showed him. He works real hard. He's not hating school any more. His teacher is over the moon.'

'He's acquiring skills other children take for granted. I was so proud of him today.'

Terry crosses his arms and chuckles. 'Look at you, Phoebe, getting teary. You've got a lovely little set-up here, so when are you going to take the plunge? Have your own kids to fuss over?'

When Benjamin throws an imaginary pass to his father, I intercept it. 'Good one, Phoebe!' he shouts as he runs to the ute and jumps into the passenger seat.

I smile at Terry. 'I'm pretty happy with other people's children.'

'You and Sinn seemed chummy at the fete. What's going on there?'

I'm about to tell Terry that whatever he might have seen at the fete was a one-off, but he works all over the district, and tends to know everybody's business. What if he finds out that I'll be at Roxburgh Estate with Sinn in a few weeks' time?

'It was nice that Sinn helped out. I'm sure I'll see him again.'

'He's a good bloke.' He grins as he opens the door of his ute. 'Reckon he'd fit the bill.'

I love my family and home, my children, job and animals. I have plenty going on in my life. Why do people think that something— or someone—is missing?

Sinn and I are attracted to each other. What else do we have in common? I don't have family in Norway. I've never been in a helicopter. I don't fly to Brussels. Or sail in Arctic waters.

I could never trust him to stay.

Did I trust Robbie Roxburgh? I must have done, or he wouldn't have hurt me so badly.

U

When Nate hasn't turned up by four thirty, I go to the horses. Camelot, standing in the yard with his neck stretched over the wheelbarrow, watches closely as I hurl in another pitchfork of straw. His rug is ripped at the neck and the tailpiece is worn from when he scratches his rump on the fence posts, but I can't afford a new one this month. I wipe hair out of my face. I can't afford a new one next month either.

'Phoebe! Are you down there?'

'Coming!' By the time I reach the garden, Nate is at the grave-yard, leaning over the spikes of the wrought iron fence. Wickham sits next to him, his tail sweeping the path.

'You got your own cemetery here, Phoebe?'

I walk quickly up the path and stand on the other side of Wick-ham. 'I think of it as a garden.'

'It doesn't give you the heebie-jeebies?'

I brush a cobweb from the cross. 'Good people live on in our memories. I didn't know the people here, but I think they were all good people. It's nice to remember them.'

He grins. 'Which one's the most memorable?'

I point to the closest grave. 'Reverend Brockman died at Gallipoli in World War One. His name is on the cenotaph in town as well. The cross is for Anna Amelia Andrews, who was only a baby when she died. That always makes me sad, thinking about the life she should have had, and how unhappy her parents must have been.'

'Born in December and died in January.' He sighs. 'Only one Christmas. My mom and sisters would cry buckets over that.'

'William Tilley, with the sandstone headstone, died on his sixteenth birthday, so that's no good either. But—' I point to another grave.

Mary Brockman, wife of Samuel and mother of John, Robert and Alfred. Loving grandmother to Jean, Elizabeth, Victoria, Anne and Mary. 16 July 1872 – 2 February 1937.

'That grave belongs to Mary, Reverend Brockman's wife. The church was decommissioned in 1929, and the graveyard was closed. I think someone must have snuck Mary in.' I smile. 'I like that.'

Nate loops his thumbs through the tabs on his jeans and rocks back on his heels. 'Reckon I do too.' He follows as I walk down the path to the back verandah.

'I only have instant coffee. Is that okay?' I speak over my shoulder.

'No way is that okay.'

We sit on the verandah with a glass of water each. The horses, ready for dinner, look over the fence.

Nate stretches out his legs. 'You still want to be a part of what Sinn and I are up to?'

'Of course I do. Isn't that why you're here?'

'We've told the Roxburgh syndicate members that they got an extra member and he was up to no good,' Nate says. 'They all denied knowing about it, but some of them were toey.'

'Martin Roxburgh in particular?'

He crosses his legs at the ankles. 'Your name won't go on the RSVP to Roxburgh's invitation—better to keep him guessing— but you and Sinn should be seen together beforehand.'

'We were seen at the fete.' When Nate sits straighter in his chair, I wish I could bite back my words. 'Not for long though. What are you suggesting?'

'How would you feel about going out with Sinn next Saturday? A drink or two at a pub in Denman. He said you don't have to. Just say the word and no questions asked.'

'It would be a set-up for the weekend away? Yes, I can go.'

Nate looks at me intently. 'You sure about this?'

Three kookaburras swoop out of the gums and land on the railing. The adult's wings are marked with blue; the fledglings are similar in size to the adult, but their brown and cream feathers are lighter and fluffier.

'If you think we need to set the scene, I'll do it.'

Nate looks like he wants to say something else, but when I extend my hand, he gives me his empty glass and stands. 'Better hit the road.' One of the younger kookaburras takes flight and the others quickly follow.

'You drove an hour to get here to tell me about Saturday? Why didn't you call?'

He blows out a breath. 'In case you were having second thoughts.'

'And you had to find that out in person?'

'Sinn thought you'd be more likely to talk to me than him.'

'So this was a test?' I stoop to pick up my glass before facing him again. 'If I'd hesitated, you'd have got rid of me?'

He grimaces. 'What happened last week, Phoebe? The night you left the house? Sinn was rattled as hell when he got back. He wouldn't say why.'

I shrug, as if being afraid of the dark is nothing to be concerned about. 'He doesn't want my help. You know that already.' I smile bravely. 'Send me the details, and I'll see him at the pub on Saturday.'

I'm walking back to the house after feeding the horses when Nate calls. He presents perfectly logical reasons for why Sinn will pick me up on Saturday. 'After all, it's a date,' he says. 'Sinn would want an excuse to spend time with you. Taking you home will suggest you're close.'

Nate must have called Sinn immediately after he left. They work together. From the very beginning, they've kept secrets. I'd be naïve to trust either of them. It shouldn't concern me that they talk behind my back.

But it does.

CHAPTER
16

By six o'clock on Saturday evening, it's raining again, the drops so fine that the wind picks them up and throws them around. Camelot pokes his head over the stable door but, even sitting on the back verandah, I can barely see him in the gloom. I twist my newly washed hair into a roll, tuck the throw more snugly around my legs and press the phone to my ear.

'Dad,' I say for the third time, 'please listen to what I'm saying. There's nothing to fear from the man at the door.'

'It's him! I told him I don't have the records. I told him he has to talk to you!'

'It's not Sinn Tørrissen. The man's name is Alex. He's delivering the groceries I ordered from the supermarket. Please let him in.'

'I don't want him here! Send him away!'

'You called this morning, Dad. You said you have no milk. You have to let him in.'

'You bring the milk. You do it!'

The function at the pub starts at seven o'clock. Sinn is bound to arrive at any minute.

'I have something else on. And I was there on Tuesday. That was only four days ago.'

'Do as I say!'

When he hangs up, I call the driver back. 'Can you leave the bags on the doorstep? My father won't come outside, but I'll try to sort something out.'

Headlights shine on the driveway. I forget what shoes I have on when I stand, and my heel sinks through a gap between the boards.

'Damn!' I wrench out the heel and tiptoe to the kitchen, locking the door behind me before scrolling through my contacts. 'Josephine. It's Phoebe Cartwright. That's right, Professor Cartwright's daughter. How are you?'

I occasionally chat to Josephine, Dad's next-door neighbour of the past ten years, over the fence, but it's only as she catalogues her physiotherapist appointments that I remember she had a knee replacement last month. I can't ask her to help with groceries. She can barely hobble around her house using a walking frame.

Sinn is walking up the porch steps when I open the door. He's in his customary black jeans, collared shirt and sweater. He looks good. He smells nice. His hair has grown; he brushes it back with his fingers. I tear my gaze away and cover the mouthpiece.

'Sorry. Come in. I won't be long.'

He nods politely, walks to Wickham and crouches by his bed. Wickham lifts his head and wags his tail.

'I'm sorry to hear that your knee is still so painful,' I tell Josephine. 'Yes, I'll help with your garden next weekend.'

'Come for lunch on Sunday,' she says. 'I'll make you lasagne, and you can take a slice to your father. I wouldn't even know he was there, love. I haven't seen him in months.'

'Thanks, Josephine.' I cross my fingers. 'I don't suppose one of your sons is with you tonight? No? That's okay. No, everything is fine. If you hear someone next door, it'll only be me. I have something to sort out for Dad.'

As soon as I disconnect, Sinn straightens. 'Phoebe? What is it?'

I collect my thoughts. 'I'm sorry you drove all the way here, but my father needs help. I have to go there tonight. We can meet at the pub later on. I'll be late … eight thirty? Maybe nine?'

He frowns. 'We should go together.'

'I was ready to go.' I smooth my hands down my pale blue dress. 'I didn't expect this.'

'We'll go to your father on the way.'

'He's an hour *out* of our way.'

'You said you'd do as I asked.'

'But that had nothing to do with this.'

'You have a coat, yes?'

I leave enough lights on to welcome me when I get home, then yank my cream wool coat from the back of a chair and hang it over my arm. Wickham, already sulking, feigns sleep as I stroke his head.

'You look after things here,' I whisper. 'I'll come home as soon as I can.'

As I tiptoe over the gravel to the four-wheel drive, Sinn strides in front and opens the passenger door, closing it behind me. He has his phone in his hand as he climbs into the driver's seat.

'Do you mind if I make a call?' he says.

'If you'd let me drive myself, you could have called without me being here.'

'The call was booked at eleven. I have to bring it forward.'

'You see!' I undo my belt. 'If I drive, you can take your call when you planned. Or you can talk while you're waiting for me at the pub.'

His lips are clamped as he leans across my legs and opens the glove box. We don't touch, but my heart hammers hard against my ribs. He takes out ear pods and clicks the glove box shut.

'Put on your belt, Phoebe,' he says gruffly.

I secure the belt again before searching my bag, pulling out a notebook and pen. 'Aren't you afraid I'll listen in?'

'If it were confidential, I wouldn't do it.'

'I won't listen anyway. I'm behind with my reports so I'll work on them.'

Other than the automatic wipers that sporadically scrape the windscreen as we drive towards the highway, the only sounds are the whir of the wheels on the road and occasional mutterings, mostly ja and nei, from Sinn. Even if I wanted to listen, I wouldn't understand.

He drives quickly but keeps within the speed limit. I mostly keep my eyes on my notebook, but every time I glance at his profile, he seems to be frowning. When we reach the outskirts of Dubbo, I point out where he should turn off. Within ten minutes, he parks at the front of my father's house.

'Ha det,' he says to whomever he's talking to, before removing his ear buds.

I take keys out of my bag, leaving it on the floor as I open the door. 'I won't be long. Five minutes? I just have to carry the groceries inside.'

'Do you want my help?'

'No.' I shake my head. 'No, thank you. He's ... he hasn't been well lately. And you know he doesn't like strangers.'

The streetlight outside the bedroom I shared with my sisters shines into the garden. When Mum lived here, there were roses, gardenias, and annuals like primulas and pansies. For a few years, the larger plants survived neglect and little water, but died well before I left home.

The groceries are piled up near the front door. I open it to darkness and turn on the light before taking the bags inside.

'Dad?' My voice is raised, but not too loudly. 'It's Phoebe.'

I'm halfway along the hallway when an additional smell permeates the stale musty scents I'm familiar with. I brace myself before opening the door to the kitchen. Even so, I take an involuntary step back. Sour milk. It's on the draining board and bench top, the sink and cupboards beneath it. A long dried puddle, brown around the edges, trails across the floor. If I breathe in, I'll gag.

My father, dressed in pyjamas and a dressing gown, sits at his desk. 'You're here.'

I walk stiltedly to the sink. 'What happened?'

'I dropped it.'

'You didn't think to tell me? I could have arranged for a cleaner.'

'I don't want anyone here!'

I find one of Mum's old aprons in the bottom kitchen drawer. The sleeves of my dress are long and fitted, but the fabric is clingy so I push it up my arms and pull on rubber gloves. I take disinfectant from under the sink.

'When did you eat last?'

'I had no milk for my tea.'

I flick the kettle on with my elbow. 'I'll heat some food once I've cleaned up, and then I'll make your tea.'

'Why are you dressed like that?'

I rinse the bench again. 'I'm going out.'

Before I mop the floor, I walk to the front door. Sinn is leaning against the car but straightens as soon as he sees me.

'I'll be another twenty minutes. I'm sorry.'

'Can I help?'

'No, thank you.'

By the time my father's dinner and tea is on his desk, over half an hour has passed. 'I'm going now, Dad.'

'Who is outside?'

'The person I'm going out with.'

'The policeman?'

'I broke up with Jeremiah years ago.'

'The man who came to see me? What was his name?'

'Sinn Tørrissen.'

'He was banging on the door.'

'That was the delivery man.'

'You gave him my records?'

I sigh. 'Yes.'

He rocks back and forth as he eats. 'You keep him away. I won't talk to him. I won't talk to anyone.'

'I'll try to get here tomorrow afternoon. The nurse will be here again on Monday. You have to let her in.'

He holds out his leg and pulls up his pants to show me the dressing. 'You do it.'

'It's an ulcer.' I shake my head, back away. 'I can't.'

On the way out, I stop at the bathroom. I scrub my hands again, and wash my arms to the elbows.

My father. His house.

Fear. Shame. Secrets. Unhappiness.

CHAPTER
17

When I walk around the car, I keep my head low even though it's not raining.

Sinn opens the door and watches as I climb into the seat.

'I'm sorry.' My voice wavers. 'There was a mess. Milk. Sorry.'

When he touches my arm, I jump. 'It's cold tonight,' he says. Leaning forward, he carefully pulls one sleeve down over my wrist, and then the other. Soft words. Gentle actions.

As he studies my profile, I try not to swallow. But the lump in my throat gets bigger. My chest is so tight that I can barely breathe.

'I can take you home,' he says.

When I shake my head, he shuts the door.

I squeeze my eyes shut. Concentrate on breathing. In. Out. In. Out.

Sinn takes off his sweater and throws it into the back before sitting behind the wheel. The heater's fan whirs over the sounds of the engine.

'We can go out tomorrow,' he says.

'It's okay. As long as …' My hand shakes when I hold it out. 'What can you smell?'

He stills for a moment. But then he lowers his head and takes my hand. My skin warms as he slowly breathes in. 'Soap,' he says.

I take my hand back. 'Are you telling the truth?'

His gaze softens. 'I always do, Phoebe.'

I nod stiffly. 'We can go now.'

He turns on the radio, a world news channel, and we listen in silence. It starts to drizzle again, and the wipers start up. There are very few cars on the highway. He glances at me briefly and then he turns away.

'Tell me about your father.'

'You know enough already.'

'You dislike him yet you care for him.'

'Because if I didn't—' I look out of my window. 'Can we talk about something else? Something non-personal?'

He turns off the radio. 'Like what?'

'Oh …' The wipers continue to swish. The wheels roll. 'Drizzle.' I point to the windscreen. 'How do you say that in Norwegian?'

'Duskregn.'

'It's a type of rain, isn't it?'

When he glances at me, I gaze seriously back. He turns back to the road and, just for a moment, I see the lift in his lip.

'Both drizzle and rain are precipitation. Drizzle drops are smaller than raindrops.'

'How small?'

'Less than point five of a millimetre in diameter. That's why drizzle falls slowly.'

'It has less weight.'

'Making it subject to the wind.'

'Which clouds does it come from?'

'Tonight?' He lifts a finger from the steering wheel as he looks at the clouds. 'Low stratiform and stratocumulus.'

'I have another question.'

His lip lifts again. 'Yes, Phoebe?'

'We've had so much rain lately. Some people say it means the drought has definitely ended, but others say it hasn't. What do you think?'

'You can look at it in different ways.'

'That's what I'm trying to understand.'

When he turns on the four-wheel drive's high beams, the drizzle is like a cloud in front of the car. There are trees at the side of the road: the trunks are silver and the leaves are glossy black.

'In meteorological terms,' he says, 'drought is a severe negative deviation from mean precipitation.'

'Things are different from what they've been in the past?'

'Meteorologists can look at deficiencies in rain over a period of months, years, decades. The drought can be over or not, depending on the period.'

'What else?'

He looks my way again. 'This is interesting to you?'

I hold my hands in front of the vents to capture the warmth. 'My kids, a lot of their parents, they live off the land.'

'Are you warm enough, Phoebe?'

I fold my hands in my lap. 'Yes, thank you.'

He turns up the temperature. 'Soil moisture can decrease through evapotranspiration. Do you know this word?'

I laugh. 'No.'

'Soil moisture is lost through evaporation, and also the transpiration of plants—where plants take moisture from the ground.'

'Plants can't grow if it's too dry. That happens a lot in our summer.'

'This might be known as an agricultural drought—if there isn't enough feed for livestock, and winter crops can't be planted, or maintained, because of insufficient rain.'

As he turns off the road to Denman, I smooth down my dress. 'Anything else?'

He glances at me. 'Hydrological droughts occur when water resources are threatened. Streams run dry. Dams don't fill. After prolonged dryness, the soil will soak up the rain and lessen the run-off.'

As we approach the pub on Denman's main street, a Federation-style hotel with a wide verandah on the first floor, he indicates and turns into the carpark. It's too late to ask him to put the radio back on. The silence is—

'Any more questions?'

I rack my brain. 'Don't you miss the ocean? When will you go back to the navy?'

He reverses into a space and switches off the engine, only turning to me as he unclips his belt.

'These are personal questions.'

When I lean forward to pick up my bag, I move so quickly that my seatbelt locks. 'You're right. Forget I said anything. It doesn't matter.'

'Phoebe. Don't—'

'Forget it!'

I unclip my belt, snatch my bag from the floor and open the door while Sinn, face set, watches me silently. It's drizzling again. When I open the back door for my coat, I hesitate. Sinn's sweater is sprawled on the top. It has the same label as the one he left at my house. Laget i Norge.

Where is the old pink sweater I lay on his chest in the storm?

When I tug at the sleeve of my coat, pulling it towards me, Sinn's sweater slips off my coat and onto the seat. As I meticulously fasten my buttons, Sinn stands over me with an open umbrella. He balances the umbrella between his shoulder and neck, securing a cuff on his shirt as I adjust my collar.

He straightens and our eyes meet. 'What about your sweater?' I ask.

'I won't need it.'

I open my mouth to argue before looking away and searching through my bag for lip gloss. I unscrew the top and pull out the stick, swiping the end quickly across my lips.

'I'm ready,' I say.

His lips are slightly open. His gaze is on my mouth. He lifts his hand slowly before, centimetres from my cheek, he stills.

I wait.

I ache.

He cups my face. His thumb glides to my chin. 'May I?' he asks.

'Yes.'

He brushes his thumb along my bottom lip and back again. When he hesitates in the middle and presses, a flood of warmth seeps through my veins. My heart thumps hard and my knees go weak.

He lets me go, his eyes still pinned to my mouth. He runs his thumb across his lip, smearing it with lip gloss.

I swallow. 'What …'

His eyes are bright. 'We're late,' he says. 'It gives us a reason.'

I open my mouth and shut it. 'Have you pretended before?' I finally say.

'Never.' He picks up a lock of hair at my shoulder, rubs it between two fingers. 'Have you?'

'If I'd had more experience …' I lift my hand like he did, run my thumb across his lip, 'I'd have worn red lipstick.'

'I wouldn't change anything.' He touches my mouth again, this time with his index finger. 'Your mouth is beautiful.'

My heart races like a wild thing. 'Vakker.'

'Veldig vakker,' he says quietly. 'Very beautiful.'

He's still holding the umbrella with one hand. Both my hands are free. Palms flat, I place them on his shoulders. Taller than usual in heels, I lean against his chest and press my lips against his.

'Fuck,' he mutters.

My mouth moves over his lips until they part. When I find his tongue, I shudder a sigh. His hand slides from my face to my shoulder and he pushes his fingers into my hair to stroke my neck. We trade shaky breaths as our lips play together. Tentative yet tempting. Tender yet—

'Oi! Police!'

Sinn pivots as he shoves me behind him, shielding my body with his. His arm is rock hard at my side and my back, keeping me in place. The umbrella, upside down, rocks on the bitumen. I peer around his body.

Bulked up with a protective vest, a truncheon and other equipment swinging from his belt, Jeremiah swaggers towards us. His curly hair escapes from his cap. 'PDA, Miss Cartwright?' he says, laughter in his voice, as he peels away from a policewoman.

She smiles in our direction. 'Sorry to interrupt, folks.' She lifts two takeaway cups in salute before carrying them to a police car parked near the carpark's exit.

'You oughta be ashamed of yourself,' Jeremiah says.

My arms, bent at the elbows, are pinned against Sinn's back. I push against his shoulder blades. 'It's okay.'

His eyes still on Jeremiah, Sinn loosens his grip. I pick up the umbrella, shaking it before releasing the catch. I hold out my hand, palm up. The rain has eased.

Jeremiah, grinning, wraps an arm around my shoulders. He kisses the top of my head. 'Hey, Phoebe. What are you all tarted up for?'

'A drink. What are you doing here?'

'Keeping Denman safe from troublemakers like you.'

'As if? What's PDA?'

'Public display of affection, idiot. You didn't behave like that when we were going out.' Jeremiah holds out a hand to Sinn. 'Jeremiah Jones. Nice reflexes, mate. What are you? Military? SAS?'

'Sinn Tørrissen,' he says as they shake. 'Navy.'

As the police car pulls onto the road, Sinn throws the umbrella into the back of his four-wheel drive and takes out a jacket.

'Ex-boyfriend?' he says as we walk towards the pub.

'Yes.'

He nods curtly. But when we reach the foot of the steps to the entrance of the pub, he holds out his hand. 'Take it.'

I pull up short. 'Already? Why?'

He pointedly looks at my mouth. 'Why not?'

Is he angry about the kiss? Even though pretending to kiss me started us off in the first place?

When I give him my hand, he holds on to it tightly. His hand is far larger. His grip is cool but firm. This is pretend. He said I have a beautiful mouth. We're attracted to each other. I have to guard my heart.

I take a steadying breath. 'How long have we been seeing each other?'

'We met when I came to your house. When I asked about the syndicate, you didn't know anything. We've dated casually since the fete. Don't lie. Be honest or avoid the question.'

Strings of lights hang from the balustrade and twist around the poles. 'Why are we here?'

'I was invited by Elizabeth and Beatrice Oldfield. You know them?'

'I know that they're sisters and they live in a big old homestead just out of town. They do charity work, but also own racehorses.'

'It's Elizabeth's seventieth birthday.'

The bar is packed with well-dressed men and women, mostly young and middle-aged, and couples who are probably here for the weekend. Two singers sit near the window and strum their guitars. When Sinn bends to speak into my ear, I smell his shampoo.

'We're in a room upstairs,' he says, tightening his grip as we weave our way through the interior—black and white decor and wide timber floorboards—to the staircase. As I climb the stairs, one hand in Sinn's, one hand on the railing, I glance at the photographs of thoroughbreds, expensively framed and hung on the wall. On the landing before the last few stairs there are three photos, larger than the others and closely grouped together.

I tug Sinn's hand. 'Wait.'

The first of the photographs depicts a newborn foal, wobbly on his legs, his coat as dark as night. In the second photo, a big black horse is racing. He's stretching out for the finish and all four hooves are off the ground. The third photograph is of the same horse, trotting through a cloud of silver mist towards the camera. He's dripping wet; his ears are pricked.

Sinn squeezes my hand. 'What?'

'It's Camelot.' I'm already certain, but peering more closely, I make out the brand on the racehorse's shoulder.

'Your horse? You haven't seen these before?'

I shake my head. 'I've never been up here. I don't mix with Denman's elite any more.'

'You did once?'

'That's how I knew Martin Roxburgh. That's how I found Camelot.'

There must be over twenty people in the wood-panelled room. I recognise Brent Green, the stud manager at Roxburgh Estate, who towers over the group of women he's with. He's not overweight, but Auntie Kate would have described him as 'big-boned'. Before his first wife left him and he married Evie, he had his own training facility, but it had to be sold in the divorce settlement. He'd be in his forties now; his hair, still thick and shaggy, is greying.

He's not far away but when I smile, he appears to look through me. It's only been five years. Surely he can't have forgotten—

'Sinn!' Either Elizabeth or Beatrice—they look very similar— leaves the group she was with and glides across the room. When she tosses her head, her hair, precisely layered and skilfully coloured, shines in shades of gold. She taps her watch. 'What time do you call this?'

'Good evening, Elizabeth.' Sinn kisses her cheek when she offers it. 'Time for an after-dinner drink.'

She laughs delightedly. 'Indeed!' Raising her hand, she summons a waiter. 'Please attend to Commander Tørrissen and—' she smiles at me, '—his lovely guest.'

Sinn lifts my hand. 'Phoebe Cartwright, Elizabeth Oldfield.'

I extend my free hand. 'Sorry we're late. It was my fault.'

'If he were mine, I wouldn't let him out at all.' Elizabeth tilts her head. 'You're familiar to me, Phoebe. Have we met?'

'I don't think so, but I've lived in the district for years.'

'No sensible person would want to live anywhere else in the world. Now,' she holds out her hand, 'let me take your coat.'

The other guests, who talk mostly about their children's achievements, property prices and thoroughbred racing, are welcoming. Sinn, while reserved, is friendly enough. When asked, he informs people about his UN committee and the type of work it does. In response, they tell him they can't think what he could find of interest out here. Which is when Sinn mentions, ever so casually, that sometimes legitimate concerns are used as a front for illegal activities. Even though Sinn says little, by the end of thirty minutes I'm aware that Elizabeth was a member of the Roxburgh syndicate. I also know that one of the other members has died, another member is a local and a fifth member lives in Adelaide.

'Martin, unfortunately, couldn't attend this evening,' Elizabeth says. 'We had such fun together, the five of us. The idea that our little diversion, our hobby, might have been used for nefarious purposes is highly upsetting to say the least.' She looks over my shoulder. 'What do you say, Brent? We enjoyed our flutters on the overseas races, didn't we?'

'You and Martin enjoyed them,' he says. 'I didn't get much out of it.'

'That I don't believe! Surely the assistance you gave Martin earned you a trip to the races in Dubai? Or at the very least, an excursion to his cellar?'

Brent barks a laugh as he lifts a glass of red. 'Maybe once or twice.'

Up close, Beatrice is smaller and rounder than Elizabeth, and somehow more familiar. She looks concerned when I tell her I don't drink, and insists on ordering me freshly squeezed orange juice. Sinn settles for a second glass of tonic water. 'I'm driving,' he tells her.

'That simply will not do,' Beatrice says. 'We have ample cars to take the guests home. Leave your vehicle here until the morning.'

Sinn reclaims my hand. 'Phoebe has to get back to Warrandale tonight.'

Beatrice's brows raise a notch. 'All that way? Why on earth don't you stay in Denman?'

'My dog and horses tend to get up early.'

Sinn squeezes my hand. 'I'll make breakfast.'

'Sinn!'

When Elizabeth calls again, and waves from the other side of the room, Beatrice links her arm through mine. 'Come with me, Phoebe. I refuse to allow Sinn to monopolise you for the little that's left of the night.'

A middle-aged man and woman are standing with Brent when we approach. Brent has his back to us, but when Beatrice places a hand on his arm, he stands back so we can join the group.

'Brent Green, this is Phoebe Cartwright, from Warrandale,' Beatrice says. 'Brent is the stud manager at Roxburgh Estate and—' she indicates the couple, '—Luke and Leanne Renford are my very dear neighbours.'

Beatrice chats animatedly with her neighbours about a boundary fence, leaving Brent and me to search for conversation.

'You're still at Roxburgh Estate?' I finally say.

He nods. 'Coming up for ten years now.'

'I've heard the facilities are even more impressive than they were.'

'Only the best for Martin.' He swirls the wine in his glass. 'You're in Warrandale?'

'I live in the old decommissioned church. I haven't seen Evie for ages. How is she?'

'No idea.' He smiles stiffly. 'We're divorced.'

Evie worked part time in the stud office at Roxburgh Estate and would laugh when Martin teased her about only turning up when she felt like it. She was attractive, chatty and lively.

'I'm sorry.'

'Don't be.' He raises his glass. 'It's not like I'm short of company.'

Sinn is still in a circle with Elizabeth and a number of other people. Beatrice is talking about furniture upholstery. When Brent puts his glass on a table close by, the waiter fills it up. I wish I had something to do with my hands.

'Are you looking forward to the yearling sales?' I ask.

'In this weather, I'm trying to keep the colts from injuring themselves.'

'Camelot still enjoys the wet. I saw the photos of him outside.'

'Didn't notice them.'

'What? There are three.'

When he leans in close, I smell the wine on his breath. 'You were lucky to get that horse, Phoebe. Bloody lucky.'

'His owner wanted to find a good home for him.'

He laughs without humour. 'He could have got a good home *and* money, given Camelot's looks and temperament. Racing on the country tracks, show horse, eventing—you paid a fraction of what he was worth.'

When the waiter hands me a glass of juice, I take it gratefully. 'Did his owner regret selling him to me?'

'His owner was a company, and I only dealt with the staff. It was Robbie who brokered the deal. You have him to thank for that horse.'

'I paid for him.'

'Two thousand dollars.' His brows lift. 'And then you dropped Robbie.'

'I had my reasons.'

Brent drinks deeply from his glass, half emptying it. 'Your father was a crazy old man, Phoebe, but you were a worker, you had to be. And you were smart. That's what Robbie and Martin liked about you. Robbie might have made a few mistakes, but you could have had him back. He would have given you anything you wanted.'

'Money isn't everything.'

He huffs. 'Only someone like you would say that.'

'Like me?'

'You've never had real money. You don't know what it's like to lose it.'

Sinn said I had to take care in *answering* questions, but he didn't tell me that I couldn't *ask* them.

I paste a smile on my face. 'Is Martin still as busy as he was with his business and the stud?'

'He and Robbie get by pretty well.'

When Sinn puts his hand at the small of my back, I instinctively move closer. His hands are generally cool, so why am I suddenly warm? This is pretend. We're working together.

'Mind if I join you?' Sinn asks.

'Brent has been the stud manager at Roxburgh Estate for ten years,' I say, smiling at Brent. 'I'm sure Martin is grateful you've stayed so long.'

Sinn steers the conversation away from Martin, asking Brent questions about rainfall, politics and Denman's population. I'm only halfway through my juice when, after nodding politely to Brent, he takes my hand.

'Time to go.'

When Elizabeth quite reasonably points out that we were the last to arrive at the party, so shouldn't be the first to leave, Sinn apologises, but won't change his mind. Eventually, her arm linked through mine, she graciously walks us to the door. She kisses Sinn's cheek and then she kisses mine.

'Happy birthday, Elizabeth. It was a lovely party.'

'Beatrice has her sixty-fifth birthday in October,' she says. 'I do hope you can join us for that.' She puts a hand on Sinn's arm. 'I shall hold you personally responsible, Sinn, if we don't see the two of you then.'

CHAPTER
18

Sinn's smile disappears well before he releases my hand at the top of the stairs. He walks behind me as we weave our way through the bar. The crowd has thinned so it's not as noisy as it was. The guitarist is singing 'American Pie'.

When we reach the car, I take off my coat, standing back as Sinn opens the passenger door.

'You appreciate I can do that all by myself?'

'Navy,' he snaps, as if that explains everything.

I wait until he's turned onto the road before I speak again. 'Why are you so cranky?'

'We need to talk.'

I kick off my shoes and smooth my dress over my knees. 'I'll go first. Why didn't you ask Brent about Martin? He seemed pretty dodgy to me.'

'Why do you say that?'

'You must have heard what Elizabeth said to him about the syndicate? How he helped Martin? That means he knew about it.

And even though he was the only person in the room that I'd met before, I don't think he would have acknowledged me if Beatrice hadn't forced him to. He mentioned my father, and he acted like it was news to him that I lived in Warrandale, even though he must have known I did because—'

'Phoebe!'

I sit back in my seat. 'Brent might not be at Roxburgh Estate when we visit, because I don't remember him socialising there, even when he was married to Evie. She worked for Martin too, but now they're divorced. She was his second wife. Did you know that?'

'You can't do this, Phoebe.' He lifts a hand off the wheel before putting it back.

'Do what?'

'Corner people, ask questions.' His jaw is so tight, his lips barely move. 'If you don't agree, we go no further.'

'I didn't corner Brent. And I don't see—'

'Do you agree?'

'I don't have a choice.' I take three deep breaths. 'Is it okay to question you?'

He sighs. 'I'll answer what I can.'

'Ages ago, you said you'd spoken to the syndicate members. Did you speak to Brent as well?'

'Yes.'

'What do you know about him?'

'He runs Roxburgh's stud. He resents losing his property to pay out his first wife. Elizabeth doesn't like him, but invited him tonight because he finds horses for her.'

'He acted as if he didn't know about the photos of Camelot in the pub, even though he was with Martin when he bought him, on behalf of someone else, at the yearling sales.'

'What does this prove, Phoebe?'

'That Brent can't be trusted.'

'Martin paid half a million dollars for your horse, yes? He trained him and raced him?'

'It was the top price that year, but that doesn't explain why—'

'Martin has shares in the hotel.'

'What?'

'You didn't know that?'

'I—no. Why are you so angry?'

He glances at me before his eyes go back to the road. 'I'm not angry with you.'

'Then why …' The trees pass by in a blur. 'I was asking about Martin when you joined us. It was a missed opportunity.'

'Tonight was an *opportunity* to show people we were going out. That was all.'

'I didn't say anything that wasn't true. I just thought—'

'Don't.'

'Don't think?'

'You have no idea what you're doing.'

'So tell me what to do! I didn't even know we were going to a party. I would have dressed up more.'

He mutters under his breath as we turn off the highway and onto the minor road that leads to Warrandale. The wipers swish intermittently at the windscreen.

'Phoebe?' He takes his eyes off the road for a moment. 'What did Green say about your father?'

'That I couldn't rely on him when I was younger.'

'How would he know that?'

'I haven't seen Martin's son, Robbie, for years, but he knew I supported myself. I guess Brent, through Robbie and Martin, was aware of that too.'

'How well did you know Robbie?'

I steal a look at Sinn's profile, his straight nose and firm, judgemental mouth. I know nothing of his past relationships. And I was only twenty-two when Robbie and I broke up, even younger than Prim is now. Robbie was unfaithful. I was naïve. Gullible.

'He was a friend when I was at uni.'

Sinn hesitates. 'Elizabeth suspected that she recognised you. Beatrice reminded her. They saw you at a fete at Warrandale. You were a child.'

'What—' A wisp of memory floats through my mind. The memory settles. 'It was the year after Mum had the stroke.'

'Yes.'

'Auntie Kate picked up my sisters and me and drove us to Warrandale. It was hot and I was sick.'

'Elizabeth and Beatrice were at the fete. Your aunt was working there. You had a high temperature. She asked Beatrice to drive you to your uncle.'

I blow out a breath. 'I would've only been thirteen. Beatrice has a good memory.'

'You wouldn't get into her car without your sisters, even though your aunt was there to look after them. You insisted you couldn't be separated.'

'I—we stayed together.'

'Beatrice knew of your father by reputation.' He changes his grip on the wheel, glances at me. 'What did he do to you?'

I lay my fingers neatly on my lap. 'Nothing.'

'You answer me literally, yes?'

'What do you mean?'

'You father did nothing on that day. What did he do afterwards?'

There are no other cars on the road, nor streetlights. But the high beams are on. I can see a long way in front of the car, and the fences either side. The rain has cleared.

Not all of my secrets need to be kept.

'There was no sexual abuse. He didn't hit us, or drink or do drugs. We had somewhere to live and we were fed. Many children are far worse off.'

'He was abusive.'

'We were neglected, but we always had each other. By the time I was fifteen, sixteen, I understood the system better. We had people we could talk to.'

'If not for your father, you wouldn't be involved in this.'

'I can't wish him away.' I sit straighter. 'Did Elizabeth know that Dad managed the syndicate? That he was responsible for paying the money into the bank accounts?'

'Do we have to talk about this now?'

'I want to be helpful.'

He frowns as he answers. 'Her accountant had dealings with him, that's all she knew. Only Martin Roxburgh dealt with your father directly.'

'Which is why you should take more interest in Brent.'

'Stop this.'

'I'm only talking to you. What's the harm in that?'

'Your father. This makes you vulnerable.'

'Don't patronise me!'

He takes a deep breath. 'What happened with him tonight?'

'Nothing out of the ordinary.'

'But you won't tell me.'

My fingers twist and untwist. 'He was afraid the delivery driver was you.'

'You said you had people to talk to when you were a child. What about now?' He hesitates. 'Jeremiah?'

'I've known him since I was a kid. Even so, I don't tell him …'

'Personal things?'

'How is this relevant?'

He frowns again. 'The syndicate. You're hiding something.'

I wait until I can trust myself to speak calmly. 'I gave you all the information I found, even though it identified me.'

'Why the delay? Why this insistence on being involved? Something scared you at my house in Denman. What?'

'I want to do what I can to put things right, and I can't trust you to protect my sisters or me. Why should you?'

'You trust nobody.'

'Have you been digging up dirt? Is that how Beatrice remembered me?'

'She remembered you were frightened. You were unwell but made her promise not to tell your father. What child keeps that from their parent?'

When I look out the window, the world rushes past. Things are different now. My sisters are safe. 'When did Beatrice tell you this?'

'You were getting your coat.'

'What else did you find out?'

'From the others? They said you were beautiful, clever, charming. They couldn't understand why they hadn't seen you before.'

'I have my work and my friends. Other than that, I keep to myself. There's nothing wrong in that.'

We pass the WELCOME TO WARRANDALE sign and the park that borders the town. The windscreen wipers swipe once before stilling again. A narrow stretch of sky peeks through the clouds. Thousands of stars—pinpricks of light—glimmer through the gap. The light on the porch shines on the driveway. I unclip my belt.

'Thank you for taking me to my father,' I say stiffly. 'I'm sorry I kept you waiting for so long.'

He turns as far as the steering wheel allows. 'Vulnerable. This word offended you? I meant ...' He tips back his head. 'Sårbar.'

'What?'

CLOUDS ON THE HORIZON

'Fragile.'

'I am not!'

His brow creases 'Følsom. Skjør. Sensitive, tender.'

When I open the door, a blast of cold air shoots into the car. 'I'm not any of those things.'

By the time I've pushed my feet into my shoes, he's standing at the passenger door. He puts a hand on the frame and holds out his other hand.

'Take it,' he says.

Matilda is oversensitive to physical stimuli, which is why she's afraid to touch anything new. Saxon is hyposensitive, under-reactive to sensory input, and seeks out touch wherever he can find it. My sensory processing isn't out of kilter. But I hesitate.

I want to touch him so much it hurts.

I'm still sitting, but do as he asks.

He leans so my knees are against his stomach. I place my fingers along his jaw and he closes his eyes. His skin is warm. His lashes are dark against his cheeks.

'Sinn?' My voice is unsteady. 'You said we couldn't do this any more.'

He opens his eyes and puts his hand on the side of my face. He strokes my cheek with his thumb.

'I want you to trust me, Phoebe.'

'Because you think I'm vulnerable? I don't—'

'Because I want you.'

'This—' My voice is uneven. I clear my throat. 'This attraction we have, it can't go anywhere. You know that?'

'I know you believe that.'

It's drizzling again. *Drops less than point five millimetres across.* They fall on his hair, tiny silver sparkles. I brush them away.

'You should put on your sweater.'

He's still leaning against my legs, the warmth of his body seeping through my veins. His hands grip my waist as I slide from the seat to the ground. I touch the top button of his shirt and trace the V of skin above it. When he bends down, our foreheads touch. His breath is soft on my lips. They meet, a delicate kiss, as I snake my arms around his neck. My breasts touch his chest. He tightens his hold.

'Jeg har savnet deg.'

'What does that mean?'

'I missed you.'

I missed you too.

We kissed in the carpark a few hours ago, but he learns my places all over again. Soft and hard. In and out. Hard and soft.

It's late. And cold. The drizzle turns to rain. *Drops over point five millimetres across.* His hair is damp, his skin slick and smooth. I rub my palms against his neck. I stand on my toes to kiss his throat, trailing a path to his chest. I tug at his shirt buttons, releasing the first and the second. His heart hammers hard against my hand as I press my palm to the warmth of his skin.

He cups my breasts, brushing the nipples lightly with his thumbs. I ache with need. 'Sinn?'

The strokes of his tongue echo the beats of my heart. When my legs wobble, he wedges a leg between them, and I lean into his thigh. His erection is long and hard. He murmurs words into my mouth but I don't know what they mean. When his hands slide from my breasts to my waist, I groan a complaint. His fingers clench and unclench.

I run my finger over the softness of his lips, the hardness of his cheekbone, the strength of his jawline. I trace his mouth. He groans when I follow the lines with the tip of my tongue.

'Phoebe.' His hands thread through my hair and cup the back of my head. When I shiver, he stills. 'You're cold.'

'We can go inside.'

He presses open-mouthed kisses down my neck and nudges the neckline of my dress with his nose. When he takes hold of the tops of my arms and lifts his face, his eyes are intent. 'I want more than a night.'

I inch back a little and look down at my shoes, wet and splattered with mud. There's a tear in the leather on my heel. I grasp his shirt.

'Phoebe?'

I search his serious face. 'More than a night?'

'Yes.'

When I take a jerky step backwards, his hands drop to his sides. I wrap my arms around my body. 'No.'

Hands thrust deep into his pockets, he walks around the four-wheel drive.

My hair sticks to my neck. My teeth chatter. 'Why can't we just—'

When he turns, the bonnet is between us. He stares into my eyes, a crease between his brows. 'I'll call tomorrow.'

CHAPTER
19

My alarm rarely sounds because I always wake up early.

Not this morning.

Wickham pokes his head around my bedroom door as I sit on the side of the bed and pull on thick blue socks. I yawn. 'Won't be long.'

He wags his tail and follows as I turn off the lights in the bedrooms and hallway. It's overcast outside. My stomach rumbles. I was too unhappy to be hungry last night. I tossed and turned for hours.

My face is pale in the bathroom mirror. There are shadows under my eyes. 'I'll cook bacon and eggs after I feed the horses,' I promise myself. Scooping my dress from the laundry floor, I shake out the creases. There are smudges of dirt near the hem. From when I ran through the garden? As if I were concerned about the rain, even though I'd been kissing him for …

Minutes? Hours? Days?

I sit on the steps to pull on my boots, yanking them over my socks and tucking in my jeans. I button my oilskin to my throat. He kissed me there. Did he leave marks? I doubt it. He was careful, in control.

I began having casual relationships when I was nineteen.

Virginity. Tick.

One-night stands. Tick.

Jeremiah was different. I *wanted* him to be different. He made me laugh. He was friendly and popular. We cared about each other. He loved having sex, but I preferred the other things we did: parties, kayaking, picnics. After a few weeks, I told him I didn't want a relationship. 'No worries,' he said sadly, hugging me when I burst into tears.

Robbie was three years older than me. When he called me his ice princess, I thought it was a compliment. He said I was part of his future, promised I could rely on him. Not many people knew how serious we were.

I liked visiting Robbie and Martin at Roxburgh Estate and so did Patience and Prim. The horses and land, the house and the stables, it was peaceful and beautiful, so different from what we were used to. Sometimes we'd stay for a weekend. My sisters shared one room and Robbie and I shared another. As a lover, he was—

I should have slowed him down when he rushed me. I should have spoken out when he hurt me. But I wanted it over and done with.

When I found out that he'd cheated, he told me I was 'freakishly' independent. He accused me of putting my sisters, work and determination to live in Warrandale ahead of our relationship. He said my frigidity was a turn-on; he'd miss having sex with me.

Sinn said he wanted more than a night. What does that even mean?

Camelot hangs around the yard as I muck out his stable. He buries his nose in the barrow, snuffling around in the fresh pile of straw. When he lifts his head, a piece of straw sticks out of the side of his mouth like a cheroot.

I pull it out and drop it in the barrow. 'That's for sleeping on.'

I knew Camelot was worth far more than I could afford, but Martin and Robbie never suggested that the owner was unhappy with the price. Neither did Brent.

Last night, Sinn shut me down when I tried to talk about him. *What does this prove, Phoebe?*

Camelot is warm beneath his rug; I straighten it over his withers before going back to the stable.

Twenty minutes later, as I'm adding soiled straw to the compost pile behind the stables, my phone buzzes. I rip off my gloves and reach into my pocket. My heart jumps around when I see the name on the screen.

'Sinn.'

'How did you sleep?'

'Not very well.' Mintie, his silver tail catching the light, trots towards the trees on the far side of the paddock. 'I'm with the horses.'

'Will you ride?'

I look up at the sky, the patchwork of clouds. 'Do you think it'll rain? Or drizzle?'

'Neither.' Another hesitation. 'Can I see you?'

'How do planes make clouds?'

'What?' I imagine his sigh. 'A plane releases water vapor. In high and cold air, the vapor freezes and forms ice crystals. It's called a contrail cloud. "Condensation" combined with "trail". Today, Phoebe? What time?'

'You're not going to lecture me about what happened with Brent, are you?'

'I'll set out reasons why you should stay out of this.'

'Oh.' I stab the fork into the compost. 'That was honest, at least.'

'I don't lie.'

Tendrils of heat rise from the mound and curl around the pitchfork. 'I've thought about what happened. I can see how you wouldn't have liked me speaking to Brent. But how was I supposed to know what to do?'

'What time, Phoebe?'

My phone buzzes again. Patience.

'I've got another call. Can I get back to you? I shouldn't be long.'

I step under the shelter of the eaves. *End call. Accept call.* 'Patience.'

'Something's happened.' Her words are high-pitched.

Fear snakes up my throat. 'Tell me. Are you hurt?'

'No, nothing like that.'

'What, Patience? What's the matter?' Even without seeing her, I know she'll be battening down her emotions in the way she always has.

'The man I told you about,' she says, 'the one who was hassling me. His name is Alan Grantham. He's my commanding officer. I'm answerable to him.'

'What has he done? Tell me.'

'He touched me in subtle ways, brushing past me in the galley, putting his hand over mine when I was on the bridge. When he called me into his cabin and bailed me up, I made it clear I wasn't interested, that he had to keep his hands to himself. A few weeks ago, at the end of a shift, he tried to kiss me. I fought back. I told him I'd lodge a complaint.'

'Have you?'

'We were in the middle of tactical exercises—there are six ships out here, a couple from the US, one from New Zealand and three of ours. He asked me to wait until the exercises were over. He told me he had his children to think about, his wife. He wanted to speak with her first, to warn her, and I agreed.'

'That was good of you.'

'The exercises were a mess. He gave me wrong coordinates and I made bad calls. When he reprimanded me in front of a bunch of other officers, I lost my temper and swore at him. I walked out. This morning, the captain asked to see me. Grantham has accused me of insubordination. There'll be a hearing.'

'What?'

'He's gone on the offensive, alleging shortfalls in my work ethic and attitude, and insinuating I make things up.'

'Have you made your complaint against him?'

'I've got no proof. And if I do it now, he'll say I'm getting back at him. Sexual assault accusations get nasty. People take sides.'

'You have to do it anyway. He can't get away with it.'

'This problem with the syndicate, Phoebe.' Her voice wavers. 'My handwriting is all over those pages.'

My chest constricts. 'Sinn thinks it's me. And the information … it might not even be important.'

'How do you know? You don't, do you? I can't believe I didn't ask questions at the time. Dad set everything up, but I improved it—the way the distributions were calculated, the payments into the bank accounts. They changed all the time; I transferred millions all over the world.'

'Are you sure you can't be up-front about this? Then it won't matter if it comes out or not. Tell your captain that Dad was abusive. You had to do what he said.'

'I lied on my application papers. I said I'd never seen a psychologist, never had a need to. Grantham is saying I'm no good under pressure and I can't take criticism. And because I had no evidence when I accused him of setting me up in the military exercises, he's alleging I fabricate things. He'll do whatever he can to undermine me. And all this shit with our father, the way I worked with him, will—'

'Patience! Forget about the syndicate. So far as anyone knows, it was me who helped Dad.'

'When does this end, Phoebe?' Her voice breaks. 'You've lied for me, protected me, ever since I can remember.'

I squeeze my eyes shut. 'That's not going to stop.'

'I don't want you to get into trouble because of me.'

'Everyone here, the people whose opinions I value, they know my past. And being involved demonstrates we're doing what we can to make things right.'

'We? You're doing it, Phoebe, not me. UN investigators are involved. It's serious.'

'I can handle it. I can handle Sinn.'

'I'll wring his neck if you get hurt.'

After we end the call, I pull the pitchfork out of the compost heap, lean the handle against the fence and walk back to the yard. Mintie, his blue-checked rug bright against the green of the grass, bends a front leg as he drinks from the trough.

He can't find out I lied. When wind blows hair across my face, I shove it under my collar. I consider the layers of clouds, from white to steely grey. *He values the truth.*

U

I sit deeper in the saddle and pull Camelot back from a trot. As his hooves clip clop on the hard-packed track, the sun, a fuzzy yellow ball, sinks beneath the tree line. We pass a giant red gum with sprawling branches and a kookaburra calls out. Others join in the laughter but Camelot ignores them. The kookaburras quieten abruptly.

'I like Sinn, and I'm attracted to him.' Camelot's ears flicker at the sound of my voice. 'But we have different agendas.'

Putting Camelot's rein in one hand, I dial Sinn's number. He answers immediately.

'Phoebe. Why haven't you called? Where are you?'

'Out on Camelot.' The fire trail is damp under the trees, dulling the sound of the horse's hooves. 'Dad's records, Sinn, the information I gave you. How important is it?'

'When will you be home? I can be there in an hour.'

'I have something on tonight.'

'What?'

'I asked you a question. You say you don't lie. When I gave you the information, you weren't sure how useful it would be. But then you said it was useful. How useful?'

'It's important.'

'Does that include the spreadsheets? The handwritten notes?'

'Leave this to me.'

'I need to know what's going on.'

'I'll keep you informed.'

'You'll tell me what you want me to know.' A low-hanging branch twitches in the breeze. Camelot shies at the shadows.

'Your father kept information from the original syndicate members. He allowed another member to join.'

'And he kept two sets of accounts.'

'You didn't know any of that was wrong. You won't be blamed for it.'

Would he say the same of Patience?

'I'll see you when we go to Roxburgh Estate.'

He curses under his breath. 'Seeing you today … It has nothing to do with my work.'

'What then?'

'You can ask me personal questions.'

'Oh.'

'Is that a yes, or no?'

'I can't.' Bird calls. Hoof beats. The scent of eucalyptus. A trickle of water that crosses the track. 'I'm sorry.'

'Do you have something to hide?'

'What would you do if I did?'

Silence. Then, 'I can't answer that.'

As I disconnect, I see a grey kangaroo, joey peeking out of her pouch, standing to the side of the track. When Camelot starts, I settle him and turn him for home.

Where no one lets me down. Keeps me in the dark. Leaves me. Hurts me.

CHAPTER

20

The wind is gusty on Tuesday afternoon, flattening the grass and forcing the leaves from the trees. The hood of my jacket blows back and hair whips across my face as I walk through the yard. Wickham flashes past and jumps over the gate.

'What's the hurry?'

By the time I close the gate behind me, Mike's ute is in the driveway. He takes off his hat and waves it as Wickham runs in circles around him.

'Phoebe!' Mike shouts. 'Gus needs a favour.' He takes a bundle out of the cab and carefully places it onto the ground. When I reach him, Lottie, her woolly ears down and pink nose curious, is looking around. I kneel on the gravel and rub her head, and she bumps it against my hand.

'Hello, baby. What are you doing here?'

'She's not doing too good, according to Gus. Now she's going on a few months old, she should be weaned like the other orphan lambs, but whenever he drops a feed, the weight falls off. He's tried grain pellets and hay, but she won't have a bar of them. The other lamb is eating grass like she's supposed to, no problems with her.'

Under her wool, Lottie's ribs are sharply defined. 'What's up, sweetheart? You're a sheep. Why don't you like grass?'

'With all this rain, Gus has a lot on his hands, trying to get his crop in and all; last thing he needs to be doing is making up bottles. He asked if you could babysit.' Mike takes two large tins of formula from the car. 'This should keep you going for a while. Milk morning and night, paddock during the day.'

'What about foxes? Do you think she'll be okay in the chicken pen at night?'

'What about your chooks?' Mike asks.

'I don't have time to care for chooks. The pen's been empty for years.'

Wickham, having little interest in Lottie, lies on the grass as Mike and I settle her into the pen, but he runs around Mike's legs as we walk back up the path. At the graveyard, Mike hesitates, looking critically at the half-open gate. When he pulls it wide, it catches on the paving.

'You sure you don't want me to fix the hinges?' He extends his leg and holds onto the spikes to inspect the gate more closely. 'I can make a new latch too.'

'You know I leave it open.'

He huffs. 'You still thinking they want to get out and about?'

I shrug. 'Maybe.'

As soon as we're back at his car, Mike puts on his hat. 'Let me know if you need a hand with the lamb.'

'I have a weekend away coming up, but that's not for a couple of weeks.'

'Where are you off to?'

'Just to Denman. With a friend.'

He grins. 'Wouldn't happen to be Martin Roxburgh's shindig?'

'How did you guess that?'

He pushes his hat further back on his head. 'Terry said you might have a fella. The Norway bloke, right?'

'Did you know he was going to Roxburgh Estate?'

'Being a neighbour of Martin's, I figured he could be.'

'Can you keep this to yourself?'

'Lips are sealed.'

'Even though you've been gossiping with Terry?'

He harrumphs. 'I was working at Martin's last week—those stables are as spick and span as that mansion he's built. Martin is out to impress, that's for sure.'

'Aren't you supposed to be retired? And doesn't Jackson McAdams look after the Roxburgh horses?'

'That was before he argued with Brent.'

'I can't imagine Jackson arguing with anyone.'

'If one more person tells him he's the spitting image of that Hollywood bloke, I reckon he'll punch their lights out.'

I laugh. 'Most men would *like* to look like Chris Hemsworth.'

'Not Jackson.' Mike shakes his head.

'He argued with Brent?' This has nothing to do with racing syndicates, so I don't think Sinn would mind if I asked questions.

'Brent's ex-wife, the second one, went to Jackson's wife Ariella for legal help. Ariella had a new bub, and there was a lot of money involved, so she passed the ex-wife on to a good mate of hers in the city.'

'Brent didn't like it?'

'Brent told Jackson that Ariella should have warned him, and when Jackson told him where to go, Brent got all hot under the collar. He said Ariella was a two-bit lawyer, and she'd punched above her weight when she'd got married.'

'What? Everybody loves Ariella.'

'Course they do.'

I'm about to tell Mike that Elizabeth Oldfield doesn't like Brent either, but—

You have no idea what you're doing.

—I promised I'd follow instructions, so I bite back the words.

After three nights of imagining Lottie shivering in the chook pen—foxes and feral dogs sniffing through the wire and eagles circling above—I lean a narrow strip of lattice across the verandah and lay a thick bed of straw on the decking. The lamb is sheltered from the rain and much of the wind in her new little pen, and there's a power point for the heat pad I bought from the pet shop in Dubbo.

When I confessed to Gus that I'd put Lottie back on four-hourly feeds, he reminded me that she wasn't a pet but a farm animal, and it might have been better to let her die like her mum had intended.

'According to the directions on the tin,' I argued, 'Lottie needs one to two litres of milk a day. If she was with her mother, she'd space out her feeds, so that's what I'm trying to do. She can gradually transition to grass.'

An hour later, and once a day since, Gus has called to see how Lottie is faring. In the past week and a half, she's occasionally nibbled on grass when I've let her out into the garden. Yesterday, she watched Mintie eat hay but refused to eat any herself.

As I wait for Kelly and Saxon to arrive, I offer her the bottle and she hungrily grasps the teat. 'Sorry to keep you waiting,' I whisper, as I wrap a blanket around her. She has a layer of fat on her ribs now, and her eyes are increasingly bright. 'I'll bring Saxon out to say hello later.'

Kelly's eyes are red and puffy when I open the door, and she looks anywhere but at me. After shaking Saxon's hand, I bring him and his mother inside, turn up the heater and invite Kelly to sit on the couch.

'Saxon?' I take his hand when he presses his face against the cushions, and encourage him to face me. 'Would you like to play with the blocks first? In a little while, we'll go outside. I've got something very special to show you today.'

He pulls on my hand. 'I want to see your dog!'

I point to Wickham, and then put my finger against my mouth. 'Look, Saxon,' I whisper, 'Wickham is in his bed, all curled up. We'll pat him after his rest.'

As soon as I put the container in front of him, Saxon buries his arms in the plastic blocks. Kneeling next to him, I hand a box of tissues to Kelly.

She blows her nose. 'Sorry. Crappy afternoon. Sometimes it gets to me.'

'That's not surprising.'

'I'm twenty-three.' She scrubs away tears. 'I didn't sign up for this.'

'You didn't.'

'I love him, but ...' She blows her nose. 'I'm doing a crap job.'

'You're a fantastic mother. The best.'

She shakes her head. 'It's hard to see past his shitty behaviour, I get that. But ...' She blows her nose again.

'Did he have a hard day at school?'

'His teacher is sick, and the substitute teacher couldn't do anything with him. He kicked the teaching assistant when she tried to pull him off another kid. At lunchtime, he hid under the demountable and wouldn't come out. He's been wired up all day.'

'Have you seen his psychiatrist lately?'

'The autism one? That's next week. Yesterday, we saw the stuck-up ADHD guy.'

'The neuropsychologist?'

'He reckons you and Saxon's speech pathologist are doing no harm, and could be doing some good.'

I wince. 'Saxon's needs are complex. We have different specialisations, and it's good that we can work as a team.'

'I told the neuro that you make the day-to-day stuff easier to put up with.'

'Saxon has to process the stimulation he gets through his senses. If he can't integrate it in a way that he understands, how can he feel comfortable? How can he settle down and learn, or socialise? Saxon is impulsive, and his medications seem to be helping with that. But we also have to find ways to support others in understanding him, as well as finding ways for him to understand others. Creating an environment where he feels comfortable will help.'

She sniffs. 'You love the balls in your pocket, don't you, Saxon?'

He pulls out one ball from his left pocket and one from the right and squeezes them. 'I can squish the balls!'

'That's great, Saxon. I'm very happy about that.' As Saxon returns to the blocks, I smile encouragingly at Kelly. 'He responds very well to teaching.'

'All I want is for him to be happy.' She leans down to rub his back. 'I want him to have friends and get on with other kids. Maybe one day he can get a job.'

'I have no doubt he will, Kelly, and as he gets older, he'll get better at expressing his feelings verbally. In the meantime, we give him as many opportunities to practise as we can.'

'Otherwise he'll tune out.'

'If it's too hard for him to process information, that's what can happen. The way he behaved at school today, that was hard, but what it's telling us is that he was so uncomfortable that he couldn't pay attention or engage.'

'He loves sitting on the bouncy ball to do his reading exercises when we're at home.' She smiles as she tidies Saxon's hair. 'And it's heaps safer for his iPad than doing it on the trampoline.'

'That could be something he can try at school. I'll talk to his teacher. If she doesn't have a problem with it, we could give it a try.' I glance at my watch. 'Do you want to catch up with your friend who works at the café? Flip through a magazine?'

She shakes her head. 'I won't be back in time.'

'Saxon's my last client today, so there's no need to hurry. In fact …' I reach for my bag. 'I asked the general store to order in tins of milk powder. Do you think you could pick them up for me? It'll save me a trip into town.'

She laughs as she stands. 'That much hot chocolate?'

'When you get back, Saxon will introduce you to Lottie.'

Ninety minutes later, after waving goodbye to Kelly and Saxon, I shut the front door and flick on the porch light. Walking through the house, I turn on the lamps. Compared to Saxon's challenges, mine are nothing, but Lottie isn't the only thing I've been worrying about in the evenings. When Sinn and I go to Roxburgh Estate, we'll have to share a room. I'm happy to make a bed on the floor, but I need a light.

My fear of the dark stems from anxiety. The sensation of being locked in the cupboard has been internalised, generalised and reinforced. Darkness scares me, whatever the context. My fear isn't a sensory processing problem like Saxon was likely born with, it's an acquired problem. It came from a traumatic childhood event.

I kick off my shoes and sit on the verandah to pull on my boots. 'I'm fine on the theory, aren't I, little lamb?'

Lottie looks up, her eyes wide and curious, as headlights shine deep into the garden.

I recognise the four-wheel drive, but can't see who's driving. Scuffing my boots on the doormat before going inside, I rush through the house to the porch. When Nate jumps from the car, I suppress a bubble of ... relief? Disappointment? Wearing brown cords and a cream-coloured cable knit sweater, he looks like a model from *Country Style* magazine.

He takes the steps to the porch two at a time. 'Hey, Phoebe.' We shake hands. 'How're you doing?'

'I'm well, thank you. But why are you here?'

A wink and a smile. 'Won't keep you long. Could we have a chat?'

I talk over my shoulder as he follows me through to the kitchen. 'I was about to settle the horses before it gets dark. It'll take ten minutes, maybe fifteen. I have instant coffee, tea, cocoa and juice. What would you like?'

When Wickham appears, Nate pats his head. 'Nothing, thanks. Can I give you a hand?'

'Do you know anything about horses?'

He squeezes his thumb and finger together. 'Zip. But I'm happy to watch the sun go down. I've got a couple of calls I can make.'

'In that case, would you like to sit outside with Lottie?'

After stabling and feeding the horses, I clump tiredly up the steps. Nate, sitting on a chair next to Lottie's makeshift pen, puts his phone in a pocket. Lottie kicks up her heels and, as much as she can in the limited space, gambols towards me.

'Hello, baby.' I laugh as I tickle under her chin. 'I've missed you too, but I doubt that Gus would approve of your antics.'

Nate stands and places another chair next to his, waiting for me to sit first. 'She's Gus's lamb? That wouldn't be Gus Mumford, would it?'

I blink in surprise. 'You know him?'

'He lives next door to Jemima Kincaid at Horseshoe Hill, doesn't he? I met him when I was working out here a couple of years ago. I knew Finn Blackwood way before he and Jet got together—we used to rock climb in Switzerland. You know Jet and Finn?'

'Jet had finished her apprenticeship with Mike by the time I moved here. I've seen her and Finn around, but I spend most of my time in Warrandale.' I smile. 'It's the centre of the universe.'

'You don't smile as often as you should, Phoebe. You've got a great smile.'

'Is that right.' I lean forward so fast that my head spins, but I pull off my boots and line them up against the pen.

He shifts in his chair. 'I have three sisters. Did I say something they wouldn't approve of?'

'Forget it.' I sit and link my hands in my lap. 'Why did you come, Nate?'

He crouches next to Lottie. 'I've never petted a sheep before. Darned cute, hey?'

'Very cute. Why, Nate?'

'Just wanted to set the scene for the weekend, that's all.'

Nate tells me that sixteen guests have accepted Martin's invitation to Roxburgh Estate. All the guests, bar a handful like Sinn who are neighbours or close friends, have been invited in the hope they'll develop an interest in the yearlings Martin wants to sell—now or in the major sales next year. Some might purchase individually; others will chip in to buy a horse together.

'Sounds like there'll be plenty of food and alcohol,' Nate says, 'no doubt in the hope it'll grease the wheels of commerce.'

'Will any of the guests have a connection to the Roxburgh syndicate?'

He whistles. 'Maybe, maybe not.'

'You're not going to tell me?'

'You got Sinn's email, right? He'll pick you up next Saturday at four o'clock.'

'I don't see why I can't drive myself.'

He shrugs. 'It's his call.'

'Does Martin know I'm coming?'

'Sinn bumped into him yesterday. When he mentioned it, he said Roxburgh looked a tad shocked.'

'That's good, isn't it? If he feels off balance?'

'Leave the overthinking to Sinn.' Lottie nibbles Nate's thumb and he smiles. 'He gets paid for it. You don't.'

'My father might have acted dishonestly, but Martin ... I don't think he'd do something illegal on purpose.'

When Wickham bounds up the steps from the stables, I take a towel and wipe his legs and feet. 'You're ready for dinner, aren't you, boy? And Lottie will be ready for her bottle.'

When Nate strokes Lottie's face, she lifts her head and searches hopefully for a teat. He grins. 'She gets a bottle?'

'You can give it to her if you like.'

'Neat!'

'Nate? Will you be at your house at Denman over the weekend?'

'Chained to my screen. Why?'

'Mintie is going to my friend Mandy's property, and a couple of girls from the pony club will look after Camelot. Mike would take Lottie, but his hip is stiff, so bending is difficult. And he has Wickham anyway. Gus is an hour away in Horseshoe, and he's flat out with his harvest. Do you think ...'

He grins. 'I can take Lottie, sure thing. How hard can it be, right?'

'I'd have to bring her to you, because she can't stay here on her own all day, but Roxburgh Estate is so close that I can easily pop over if I have to. Your back garden is fenced, so she can graze. And the verandah is sheltered, so all you'd have to do is block it off at one end at nighttime.'

He pulls out his phone and takes a photo of Lottie in her pen. 'I can recreate this, no problem.'

'I'll bring plenty of straw and make up her formula. I'll also bring her heat pad. I'll write everything down.'

His phone buzzes as I'm warming the milk. 'Hey, Sinn,' he says, as he steps back onto the verandah.

It's been two weeks since I've heard from Sinn. I eavesdrop shamelessly.

'That's right … Sure, buddy … Nope … I'll tell her.'

Nate takes my arm as I step over the lattice into the pen. Lottie grasps the teat and hangs on like a limpet when I offer it, her throat working furiously.

'Lottie!' I laugh as I hold the bottle with both hands. 'Ease up.'

Nate laughs too. 'Gotta go,' he says into the phone. 'It's my turn to feed the baby.'

I put my thumb to the side of Lottie's mouth, prising it open. 'Hurry up, Nate.' I hold out the bottle. 'Before it's all gone.'

Nate looks away and frowns. 'What?' he says into the phone. 'Why?' He huffs. 'If that's the case, why didn't you come here your—' He holds the phone away from his ear. 'Better give her the bottle back, Phoebe,' he says.

Lottie, tail spinning wildly, latches onto the teat.

Nate puts the phone to his ear again. 'Of course I get it! You think I'm an idiot?' He disconnects, glaring at the phone before shoving it into his pocket.

'What's the matter?'

He smiles stiffly. 'Gotta get back to my desk.'

'Is Sinn okay? I mean, is everything okay in Denman?'

'Yeah, all good.'

When milk dribbles down Lottie's chin, I adjust the angle of the bottle. 'So why do you have to get back?'

He lifts a brow. 'How about you ask Sinn that on Saturday?' Leaning low over the pen, he runs his fingers across Lottie's woolly shoulder. 'Don't you worry, little buddy. We'll get our own back.'

'Sinn won't mind, will he? That you'll be looking after her over the weekend?'

'You know what, Phoebe?' He grins. 'I can't wait to tell him. He's gonna *love* it.'

CHAPTER
21

At three fifty-five on Saturday afternoon, I'm sitting on the lawn in the front garden while Lottie, in a dog harness at the end of a lead rope, lies happily in the grass.

'I wish you'd eat it,' I tell her. 'It'd do you good.'

When Sinn's four-wheel drive turns into the driveway, I jump to my feet. And by the time his door slams shut, I'm leaning over Lottie, encouraging her to walk into the plastic crate I borrowed from the vet.

'Phoebe.'

I twist and look over my shoulder. 'Thanks for doing this.' My words tumble over each other. 'I would have brought her over, but Nate said you still wanted to pick me up.'

His face is grim. His eyes are blue-grey. He doesn't say a word as he reaches for Lottie, wrapping his arms around her middle and lifting her into the crate. She completes a cramped circuit before lying on the straw and staring trustingly through the grille.

'Poor baby.'

When I sense Sinn's gaze on my face, heat moves up my neck. Last time we were here, I invited him into my bed. *He doesn't do one-night stands.*

After brushing grass from my yellow dungarees, I fold the cuffs of my navy blue sweater. When I feel his gaze again, I look up. 'I'll change before we go to Roxburgh Estate.'

He yanks down the cuffs of his jacket. 'Why?'

'Nate said the people there will be well off.' I lift my arms to adjust my ponytail. 'They'll probably dress up for dinner.'

'There's no need to change.'

Sinn starts the engine as soon as Lottie's supplies are loaded in the back and I'm seated. He glances in the rear-view mirror to check on Lottie before pulling onto the road.

After a few minutes, he points to the radio. 'What would you like?'

'I don't care.'

His eyes narrow, but he streams a podcast, a lecture by a professor at the National Oceanography Centre at Oxford University, who talks in technical language about atmospheric and oceanic modelling of sea surface temperatures, global warming and cooling rates and greenhouse gas concentrations in the North Pacific and North Atlantic Oceans.

I listen politely, but we're barely out of Warrandale when Sinn asks whether I'd like something else.

'This is about warming oceans, and weather, isn't it? Where does radiatively active gas come from?'

He looks at me suspiciously, as if I'm having a go at him. 'It can be produced anthropogenically, pollution from human activity, or naturally. When it's absorbed or emitted, it will affect atmospheric radiation.'

'Sea temperatures were recorded way before anybody knew what global warming was. That's what Professor—' I turn in my seat. 'What was his name?'

'Tan.'

'That's what Professor Tan just said, isn't it? Why would sailors do that? To see whether it was warm enough to swim?'

His lip lifts, just for a moment. 'Sea temperatures can be used to check bearings and also predict weather patterns.'

'So they can work out if a storm is coming? That's interesting.' When I hear the rustling of straw, I turn in my seat. 'I can't see Lottie.'

He reaches across me to adjust the visor. 'This has a mirror.'

As I turn to face the front again, my shoulder brushes his arm. It's a momentary touch, a fleeting moment in time. But my heart is jumping around as I angle the visor to see Lottie, now curled up and fast asleep. I fold my hands in my lap.

What seems like a lifetime later, as Professor Tan winds up his lecture, we turn down the laneway to Sinn's house and he parks on the gravel near the fig tree.

After setting Lottie, still in her crate, on the front verandah, Sinn says something about packing a bag. 'I'll tell Nate we're back.'

When Nate appears, he pulls me into a brotherly hug. 'How're you doing, Phoebe?'

'Fine, thanks.'

He picks up the crate. 'Remember me, Lottie? I'm Uncle Nate.'

'Thanks for looking after her,' I say, as I gather up her supplies. 'I think I have everything she'll need.'

'Sinn fashioned a pen.' He grins. 'Come and tell me whether it'll be good enough.'

Stepping onto the expansive back verandah, I jerk to a stop, dropping the bags at my feet. A structure with a timber frame, whitewashed weatherboard panels, a split door and a pitched roof sits neatly on the decking. Immediately in front of the miniature house is a yard with a picket fence and gate.

'What the—'

Nate laughs. 'Sinn likes a project. Neat, hey?'

I'm still flustered when, ten minutes later, we sit at a table that overlooks the back garden, my list of instructions in front of me. Lottie jumps around on the lawn, looking up at us occasionally.

'I've got her down to three milk feeds a day,' I tell Nate. 'She'd like more than that, but I fear it would make her even less interested in what she should be eating. She spends her days outside, but I bring her in around five when it gets cold. She has her night feed around six. After that, she'll be ready to go to sleep.'

When Sinn appears, closing the door behind him and leaning a shoulder against the doorframe, I push back my chair and stand. He's changed out of his pants and jacket into black jeans, and is wearing a dusky blue sweater over his shirt. Did he dress down for me? I tighten the straps of my dungarees.

He points to Lottie's stable and pen. 'This is suitable?'

'It's …' I search for the right words. 'What you've built is appropriate for a princess, Sinn. In fact, I'd call it a palace. Nate said you made it all yourself.'

He shrugs. 'My father taught me.'

'I see you've fenced half the lawn as well.'

'The pool was a hazard. Azaleas are poisonous to sheep.'

'How do you know that?'

'I looked it up.' He points. 'She has water in the tub.'

'How long did all this take?'

When he hesitates, Nate jumps in. 'Two nights, most of a day.'

I take a step towards Sinn, my hand raised, but I can't think what to do with it. Shaking is too formal. A hug is impossible. I put hair behind my ear.

'It's beautiful. I—Lottie is very lucky.'

Sinn looks at his watch. 'We're late.'

The trees at Roxburgh Estate are mostly introduced species—oaks, maples and windbreaks of firs. In summer, the poplars are splashes of green; in spring they're dotted with buds. Behind the post and rail fences are thickly grassed paddocks where the broodmares and foals spend their days. The fork off the driveway fifty metres from the cattle grate will lead to Robbie's house. Martin wanted him to build on land with views of the valley, but Robbie preferred a site near the river. When he asked where I'd like to live, I refused to state a preference. Deep down, I must have known I'd never come home to Robbie.

When Sinn lifts a hand from the wheel to turn off the radio, I jump. He looks at me sternly before facing the driveway again, slowing the car to a crawl as we pass a tall, slender woman leading two mares towards the stable block. She's probably in her early thirties, and very attractive. Sinn nods an acknowledgement in response to her wave. And then he turns to me.

'Roxburgh has invited sixty people to dinner.'

'But only sixteen for the weekend?'

'Others—friends, associates, neighbours—come and go.'

'Did Martin invite you to stay because you're a new neighbour, or did you ask for an invitation?'

'I didn't ask, no.'

'Because that would be too obvious? He might have worked out you were spying?'

'I'm not.'

'Investigating, then. Secretly.'

'Elizabeth Oldfield suggested to Martin that I be invited.'

'Did you suggest it to Elizabeth?'

He hesitates. 'She and Beatrice will also be here.'

When the driveway curves to the left, the house appears. Built in the early 1900s, the original homestead would have been a one-storeyed brick bungalow with a verandah. Martin added an extra level, built a wing to the side and another at the back, and then he cement rendered and painted it all. The gardens and land are beautiful but the house, while impressive, isn't particularly attractive.

Sinn finds a spot in the parking area and reverses into it.

We unfasten our seatbelts and he turns towards me. 'Are you sure you want to do this?'

I nod with far more confidence than I feel. 'Yes.'

A young woman from an events management company greets us in the foyer and, after looking Sinn up and down appreciatively and raising a brow at my dungarees, she marks us off a list.

'You're the last to arrive,' she says, before telling us our bags will be taken to our room, and dinner is about to be served. Walking soundlessly over thick woollen rugs, we follow her across an atrium to an outside courtyard at the rear of the house. In addition to the electric lights, there are candelabra, filled with tall white candles, on the trestle tables. Gas-powered lamps provide warmth and additional light. The women are mostly late middle-aged and are very well dressed; many of the men wear ties and jackets. My navy sneakers are relatively new, but I'd never wear them to a semi-formal dinner. I tidy my hair and smooth my hands down my dungarees.

As if he reads my thoughts, Sinn casually slides a hand down my arm and grasps my fingers. When he whispers in my ear, my heart skips a beat.

'Vakker.'

'What?'

'You know this word.'

Beautiful. 'Yes.'

On the other side of the courtyard, beyond the sandstone pillars, is a rectangular garden. Strings of fairy lights dance from tree to tree and the branches of a gum, luminescent silver, glisten through the darkness. Martin, his sandy hair thinning, would be in his late sixties by now. Strongly built but not very tall, he hangs his jacket on the back of his dining chair before saying something to the woman standing next to him. He walks purposefully towards us.

I pull my hand free of Sinn's, but before I can hold it out, Martin grasps my shoulders and kisses my cheeks.

'Miss Phoebe,' he says, jovially. 'Welcome back to Roxburgh Estate.'

I smile. 'Hello, Martin. You look very well.'

'And you're even prettier than you were.'

Sinn holds out his hand. 'Good evening, Martin.'

Martin shakes Sinn's hand enthusiastically. 'When you told me you were bringing Phoebe along, I could hardly believe my ears.'

I look out to the gardens. 'Everything looks lovely.'

'There'll be plenty that'll be new to you, because last time you were here …' His brow creases, then clears. 'It was the year that Robbie's house was built! And if memory serves me correctly, and I'm sure that it does, we'd only just laid the foundations. That would make it over five years ago.'

'I guess so.' I shift my weight from one foot to another. 'I feel a little underdressed.'

'What?' He runs a finger around the inside of his collar. 'You're the only two here who look comfortable.'

Sinn reclaims my hand. 'We look forward to the weekend.'

Martin nods. 'As Elizabeth tells me you've never been to a thoroughbred stud, this weekend is well overdue. In fact, it's the least I could do to welcome you properly to Denman. On that, how are you going with your work?'

Sinn's thumb brushes against my knuckles. 'Slowly.'

'Elizabeth worries terribly about this palaver, but as I say to her, it wasn't our fault that some overseas ne'er-do-well rode rough shod over our syndicate.'

'We hope to find out who it was.'

'Good on you.' Martin turns to me again. 'How are your sisters? I thoroughly enjoyed having the three of you here in the holidays. Not that you weren't around at other—'

'Patience and Prim are well. Thank you.'

Sinn's smile is definitely stiff. As are his fingers. Perhaps because seeing us together doesn't seem to have unsettled Martin like we thought it might? Or because Martin is behaving like he only saw me last week? I had no idea he'd be so friendly and welcoming.

Should I have told Sinn about Robbie? What difference would it make anyway?

I recognise some of the people at our table from Elizabeth Old-field's party. She and Beatrice are sitting at another table but wave and smile as we take our seats. As entree is served and the woman on his right asks Sinn about Norway, I introduce myself to the retired paediatrician from Sydney, William, who is sitting on my other side. He tells me, sotto voce, that his daughter only brought him along because her partner couldn't make it at the last minute. And, as he knows even less about the horse-racing industry than I do, we spend much of the meal talking about children and different approaches to the treatment of challenging behaviours.

By the time the coffee orders are taken, I'm holding back yawns and pushing dessert around my plate. Sinn, who's been listening politely and nodding appropriately to the guests around him, puts his hand on my wrist.

'Tired?'

He was cross when he picked me up from home. He's barely spoken to me since. His touch should feel unpleasant or at the very least unwelcome. But it's all I can do not to turn my arm and grasp his hand.

'I was up early.'

'Let's go.'

He smiles charmingly as we say a general goodbye to the others at our table.

William stands and touches my arm. 'Your companionship this evening has been not only delightful, but also insightful. I hope to see you again over the course of the weekend.'

I smile. 'I'll come searching.'

Sinn takes my hand firmly as we make our way to Martin. Other guests at his table are leaning back in their chairs, all with glasses of wine in front of them.

Martin, his cheeks flushed, waves us in. 'Welcome, you two! Coming for a nightcap?' He holds up his hand, attracting a waiter's attention. 'Two more chairs over here, please!' When he faces us again, he rubs his hands together. 'Now then, what are you drinking? I have an excellent bottle of—'

'Thank you, Martin,' Sinn says. 'We've come to say goodnight.'

'What?' Martin says. 'It's barely eleven. One for the road! Phoebe? Champagne? Wine? Or a cocktail? What's your poison?'

'Not for me, thanks, Martin.'

'What do you—' He purses his lips. 'Now I remember! You don't drink, do you?' He turns to the man next to him. 'This is the one person I'd trust with a key to my cellar.'

'I don't think you'd trust anyone with that, Martin.'

He laughs. 'Hot bloody chocolate! *That* was your weakness. How about that, then? I'm sure the kitchen could rustle something up.'

Martin is at the very least tipsy and very possibly drunk. Wouldn't this be an ideal time for Sinn to catch him out?

'We could stay,' I say, smiling encouragingly at Sinn. 'Or you could stay while I go to our room?'

Sinn turns to me, eyes wide in warning, before putting a hand on my shoulder and kissing my mouth. It's not a long kiss, but a lingering one. My heart hammers hard against my ribs.

Lifting his head, he looks into my eyes. 'I'd prefer we go to our room together.'

Martin laughs and slaps the table. 'Fair enough!'

I'd thought Sinn's kiss was intimate but perhaps it was calculated? His arm slips possessively across my back. The ends of his fingers sit at my hip. 'Goodnight, Martin.'

As we approach the event manager, still stationed in the foyer, Sinn's hand drops to his side. The woman consults her list before leading us down a hallway to the old part of the house.

We're a few paces behind her when Sinn slows. 'Tell me about your association with Roxburgh,' he says quietly.

'I told you I knew him.'

'You know him well.'

'This is why you've been so cranky all night, isn't it?'

'You said you were acquainted through his son.'

'I met Robbie when I was at university.'

'But you were at this house often, yes? With your sisters?'

The event manager stops at a stained timber door at the end of the hallway, opens it wide and steps back. An antique sleigh bed with matching side tables and lamps with silver shades and crystal bases faces a bay window with a window seat. The cushions are different shades of pink with tassels on each corner. 'Voila,' she says.

'What a lovely room.'

She walks around the bed and opens a door to a verandah, indi-
cating a small table and two wicker chairs. 'Yours is the only room
with access to this space, so it's perfectly private.' After closing and
locking the door, she opens a door to an en suite. 'I trust you'll have
everything you'll need.'

'I'm sure we will.' I force a smile. 'Thank you very much.'

Sinn closes the door behind the woman. 'Martin Roxburgh,' he
says. 'Your association?'

I walk past Sinn to the window seat and place my case next to it.
'He didn't seem worried about the syndicate, did he?'

Sinn's jaw is clenched. 'No.'

A soft pink blind, curved to fit the bay window, is rolled down
to the sill. I unfasten a tassel that holds back a heavy floral curtain
and pull it across the window.

'I'll sleep in here. It's like a little room.'

'Take the bed,' he snaps.

'No, thank you.'

'I have a call at four am. I'll go outside to take it.' He throws his
sweater on an armchair. 'This will do until then.'

I march determinedly past him and pull a thickly feathered
doona and pillow from the bed. 'There are two blankets and—' I
count, '—five more pillows. That will be enough for you, won't it?'

'I won't go near you, Phoebe.'

'I know that!'

'So take the bed.'

My first client arrived at eight o'clock and I saw four more clients
after that. I ran around in circles organising Lottie, Wickham and
the horses. I sat for hours at a trestle table, far too anxious to do
more than pick at my food. Should I shove him in the chest and

tell him that? Should I remind him I'm not stupid? That I fully appreciate I'm not welcome?

I take a steadying breath. He's not welcome in my life either. Besides working out what happened with the syndicate, there's nothing between us.

Irrespective of the way his lip lifts when he smiles. The way it feels when he touches my hand. The way he built Lottie a palace.

I cross my arms and uncross them again. 'I know you won't go near me.' I sit on the window seat and untie my laces. 'But there's plenty of room for me here.' My words escape in a rush. 'Please, Sinn. This is where I want to sleep.'

Not giving him a chance to argue further, I slide to the floor and open my case, turning my back as I take out pyjamas and a toiletry bag. I walk quickly to the bathroom, shut the door and carefully turn the lock. *Clunk!*

It's not unreasonable to lock it. It would seem unreasonable *not* to do so. But I imagine Sinn standing stiff and offended on the other side of the door.

I shower quickly so I don't keep him waiting. Or has he showered already? He was dressed formally when he picked me up—he only changed afterwards. My hair drips onto my pyjama top when I take the towel from my shoulders to wipe steam from the mirror. Even through the fog, my face is pale. I clean my teeth and zip my toothbrush and toothpaste away. I scoop my clothes from the floor.

I'll read. And then I'll sleep.

'All yours,' I say as I walk to my bag, store my clothes and take out a book, *Sensory Processing: New Directions.*

Sinn is muttering as he walks into the bathroom, and I can't make out his words. I wait for the sound of the lock, but—nothing. I tiptoe past the door and unplug the desk lamp from the table next to the chair, plugging it into the power point near the bay window and threading the cord under the curtain.

When Sinn comes out of the bathroom, my head is on the pillow and I'm wrapped snugly in the doona. My damp hair is pushed to one side and my book is open and propped on my chest. Sinn won't be able to see me because the curtain is closed, but I noisily turn a page back and forth so that he can hear me.

Reading calmly by the light of my lamp.

My eyes are scratchy with sleep when Sinn turns off his light. I close my book and put it carefully onto the floor. I hear him turn over. Silence. Is he asleep already? Pulling the doona up to my chin, I rub the bottom of one foot over the top of another, hoping to heat them up. I should have worn more layers. Long pyjama pants not short ones. Definitely socks. The room is warm enough, so why …?

A draught sneaks under the window, along the sill and over the edge. I shiver as I cocoon myself and roll onto my side.

CHAPTER
22

My eyes open slowly.

Darkness.

My breath expels in a rush.

Think.

I lift a hand. Nothing. My head jerks left and right. Nothing.

I shiver. I sit up. I stare through the black. I look for a glimmer or shard or pinprick of light. Nothing. Behind me is a wall. Another wall, hard and cold but smooth like satin, is on my left. Reaching desperately to my right, I lose my balance.

I fall.

Folds of impenetrable black, smothering blankets of darkness, wrap around my face and steal my breath. The harder I fight, the closer they press, pinning me down in the dank deep earth and—

A lost and frightened whimper fills the void around me.

'Phoebe!'

I pant in giant gasps.

I hear a curse. See a light.

The blanket lifts and I look wildly around me. The sleigh bed with five pillows. The tables either side. My bag on the floor.

I'm not locked in.

I can get out.

I've fallen off the window seat and into the curtain. The doona is twisted around my waist and legs.

Like a mermaid.

Sinn kneels by my side. My fingers are clawed around the curtain. He opens them up and releases it, pushing it to the end of the rail.

'Kjære.'

He's wearing sweatpants. His chest is bare like it was in the shed. It was dark there too, but …

Floods of tears course down my cheeks. I shiver and shake. Resting my forehead on my knees, I wrap my arms around my shins. I turn my head to the side, away from him.

'I'm sorry.'

He pulls the doona free of my legs and wraps it around my shoulders then sits on the floor, leaning against the window seat. He pulls me onto his lap and gathers me close. When he rubs his face against mine, his bristles are rough.

'Sweetheart …'

I hiccough as I hide against his neck. I breathe him in, find his scent and warmth. He rubs my back with long firm strokes.

'Phoebe?'

My sobs ease slowly. My body softens. My head sinks to his chest.

'Sorry,' I choke.

He rests his chin at the top of my head as he combs through my hair. Then he takes my face in his hands and wipes my tears, his fingers slipping and sliding. I smother a tremor. Quietly sniff. I look away, over his shoulder.

His shoulder is naked.

I squeeze my eyes shut and wriggle off his lap. 'I'm—' I swipe tears from his chest with the palm of my hand. He stiffens and I freeze, pulling back. I inch further away. 'I'm sorry.'

'A nightmare?'

I focus on the lamp. 'You moved it.' I stare at my tightly linked hands. 'You turned it off.'

'You were asleep.'

'I woke up. I need a light on.'

'What?'

'I need a light. I'm scared of the dark.' My words come out in a rush.

'You're—' He puts his hand over mine. 'The dark?'

I nod jerkily as, still wrapped in the doona, I scramble off the floor and perch on the edge of the window seat. 'I need a light, but tonight …' I take a shaky breath. 'You turned it off.'

'Jeg gir opp,' he says slowly before standing. He rummages in his bag for a T-shirt and pulls it over his head, the white stark against the brown of his hair. He returns to the seat, pulling the doona more cosily around my shoulders and twisting the corners, tucking them in at my front. His hand is perfectly steady when he puts hair behind my ear. 'Phoebe? What the fuck?'

I sniff and wipe a hand across my face. 'Martin and Robbie Roxburgh. I have to tell you about them.'

'Not now.'

My stomach rumbles. 'Oh.' I put my hand against it and look away.

'I'll find the kitchen,' he says. 'What can I get you?'

'I've already eaten.'

'A bread roll and a lettuce leaf.'

'I'm fine.'

He sighs. 'Sjokolade?'

When Sinn closes the door behind him, I untangle myself from the doona, blow my nose, wash my face and pull on socks. It's only two in the morning, but I secure the curtain with the rope and tassel and open the blinds. The moon is a sliver but the stars shine brightly in a velvety sky.

I'm sitting on the window seat again, pulling a sweater over my pyjama top, when the door handle turns. Sinn places two steaming mugs on a side table and carries it to the window seat. When he hands me the hot chocolate, I move the teaspoon to one side and blow on the surface.

'Thank you.' I scrape the bottom and the darkness of the chocolate bubbles to the top.

'Too strong?'

'No.' My lips wobble into a smile. 'I like it strong.'

He closes his eyes for a moment. 'Jeg gir opp.'

'You said that before.' I lick chocolate from the corner of my mouth. 'What does it mean?' When I lift my legs onto the seat and stretch them out, he lays the doona across them.

'It means "I give up."'

'On me?'

'Nei, Phoebe. No.'

When he switches on the lamp on the far side of the bed and turns off the lamp on the floor, the colours in the curtains fade to pastel. He sits on the other end of the window seat and stretches out his legs so they line up with mine. We touch through the doona and my heart jumps around.

He sips his coffee. 'You look for light, yes?'

'I— Yes.'

'Like the stars?' He looks out of the window and I follow his gaze.

'Whatever I can find.' I take another sip of chocolate. 'Do you know about stars as well as the weather?'

His lip lifts. 'Yes.'

'Our sun is a star, isn't it? Why can't we see the planets?'

'They aren't bright like the stars.'

He must have put half a cup of cocoa in the hot chocolate. And also ... I hold up the mug. 'You put a lot of sugar in, didn't you?'

'Kilojoules.'

We drink in silence and when I finish, he takes my mug and puts it on the table next to his. He leans forward and holds out both hands.

'Come here.'

My eyes sting. They must be red and puffy. Is my nose red too? 'Do you feel sorry for me? Do you think I'm fragile?'

'No,' he says firmly. 'Lie down with me. We'll search for the light.'

I crawl across the window seat and lie on my side between his outstretched legs, so I'm facing the window with my cheek on his chest. He gathers the doona closely around us and leans back again. One of his arms crosses my waist so his hand is on my hip. He nuzzles through my hair to the side of my neck.

'Tell me what you know about the stars,' he says.

'I know there's a reason why they twinkle.' His chest is hard with muscle. His heart thumps steadily. 'But I can't remember what it is.'

'Astronomical scintillation.'

'And what is that?'

He strokes my hair with the back of his hand. 'A star's light is diffracted by atmospheric interference.'

'I'm not sure what that means, either.'

He sighs against my cheek. 'As a star's light enters our atmosphere, it passes through air pockets. These are affected by the wind; they have different temperatures and densities. The light gets ...' he says something in Norwegian. 'I can't think, Phoebe. What does a ball do when you throw it on the ground?'

'Bounces?'

'The light gets bounced around, it gets diffracted.'

'It bends?'

I feel the lift and fall of his chest against my back. 'Light waves from a star come from a single point. The diffraction makes the brightness appear to change.'

'But it doesn't really.'

He points to a star near the horizon. 'That star is further away. It appears to twinkle more than other stars, because there is more atmosphere between us.'

'Are you telling me about the stars so I can search for them?'

'They are lights.'

'It takes time for my eyes to adjust after a light is switched off.' When I lift my face, I breathe against his neck. 'Sometimes it's cloudy.'

'Behind the clouds, there is light.'

'I'll try to remember that next time.' Our mouths are only cen-timetres apart. 'Are you afraid of anything?'

He bends a leg, changing his position and shifting mine. 'You scare me.'

'I don't believe that.' He moves his leg again. 'Do you want me to get up?'

He growls as he tightens his arms around my front. 'No.'

'I manage my fear. Usually, I do.'

He shifts his position again, back to the way it was. His erection, long and hard, presses against the inside of my thigh.

'Oh.'

He puts his fist under my chin and tips it up. 'Yes.' He brushes a kiss against my mouth. 'Take the bed, kjære. Sleep.'

I twist out of his arms and sit. His hair is glossy in the half-light. I push it back and run a finger down his forehead and nose, over his mouth to his chin. 'I didn't thank you properly before.' I kiss his cheek. 'I love it.'

'What?'

'Lottie's palace.'

For an instant, his eyes are shadowed. Then he blinks and they clear. 'I like to use my hands.'

I reach for his hands and run my thumb over a cut on his index finger. 'They're good hands.' When I bend down and press my lips on the mark, he mutters a curse.

'Phoebe,' he says. 'I don't have the language for you.'

'Your English is perfect.'

He pulls a hand free and touches my mouth. 'This is perfect.' He runs his other hand down my arm then grasps my hip. 'This is perfect.'

I rest my hands on his chest, opening my fingers wide. His heart-beats are strong and steady. 'Thank you.'

'Tell me why you are frightened.'

'I already did.'

'Your father hurt you,' he says. 'I won't.'

'You wouldn't mean to.'

He puts his finger on my mouth and pulls down my bottom lip, just a fraction. When he presses a fingertip to the dampness, warmth steals through my body.

'Explain what you mean,' he says.

I can't afford to fall in love with you. 'You're taking a break from the navy. Don't you miss the ocean?'

'You asked me this before.'

'I didn't get an answer.' I speak through a yawn.

He stands, lifting me and the doona with him, one hand at my back and another behind my knees. The doona drags along the floor before he deposits it with me in the middle of the bed. He sits next to me, leaning back against the bedhead.

'I have cousins. Nate told you this?'

'Tor's wife is expecting twins.'

'He and Per are also twins, four years older than me. Tor was raised by his mother and stepfather in France. Per lived with his father, and grew up where I did in Bergen, a navy town. He's a scientist and an officer. I wanted to be like him.'

'We're far from the ocean here.'

Turning towards me, he runs his hand up my hip to my waistband. When he touches my skin, he hesitates. *Please. Please. Please.* His hand slips under my pyjama top. His face is flushed. His eyes are bright.

'I should go,' he says.

I grasp the hem of his T-shirt. 'Can you take this off first?'

He closes his eyes. 'Phoebe.'

'Your pulse.'

He takes my hand and guides it to his jaw. 'This is not enough?' When I shake my head, he pulls off his T-shirt and throws it onto the floor. His chest muscles are clearly delineated. His abdominals form neat rectangles that march down his torso. I put one hand on his heart, one on his pulse and count to ten.

And then I take off my sweater and top.

He stares. Lifts a hand and drops it. His eyes go from my breasts to my eyes and back to my breasts. 'Vakker,' he whispers. He cups one breast, lifting it and running a thumb across my nipple. He dips his head and circles my other nipple with his tongue. I squirm with need, running my fingers through the silky thickness of his hair as he strokes and nudges and sucks. He trails kisses down my cleavage, soft and slow then hard and fast. He kisses my mouth, lips dancing and playing. But then, breaths harsh and uneven, he lifts his head.

'Enough.'

I fight through the fog in my mind. 'Why?'

He groans as he lies on his back. He strokes a lock of hair that drapes across my breast. 'Come here.'

I do as he asks, falling against the warmth of his chest.

'You've stayed alone in your house ever since you came to Warrandale.' His voice is gruff.

'I don't need to live with anyone.'

'Never?'

'Do you live with anyone?'

'I told you. No.'

'Have you ever?'

'Not for long, but yes.'

'I have had sex, Sinn, plenty of times.'

'The last time?'

I look straight ahead. 'I can't remember.'

'You'd have sex with me?'

I close my eyes. 'I wish you'd stop *analysing* everything so much.'

He feathers a kiss on one of my eyes and then the other. 'Look at me, Phoebe.'

Our legs scissor together—his leg, my leg, his leg, mine.

'What?'

'Leave me to do my work.' He briefly kisses my mouth. 'Then we sleep together.'

'That's not fair.'

'I care about you. What do you feel?'

A gold-framed print of pink roses and white peonies hangs on the wall. 'I like you and I like Lottie's palace. But you don't belong here.'

'Sex won't be enough. I want more.' His face is set. His hair is messy. His chest is bare.

'So that's it?'

He closes his eyes. Nods. He's cranky but concerned. He's confused and—

I wrench my gaze away, roll onto my back and stare at the ceiling. I count the nymphs with flowers in their hair that dance around the cornice. *One. Two. Three.*

'Phoebe?' He comes up on an elbow and kisses my mouth. He brushes my breast with the back of his hand. 'Tell me about the senses. Tell me how they work.'

'Why do you want to know that?'

'I want to know you.'

I do my best to focus. 'The skin has receptors—they give a sense of touch. Sight, sound, taste and smell are external senses. The senses gather information from what's happening in the environment.'

He strokes down my side. 'More.'

'Our minds don't process sensory information one sense at a time, but all at once.'

He nudges my nipple with his tongue, a velvety sweep. My toes curl into the mattress.

'There are other senses too.' I stroke his hair, 'like proprioception, a sense of space. Senses tell us how our bodies move, and where they are in space and time.' I run my hands over the smooth skin of his shoulders then lift a leg and wrap it around his thigh. I press against him in an attempt to ease the ache.

With a groan, he kisses me again, but this time it's different. Demanding. Passionate. Hard. Possessive. He doesn't hold back. He isn't my lover but ... this is what he'd be like as a lover.

But just as I sense it, it slips away. He regains control. His mouth and hands become gentle. He smooths my hair on the pillow. Slowly and deliberately, his hand slips down my body and under the waistband of my pyjama pants. He traces the lacy edges of my underwear before kissing me again, an intoxicating kiss that sends warmth through my body.

He lifts his head as his fingers slip under the lace. 'Phoebe? Can I touch you?'

I groan and lift my bottom, pressing against his hand. 'Mmm.'

He grazes my breast with his cheek. 'Say it, sweetheart.'

'Yes.' I thread my fingers through his hair as he kisses my mouth and strokes between my thighs. He teases, his movements measured. His breathing deepens as he plays.

'So soft,' he whispers against my mouth. 'Sweet.'

His fingers slip and slide. He touches around and inside me. My skin burns, my hands shake, my breaths are little gasps.

'Sinn …'

'I won't hurt you.'

I squeeze my thighs together and press hard into his hand, moving against his fingers.

When I sob my release, he captures it. 'Kjære,' he whispers.

The word on his lips. The look in his eyes. The scent of his skin. His taste on my mouth and his hands on my body.

Sound, sight, smell, taste, touch.

♘

When I open my eyes, I'm gathered close to his side and the doona is tucked around my shoulders. My arm is draped over his chest. Like he belongs to me.

I lift my leg over his hip to bring him even closer and his erection presses against the inside of my thigh. I rise up on an elbow.

'Sinn?' My voice is raspy with sleep. I reach for him beneath the doona but he captures my hand.

'Go to sleep.' When he settles my head on his chest again, I sink into the warmth of his body.

'But you didn't—'

He lifts my chin with a finger. 'You like what I built for the lamb?'

I yawn. 'Very much.'

'It won't fall down. You know this? You trust it?'

'Yes.'

'For now, this is enough.'

When Sinn's alarm thrums, I cling on to him. For an instant he holds on too, before sighing and kissing my neck. His stubble, rough against my skin, sends warmth through my body. Besides the glow of the lamp, the room is in shadows.

'Sleep, Phoebe.' He brings the doona around my shoulders and tucks it in.

Has he slept? He rummages in his bag before walking across the carpet, head down as he buttons his shirt. He closes the blind at the window, then goes into the bathroom. The door to the verandah opens and closes. I hear his voice on the other side of the wall: ja, nei and a steady murmur of incomprehensible words.

Last night, he said he didn't have the words for me. What did he mean? My mind, foggy with sleep, can't tie the threads together. I reach for his pillow, still warm, and hold it in my arms.

It smells of him.

CHAPTER
23

The sun filtering through the blind is brighter than the lamplight when I wake. My pyjama top is draped at the end of the bed. I pull it over my head and comb through my hair with my fingers. My chocolate mug and Sinn's coffee mug are side by side on the table. His bag is zipped closed. I hear him outside—another call?

I step over the threshold to the verandah. He has ear pods in his ears and a laptop. An empty coffee pot, a cup, saucer and the remnants of a bowl of muesli sit on a tray to the side of his chair. He looks up, taps his ear pods and holds out his hand, beckoning me.

'You should have woken me up,' I whisper.

'Why?' He smiles. 'You curl up like a lynx.'

'It's already seven thirty. Breakfast is served from seven to nine.'

'I've eaten.'

'Do you always raid people's kitchens?'

He shrugs. 'I was hungry.'

'At nine o'clock, we're supposed to go to the arena to see the yearlings.'

He takes my hand. 'I don't want to buy a horse.'

'That's not—' I swallow. *What does he want?* When his hand trails up my arm, the burst of heat that shoots through my body catches my breath. He tugs my hands and I kneel, leaning against his legs.

He kisses my mouth and I taste coffee. He must have the call on mute, but I'm sure there's a conversation going on.

'How are you going to catch anyone out if you don't concentrate on—'

'I know my job,' he says, taking out his ear pods before kissing a trail to my collarbone. 'Please, Phoebe, stay out of it.'

'Yes,' I say, as I stand. 'I mean no.'

His eyes are smiling when he squeezes my hand, but he doesn't speak again as I back away. I quickly dress in jeans and a sweater, brush my teeth, splash water on my face and tie up my hair. Walking down the corridor, I apply lip gloss.

The sun is out, but large market umbrellas shade a number of tables in the courtyard garden. A row of silver bain-maries and other breakfast supplies are lined up in front of a hedge of orange blossom shrubs. White-aproned wait staff walk around with coffee and teapots. When I request poached eggs, a young Irish chef insists on cooking them fresh, piling them on top of sourdough toast and, with a flourish, adding grilled tomato to the side of the plate.

He grins. 'Enjoy.'

A number of guests sit at one table, but I don't see my doctor friend William or Elizabeth or Beatrice. Martin is sitting alone at another table, his hands circling a mug of black coffee.

'Good morning,' I say. 'Is it okay if I sit here?'

He rubs his red-rimmed eyes. 'I've said no to everybody else.'

'Oh.' I step back. 'I'll sit else—'

He barks a laugh as he leans forward to pull out a chair. 'You're an exception.' As he sits back in his chair again, he winces and touches his head. 'I'm waiting for the painkillers to kick in.'

I put my plate on the table and take the chair he offers. 'Did you have too much to drink?'

He grimaces. 'Yes, my teetotal friend, I did.'

'You shouldn't take analgesics on an empty stomach. Maybe you should eat something?'

He opens his mouth to disagree, but then looks with interest at my plate. 'I presume there's bacon at the buffet?'

'Sausages, mushrooms and hash browns as well, but if you're not feeling well, maybe you should keep it simple.' I push my plate across the table. 'Why don't you have mine, and I'll go get some more.'

'I wouldn't dream of it.'

'Eat it, Martin, before the tablets burn a hole in your stomach. I'll bring back some bacon as well.'

Suddenly serious, he puts a hand on my arm. 'I missed having you here, Phoebe. But being Robbie's father, I didn't think it right to muddy the waters and tell you that.'

I refold my serviette. 'You weren't angry I left Robbie?'

'It saddened me. But I always hoped that, in time, you'd forgive my errant son.'

'I'm sure it's only a matter of time before he gives you the grand-child you were always nagging him about.'

Someone touches my shoulder. 'This is like old times.'

The hairs at the back of my neck stand on end. When Robbie didn't appear at dinner last night, I hoped that meant ...

Martin laughs. 'Were your ears burning, my boy?'

Robbie is taller and more athletic than his father, but shares similar facial features. His hair is still light brown, and cut short. He's thicker set than he used to be.

'Hello, Robbie.'

When he holds out his arms, I hurriedly stand, taking his hand to control the embrace. Even so, he presses me into a bear hug and hangs on for too long.

Stepping back, he smiles into my eyes. 'I couldn't believe it when Dad said you'd be here.'

'I came with a friend.'

'Lucky bastard.' He looks around. 'Where is he?'

'On his way.'

Martin walks gingerly towards the buffet and Robbie takes the seat on my other side. He signals to the waiter for a coffee before angling his chair towards mine.

'If possible, you look even better than you did. Hardly any older though.'

I nod stiffly. 'You look well too. Do you still play polo?'

'Whenever I can. Still cloistered in that church of yours at Warrandale?'

'My practice is there as well. Do you live here?'

'And in Sydney.'

I slice through one of the eggs and gooey yolk spreads over the toast. Martin is at the buffet, lifting up lids and peering inside, when Sinn walks through the doors to the gardens. He wasn't happy that I used to be close to Martin. Will he mind I haven't said much about my relationship with Robbie? After my nightmare, I was going to tell him we used to be together. A flush creeps up my neck.

'That's him?' Robbie asks.

'He doesn't know we dated.'

'Dated? Is that how you'd describe it?' His brows lift. 'How long have you been with him?'

'A few weeks …' I aim for a nonchalant shrug. 'He won't be in Australia for long.'

When Martin shouts out, Sinn, dressed casually in jeans and a sweater, changes direction, joining him at the buffet. Eventually the men walk towards us, Martin with a plate and Sinn with a cup and saucer. I pick up my fork, toying with the sprigs of parsley that garnish my tomato.

Sinn, hair damp, puts his face to my cheek. 'Kjære.'

'Hi.'

Robbie rises from his chair and holds out a hand. 'Robbie Roxburgh.'

'Sinn Tørrissen.'

'Welcome to Roxburgh Estate. Dad tells me you have something to do with the UN.'

'I'm on secondment there.'

When Robbie sits next to me again, Sinn has no option but to walk around the table to Martin's other side and sit opposite. Our eyes meet.

'The food is lovely.' My voice is stilted.

He frowns as he nods towards my plate. 'Can I get you something else?'

'No, thank you.' Being hemmed in by Sinn and Robbie is suffocating. I put a forkful of toast into my mouth and force it down.

When Martin launches into a spiel about the state of the property market, Robbie joins in, telling Sinn about the new high-rise development he's involved with in Sydney.

'My boy's almost as busy as I am these days,' Martin says.

Robbie laughs. 'Someone has to earn a decent living, Dad, given the fortune you sink into this place.'

'Martin always said spending money on Roxburgh Estate made him happier than anything else in life,' I say.

Even from the corner of my eye, I see Sinn stiffen. Because I mentioned money? Does he imagine I'm trying to trick Martin into telling us something?

Martin smiles. 'You remember correctly, Phoebe. And I must say, Robbie has a hell of a cheek, baiting me like that. Wait till he has a wife and son to care for. They don't come cheap.'

Robbie slaps the table and hoots. 'You have three ex-wives, Dad. It triples the expense.' He turns in his chair and puts his arm along the back of mine, smiling broadly. 'One of the many things you liked about Phoebe was that she wouldn't rob me blind.'

My gaze flies to Sinn, but other than a slight narrowing of his eyes, he doesn't react.

Martin pats my arm. 'I wanted you and Robbie to have a long and happy marriage, as you are well aware. Divorce was the furthest thing from my mind.'

Robbie smiles again. 'Dad was almost as miserable as I was when we broke up.'

'I told you not to—'

'Chill, Phoebe.' He flicks my ponytail. 'You were the one who ended it. Anyway, according to what you said earlier ...' He smiles in Sinn's direction. 'Sinn won't be here for long. Why would he care?'

I fold my serviette and unfold it again. 'I wish you'd all stop talking about what happened years ago.'

Sinn lifts his cup with a perfectly steady hand. His eyes are icy when he looks at me over the rim.

'I didn't comment,' he says.

I put my fork and knife together and cover my food with my serviette. 'I have things to do,' I say as I stand.

Robbie stands too. 'Better go make some calls.'

'Leaving already?' Martin, his elbow on the table, picks at a rasher of bacon. 'You haven't eaten anything yet.'

'I only came to see Phoebe.' Robbie pulls a card from his wallet and holds it out. 'Keep it somewhere safe.'

'Why would I need it?'

'I told you to call when you'd calmed down.' He winks. 'Still waiting.'

I take the card to get rid of him, but no sooner has he gone than Sinn stands too. He kisses me, a press of his cheek against mine.

'I'll see you back at the room.'

Not wanting to leave Martin on his own, I return to my chair, waiting until Elizabeth and Beatrice join us before saying good-bye. As I walk across the gardens, I create a list in my mind of all the 'important' things I have to think about. Cleaning my teeth. Calling Mike to check on Wickham. Emailing my aunt to let her know I won't be able to do my Zoom call with Mum until tonight. Texting Nate to see that Lottie is okay.

Sinn isn't in the room, but he's tidied the bathroom and packed all his things away. He's straightened the bedclothes and neatly folded my pyjamas. Did he notice that his pillow had come over to my side of the bed? I push the thought from my mind as I make my calls from the verandah, before packing my bag and leaving it near the door next to his.

When I walk from the room, Sinn is in the hallway, leaning against the wall with his hands in his pockets.

I take an involuntary step back. 'Oh.'

'Why didn't you tell me about Robbie Roxburgh?'

'I didn't know he'd be here. I— Why does it matter?'

'You were going to marry him.'

'He asked me to, but I don't think I would have.'

'What does that mean?'

'Why do you care?'

'You should have told me.'

'I don't know about your girlfriends!'

He walks a few steps down the hallway, spins on his heel and strides back again. 'That's not—' He clamps his mouth shut. 'I don't care about the relationships you've had, but Robbie is Martin's son. I should have known.'

'I was going to tell you. Last night, I tried.'

'After you woke up screaming.'

I push past him. 'I don't want to talk about it.'

'None of it?'

'I want to forget!'

'I don't!'

We're at the end of the hallway when he catches up. 'Is there anything else I should know?'

'How can I answer that, when you won't tell me what you're looking for?' I step in front of him and cut him off before we reach the crowd of guests assembled in the courtyard. He pulls up sharply and puts his hands behind his back. As if he doesn't want to touch me.

I study my boots before looking up. 'I want to help, Sinn.'

He looks over my shoulder. 'Pretend we're together.'

'That's all?'

'If you can't do that, we leave.'

'Is this a punishment?'

His swears under his breath. 'Through your father, you were associated with the syndicate. We thought Martin might care about that. He doesn't.'

'I bet you haven't even asked him about—'

'Phoebe! You lack objectivity.'

'I'm a good judge of character!'

'You said you'd do as I asked.' He looks at his watch. 'We go to the arena and tour the stables. I've arranged to meet with the syndicate members at lunch. We have an afternoon drink with the others.'

I tear my gaze away. 'I should have told you about Robbie. I'm sorry I didn't. If you ask me questions about him, I'll answer them honestly.'

He crosses his arms and uncrosses them. 'You told me you were at university with him.'

'I said I was at uni when we met. He said he wanted to marry me. I never agreed.'

'According to Martin, Robbie was building you a house.'

'I didn't ask him to!'

Muttering under his breath, Sinn takes my hand. 'Come.'

CHAPTER
24

Elizabeth and Beatrice stand at the top of the path that leads to the stables.

Elizabeth beckons. 'Phoebe, my dear. We only saw you briefly at breakfast. You must join us this morning. We insist.'

Prising my hand free of Sinn's, I follow Elizabeth and her sister to the indoor arena, an enormous high-ceilinged shed with tiered seating on two sides. The floor, double the size of a dressage arena, is carpeted with wood shavings. Beatrice waves Sinn away when he explains he has to make a call.

By the time he returns, I'm seated between the sisters. Declining Elizabeth's invitation to sit next to her, Sinn joins a man sitting on his own behind us. When an announcer introduces Martin, seated in the front row, he turns and waves to everyone. Then Brent, dressed smartly in chinos and a shirt, walks through the double doors holding a spirited pitch-black thoroughbred at the end of a lead rope.

Elizabeth gasps. 'What a divine creature.'

Beatrice leans forward, her eyes open wide. 'Yes, indeed.'

When I refer to the catalogue, it confirms my suspicions. 'His name is Lancelot. I have his half-brother.'

Elizabeth's perfectly sculpted brows draw together. 'I beg your pardon, my dear?'

'My horse Camelot has the same sire.'

'Goodness me! Did Camelot race?'

'He was retired as a four-year-old.'

'Was he injured?'

'No. But he wasn't fast enough for Group One.'

'He looks like Lancelot?'

'A carbon copy.'

'Then why haven't I seen him in the show ring or dressage arena? He's *magnificent*.'

'I ride him at home.'

'That's *all* you've done with him?' Elizabeth says. 'A horse with his confirmation, his bearing?'

'He has a beautiful nature.'

'Which would have made him even more valuable as—'

'Look, Elizabeth.' I point to a fine-boned chestnut mare, her strapper running next to her as she trots briskly into the arena. She tosses her head and pulls on her lead rope as she dances after Lancelot. 'Isn't she lovely?'

'She certainly is,' Elizabeth says, consulting the catalogue. 'And likely to be a great deal more affordable than Lancelot.' She leans over me and taps Beatrice's arm. 'Look sharp, my dear. I fear the mare won't have the build to make her competitive at the top level, but isn't she a gem?'

After the twelve horses have been brought into the arena, paraded and led out again, we walk to the stable block, a long double row of stables with a wide central aisle. Some horses look curiously over their half-doors while others gaze cautiously from the shadows.

We're approaching the final stable in the row when Brent leans over the door and looks me up and down. 'Phoebe.' He smiles at the sisters. 'Morning, Elizabeth, Beatrice. What do you think of Lancelot?'

'A great deal.' When Elizabeth peers over the door, Lancelot, his black leather halter barely discernible against the darkness of his coat, gazes back. 'Phoebe informs us he shares her horse's sire.'

'The sire's studbook closed last year, so we were glad to get another horse out of him. This colt's fierier than Camelot ever was, but to look at them as yearlings? Spitting image.'

'Elizabeth,' Beatrice calls out from further down the row, 'you must see this mare!'

As Elizabeth walks away, Brent unlatches the half-door. He winks. 'I've told the strappers not to let the guests into the stables. But you know your way around a horse. Come and take a closer look.'

I can't think up a sensible reason not to join Brent. The stable is brightly lit with a high window at the back and fluorescent strips attached to the rafters. When I hold out my hand, Lancelot, his coat glistening onyx, warily sniffs my palm.

'Hello, beautiful boy.'

Brent closes the door behind him and leans against it. 'Thought this might be a good time to have a word, Phoebe.'

I step closer to Lancelot. 'About what?'

'You and Tørrissen are joined at the hip from what I hear.' His smile goes nowhere near his eyes. 'How'd you get together?'

Weeks ago, Sinn told me to stick to the truth when I could. So even though I'd like to tell Brent to mind his own business, I hold back.

'He got roped in to setting up the audio for the Warrandale fete.' *He kissed me senseless behind the pavilion.* 'I guess that was the start.'

Brent purses his lips. 'Nothing to do with your father, then?'

I stroke Lancelot's neck, warm and satin smooth. 'What are you getting at?'

'You were at Elizabeth's party when the Roxburgh syndicate came up. From what Martin tells me, and what Tørrissen's hinted at himself, that's what he's interested in.' He leans an elbow on the door. 'Your father managed the syndicate, so Tørrissen would want to talk to him.'

'My father has dementia. He's not capable of helping Sinn.'

'Is that what they're calling it?' He huffs. 'No offence, Phoebe, but your old man was crazy as a cut snake at the best of times.'

I glance over Brent's shoulder, willing Sinn to appear. He'd likely accuse me of meddling in his business, but he'd also know what questions to ask.

'I'm sure Sinn would be happy to talk to you about the syndicate.'

'I prefer to talk to you.'

'He doesn't talk to me about work. And I have as little to do with my father as possible.'

Brent stretches out his legs. 'You helped your old man out though, didn't you? When you were at home.'

To hide my sudden shakiness, I run my hands down Lancelot's shoulder. As I trace his brand, similar in design to Camelot's, the colt turns his head towards me, blocking Brent from view.

Brent tugs on Lancelot's halter and pulls him round again. 'What's up, Phoebe? You've gone all quiet on me.'

'I'd better get back to the others.'

'The professor was lucky, having you on side when he was off with the fairies. And let's face it, that was most of the time.'

'Why bring this up? What's it to you?'

'It's best we keep some things to ourselves, Phoebe—in the family so to speak.' He takes a step towards me. 'Tørrissen isn't like us, growing up poor, trying to improve on the cards we've been dealt.'

'You sound like you've got something to hide. I don't.'

Three other guests appear at the door. 'You must be Lancelot,' a portly man says, placing his glasses on the end of his nose to read the catalogue before taking them off to peer at the horse again. 'What do you say, Mr Green? Is he beyond my means? Would he go for more than four hundred?'

Brent barely acknowledges the man, nodding abruptly before turning his back. He strokes Lancelot's neck, his hand stopping just short of mine. 'Just like you, Phoebe, I've got to watch out for guilt by association. If something dodgy was going on with the syndicate, or with what happened later—and I'm not saying I had any idea about that—I don't want to get the blame for it.'

'If you didn't do anything wrong, why would you?'

'Things can get twisted around, and—' he smiles unpleasantly, '—unlike you, I can't hop into bed with Tørrissen to straighten them out.'

Brent's scent is nauseating. His lids are heavy and his face is flushed. I doubt he'd be funnelling tens of millions of dollars through a syndicate, but he could know something about it.

'You've always worked closely with Martin on anything to do with the stud,' I say. 'Is that where things got twisted? Is that what you're scared about?'

'I'm not scared, but I have a lot of bills to pay. Martin is a good boss and a generous one—it's not in my interests to cause him grief. Not only that, Elizabeth pays me on top of my wage to source horses. Those sisters are so prim and proper, even a whiff of scandal would have them running for the hills.'

'Phoebe!'

Martin appears at the door, smiling as he looks over Brent's shoulder. 'If you think you can come in here and take another one of my horses, you've got another thing coming. Get out of this stable immediately.' Brent turns and Martin waggles a finger in his direction. 'And you? You're monopolising not only my horse but my guest.'

'All in the line of work, Martin.' Brent calmly loops Lancelot's lead rope around his hand. 'Phoebe's invited me to Warrandale to see Camelot. Means I can tell buyers, first hand, how the mature version of Lancelot turned out.'

'I suppose that's fair enough then,' Martin says jovially, walking to the centre of the aisle and lifting an arm. 'Sinn! I've found her! Over here!'

Brent turns back to me. 'I'll be in touch,' he says, taking out his phone and scrolling. 'What do you know? I've got your number in my contacts already.'

'Can you move out of the way so I can get past?'

Unlatching the door, he opens it a crack. 'Would you like some advice?'

Sinn has taken off his sweater and draped it over a shoulder. Even though he's on the other side of the aisle, his eyes are on me.

'I think I'll get it whether I want it or not.'

'Take it from me, pillow talk can be a dangerous thing. I don't think it'd be in either of our interests to share this conversation with Tørrissen.'

I nod woodenly as I slip past. 'Goodbye, Brent.'

The event manager is subtly herding guests towards the exit and I'm forced to dodge around them to reach Sinn. His jaw is clenched, but when I hold out my hands, he takes them. He dips his head and presses his cheek against mine.

'Phoebe.'

He might be cranky and arrogant, but he's also honest and mostly kind and he's trying to do his job. His sweater is still on his shoulder; I pull a hand free to straighten it.

'I need to talk to you.'

'After lunch.'

'Now.'

He says something to Martin before, keeping hold of my hand, we walk towards the house.

'Sinn? Can you slow down please?'

Other than tightening his fingers, he ignores me. 'I left you with the Oldfields. Why go off on your own?'

'Last night, you deposited me with William. Do you think I need twenty-four-hour care?'

He jerks to a stop. His eyes narrow. 'Yes.' He starts walking again, but not quite as fast.

'Why are you holding my hand?'

'We're supposed to be together.'

'It's not very convincing when you scowl at me like that.'

He stops abruptly again. 'Do I frown? Is this what you mean?'

'A scowl is more than a frown. It's more ... ferocious.'

His eyes darken. He dips his head and kisses my mouth. All of a sudden, my legs are unsteady. As he lifts his head, I put my hand on the side of his face.

'What was that for?'

'I'm not ferocious,' he growls.

I stand on my toes, lean against him and speak against his lips. 'Not very often.' My kiss is soft and sweet, but desire flares like wildfire. As if it has a mind of its own, my hand slips inside his shirt.

He wraps his arms around me. 'I want you safe.'

'Why do you worry so much? When I was the one who saved you?'

He mutters something unintelligible before gripping my hand and walking away again.

'Why were you with Green?'

'He called me into the stable. That's what I wanted to tell you about. He acted like he knew something about the syndicate, but he wouldn't say what it was. He also said he didn't do anything wrong, but he would say that, wouldn't he?'

'You asked him questions?'

'Just follow-up questions.'

Sinn whispers a curse.

'Brent said he and I should keep things to ourselves and not tell you anything, and that we had to be careful of guilt by association.'

He nods stiffly. 'That is all?'

'Well ... more or less, but it's useful information, isn't it?'

'No. Forget it.'

'Aren't you going to talk to him again? He could know about your target. I don't like being dragged into this any more than he does, but we don't have a choice, do we? If it might help.'

'Leave this to me.'

'You're not going to pursue this?'

'I have no interest in Green. And you're to stay away from him.'

I yank my hand free. 'Why?'

The events manager is waving, directing us to the bathrooms to freshen up before lunch. Martin and Elizabeth approach with the portly man who thought Lancelot might be too expensive. Was he one of the syndicate members? Brent was rude to him. Should I tell Sinn that? But why would I bother when he doesn't listen to me any—

'Phoebe?' He squeezes my hand. 'Sit with Beatrice at lunch.'

'Not Brent?' I smile stiffly. 'That was something else he said. When Martin appeared, Brent told him he was coming to—'

'Forget him.' He smiles over my shoulder. 'Beatrice. Thank you.'

Beatrice puts her hand on his arm. 'Did you think I'd forgotten your lovely Phoebe? Shame on you, young man.' She links her arm through mine. 'Come, my dear, leave the others to their boring private lunch. William will join us, so a merry band of three we shall be.'

Sinn and I only drink tonic water and lemon squash at the farewell cocktail party, but it's well after six by the time we can say our polite goodbyes and join the queue of hire cars on the driveway. Ever since Sinn found me after lunch, sitting on the verandah outside our room, he's been courteous in a tight-lipped and reserved kind of way. No kisses. No handholding. Time to stop pretending.

He glances at my phone, vibrating on my lap, as we near the end of the driveway. 'Answer it, Phoebe.'

'It's my aunt.' I send a text: *Will call as soon as I can.* 'My mother lives with Debra and her husband. I thought I'd be home an hour ago and promised to call. I also told Nate I'd give Lottie her bottle when I got back to Warrandale. She'll be starving, and picking her up will make us even later and—'

'I'll take you home now.'

'What about Lottie?'

He calls Nate on speaker. 'Phoebe has to get back. Can you feed the lamb—'

'You'll need to mix more formula,' I interrupt. 'For tonight and in the morning. Boil the water first, then three scoops per bottle. Have you sterilised the bottles?'

'All good.'

'Take her to Phoebe tomorrow,' Sinn says. 'I can't do it. My flight leaves at eight.'

'Hey, Lottie,' Nate shouts. 'You get another night with Uncle Nate!'

Sinn is doing a U-turn when my phone rings again. This time, I answer. 'Debra. Is everything okay?'

'Yes, love, but is there any way we can do the call now? Barbara's been sitting in front of the screen for the past few hours. I told her you'd be calling later today, but she knows it's Sunday and after all these years, she's used to a call at lunchtime. As you know, she gets a little upset if things don't go to plan.'

I glance at Sinn. 'Do you mind if …?'

'No.'

'I have to connect on Zoom so we can see each other. It'll be on speaker.'

'Do it, Phoebe.'

Mum smiles when the call comes through. 'There she is! Look at my darling. There she is.'

'Hello, Mum. Sorry I was late. How are you? It's Phoebe.'

'I've been worried about you, being away from home at university.'

'I'm in Warrandale, Mum. Prim is up north, but she's enjoying studying there. Did you get her last email?'

'Yes, Phoebe,' Debra says, 'Barbara loves getting Prim's news.'

'What about your sister on the ship?' Mum asks.

'Patience is well too.'

'What about you, love?' Debra asks. 'Tell us what you've been up to this week.'

'I've been away for the weekend, which is why I'm not home yet.'

'Where did you go?' Mum asks.

'A horse stud in Denman. It was very fancy.'

'Have I been there?'

'I don't think so, Mum.'

'What about your sisters? Did they go with you?'

'Patience is still at sea. And Prim is in Darwin.'

'Have I been there?'

'I don't think you have. After you finished your doctorate at Oxford, you mostly travelled around Europe.'

'I did, didn't I?'

'We have some lovely photos of you and all your friends. Tell me about your week, Mum? Have you, Debra and Ray been busy with the dairy?'

Mum turns to Debra. 'We've been very busy, haven't we?'

Debra prompts Mum about her visits to Carol, and what's been happening on the farm. 'One of our old heifers had twins, didn't she, Barbara?' she says. 'We've been worried about one of them because he was so small, but we think he's come good now.'

'I'm still feeding Lottie. She should be weaned, but she's not too keen on grass.'

Debra smiles. 'You're far too soft-hearted, Phoebe. Leave it too long and you'll never get her back in the herd.'

By the time I disconnect, we're only ten minutes out of War-randale. I glance at Sinn, who takes his eyes from the road for a moment.

'Can I ask a personal question?' he says.

'Only one?'

'Your mother had a stroke?'

'She's remarkably well physically, but her memory was badly affected.' I tell him my mother's story as I look out of the window. There are fewer clouds tonight; the stars and moon are bright above the trees. 'She lost a lot of her long-term memory, and her short-term memory comes and goes,' I finish.

'She confuses her children?'

'Mum has always recognised our faces but can't differentiate between us. In some ways …' My voice wavers. 'Debra says she sees all of us whenever she sees any one of us. I think that's a nice way of looking at it.'

'When she moved to New Zealand, you and your sisters stayed behind?'

'It wasn't what Mum would have wanted if she'd had the capacity to decide.' My fingers thread together in my lap. 'Debra's children were teenagers and having Mum was enough to take on. Carol had younger children. Anyway, my father would never have agreed to let us go.'

'What happened to him?'

We pass the Warrandale sign. 'Why do you want to know?'

A few cars are parked outside the pub. Hendrika is on the footpath and, even though I doubt she recognises Sinn's car, she waves.

'I want to understand,' Sinn says.

It's dark when I close my eyes, but whenever I want to, I can lift my lids. 'He was unhinged by Vietnam, and even though he was respected academically, he hated the bureaucracy. As much as he was capable of seeing beyond his own problems, he loved Mum, but mostly he respected her intelligence. So what happened … it couldn't have been worse in his eyes.' My words run together, but now I've started, I don't seem to be able to stop. 'Only it *was* worse, because Mum only developed high blood pressure after she became pregnant with me. And when she did have the stroke, it happened during a routine medical procedure. That played into Dad's paranoia.'

'He blamed you?'

'Me, my sisters, the doctors, the government. He became a milder version of what he is now.'

'People must have known.'

'There were no bruises. We were fed and clothed. He supported our education—that was important to him. Maybe we would have been better off in care, but he would have fought hard to keep us. I was compliant and helpful. Patience was rebellious but freakishly clever—he saw that as a reflection of his own intelligence. He barely acknowledged Prim, but he didn't want the government to take her away.'

Sinn swears quietly. 'You told no one in your family?'

'Debra knew it was hard for us, but we gave away as little as we could—if she'd complained to Dad, he would have made things even harder for us. We were afraid we wouldn't be allowed to go to Warrandale if we'd said anything to Auntie Kate or Uncle Bob. The most important thing was to stay together until we could live independently.'

The porch light shines brightly onto the steps and across the driveway to the liquidambar trees, their tumbles of leaves piled up in drifts. Unfastening his seatbelt, Sinn turns towards me as I reach for the door handle.

'Thanks for—'

'Wait, Phoebe. I'll be gone for two weeks.'

'Where are you going?'

'Overseas.'

'Can you be more specific?'

'We have to talk.'

'I haven't stopped talking since we left.'

'Thank you for explaining about your family.'

'You knew a lot of it already.'

'Now I know more. I know you better.'

I link my fingers together and pull them apart. 'Ever since we met, it's been … I've been …' I shake my head. 'However well you think you know me, it's a lot better than I know you.'

'What do you want to know?'

'A lot, but …' I reach into the back for my coat, laying it over my knees. 'Nate told me you took this job after the court martial. Why take a break when you were exonerated? Will you go back?'

'I can't say.'

'You got to eavesdrop on my conversation. I answered your questions.'

'Your questions are different.'

'You wouldn't let me help this weekend. You have no faith in my opinions.'

'Even though you don't trust me …' His eyes go to my mouth. He lifts a hand and drops it again. 'You would have let me—'

'I don't want to talk about that.'

'You're vulnerable.'

'I am not!'

He blows out a breath. 'The nightmare. You're afraid—'

'You shouldn't have turned out the light.'

'I didn't know.'

'You didn't need to know.'

'For fuck's—'

'It wasn't relevant to why I was there.' I fold my hands in my lap. 'You promised I could be involved if I did as I was told. You lied. You only took me with you to shut me up.'

'You didn't tell me how close you were to Martin, or about your relationship with Robbie. You spent time alone with Green.'

'I explained the circumstances. And when I told you what he'd said, you refused to listen.'

'I did listen.'

I blow on my hands. 'There's listening and there's *listening*.'

'This assignment will end, Phoebe. It will be easier.'

'When will it end?' Through the gloom, I make out the shoots on the trees. 'How long will you stay afterwards?'

He hesitates. 'I don't know.'

His door slams shut immediately after mine, but I beat him to the boot, opening it by the time he catches up. I position my bag on the tailgate so it forms a barrier between us. I force a smile.

'Say goodnight to Lottie for me, and ask Nate to text when he leaves. I'll make him breakfast, or morning tea.'

'Last night, Phoebe,' Sinn says as he searches my face, 'I didn't want to fuck things up by having sex.'

'I understand that. And now things are back to how they were.'

'Are they?' he says.

'You don't have to look after me. I have my own ways of dealing with things.'

'On your own.'

I point to the porch. 'My neighbours used to think I left lights on by mistake, but now they understand. You call me vulnerable, but they don't have a problem with it.'

'They leave you alone. You push them away if they get close. That's what you want from me.'

I don't know what I want from you. That's why you scare me. 'You don't respect my views. You don't share information. You've never even acknowledged that I saved you.'

He opens his mouth and shuts it. Then says only, 'Thank you for looking after me.'

'You were too cold to shiver. I couldn't find your pulse.' I pull the bag closer, hug it to my chest. 'You think you're indestructible, don't you?'

'Look at me, Phoebe.'

His brow is creased and there are lines at the sides of his eyes. I woke him at two. He was up again at three thirty. My eyes slip to his mouth. I wish it were simply desire.

I wish it didn't hurt.

I wish I could trust him.

'Will you kiss me goodbye?' he asks.

How would it feel to kiss him goodbye forever?

I've already stepped back when headlights appear on the road. Mike slows, indicates and turns into the driveway. Wickham's front paws are on the dash and he's peering through the window.

Mike's thick straight hair is brilliant white against his tanned and weathered face. He sits at the kitchen bench as I brew a strong pot of tea and open his favourite biscuits. Wickham sticks to my heels like glue as I pour the tea into a mug and add milk.

'Sinn seems like a nice enough bloke, Phoebe. A bit stiff maybe, but good firm handshake and looked me in the eye.'

'Yes. I would have come for Wickham.'

'You think I'm too old to crank up the ute and drive two miles down the road?'

'I didn't want to put you out, that's all.'

'And that's your trouble. You think you're putting people out when you ain't.' He bites a biscuit in half, crumbs tumbling onto his sweater. He points to the stove. 'Watch that milk don't boil over.'

I turn off the hotplate and pour the milk into a nest of powdered chocolate. Less than twenty-four hours have passed since Sinn made me hot chocolate. It feels like days.

I smile bravely. 'It's good to be home, Mike.'

'Then why d'you look so blessed miserable?'

CHAPTER

26

Mist rises from the valley the following morning. Mintie is still with Mandy, but Camelot nickers as I walk around the puddle at the gate to the yard, and stands quietly as I take off his rugs. He has scars on his rump because he slipped in the mud and got tangled in blackberry bushes. When he baulked at a fallen log, throwing me over his head, he took a patch of hair from his fetlock that has never grown back. He has a permanent lump under his chin because he insisted on snooping in an ant's nest in the rain. I run the brush over his back and sides where the saddle blanket will go, and comb through his tail with my fingers.

'I think you're more handsome than Lancelot.'

He never wanted to be a racehorse. And as a show or dressage horse, he would have been trained for hours in indoor arenas and booted, rugged and hooded all year round to make sure he stayed perfect. I'm sure he prefers to live here.

It's where I belong too.

Benjamin, my first client of the day, has only been here for twenty minutes when he sinks to the floor and buries his face in Wickham's fur. 'Fair go, Phoebe. More writing? When can we go outside? Today's lesson *really* sucks.'

I smile and tap his shoe with my pencil. 'Have you looked outside? It's pouring with rain. Your teacher won't be happy if you go to school dripping wet.'

'She won't care.' Wickham watches as Benjamin slumps back into his chair, picking up his pencil before laying his arm on the table and leaning an ear on the inside of his elbow. When he reaches for the exercise book, I pull it away.

'It's impossible to get a good pencil grip in that position.' I sit next to him. 'How about you mirror my actions?'

'What?'

'Like a football drill.' I put a blank sheet of paper in front of me and open his book to a new double page. 'You have to copy what I do.' I sit ramrod straight and exaggeratedly push back my shoulders. I pick up a pencil and place my fingers, one by one, around it before stabbing it in his direction. 'Just for fifteen minutes. I dare you.'

He laughs as he mimics my posture. 'Sure, I'll give it a go.'

Benjamin copies my lines of text word for word, biting his lip in concentration as he forms the letters while keeping within the lines. Every few minutes I shake my hands and stretch out my fingers and he does the same. Then, when he's getting bored again, I put down my pencil and swap our work.

'Now we give feedback.'

'What?' He scoffs as he looks at my page. 'You write like a computer.'

'Only when I'm getting my fingers accustomed to doing what they need to do.'

'Sensory stuff, right?'

I hand him a sharpened pencil. 'For writing your feedback, I'd like you to form letters in a relaxed way, like you would when you have a test at school.'

'Tests aren't relaxing.'

'True, but most people write less carefully in a test.'

'I can write quicker?'

'So long as it's legible.'

I write notes down the margins of Benjamin's work. *Fantastic. Excellent. Give up football and write full time! Great work. Wow! Amazing. I'm impressed.*

He writes on my page too. *Try harder. This sucks. Disappointing. I give up. What a mess. This is crap. Wickham could do better than this.*

We're both laughing when there's a knock at the door. Sinn's four-wheel drive is parked on the driveway.

'Nate's early.'

'Who's Nate?'

'He's been looking after Lottie for me. C'mon. The rain has stopped. We can stretch our legs.'

Nate, with his customary sparkling smile, takes Lottie out of her crate and carries her into the garden. When he puts her on the grass, she gambols towards me and butts against my legs. It's only been two days since I've seen her, but I'm sure that she's grown.

'Hey, Phoebe.' Nate winks. 'Told you I'd bring your baby back.'

After we settle Lottie in her pen on the verandah, Benjamin is so busy telling Nate how much American football sucks compared to Aussie Rules, he hardly complains when I set pegs in front of him on the dining table and tell him to get back to work.

As he clips the last of the pegs onto the container with his thumb and little finger, Terry arrives, holding the take-away coffee I asked him to collect from the café.

'One large Americano with milk,' he says, pumping Nate's hand as he gives him the coffee, before shooing Benjamin out to the car. 'Off to school, little fella.'

After they leave, Nate and I sit at the table eating toasted sandwiches. I take another sip of hot chocolate.

'Thanks again for bringing Lottie home.'

'Sorry I couldn't fit her shed in the car,' he says, smiling appreciatively as he finishes his coffee.

'It would be much too big for my verandah anyway.'

'Sinn says he'll take it apart when he gets back. He reckons he can set it up in your garden.'

Do I want that reminder after he's gone? No.

But …

'When Lottie doesn't need it any more, it would make a perfect cubby house. My younger children would love it.' I shrug. 'If it wouldn't be too much trouble, I'd like it here. Can you tell Sinn that?'

'Why don't you tell him?'

'I don't want to put him on the spot.'

Nate tips his head to the side. 'Did you happen to do that over the weekend?'

I push my plate away. 'I doubt it.'

'Couldn't get much out of him last night, but I heard him bitching to Lottie when he fed her early this morning.' He grins. 'Didn't seem too happy with you.'

'He rarely is.'

'I've worked with guys like him before,' Nate says. 'Can't be easy for him, acting against his nature, tripping over a woman he has reason to distrust.'

I cross my fingers under the table. 'Because I helped my father?'

'He's sticking his neck out for you.'

'I didn't do anything dishonest.'

'*We* know that, but it still leaves him open to criticism. That's why he's monitoring every step.'

'Sinn won't let me monitor his steps. He clams up every time I ask him anything.'

Nate looks around as if searching for something to say. When he reads Benjamin's scrawl on my page, he looks up. '"Wickham could do better than this"?'

I smile. 'Benjamin and I were giving feedback on each other's writing exercises.' I show him the workbook. 'My comments were a little more encouraging.'

After studying the page for a while, Nate stands. 'Guess I'd better get back to work.'

I hand him the brightly wrapped package that's been sitting at the end of the table. 'This is for you. Thanks again for caring for Lottie.'

He hesitates before taking the gift, puffing out his cheeks as he unwraps the tissue paper and examines the mug and small plate, painted with gum trees and sheep, and made by a local potter.

'This was real kind,' he says, rewrapping the items and heading down the front steps. He turns when he gets to the bottom. 'I'll see you when Sinn gets back.'

I line up cushions on the sofa, put my folders in neat piles on the table and rearrange the toys in the sensory bins.

When Sinn gets back.

CHAPTER
27

The wind is brisk but the sun is warm the following Sunday afternoon as I hang a load of washing on the line. Shifts of wispy clouds skate across the sky, and the liquidambar trees burst with bright green leaves.

'Phoebe!' Mr Riley shouts from the road, his ancient Akubra pulled low over his brow. 'Spare me an hour? It's time I got the sheep pens and shed in order, and Tom's turned his ankle at the footy.'

I'm hardly a substitute for Mr Riley's grandson—twenty-one, six feet two and built like a Hereford bull—but I whistle for Wickham, secure Lottie in the chicken coop and lock the front door. When I snap my fingers and point to the tray, Wickham bounds over the side. He snuffles among the buckets, tools and other gear until he finds a spot behind the cab. Mr Riley waits until we're both settled before pulling back onto the road.

When we turn off and bounce over the potholed laneway to the lopsided gates of his property, Mr Riley harrumphs. 'I'll never find a buyer if I don't get this lane graded.'

'I don't think the bumps will be a problem, not when your buyer will most likely have a tractor to smooth them all out. The land is fenced, and both dams are full.'

'It's hard to make a living off a few hundred hectares.'

'Many farmers supplement their income with other work. This is a lovely property.'

'Would you buy it?'

I laugh. 'Of course I would! But it'll take me another twenty years to pay off the church.'

'I didn't get time to get a crop in this year.'

'There's plenty of grass. I've never seen the paddocks so green.'

He grumbles as he pulls on the handbrake. 'It's too wet to cut for hay.'

'We've had a lot of winter rain, so maybe we'll have a dry spring? The grass can be baled up at the end of the month, ready for the summer.'

'It's not like I'm praying for drought.'

The shed's corrugated roof glimmers in the sunshine. 'I didn't think you would be, but since you're keen to sell, it might be good to focus on the positives. The land is close to the town.'

Mr Riley pulls up outside the shed and we get out of the ute. 'No one will pay me what it's worth if it looks like Steptoe's junkyard. Now the squatters are out, I want to put things to rights.'

It was three months ago that I moved the hay into the corner of the shed, rolled Sinn onto my coat and covered him with sacks. I took off my sweater and laid it on his chest. A week has passed since I last saw him. And not a word since. Do I spend another week waiting? When I don't even know what time zone he's in? He said he'd be 'overseas'.

'Ha!'

Mr Riley puts his hand to his ear. 'What's that?'

'Nothing,' I say, turning to examine decades of discarded odds and ends. 'We can take the fence posts and wire, machinery parts and other smaller items out of the pens. Perhaps Tom can pick them up in his truck and take them for recycling?'

'I'll ask him.'

'The shed doesn't look too bad inside—most importantly it's weatherproof—but you'll want to clear a space to store the hay when it's cut.'

'I'm not giving hay to a buyer who won't want to pay extra. I'll give it to my sons.'

'In that case, I can tidy the shed and sweep it out. If I clean the windows, twice the light will shine through. The buyer will be able to see that, with a little modernisation, the shed could be used not only for shearing, but other things as well.'

An hour stretches to three so it's well after four o'clock by the time Mr Riley, as filthy as I am and sagging with exhaustion, agrees that we can finish our work next weekend.

I'm holding in a yawn and examining the scrapes on my hands when he pulls up outside the church. 'Drive carefully, Mr Riley. I'll see you next Saturday.'

'I hope them squatters don't come back now the shed's clean and tidy.'

'I'll keep an eye on it.'

'Jeremiah won't want trouble—I'll warn him too.'

Wickham jumps from the truck and sits at the steps of the porch, head tilted as he waits for instructions. 'How about you stay inside so you don't roll in the grass and get wet again?' When I open the front door and point, he reluctantly walks through.

Lottie peers through the chicken wire and bleats as I pass. 'I'll bring you up to the house after I've seen to—'

The yard, where Camelot always waits, is empty, and even though Mintie is on the far side of the paddock, there's no sign of Camelot there. His stable door, held open during the day with a hook, is closed and bolted shut. He couldn't have locked himself in there, so how—

A clang, metal on metal, shatters the air. There are voices, loud indecipherable sounds, behind the stables. Two men yell and shout. I hear the whinny of a horse, high-pitched with fear, and iron shoes on concrete.

The stable wall bulges and cracks.

'Camelot!'

The shouts cease abruptly. But the clangs, like cymbals, blast faster and faster.

I frantically bash the bolt with the palm of my hand as Camelot paws against the door and kicks the walls. But when the bolt shifts in the barrel, my hand slips.

'Oh!'

The metal edge of the casing catches my forearm near my wrist. Blood oozes from the gash in a thick dark line, and smears across my fingers. I shove my arm between my thighs to stem the flow before I grasp the bolt again, pulling and yanking until it releases.

The door bursts open and rams into my hip, throwing me backwards. Camelot leaps from the stable, his eyes wide with terror. His knee glances my side, and I fall. Pain flashes through my shoulder as I roll into a ball and bring an arm over my head. His body stretches out above me and I wait for the crush of his hooves—

My cheek is pressed into the earth. My hands are clawed into fists. It's deathly quiet. No men. No horse. The mud is cold and deep.

The air is damp and dark. A low-pitched moan escapes me. Blood in my mouth.

I uncurl slowly. Wipe my eyes and blink against the grittiness. The dark is ...

Am I buried in the mud? I hold on to it tightly but it leaches through my fingers. I suck in breaths, short and sharp in the nothingness.

There's something I have to remember. I have to remember ...

I can get out.

Can I get out?

I roll onto my back and lift my arm. No dirt above me. I roll onto my side again, push my hand into the mud and sit. My body hurts. Warmth flows down my cheeks. I wipe my eyes, stinging and scratching and blind. My throat constricts and I struggle to breathe, but a memory tugs at the back of my mind.

I should look for the light.

Tiny pinprick stars. Stars that shine brightly. Stars all alone. Stars in constellations that sweep across the sky. Above the treetops, wafer thin and palest gold, a crescent moon glows softly. The moon and the stars.

I'm not locked in.

I can get out.

All of a sudden everything, all of my senses, sparkle and fizz. Lights in the sky. The whistle of the wind in the grass and the trees. The dankness and grittiness and taste of the dirt.

My arm stings. My shoulder pounds.

A snort. Camelot, a shadow horse, stands against the railings in the corner of the yard. Why is he—

The yelling. The clanging and crashing. My heart bangs fiercely as I look around the yard.

All I see is Camelot.

'Hey,' I whisper. 'It's okay.' When I put my hand on the ground to push myself up, a lightning rod of pain shoots down my arm and a wave of nausea roils in my stomach. I hang my head between my knees, gag and spit out. I roll my tongue around my mouth, collect the dirt and bile and spit again. When I move my left shoulder, the pain repeats. Something hit me. Something—

Camelot.

When I move my right hand, my arm stings like nettles. What happened to it?

I sliced it on the stable door.

Prioritise.

Holding my left arm close to my side with my right hand, I kneel carefully. I sway. I focus on Camelot as I fight to get my balance and then shuffle on my knees across the yard to the railing. On the third attempt, I grip a post and stand. Camelot, as if on tiptoes, walks cautiously towards me.

'It's okay.'

He dips his head and presses his nose against my stomach, asking for a scratch. He snuffles against the pocket near my hip.

I lean against his shoulder. 'What happened back there?'

Headlights cast an arc on the road and Wickham barks from inside the house.

'Phoebe!' The back door crashes open. Jeremiah looks over the railing. 'Where are you?'

'Jeremiah!' My voice catches.

Wickham and Jeremiah run down the steps to the garden. Behind them, the sheets on the washing line flap in the breeze. I bite hard on my lip, hold my arm even closer to my side, lower myself to the ground and put my head between my knees.

Suddenly I'm cold. Shaking and shivering. When Sinn was cold, I took off my sweater and laid it on his chest.

Why think of Sinn?

Why now?

U

'You must've popped your shoulder.' Jeremiah opens the front passenger door of the police car. He looks uncertainly at me, leaning shakily against the bonnet. 'An ambulance would have pain relief on board, but you'd have to wait an hour.'

'I don't need—' I walk around the car, clenching my teeth as I back towards the door and tentatively bend my knees. 'I can come with you.'

'Lucky me.'

Holding my left arm closely to my side, I lower myself to the seat. 'Ow!'

'That was the easy part. Now you've got to turn.' Jeremiah squats next to me and supports my legs. 'Ready to pass out?'

As I lift my legs into the car, my shoulder spasms and jerks. I double over and my forehead hits the dashboard. I blink back tears.

'Jesus,' Jeremiah says. 'You okay?'

Another spasm. But then …

I suck loud breaths through my teeth. 'Oh.' I lean against the headrest and tentatively wriggle my fingers and turn my wrist. 'I think it's slipped back in.'

Jeremiah unzips a medical kit. 'As easy as that? Must've only been a sublux, a partial dislocation.'

I shudder a breath. 'Thanks for your sympathy, Dr Jones.'

'I've told my sergeant I'm taking you to Dubbo Hospital.'

'How did you know to come?'

'Mr Riley came to the station to tell me the shed had been cleaned up, so the squatters might be back. I was clocking off, so thought I'd drop by for a laugh.'

'Funny.'

'That's what I thought. But when I got here, Wickham was howling and the front door was unlocked. The lights were off.' He picks up a lock of my hair, thick with mud, and grimaces.

I tentatively take my right hand from my left arm and touch around my shoulder joint. 'It feels bruised, but—' I bend my elbow, '—I think it's okay now.'

Wickham, sitting in the back, pushes his head between the seats and nudges my leg. Jeremiah pulls a length of cloth from the kit and fashions a sling.

'This'll do until the doctors check it out.' He wraps my cut arm securely in gauze. 'Quit bleeding on my upholstery.'

After checking me over, the triage nurse at the emergency department tells me it's a quiet night, and I'm well enough to be cleaned up before having more tests. I sit on a chair under a steaming shower while a sweet-faced nursing student with curly brown ringlets squeezes soap all over me. Without congealed blood and mud to bind the skin, the cut on my arm bleeds a river down the drain. We wrap it in a towel while she rinses my hair.

The radiologist and emergency doctor hook me up to an ultrasound machine and examine my shoulder, the radiologist smiling encouragingly when she reports that there seems to be no deep tissue, nerve or ligament damage.

I clumsily tie the laces on the hospital gown. 'It's hardly even sore.'

She feels along my arm. 'No numbness or tingling?'

'When it first happened I think there was, but now it's fine.'

'A millimetre shift in the shoulder socket can be excruciating. You'll be stiff tomorrow, but that's likely to be bruising at the site.' She points to the purple shadows creeping down my arm. 'A horse hit you?'

'He didn't mean to.'

The other doctor rolls her eyes. 'Ice it regularly and don't lift anything heavy until you see your GP. Dr Gupta?'

'Yes.'

'He'll put you in touch with a physio,' she says. 'You're lucky the plastic surgeon is on call tonight. Your other arm will need sutures.'

When Jeremiah, his blue police shirt smudged with mud and grime, holds up a cardboard box of juice, I drink through the straw.

'Ow.'

'You said it didn't hurt much.'

'It's my lip. I think I must've bitten it.'

'And here's me thinking you'd overdone the botox.' When the doctor laughs, Jeremiah winks. 'When will she get the stitches done?'

'We'll anaesthetise the wound and scrub it clean.' She draws in the air above the cut, which extends from the knobbly bone at my wrist to halfway up my forearm. 'The cut isn't deep, and the edges are mostly straight, but sutures will minimise scarring.'

'Might need to get a new bolt for the stable, Phoebe.'

'Thanks for the advice.' I smile sweetly. 'Can you go to the car to check that Wickham is all right?'

It's after midnight by the time we arrive home. Mandy, looking smart in spotless jodhpurs and a hot pink polo-necked sweater, her grey hair plaited neatly, waits at the door. After sending Jeremiah to the laundry with rapid-fire instructions on what to do with my clothes, she turns to me.

'Camelot walked into his stable for his feed, not at all perturbed, but I'd get someone to look at the holes he's kicked in the walls. Lottie, bless her woolly socks, is fast asleep on the verandah. And Wickham's dinner—' when she points, he sits and lifts a paw, '—is waiting for him in the kitchen.'

I stroke Wickham's head. 'Go get it, boy.'

As he darts through the living room, Mandy tucks the hospital blanket around my shoulders. 'You're as white as a sheet. Let's get you stabled for the night.'

Dressed in old flannelette pyjamas Mandy pulls from a bottom drawer, I sit on the end of my bed. Mandy brushes my hair and secures it into a braid, as if I'm one of her ponies.

'That'll stay in for a day or two,' she says. 'I'll stay tonight.'

'I'll be—'

'No arguments.'

I puff out a breath. 'The doctors said to rest for twenty-four hours. If the shoulder is still okay after that, I can use a sling and get back to work. You have your own work to do and—'

'I'll see to your horses tomorrow morning. After that, I'll get back to mine.'

As Mandy walks out, Jeremiah, his cuffs wet from the sink, walks in. He flicks on the lamp before turning off the overhead light. I sit up against the pillows and he perches on the end of the bed.

'I'll come back with my sergeant tomorrow, and we'll have a proper search in daylight.'

'Did you get that emergency doctor's number? I think she was more interested in you than anything I had to offer.'

'Sure I got it. Didn't want the night to be a complete write-off.' He grins. 'You want me to call the guy you were snogging in Denman?'

'Snogging?' I fold my hands in my lap. 'No, thanks.'

'Why not?'

Because I'm cold and sore. And because, unaccountably, it hurts that he's not here.

CHAPTER
28

I'm wide awake at dawn. Stiff shoulder and hip. Throbbing arm. My bottom lip is puffy and tender. I touch my forehead, bruised from where I hit it on the dashboard. Mandy, whistling as she walks down the steps, will send me away if I offer to help, so I focus on the morning sounds: birdcalls, Camelot's nicker, Lottie's bleat, the clatter of buckets and the squeaking gate.

I must doze, because by the time I roll out of bed and plant my feet on the carpet, Mandy is clattering about in the kitchen. I wiggle my fingers, peeking out of the bandage that extends past my wrist. I gently extend my other arm to test my shoulder. Wickham appears and I stroke his chest.

'That'll teach me to keep you shut inside.'

Mandy looks up from a bowl of cereal. 'I hope I didn't wake you. How do you feel? Juice? Toast?'

'Both would be great, thank you.' Lottie's little hooves clip-clop on the verandah. She presses her nose against the fly screen and peers inside as I perch on a stool. 'Good morning, baby.' I lean an elbow on the bench without thinking, but only feel a twinge in my shoulder. I hold up my other hand. 'I'm not sure I can write very well wrapped up like this, but I should be okay to do most things.'

Her brows lift. 'Complete rest today, and restricted activities until you see Dr Gupta for a check-up on Friday—though Jeremiah said the stitches won't come out until the following week. I'll be back to stable Camelot and Mintie tonight.'

I return to the bench with my laptop and phone. 'I was supposed to be at Horseshoe Hill Primary this afternoon. I'll have to reschedule.'

Dropping slices of bread into the toaster, Mandy looks over her shoulder. 'It's only seven o'clock, Phoebe. Wait until you've eaten. Honey?'

'Yes, please. I should have got up earlier.'

She glances towards my bedroom door. 'You leave the light on all night?'

'I— yes.' We both start when the toast pops up. I put my phone on my laptop and push it to the far side of the bench. Mandy spreads the honey, handing me the plate with a glass of juice. 'Thanks.'

Her brows lift. 'Might I don my psychologist hat?'

'Go for it.'

'Some people are more likely than others to be susceptible to fears. Throw in your challenging childhood, which would have included one or many traumas, and phobia becomes more likely. Are you afraid of going to sleep?'

'I sleep fine.'

'Keeping the light on all night works well as an avoidance strategy, but doesn't address the underlying issue.'

I tear off a length of crust. 'I know the theory. We don't know what's around us or what might harm us when it's dark. We lose our visual sense and that can be frightening.'

'A phobia is excessive and irrational. It impacts on everyday life.'

I nibble the crust, being careful of the cut on my lip. 'How did you know I panicked last night? I was over it by the time Jeremiah arrived.'

'You had a panic attack after Camelot knocked you down?'

I blow out a breath. 'Damn. I thought that's what you were talking about.'

She hides a smile. 'What happened, Phoebe?'

'It probably only lasted a minute or two, but I was lying with my face in the mud.' I put my hands in my lap, tracing a crease in the bandage. 'I had no idea how I'd got there. I thought I might be buried. Not that that's so unusual.'

Mandy pushes my juice closer. 'Drink up.'

'I imagine I'll never get out of the dark when it happens.' My voice is thin. When I wrap my hand around the glass, it dampens the bandage. 'Sometimes it's a well. Sometimes it's quicksand, or a hole. I'm aware I need to find out what's around me, but I don't want to know, if that makes sense.' I take a sip of juice before wiping my fingers on my sleeve.

Her eyes are kind. 'You were in the mud. What happened next?'

'The cognitive therapy stuff kicked in. I tried to replace my negative thoughts with more positive, realistic thoughts. I reminded myself that I could get out. And this time, there was something else as well, something I had to look for.'

'What was it?'

'I saw the stars.' I smile bravely. 'It was lucky I was lying outside at the time.'

'It's good to look on the bright side.'

'Is that a psychologist joke?'

'Not a bad one, all things considered.'

'You think I need more therapy, don't you? I'm avoiding things rather than facing up to them?'

'You know the drill. Desensitisation is a start.'

'Maybe I should put the lamp further away.'

'Visualise ways around the fear when you're not in a panicked state, just as you've done in the past.' She clatters plates in the sink. 'Why do I get the feeling things are worse lately?'

'They are. My father ... other stuff ...'

'You're not inclined to share the load?' She leans over the bench. 'Jeremiah suggested you call Sinn. To be honest, he pre-empted what I was going to suggest, particularly with your sisters so far away. You're no longer intimate?'

Lying on the window seat and looking at the stars was intimate. What happened later was intimate. But would that have happened if I hadn't had the panic attack when I woke up in the dark? *Will you kiss me goodnight?*

I open my mouth and close it. Then say, 'Intimate?'

She hides a smile. 'I've heard he's extremely good looking.'

'He is, but—' I take a large bite of toast, chewing slowly. 'Whatever we had was tentative. He's away. I don't know when he'll be back. We don't have a commitment, nothing like that.'

When Lottie bleats, I use it as an excuse to go outside. She's standing at the top of the verandah steps, looking over her shoulder as if asking for permission to go to the garden. It's cold outside, but the sun is out. When I put my hand under her tummy and lift, she leaps into the air and gallops down the steps before bouncing across the grass to the washing line. She splays her knobbly front legs and lowers her head to the grass.

'You're doing well, little lamb.' I sit on the step and watch a line of ants follow an invisible path up the railing.

How am I doing?

My father. My fears. My future.

How can I have so much less certainty than I had only months ago?

CHAPTER
29

The following week, Jane calls in tears to cancel Matilda's appointment because she had a difficult day at preschool.

'Take her home where she can be comfortable,' I say. 'If you don't mind an early start, I can squeeze her in at eight o'clock tomorrow morning.'

'It's not fair to cancel with such little notice.'

'I've been meaning to weed the graveyard for weeks. I'll do that instead.'

'Are you sure you're up to weeding?'

'I haven't used the sling in a week, and I'm getting the stitches out tonight. It's been ten days.'

Wickham trots at my heels as I walk down the path, finding a shady spot under the shrubs as I sit on Mary's grave. The trowel pushes easily into the soil at the side of the headstone, still moist from last week's rain.

'I hope all is well with your family, Mary. With all those sons and granddaughters, you must have a lot of descendants by now.'

When my phone, lying on the granite slab that covers Reverend Brockman's grave, rings, I pick it up, fumbling as I swipe with my gloves.

'Hello, Nate.' Laying the phone next to me, I put it on speaker. 'Is everything all right?'

'Sure it is. How's our baby?'

I smile. 'She doesn't need a bottle any more, but I swear she would have had a tantrum last night if I hadn't given her one. I guess that means she's reaching the toddler stage. What have you been up to?'

'Staring at a screen—multiple screens.'

'I haven't heard from Sinn since he left.' I rush my words, determined to say them. 'Is he okay?'

'He's been in the air for the past thirty hours, but his plane's due in Dubbo any minute. Can we bring Lottie's shed to you on Saturday? Sinn should be on top of things by then.'

'Have you worked out what happened with the syndicate?'

Silence. Then, 'I can't answer that.'

I yank out a dandelion weed. 'Can I get back to you about Saturday? I promised Mr Riley I'd help him clean up, but then I hurt myself and had to pull out. He's picking me up early in the morning.'

'You didn't take a tumble from that horse of yours, did you?'

A second dandelion weed has a sphere of fluffy white, and I break it off at the base of the stem. Maybe I can get Matilda to blow on the seeds tomorrow.

'It's a long story, but two men came to the stables when I was out. They deliberately frightened Camelot, and he bowled me over.' Grass on Florence's gravestone obscures the engraving; I trim the spindly spears with secateurs. 'The stitches are itchy and driving me crazy. I can't wait to get them out.'

'What? Stitches?'

'A few subcutaneous, but most are on the outside.'

'How many?'

'Twenty-five.'

'Sheesh.'

'They're very small.'

'When did this happen?'

'The weekend before last.'

'Did the police get called?'

'Yes, but they couldn't find out who it was.'

The quartz on the reverend's gravestone sparkles silver and bronze in the sunshine. The top of Anna Amelia's grave, shaded by the church, has a blanket of bright green clover. I dig with the trowel around her little white cross, taking care to remove all the bulbs as I ease onion weed out of the soil.

'Are you still there, Nate?'

'Sure.' He sounds distracted.

'I'll talk to Mr Riley, and call about the timing for Saturday. You and Sinn could come, even if I'm not here.'

Will I see Sinn? I wish the answer to that question didn't matter so much. I lean against the gate and stretch out my arm, swallowing sadness as I complete a set of the exercises the physio gave me. I rub around my wrist and flick dirt off the bandage, before picking up the trowel again. William Tilley was the boy who died on his sixteenth birthday. I lean over his grave and clumsily dig out a clump of paspalum grass at the side of his headstone. 'I'll start with you next time and do this properly, I promise.'

Just in case Dr Gupta is running late, I feed the horses early. Mintie, delighted, trots ahead of me through the yard to his stable, with Camelot walking calmly behind. Afterwards, careful of my shoulder, I shovel small amounts of straw and manure out of the barrow and onto the compost heap before heading back to the graves to collect the tools.

'How did I miss that?' Wickham lies near the bucket as I sit on the edge of Mary's grave and dig up the clump of onion weed between her and the reverend.

'Phoebe!'

Sinn? I push hair behind my ears, wipe my hands on my jeans and curse like he does.

'Phoebe!'

'I'm in the graveyard!'

He's wearing city shoes and smart navy pants. His shirt is starkly white and his hair is glossy dark. He walks purposely towards me, not scowling, not smiling. Serious.

I put the trowel down. 'What's the matter?'

He stops on the other side of the fence and holds onto the spikes. 'You tell me.'

'What do you mean?'

'Nate called.'

There's a small hole in the neck of my long-sleeved T-shirt where, years ago, it snagged on a barbed wire fence. My bra strap has fallen down my arm. I'll smell of horse and probably manure. I pull off my glove and examine my nails. Filthy.

'Nate said you'd come on Saturday.'

'He said you might not be here.' He walks through the gate and crouches down next to me. He smells of soap. His clothes are barely creased.

I pull off my other glove and line it up on my knee with the first one. I look at him suspiciously. 'I thought you'd just got in.'

'I hired a car.'

'You had a shower too?'

'In Sydney.'

'Oh.'

His gaze goes to my hand, still bandaged around my thumb and up my arm. This morning the covering was crisp and clean; now it's limp and dirty.

'What the fuck, Phoebe?' he says.

I run my tongue along my bottom lip. The split has healed. 'I'm fine.'

He sits next to me on the grave, our thighs lined up, and stretches out his legs. The elastic sides of my riding boots are faded and dimpled with wear. His shoes are black like the letters on William's headstone. I missed Sinn. I missed the flutters in my chest, the quickening of my heartbeats and the tingling in my fingers and toes. I missed the different shades of grey in his eyes. But how does he feel?

'Sinn?' A whisper. 'Why did you come?'

'You should have told me about this.'

'What was there to say? I hurt myself, Jeremiah took me to the hospital, the doctor patched me up.'

'Jeremiah is the officer we saw in Denman?'

'He arrived just after I fell.'

Sinn stares at my hand, pale and grubby on my knee. 'Twenty-five stiches?'

I draw a line up my forearm. 'It wasn't deep, but long and close to my wrist.'

He lifts a hand and drops it. He swallows, rubs the back of his neck. 'This could relate to the Roxburgh syndicate. Did you consider that?'

'What? Oh.'

'These men, what happened?'

'In addition to a lot of clanging, I heard two voices, but they were behind the stable and I couldn't make out the words. They mightn't have known I was there.'

Sinn's eyes close for a moment. When he opens them again, they stare straight into mine. He leans over my lap and bumps my shoulder. I bite back a yelp.

'What?'

'Nothing. It was nothing.' I pick up the trowel and turn the soil.

He stands. 'I'm staying here.'

'What for?'

'Until I know more.'

'I haven't asked you to stay.'

His mouth firms. 'This is work.'

I stand carefully, making sure I don't put too much weight on my arm or jar my shoulder, and throw the trowel in the bucket. When I link my hands, Wickham tips his head to the side as if trying to make out a signal. 'How could this relate to the syndicate?' I say.

'I don't know.'

'You won't say.'

'If I wasn't here, Nate would be.'

When I take a step back, Mary's gravestone nudges my hip. 'It's nothing personal?'

'It can't be.'

Wickham tenses, before spinning around and charging up the path.

'That'll be Dr Gupta.' I run my hands down my jeans. 'How am I supposed to explain you?'

'We were together at Roxburgh Estate,' he says brusquely. 'We maintain the pretence.'

I suppress the lump in my throat as I pick up the dandelion clock, holding it carefully in my palm as I walk through the open gate.

U

Sinn sits opposite Dr Gupta at the table, his hands circling a mug of instant coffee I'm certain he won't drink. He listens attentively as Dr Gupta describes the Oslo hotel he stayed in when he visited Norway. I wash strawberries in the kitchen and put them on the table.

'Are you sure you don't mind waiting while I have a shower?'

Dr Gupta looks over the rim of one of Mum's fine china teacups. 'I arrived early in the hope of receiving my customary beverage.' He returns the cup to the saucer and smiles. 'I'm on my way to visit my daughter, who won't be home from work for an hour. Please, Phoebe, take as long as is needed.'

I leave my hair loose after the shower, brushing it smooth before twisting it into a rope and towelling the drips from the ends. My faded blue tracksuit jacket is old and the cuffs are stretched; I roll the right sleeve up past my elbow to expose the bandage as, my fluffy socks silent on the floorboards, I walk quickly down the hallway. The dining table has been cleared of books and other materials—now placed in neat piles on the floor—and Dr Gupta has laid a plastic-backed sheet and a metal kidney dish containing scissors, tweezers and other paraphernalia on the timber surface.

Sinn looks at me critically when he sees me at the door. As he pulls out a dining chair, Dr Gupta smiles.

'Yes, Phoebe, please make yourself comfortable.'

I look over his shoulder to Sinn. 'I don't want to hold you up.'

He smiles stiffly. 'I want to be here.'

Dr Gupta unravels the bandage. 'It turns out Sinn is not only from Bergen, where my cousin makes his home, he knows him—a professor at the university—by reputation. What a small world.'

Sinn takes a chair on my other side, leaning forward with his elbows on his knees.

Dr Gupta points to my tracksuit top. 'Can you remove this please? I'll examine your shoulder first.'

I hold my breath as I ease my arm out of the jacket and pull it off, laying it across my lap.

Sinn sucks in a breath. 'What the ...'

I keep my eyes on the dish. 'It wasn't Camelot's fault.' The bruises, fading now, extend from my shoulder to my collarbone and halfway down my arm. 'It looks much worse than it is.'

'You have consulted the physio?' Dr Gupta says. 'What does she say?'

'I've been twice since the sling came off.' I hold my arm out and then lift it high. 'It's only a soft tissue injury, with no ligament damage. She says in a month or two, I'll be able to do everything I usually do.'

He lifts his brows. 'You can get back on the horse?'

I smile. 'I've already done that.'

Sinn has creases at the sides of his eyes, the lines he gets when he doesn't sleep. He takes my hand. *We should maintain the pretence.* He runs his thumb over my knuckles. 'I wish you wouldn't, Phoebe.'

'Exercise is good.'

'So long as you don't fall,' Dr Gupta says, as he feels around my shoulder joint.

'I keep Camelot to a walk.' When the doctor presses more firmly against a bruise, I wince.

'Even a partial dislocation can cause instability and require surgery, but this one, as you say, is healing well.'

'A shoulder subluxation?' Sinn says.

'Anterior,' Dr Gupta says. 'Thankfully, the top of the humerus slipped back into the socket on the way to the hospital.' He gently taps my forehead. 'This bruise has faded too I see.'

I hold out my bottom lip. 'All good here too.'

'So now to your arm,' Dr Gupta says. Sinn stands as Dr Gupta takes off the bandage, exposing the waterproof dressing the surgeon applied. He prises a corner of the tape free of the skin.

I hold my breath as he peels back the tape. 'I've kept it dry.' The scar, a thin red line crossed by spider's leg stitches, is longer than I remember.

Sinn mutters something under his breath.

Dr Gupta lowers his head as he takes the scissors and tweezers, snipping and pulling out stitches one by one. I grit my teeth.

'Ow!' When a spot of blood appears in the middle of the cut, Dr Gupta presses gauze against it before continuing to cut and tug. Suddenly queasy, I look away and take deep breaths. When I shudder, my arm moves. 'Sorry.'

Sinn crouches by my side and puts a hand over mine. 'Phoebe?'

Butterflies cruise around my stomach as he prises open my fingers, clenched tightly around the tracksuit jacket.

'Let me have it, kjære.'

He pulls the sleeves the right way through before standing again. Taking care not to get in Dr Gupta's way, he drapes the jacket around my shoulders. When I lean forward, he smooths it down my back.

I think it's only to distract me that the men talk about Oslo and Bergen again. Snip. Tug. Snip. Tug.

When Dr Gupta declares he's done, I have another look.

'It's very neat.'

He indicates the spot that bled. 'I could put another steri strip there.'

I shake my head. 'I'll be careful. I promise.'

He finds a roll of tape in his bag. 'Cover it with this during the day, and bandage it as required to keep it clean. You took the antibiotics the hospital gave you?'

'And I had a tetanus shot.'

'Any signs of redness or fever, call me immediately.' He smiles as he collects his instruments. 'Resume your usual activities, but no heavy lifting until the physiotherapist gives permission. This will be another few weeks at least.'

Sinn comes with us as I walk Dr Gupta to the door. The men shake hands and Sinn takes an overnight bag from his car. We stand side by side on the porch as the doctor lifts his hand in salute.

As soon as he drives away, Sinn turns to me.

'Where do I sleep?'

30

For the next hour, Sinn and I are unfailingly courteous.

'You can sleep in the spare room. Take either bed. They're both made up.'

'Thank you.'

'There's only one bathroom. I've put spare towels in there.'

'I raked the yard. Lottie is on the verandah.'

'Thank you. I'll feed her later.'

'I put the bucket and gardening tools in the shed.'

'Jeremiah is joining us for dinner at seven. I told him you wanted to talk to him.'

U

As I push stir-fried chicken and vegetables around my plate, Jeremiah scrapes his clean. 'Not hungry, Phoebe?'

'I had a late lunch.'

'Why're you so quiet?'

I scoop up a forkful of rice. 'The men who frightened Camelot are likely to be locals, aren't they? Maybe I offended them.'

'Because you wouldn't let them buy you a drink?' His gaze shifts to Sinn. 'Phoebe's the last person in Warrandale anyone would hurt. We can't think why she'd be targeted like this.'

'They mightn't have known I was there.'

'Until they walked past you, unconscious in the mud?'

'I might've been conscious. I just can't remember.'

Sinn's cutlery clatters on the plate. 'Can I speak off the record?'

Jeremiah leans back in his chair. 'Shoot.'

'You know Phoebe's father?'

'He's an abusive prick.'

I line up the salt and pepper shakers. 'Jeremiah …'

He nods towards my food. 'You going to eat that chicken?'

'Help yourself.' I hand him the plate.

He smiles at Sinn as he picks up his fork. 'Keep going, mate.'

Sinn puts his serviette on his plate. 'Professor Cartwright has links to a syndicate. Before it was disbanded, it was infiltrated and used to launder money. If the person who infiltrated the syndicate, or their associates, believe Phoebe knows more than she does, she could be seen as a threat.'

Jeremiah whistles. 'You reckon that could be behind this? Why didn't you say anything, Phoebe?'

'Because—' I look pointedly at Sinn, '—I didn't think of it.'

'It's unlikely,' Sinn says, 'but we don't know enough to rule it out.'

'I'm glad you're staying with her, mate.'

When I hold in a yawn, Jeremiah drains his glass. 'You sending me a message?'

I glance at the floor, the piles of books and reports. 'I have clients from eight. I have to prepare.'

Sinn asks Jeremiah questions about the police investigation for another ten minutes and then, as I clear the table, Jeremiah takes him to the stables to show him where the police found the foot-prints. I'm gathering my files when they return to the house. I walk Jeremiah to the door, closing it behind us.

'Thank you for coming.'

'Bit heated in there.'

'What do you mean?'

'Is Sinn the first guy you've had since Robbie?' He grins. 'You can't take your eyes off each other.'

'We're not together.'

'No?' He walks down the steps. 'That's a pity, because excluding myself, I reckon he's the only decent bloke you've ever been out with.'

'Go home, Jeremiah. And please don't gossip about me.'

'You deserve better than Robbie. You even deserve better than me. I told Sinn that.'

'Jeremiah ...'

He winks. 'He politely suggested that if I'd ever hurt you, he'd break my neck.'

I push against his chest. 'Please stop.'

'When I told him it was my heart that got broken, he liked me much better.' He slowly shakes his head. 'Poor fucking bastard.'

Sinn is drying the dishes when I walk into the kitchen, and Lottie is bleating plaintively outside. Immediately I step onto the verandah, she quietens. 'This is the *last* time I give you a bottle. I know I said that last night, but this time I mean it.'

By the time I go back to the kitchen, Sinn is shaking the bottle of formula. He follows me outside and leans against the wall as I sit cross-legged on the ground in front of Lottie's pen. She stands on the straw with her neck stretched over the lattice as the rain pitter-patters on the roof.

'Here you are, baby.'

'Will she go back to her herd?'

I run my fingers over her ribs. 'Gus and I aren't sure yet.'

'I should put her shelter in the garden by the trees, yes?'

My shoulder pulls when I swap hands. 'Thank you.'

'Let me.'

Crouching so closely behind me that his body keeps out the chill, he takes hold of the bottle. When our fingers touch, my breath hitches. My skin warms.

'Baby,' he repeats.

The deepness of his voice, the touch of his arm, his slow and steady breathing, his intoxicating scent. I'm painfully aware of all these things as Lottie, chin up and tail spinning, sucks on the teat.

When she's finished, I lean forward, wiggling my finger in the side of her mouth to loosen her grip. She blinks at me twice before relinquishing the teat and teetering to her mound of straw.

'After Nate gets here tomorrow,' Sinn says, 'I'll go to Denman and dismantle the shelter.'

'Thank you.' I look past him to the stables, dimly lit under the beam of the spotlight. 'I have to check the horses.'

He stands abruptly, walks to the top of the stairs. 'You ate very little.'

'And you haven't slept.'

'I'll go to the stables, lock up.'

My shoulder aches. My head is foggy. I stand at the back door and flick the verandah light on and off. 'Can you keep this one on, and also the porch light at the front? The hallway and bathroom lights too.'

'I understand.'

When I open the door, Wickham charges through the gap and scampers down the steps, sitting at Sinn's feet.

'Flink bisk,' he says tiredly.

'What does that mean?'

At first he looks as if he doesn't know why I asked the question, but then his expression clears. 'Good dog,' he says, as he turns away.

Wickham scampers ahead but, when Sinn whistles, he comes back to heel. Mintie nickers and Camelot, black as the night, peers over his stable door.

U

My bedroom door is closed as I sit on my bed in shorty pyjamas, my back against the headboard and my files spread out around me. Matilda and I can eat toast together tomorrow, and then spend time with Wickham. From nine to twelve I have appointments with two new clients, referrals from the hospital. Benjamin will be here at lunchtime, and after that I'll drive to Horseshoe Hill to complete a second round of assessments for a ten-year-old child.

Then home again.

If it wasn't for the spotlight, I wouldn't be able to see Sinn between the gap in the curtains. For the past ten minutes, he's paced lengths of the garden near the paperbark trees. I have no idea what he's doing. Or thinking.

The back door opens and closes and the key turns in the lock. My eyes scratch. Yawning, I bunch up files and put them on the floor before carrying my lamp to the door. I've been leaving it in the open doorway as Mandy suggested, but not tonight.

Why didn't I go to the bathroom when Sinn was in the garden? Do I *really* need to go right now? No. I can wait till morning.

After an hour of dozing, I conclude I *do* have to go to the bathroom. Surely Sinn will be asleep by now? The spare room is next to mine, at the end of the hallway. The door is open. The light is on. I walk quietly in my ugg boots, shutting the bathroom door silently behind me.

When I emerge, the light in the living room glows through to the kitchen. I'm reaching for the switch when I see Sinn's arm, hanging over the edge of the couch, his fingers touching the floor. He must be on his back. Asleep?

Wickham opens an eye as I creep past his bed.

When I laid Sinn on the hay bales, he was pale and icy and barely alive. Sleeping on my couch, his breathing is deep. His lips are slightly open. His hair falls onto his forehead and his lashes are inky black. He's pushed the smaller cushions onto the floor and other than taking off his shoes, he's wearing what he had on before. His shirt has pulled out of his pants and his sweater is twisted.

The weather is warming up, but it's chilly at night. Do I wake Sinn up so he can go to bed? He doesn't look uncomfortable, but he has no room to move and is bound to get cold. When I turn on the oil heater it clanks and clunks. I hold my breath but he doesn't stir. I step a little closer and see colour in his face. I watch the rise and fall of his chest. *One. Two. Three* … I back away.

Sinn's bag is in the spare room, but it doesn't look like he's even sat on either bed let alone laid down on one. When I moved out of my father's house, I took everything belonging to Patience and Prim, including their toys. I gather Prim's stuffed horse and cow families from her bed and find room for them on the bookcase next to Patience's dolphins, then yank off the doona and scoop up two pillows. My sisters have never complained, but without covers the single bed doesn't look any bigger than the couch. Patience is small. Prim is the tallest of the three of us, but nothing like Sinn's height. Is that why he's sleeping in the living room? Or did he fall asleep by mistake? Wickham looks up again as I pass, before curling up even more tightly and burying his nose under his paw. The heater, slowly warming, clanks again.

Sinn stretches. He runs a hand through his hair and opens his eyes. He jerks upright when he sees me, planting his feet on the floor.

'Phoebe.'

I hold out the pillows and bedclothes. 'You were asleep.'

'What are you doing?' he asks.

'These are for you.' When I open my arms, he catches the doona but the pillows tumble onto the floor. Instead of reaching for them, his eyes stay on me. All of me. Patience gave me the pyjamas last Easter. The fabric is white cheesecloth embroidered with tiny yellow chickens. The shirt clings to my breasts and the shorts cling to my thighs. My skin warms.

He swallows and holds out a hand. 'Come.'

I sit on the far end of the couch, much of the doona bunched up between us. My back stiff like his, I stare straight ahead through the coloured panels of the stained glass window.

'Is this where you wanted to sleep?'

'Yes.'

'Why not the spare room?'

'Jeremiah said you'd be the last person anyone would want to hurt.' He hesitates. 'Look at me, Phoebe.' When I do as he asks, his eyes narrow. 'I believe he was right.'

'I was worried you'd get cold.'

He pulls the doona over our laps. 'You don't know what you want.'

I could pretend not to understand, but— 'No.'

'Nothing happens with us, Phoebe, until you do.'

I pick up a pillow, sit further back and smooth the pillowcase over the foam.

'Your shoulder,' he says, 'your arm. Are they painful?'

'They're fine, thank you.'

'I wish you'd told me.'

'You're secretive too.'

He hesitates. 'About my work, yes.'

I move closer, turning and bringing my knee up onto the couch. 'And other things. You won't talk about the navy, either.'

'What do you want to know?'

'Do you miss it?'

He smooths out the creases in the doona. 'I liked the camaraderie, the work and physical demands.'

'Does that mean you'll go back?'

'I disobeyed a direct order, many of them.' He rubs a hand around the back of his neck. 'In a conflict situation, in combat, this is unforgiveable.'

'Even though what you did was the right thing to do?'

'Junior officers followed me. I put their careers at risk.'

'But not their lives. You were exonerated.'

'My cousin Per is a flaggkommandör, a senior commander. He had no input, but some believe this saved me.'

'You'd do the same again, Sinn, wouldn't you? If you believed you were right.'

His eyes are dark and sombre. 'A commanding officer wouldn't want to hear that. I won't have the opportunities I had.'

'You're on secondment now. Can you keep the job you're doing?'

'Possibly.'

'You're a meteorologist. You know about solar systems and satellites. And you can build things.'

'A shelter for a sheep? A hut in the forest?' He smiles. 'Yes.'

I shuffle even closer. Our thighs bump. 'You should smile more.'

Besides the shift of his gaze to my mouth, he's motionless. But when I lean away, he takes my hand, rubbing his fingers over my palm before placing it back on the pillow.

'Go to bed, Phoebe.'

'Why?'

'I shouldn't touch you.'

Every cell of my body wants him to touch me. I link my hands. 'Consciously we might think we don't want something, but subconsciously we do. Our body does. Feelings aren't always logical or consistent.'

When he shakes his head, his fringe falls onto his forehead. 'What do you think my feelings are?'

'You want to find out about the syndicate, and me being hurt like I was could, by the smallest chance, be related to that. You're annoyed that you didn't find out about it straight away.'

'There's more.'

'What?'

He takes my arm and turns it, exposing the narrow red line and the stitch marks. He lowers his head and, so softly that I barely feel it, he runs his lips along the scar. He presses his mouth on the part where I bled. 'Poor baby.'

I don't feel poor. I feel hot and needy and—

'Sinn?' A question and a plea.

He cups the side of my face and kisses my mouth, his tongue searching and seeking and finding every single little place there is to find. When he lifts his head, our breaths are rough. My hands slide from his chest to his neck. I pull at his sweater.

'Take it off.'

He yanks it over his head. With shaking hands, I undo his buttons and open his shirt and splay my hands on his chest. I trail open-mouthed kisses down his collarbone and sternum.

'Phoebe.'

My name on his lips. His scent and taste. The touch of his hands on my body as they slide down my sides and take hold of my waist and—

'Oh!' Our shoulders connect. My eyes water and I blink.

He freezes. 'Fuck.'

His arms are linked around me. I grasp them. 'It's fine.'

'It.' He frees his arms and undoes my top button. 'Is.' He undoes my next button. 'Not.' The air is cold on my skin as he carefully slips my pyjama shirt over my shoulder. 'Fine.'

The bruises are faded but colourful. Black, purple, blue and yellow. 'Sinn?' Desire, frustration, uncertainty. 'Please?'

He dips his head and feathers kisses over my shoulder and down my arm as I stroke the hair at his nape. His hair tickles my chin when his lips follow the line of fabric from my throat to my cleavage. My nipple is just out of sight.

'Mmm.'

He stills. Straightens. He looks over my shoulder. His hands as unsteady as my breathing, he adjusts my shirt and does up the buttons.

I moan. 'Not fair.'

Lifting my hands, he puts them on his chest. He covers them with his before kissing my neck.

'I'm having a cold shower,' he says. 'You're going to bed.'

His expression is stubborn. He runs the pad of his thumb across my mouth before kissing me swiftly. Then he stands and holds out his hands and I take them. Our eyes lock. Stormy blue on unpredictable grey.

'Goodnight, Phoebe.'

I sigh, then stand on tiptoes and kiss his cheek. 'Goodnight, Sinn.'

CHAPTER
31

The sun peeps through the curtains as I follow Dr Gupta's instructions, putting a line of tape over the cut on my arm and applying a bandage to keep the wound clean. As I pull on old jeans and a long-sleeved T-shirt, kookaburras call out. There's another sound as well—a rhythmic thump and ... digging?

My bedroom window looks onto the stables but I can also see the trees at the bottom of the garden. The rain has cleared but the grass is wet. The sun looks for gaps through the softly rounded clouds. Sinn, wearing a T-shirt and jeans, is bending over a shovel near the paperbark trees. An arc of soil flies into the wheelbarrow.

Lottie, front legs splayed wide, grazes near the yards. As I sit on the steps of the verandah and push my feet into my boots, Wickham charges across the garden, tongue lolling happily. 'How long have you been up?' He wags his tail and licks my hand before jumping down the steps again, sitting and lifting a paw.

When we get close, Sinn straightens. He glances at the patch of ground he's levelled and the deeper excavation around it. 'Do you want the shelter here?' he asks.

What would he say if I told him I wanted it somewhere else? 'It's a good spot. Thank you.'

'It faces north. There will be sun all year, but the trees will shade it in the summer.'

I like him. I'm hopelessly attracted to him. Am I learning to trust him?

I'm terrified I've fallen in love with him.

'What time did you start this morning?'

'Before five.'

I consider his work site. 'Are you building an underground carpark for the palace?'

'Trenches for the foundations.' His face has more colour than usual. His T-shirt is damp and sticks to his body. His arms glisten with sweat and his muscles are taut. His body is—

'Phoebe?' He tilts his head to the side to capture my gaze. His eyes are bright, his expression amused. He's clearly aware I was staring.

'Yes. Of course.' Camelot has his head over his stable door. Mintie isn't tall enough to do that, so all I see is the tip of his nose. 'I'd better get to work.'

U

When I answer the front door later in the morning, Jane, wearing black yoga leggings with see-through panels and a matching short-sleeved top, has her back to me. Sinn's hire car is at the end of the driveway with the boot open. He takes out bags of cement and pieces of timber he's found somewhere in Warrandale, probably at Mike's foundry, which serves as an unofficial hardware store, and throws them into the wheelbarrow.

'Phoebe?' Jane is facing me now. She waves her hand in front of my face. 'I asked where you found him?'

Matilda is still in the car but the window is open. She waves. 'Phoebe! Here I am!'

'How is Matilda today?'

'Much better after a sleep. Thanks for rescheduling.' She raises her brows. 'For the third time, Phoebe, where did you find him?'

'Sinn? He's making a shelter for Lottie. When she doesn't need it any more, I'm going to convert it to a cubby house.'

'This is the guy Terry talked about?'

'Terry is a gossip.'

She smiles. 'If he'd mentioned the abs and pecs, I'd have been on your doorstep weeks ago.'

'He's— It's complicated.'

'A man with his looks? Who's good with his hands?' She smiles again. 'It shouldn't be.'

Sinn glances our way before wheeling the barrow down the side of the house. I walk determinedly to Matilda.

'I have to show you something!' she says.

'The new car seat,' Jane whispers. 'Once I took it into the house like you suggested, she was so much more open to it. By the end of last week, she insisted on being strapped in to watch TV.'

After admiring her seat, I open the door and Matilda jumps out. 'Let's go, sweetheart. We've got work to do.'

'Mintie!' she says. 'I want to see Mintie!'

I put my hand on my stomach. 'Did you hear that, Matilda? My tummy is grumbling. I think I'd better eat toast before we play outside. Would you like toast too?'

'I don't want jam!'

'I have honey. No lumps, I promise. And after you eat it up, you can feed Wickham your crusts.'

'I can use sticks!'

I grimace as I turn to Jane. 'I had no idea she'd take to them so well. How are you coping?'

Jane laughs. 'I love the chopsticks. No more meltdowns about one food group at a time.'

'They're not much good for yogurt and ice cream. I'll work on spoons when we play with the dough.'

Matilda runs in front of me and darts through the door. 'I want to blow Wickham a kiss.'

After Matilda eats bite-sized pieces of toast and honey with chopsticks, coping with the mixture of textures relatively well, we practise scooping up little balls of dough with a plastic spoon. As a reward for trying something new, I allow Matilda to blow dandelion seeds into the sink.

'Great work! We need Wickham for our next game.'

As Wickham pricks his ears, she looks at him suspiciously. 'He's not allowed to touch.'

'He won't touch you if you don't want him to. But when you're ready, I think you could touch him, like you touch Mintie's tail.'

Sinn is laying formwork for his foundations by the time Matilda and I sit on small plastic chairs on the verandah. I have bowls of water, small sponges and watery shampoo.

'Wickham. Come.'

When Wickham sits at my feet with his head on my knee, Matilda is curious. I wet the sponge and lift Wickham's ear, carefully dampening the fur.

'Can you help me please, Matilda?' I hold out the sponge. 'You can dip this in the soapy water.'

She recoils. 'No!'

I hand her a dry sponge. 'Try it with this one.'

She dips the corner in the bowl. 'I don't like it when Mummy washes my hair.'

'That's why we thought you could try something different. If you can wet and shampoo and rinse your own hair, you might like it more.'

Matilda grabs her plaits. 'No!'

'Today we're washing Wickham, Matilda, and he likes to have a bath. There's nothing at all for you to worry about.'

Matilda squeezes tiny portions of water over Wickham's ears with the sponge, and then, with encouragement, uses a plastic cup to rinse off the shampoo. My leg is soaked by the time we've finished, and Wickham is almost as wet as he was when he rolled in the grass this morning.

'Great job, Matilda. Now we have to dry Wickham so he doesn't get cold. Do you think you could help me with that?'

'Mummy makes my towel warm.'

I laugh. 'I'm sure Wickham would like that too. Come with me. How long should we put the towel in the dryer?'

Ten minutes later, when Matilda, through the heated towel, puts her hand on Wickham's head, I'm not sure which of the three of us is more surprised. 'Good doggy,' she says, bouncing her hand up and down. 'You were very brave and you don't have to do it again until next week.'

We're tidying up when Sinn walks across the garden, stops at the tap and drinks from the hose. When he squirts water on his hands and splashes his face, Matilda stands and points.

'He's wet like Wickham.'

'Sinn, this is Matilda.'

He runs his fingers through his hair as he walks towards us, and a drip trickles down his cheek. He stops at the bottom of the steps.

'Hello, Matilda.'

'Matilda is learning to wash and dry her hair,' I explain.

'The soap didn't go in Wickham's eyes because he kept them shut,' Matilda says. 'Phoebe dried Wickham but you've got drips.'

'Do I need a haircut?' he asks.

Matilda jumps to her feet and rubs her hands down her jeans. 'No cutting! No cutting!'

'I didn't—'

I hold out my hand. 'It's okay.' I crouch to Matilda's height. 'I'm not going to cut Sinn's hair, Matilda, and neither is he. But even if we did give him a haircut, it wouldn't hurt.' I hold the end of my ponytail. 'It doesn't hurt when you have your hair cut.'

'I don't like it!' Matilda's hands flap in agitation like the wings of little birds. 'I like ... I like ...' Her eyes fill with tears.

I kneel next to her. 'Let's link our hands.' I thread my fingers together. 'Or we could put them around our tummies.' I cross my arms over my front. 'When we feel comfortable, it's much easier to say our words.'

Matilda crosses her arms like mine. Her mouth pinches in concentration. 'Elsa has long hair and you have long hair and I like it.'

Sinn puts his foot on the bottom step. 'I like it too, Phoebe.'

Wrenching my eyes away, I rub my wet jeans with Wickham's towel. 'Yes, well ... Matilda? Do you remember what Sinn was doing in the garden?'

'Are you *really* making a palace for Lottie?' Matilda asks. 'Will it have a tower like Elsa's palace?'

Sinn looks from Matilda to me. 'Does Lottie want a tower, Phoebe? Will you commission one?'

I laugh. 'I don't think so.'

'Can Wickham go in the palace?' Matilda asks.

Sinn nods. 'It will be big enough for him, yes.'

Matilda taps my arm. 'Should I tell him what I did with Wickham?'

'I'm sure he'd love to hear about it.'

When Matilda hesitates, Sinn crouches at the bottom of the steps. His teeth flash white. 'Yes, Matilda?'

She points to Wickham. 'I touched him.'

When Sinn glances at me, I nod encouragingly. 'Matilda doesn't like to touch new things, but today she touched Wickham for the very first time.'

'He had a towel!' Matilda says.

'Yes.' I smile. 'You wet his fur and touched him through the towel.'

'How old are you, Matilda?' Sinn asks.

She holds up four fingers. 'This much, but—' she holds up five fingers, '—I'm going to be this much when it's my birthday.'

'Almost five?' He whistles. 'My cousin Per's daughter is three.'

'What's her name?'

'Annalise Marguerite Amundsen. She lives on a ship and has a dog called Olaf.' He's smiling as he stands. 'Can you guess why?'

'I know!' She jumps up and down on the spot. 'He's like Elsa's snowman! He's got white fur!'

Sinn's eyes crease at the corners. 'Yes.'

Matilda skips a wide path around him as she runs into the garden. 'Mintie,' she shouts. 'I'm here!'

I'm sitting at the table updating my notes when Nate does a U-turn in the four-wheel drive and parks behind Sinn's rental. By the time I open the front door, Sinn, hair still wet from his shower, is striding through the garden, his overnight bag slung over a shoulder.

The men shake hands. 'Hey, buddy.' Nate's hair is attractively unkempt. 'Good to have you back.'

'Did you look at what I sent through last night?'

'All good.'

After Sinn transfers his other bags from the rental car to the four-wheel drive, Nate slams the rear door.

'Keys?' Sinn holds out his hand. 'I'll take the five o'clock call in Denman. I won't be back till seven.'

'What?' Nate frowns. 'I need an hour at least for a proper debrief. And I've been busy too. There's something you should know about—'

'Hi, Nate.'

He spins around, frowning as if I've interrupted something. 'Phoebe.' He opens his arms as he walks towards me.

I walk down the steps. 'Is everything okay?'

'Sure it is.' He pastes on a smile. 'Great to see you.'

Sinn extends a hand, blocking Nate's path. 'Watch her shoulder.'

Nate pulls up short. 'How're you doing?'

'Fine, thanks. I'm sorry to put you out like this.'

'We thought a bit of company might be good.'

'Lottie is out the back if you want to say hello. She's much bigger than she—'

'Better set up first.' He glances unhappily at Sinn. 'As I'm flying solo here all day.'

When Sinn takes my hands, I run my thumbs over the back of his. He only hesitates a moment before dipping his head and kissing my mouth. It's barely a touch, but flashes of lust shoot straight to my toes.

'See you tonight,' he says.

'Better get this car unloaded,' Nate says loudly, opening the back door and lifting a computer screen off the seat. He balances a box, containing a coffee plunger and bean grinder, on his hip.

I touch a tiny scratch on Sinn's cheek. 'You won't be back until late?'

'Order something to eat and I'll pick it up.'

Nate insists he can work anywhere, but I offer him the table in the living room. Within an hour, his two screens and laptop have taken up much of the space, but my new clients are happy to spend time with Wickham, Lottie and the horses. Benjamin whoops when he works out we'll be outside for his session, and it's only after he's left that I tell Nate about my appointment in Horseshoe Hill.

He pulls out his phone. 'Better let Sinn know,' he says crisply.

'What?' I put my keys in my pocket and sit at the table. 'You said I could do what I usually do. I'm going to the primary school at Horseshoe Hill and then I'm driving home.'

He puts his phone on the table. 'Don't let me down, Phoebe.'

'Why would I do that? What's going on, Nate? Are you okay?'

He smiles stiffly. 'Got a heap of work.'

'Are you sure that's all it is? Can't you take a break to visit your family? Or have a holiday?'

He shakes his head. 'Afraid not.' He closes all the documents on his screen. 'But while you're here, can I ask you something?'

'Sure.'

His phone lights up and he glances at the screen before flipping it over. 'When Sinn and I were at Martin Roxburgh's stud a few weeks ago, I met Brent Green. He couldn't get on to Sinn last week and called me.' His brows lift. 'You know Brent?'

'He's the stud manager at Roxburgh Estate. I saw him the weekend Sinn and I went away.'

'But that wasn't the first time you'd met, was it?'

'You're not talking about the party Sinn took me to, are you? Elizabeth's party?'

He shakes his head. 'Way before that. Green told me you'd known each other for years; you were old mates.'

'I wouldn't say that.' I examine my nails, marked with green dough. 'Why were you talking about me anyway? Sinn said he didn't care about Brent.'

Nate looks at his screen—even though it's faded to black. 'You shouldn't assume what we care about and what we don't.'

'I'm repeating what he said.'

He smiles stiffly. 'Brent said he hadn't seen Sinn in a while. When I told him he was away, he asked whether you two were still together.'

'Does this relate to the syndicate?'

'He suggested you might know more than you were letting on. Did you tell him you gave us your father's documents?'

'No!'

'He mentioned your sister.'

My heart rate triples. 'What?'

'He said Patience might know something.'

I count to three before answering.

'She left home straight after school.' The stained glass window captures the afternoon sun. 'She doesn't know anything.'

'Why didn't you tell Sinn about Robbie?'

'It wasn't his business.' I lift my chin. 'It's not yours.'

He holds out his hands, palms up. 'Sinn kissed you goodbye. You like each other for real, right?'

I stand. 'I'll be back before four.'

'Wait.' His cheeks puff up, he blows out a breath. 'Sinn is a friend as well as a colleague. I also like you, which is why I don't want trouble. Are you sure you've told us everything we need to know? There's nothing you've left out?'

'I suggest you talk to Sinn. He was the one who shut me down when I said I didn't trust Brent.'

'I'll tell him what Brent said, same as I told you.'

'Good.' I nod stiffly. 'You do that.'

'If anything comes up, you'll be at the school, right?'

Nate's words replay uncomfortably in my mind as, twenty minutes out of Horseshoe Hill, I pull into a narrow dirt road that leads to Gus's property. I can't see his weatherboard cottage from here, but the paddocks between it and the road are dotted with sheep. I close my eyes. What is Brent up to? Why would he talk to Nate about Patience?

I dial the office at Roxburgh Estate.

'Brent Green.'

'It's Phoebe Cartwright.'

Silence.

'You haven't seen Camelot yet. I thought you wanted to compare him to Lancelot.'

'And I got the impression you weren't too keen on a visit.'

Gus's sheep bunch together. And then I see Banjo, Gus's red and black kelpie, running along beside them. Patterson, his brother, is black. He runs behind the sheep and gathers up the stragglers. I turn on the ignition and wind down the window, but I'm too far away to hear the bleats.

'You still there, Phoebe?'

'You spoke to Nate Gillespie. Why did my name come up?'

'You and Patience?'

I grip the phone. 'Yes.'

'That's why you called, isn't it? You're hiding something.'

'Why would I do that?'

Another silence, even longer. 'How about I come over? We can have a chat while I check out Camelot. I'm on my way out, as a matter of fact, taking the rest of the afternoon off.'

'Sinn will be staying at my house tonight. Nate is there now.'

'So where should we meet?'

'Do you know Mr Riley's property? I could meet you there with Camelot. At the old shearing shed just up the road from the church. Four thirty?'

CHAPTER
32

After I tighten Camelot's girth, I lead him to the old-fashioned stile—thick pieces of wood set parallel to the fence. Standing on the tallest block, holding the pommel, and bracing myself to support my shoulder, I swing my leg over the saddle and draw in the reins. Wickham and Nate appear on the back verandah.

'Won't be long,' I shout.

Nate strokes Wickham's head when he sits happily at his feet. 'You sure got a sook for a dog, Phoebe.'

'He likes to make new friends.'

'When will you be back?'

I glance at my watch. It's almost four fifteen. 'I'll be an hour, no more.'

Brent, the front door of his black Land Rover marked with the Roxburgh logo—a thoroughbred's head and neck outlined in gold—drives past as Camelot and I approach Mr Riley's shed. He parks around the bend and out of sight. The door slams.

'Phoebe.' He tucks in his shirt as he walks towards me.

'Hello.' I slide from Camelot's back but hold onto his rein. When Camelot turns his head, rubbing it against my stomach, I scratch under his forelock.

'He's got too much weight on him,' Brent says, holding out his hand so Camelot can sniff it. 'But he's a fine-looking horse, the spitting image of Lancelot.'

'He's leaner in summer when he gets more exercise.'

'Mind if I take a few photos?'

I tidy Camelot's forelock before standing at the end of the rein. As Brent walks around Camelot, the horse tenses and skitters. I put a hand on his shoulder and bring him around again.

'Steady, boy. You must remember Brent.'

'Course he does.' Brent looks pointedly down the lane towards the church. 'You didn't bring the boyfriend, then?'

'I told you he wouldn't be back until tonight. Nate is there though. I said I'd be home around five.' When a cockatoo flies out of the gum, two more follow, flapping and squawking. 'What did you want to talk to me about? Why couldn't we do this over the phone?'

He looks towards the shed. 'Can we go in there?'

'No. Mr Riley doesn't approve of trespassers.' I step closer to Camelot. 'You obviously have something to tell me. Why don't you say it?'

He puts his hand on the gate, trapping me between him and my horse. His face is flushed like it was when we talked in the stable. Tiny veins criss-cross his nose. 'The syndicate members' advisors assumed it was you who helped the professor. Tørrissen accepted what they said, but I knew different.'

'I don't know what you mean.'

'It was Patience.'

'Then why didn't you tell Sinn that?'

'I didn't have a reason to. Now I might.' He rests an elbow on the gate and puffs out his cheeks before loudly exhaling. 'I could've been indiscreet. I don't want it coming back to bite me.'

'What did you do?'

'Patience isn't talking. Why would I?'

'She didn't do anything wrong.'

I hadn't been going out with Robbie for long when Brent, swimming a horse, slipped and chipped an eyetooth. After Martin offered to pay whatever it cost to get the tooth fixed, Brent had a gold cap fitted. When he laughs, the tooth glistens dully.

'I drop Patience's name in a chat to Gillespie, and all of a sudden, I get a call from you. What's going on?'

Camelot's rein slips through my fingers as the horse lowers his head to tug happily at the grass. 'Patience was young. She didn't know anything.'

'Given your old man was a nut job, I bet she knew everything.' He leans in closer. 'Every quarter, the professor sent out the syndicate's spreadsheets. They set out what'd happened with the investments, the wins and losses, the payments to different accounts.'

'So?'

'One day about seven, eight years ago, New Year's Eve I think it was, the professor emailed Martin a spreadsheet.'

'I …' I nod stiffly. 'Okay.'

'The spreadsheet had Martin's name on it and looked much the same as what was usually sent through. Martin never looked at them, and neither did I before I filed it. But then I get a call from your dad, screaming and ranting, telling me to delete the email and attachment.' He grunts. 'Like I said, he was crazy, so back then I thought nothing of it. But now things are different.'

'How?'

'It's obvious, isn't it?' His grin is a stretch of his mouth. 'Tørrissen believes the syndicate was infiltrated. That night, I reckon your old man sent the wrong spreadsheet.'

'What does that have to do with Patience?' The shadows are lengthening. I bunch my cuffs in my hands and hold back a shiver. 'Get to the point.'

'The day after your father called, I get a call from your sister. How old would she have been? Seventeen? Eighteen? She said she was giving her dad an extra bit of help with the paperwork. Sweet as pie she was, apologising for the professor's behaviour, and explaining he sent through another client's document by mistake. She would have been doing your father's bidding, making sure I'd deleted it like he'd told me to.'

'Had you?'

He shrugs. 'Why wouldn't I? I thought he'd put a wrong decimal point somewhere in the calculations. That was the type of thing that'd set him off.'

'This doesn't prove anything.'

'About Patience? I don't know about that. Because when I had her on the phone, I happened to mention I was still waiting for a response to something I'd queried months ago, a calculation in an end-of-year statement Martin's tax accountant had been banging on about. And guess what? Pretty much off the top of her head, Patience went through the numbers with me, explaining that statement with reference to the statement from the year before. Knew everything inside out. I was impressed, to be honest. Probably why I remembered it, thinking what a smart little cookie she was.'

'She was like me. She helped with the admin.'

'Way more than that, Phoebe.' He turns, placing his hands on the top rail, then using the bottom rail to scrape mud from his boot.

'It was the professor who let a crim into the syndicate, wasn't it? And did all the paperwork? I'd lay a substantial bet that Tørrissen's worked that out already.'

'I have no idea.'

'He doesn't tell you what he's up to?'

'No.'

'And you don't tell him about your sister. Then again, I guess you and Tørrissen have got other things to be doing than talking.' He looks me up and down. 'You're easy on the eye, Phoebe, and just like your sister, you're a smart little cookie.'

I take a step back. 'I'm going home.'

'Not so fast.' Brent grabs my bandaged arm and yanks me close. His fingers clench, dig into my wrist. Camelot startles and skitters.

'Let me go!'

'Hear me out.'

'You're hurting me!'

The tops of his fingers turn white. 'You don't want Tørrissen to know about Patience. Admit it.'

I pull back but his hold is too firm. My scar stings and throbs. Pins and needles shoot through my fingers. 'Let me go!'

'Shut up and listen.' His breath is stale; nausea claws its way up my stomach. 'I want two things, two little things. One, keep clear of Tørrissen. He's dangerous to you, your sister, and to me.'

'I don't know what you mean!' When he twists my arm, my eyes water. 'Ow!'

He loosens his grip, but not by much. 'Two, keep your mouth shut about anything you might've seen or heard at Roxburgh Estate.'

'What are you talking about? I didn't see or hear anything.'

'In that case, you'll have nothing to keep quiet about. And that'll be in Patience's interests too. Because if you keep your mouth shut, then so do I. We both get what we want. Isn't that right?'

He lets me go so suddenly that I stagger backwards. I rub my arm and open and close my fingers. Camelot's bit clicks and jangles.

'You ...' I take another step back. 'It was you who came to my house, wasn't it?'

Another stretch of his lips. 'I don't know what you're talking about.'

'There were two men. They scared Camelot.'

'Heard you had an accident. I wasn't there.'

'Who were they? Did you put them up to it?'

I jump when he straightens his shoulders, but he walks past me to the lane, peering down the road towards the church before walking back again. I move to the other side of Camelot and take hold of the stirrup iron.

Brent looks at me over the saddle. 'Whoever came to the church, maybe they wanted to give you a reminder, a warning.'

'About what?'

'It's no secret you've stayed clear of men since Robbie, so why take a chance on someone like Tørrissen? Snooping around like he is, he's bound to bring bad luck.'

'And that's why my horse was frightened? As a warning to stay away?'

He takes out his keys and stabs the air. 'What gives him the right to ask questions? To push his weight around?'

I hold my breath until Brent slams the door to his car and only release it when the car is out of sight. My legs unsteady, I walk to the gate and lean against it. But that's not enough—my legs buckle and I slip to the ground, bringing my knees to my chest and lowering my head. I breathe in through my nose and out through my mouth until my head clears and I don't feel quite so sick. A large black butcherbird with a long sharp beak hops up the laneway, peering at me with suspicion as he pecks at the ground, his glossy feathers stark against the gravel.

'How do I ...' Another deep breath. 'I don't know what I've seen or heard,' I tell the bird.

He hops a few more steps before flying above the gums and into the clouds. It's getting dark. I'm cold. I lift my sleeve where Brent grabbed my arm.

I laid a strip of tape over the scar. I wrapped the bandage around and around and around. But that was to keep my arm clean, not to protect it from a thug.

When I pull myself up by the post, Camelot lifts his head. 'It's time to go home,' I say, my voice soft and shaky.

The horses munch on hay as I sit in the corner of Mintie's stable and send an email:

Hi Patience,

As soon as you can, I need you to call. I saw Brent Green today. He knows you helped Dad, that you understood the numbers. He frightened me—grabbed my arm and told me I had to stay away from Sinn and keep quiet (I don't even know what I'm supposed to keep quiet about!). He said he'd tell Sinn you knew what Dad was up to if I didn't do what he wanted. Brent might be hiding information that could be useful to Sinn. Even if he isn't, I think he feels threatened by Sinn, and I'm afraid he'll go after him (or somebody else) next. I don't want anybody else to be hurt.

I want to brief you properly before I talk to Sinn. It's Friday night here, and Sinn will be staying for the weekend, so I'll give you until

*midday on Sunday to get in touch. Whatever happens, I'll do my best
to cover for you.*

Love Phoebe

U

Sinn and Nate, both with mugs of coffee within reach, are at the table behind their screens when I walk into the living room after dinner and a shower. I've removed the dirty bandage and tape. The cuffs of my pyjama top fall over my hands.

'Can I get you anything before I go to bed?' I ask.

Nate looks up. 'All good, thanks.'

When Sinn stands and taps his ear pod, I glance at his screen. Six people are waiting to be let into a Zoom call.

'Have you found your munitions dealers yet?' I whisper.

He opens his mouth and shuts it again. 'I can't say, Phoebe.'

'I didn't really expect you to.' I walk around the table. 'Nate?'

Distracted, Nate adjusts his headphones. 'Yeah.'

'You've been staring at that screen all day.'

'Be a few more hours yet.'

'Would you like to stay the night too?'

He glances at the couch. 'If it's okay with you, I'll crash there.'

'There are clean sheets on the beds in the spare room.'

When Sinn turns in his chair, I feel his gaze on the side of my face. He takes out his ear pods. 'Phoebe? Are you all right?'

'Yes.'

'Sorry to take over here.'

'What you're doing is important. I understand.'

He stands and takes my hand, his grip cool and firm, and we walk to the hallway. 'Nate said you went out today.' His eyes are dark and serious.

'I had a school visit.'

'If I'd been here, I would have come with you.'

'I don't need a chaperone.'

He lowers his head as he takes my other hand. 'Nate also said he'd taken a call from Brent.'

The skin on his hands is darker than mine; his nails are short and clean. 'I warned you not to trust him.'

'Telling you to stay away didn't mean I trusted him,' he says. 'How often did he see your family?'

'Hardly ever.' I repress a shiver. 'Can we talk about this later?'

He squeezes my hand. 'What's happened?'

'I'm tired, that's all.'

'Last night on the couch … Did it upset you?'

'No.'

'You've said ten words to Nate. Less to me.'

'You've been working, and …' I shake my head. 'It's the end of the week.'

'Sinn!' Nate calls. 'We're waiting!'

I step back but Sinn keeps hold of my hand. 'Thanks for dinner.'

'Ordering takeaway?' When I smile, his gaze goes to my mouth, sending waves of warmth through my body. I study our hands again, 'Ming Ong called. She thought you must've made a mistake—your tip was more than the bill.'

'I'll finish Lottie's shelter tomorrow morning.'

How does he do this? Engender lust and longing and love and …

'You shouldn't …'

He frowns. 'What?'

'Mr Riley is picking me up at seven.'

He runs his thumb over the back of my hand. 'What about your shoulder?'

'It's not heavy work. I'll be careful.'

'It will rain in the afternoon.'

'You're certain?'

He lifts my hand and kisses my wrist. 'You'll be at the shearing shed, yes?'

'Yes.'

When he threads our fingers together, the sleeve of my pyjama top slips down my arm. The circular bruises are stark against the paleness of my skin.

'What the fuck?'

I tug my hand but he holds tight. 'It's nothing.'

His eyes capture mine. They silently interrogate. 'Phoebe? What?'

'I got twisted up in Mintie's lead rope.'

He runs his index finger over the mark on my wrist.

Should it hurt? Yes. Does it hurt? No.

He wouldn't hurt me.

Not in that way.

If I told him the truth, would he put his arms around me? Would he defend my sister no matter what she'd done?

He doesn't know her, or love her. He can't protect her, or put her first.

Would he tell me he'd forgive me for so many lies? How could he?

Truth. Love. Trust.

When I tug again, he releases my hand. 'It's fine, really.'

'Sinn!' Nate shouts. 'They're getting pissed!'

'You have to go.'

His hand goes to my waist. 'Kiss me goodnight.'

What about tomorrow night? And the night after? He won't want my kisses when he knows the truth.

I press my cheek to his. 'Goodnight.' My voice breaks.

It's his turn to step back. 'Nate will leave tomorrow. We'll talk.'

Sinn's and Nate's voices drift down the hall as I walk from the bathroom to the bedroom. I close the door to shut out the sounds. The lamp in the corner of the room lights a path to the bed. I lie on top of the covers and, in the same way I showed Matilda, fold my arms across my middle. I press hard against the inside of my arm to ease the ache.

But that doesn't help with the ache in my heart.

Brent hurt me.

Robbie hurt me.

My father hurt me.

It's wrong to hurt Sinn.

By Sunday night, I'll tell him as much of the truth as I can.

CHAPTER
33

Dawn seeps through the window as I tiptoe to Sinn, lying on the couch in a tangle of bedclothes. His eyes are closed, his lashes long and dark against his cheeks. I leave my note, folded in half, on the side table next to the couch.

Sinn. Mr Riley is waiting outside. I'll be with him at the shed all day, and he'll bring me home about five. I've fed the horses and let them out, but can you see to Lottie? I have Wickham with me. Phoebe.

Wickham keeps close to my side as I silently open the door and close it behind me. As I run across the garden, Mr Riley, twenty minutes early, slams his truck into gear and revs the engine. A gust of wind sweeps up the valley; dry liquidambar leaves flurry at my feet. I brush the ends of my ponytail out of my eyes and point to the truck. Wickham, eyes bright with adventure, leaps on to the tray.

'Morning, Phoebe.' Mr Riley, his beanie so low that only one bushy brow peeps out, nods a gap-toothed welcome. When he shoves mud-caked gumboots and a raincoat from the seat, they join crumpled papers and a cow drenching hose on the floor. 'Make yourself comfy. Big day ahead.'

'We've had a cold start to spring.' I pull the cuffs of my jacket over my hands as I peer through the windscreen. 'It might rain this afternoon.'

'Best to start outside then.'

By lunchtime, Mr Riley is shaky on his feet, so I insist he rests on one of the railway sleepers we've dragged to the pens. I hand over sandwiches and a muesli bar before pouring from thermoses—hot chocolate for me and strong milky tea for him. His colour is better than it was, but he's still very pale. He had a pacemaker fitted last year.

I top up his mug. 'Selling this land will give you more time to put your feet up.'

'It ain't sold yet,' he complains, 'and the real estate bloke said buyers are thin on the ground. Mightn't happen till next year, he reckons.'

'You could get lucky.'

Wickham, lying near the entrance to the shed, looks up and sighs.

'He should be chasing sheep, a dog like that,' Mr Riley says. 'What's his problem?'

'Wickham has other talents.'

'What's he like as a guard dog? He could work up here, keep an eye on things after dark until I find a buyer.'

I laugh as I store the thermoses in my bag. 'He wouldn't enjoy that at all. Anyway, he works with me.'

By the time I chock open the doors to the shed with a fence post, it's almost five o'clock. It hasn't rained yet but the sky, thick with steel-wool clouds, hides much of the light. Mr Riley searches in his pockets.

'Are you looking for your beanie? You put it down the back of your gumboot.'

He grunts as he pulls the hat over his ears. 'Time to get the shed in order.'

'I tidied it last time we were here.'

'That was before them squatters came back.'

This morning when we pulled up on the laneway, Mr Riley spotted the tyre marks etched in the ground near the gate. Brent's Land Rover. It set him off on a search, and he imagined all sorts of things. Finding mud from a scraped boot on the bottom rail of the gate didn't help.

'There's no sign of them now.' A pitter-patter starts up on the roof. 'You'd better get home, Mr Riley. Will your grandson help you unload the truck?'

He pulls an old silver watch from his coat and peers at it worriedly. 'Being Saturday, Tom will be off to the pub by dark.'

'Let's cover the load so you can get going.'

He scratches his head. 'The girl from the real estate is taking photos on Monday.'

'In that case, I'll finish tidying the shed. Then I'll walk home.'

'You'll stack the bales? And do a bit of sweeping?'

Once I'm standing on the tray of the truck, securing tarpaulins over tools, ancient farm equipment, and the other odds and ends Mr Riley wants to keep, the drizzle turns into rain. But I don't want to delay him further by going back to the shed for my coat.

'Phoebe!' Mr Riley says. 'What's going on? You got your head stuck in the clouds?'

He cusses, undoing half of my knots and retying them before stomping to the cab. I jump to the ground, my shirt sticking to my back.

'Drive carefully, Mr Riley.'

'Mind you bolt those doors.'

It's darker in the shed than outside, but there's plenty of light to work by. Enveloped in dust, I climb to the shearing platform and sweep fragments of fleece, dirt and leaf litter into a pile before crouching with a brush and pan.

'Phoebe.'

Sinn, hair wet and dark, wears a waterproof jacket with the hood pushed back. Wickham barks a greeting.

My legs are suddenly shaky. 'I'm almost done.'

The light is too dim to see his expression, but I sense that he's frowning. 'Why didn't you wake me this morning?'

'Mr Riley was early. I left you a note.'

'You said you'd be with him.' He repositions the post holding the door open, widening the shaft of light.

'Didn't you drive past each other? He's only just left.' I wipe an arm across my face. 'Is everything okay?' I empty the pan into the bucket and shuffle to the end of the platform, sitting with my legs over the edge. Just before I jump, he reaches me. I suck in a breath as he plants his hands either side of my legs. 'Sinn?' My voice is a squeak.

Jaw tight, he leans forward, his abdomen pressed against my knees. 'You said you'd be back at five.'

I'm shaky with agitation and heated with need. 'I said about five.'

'You don't do what you should.' He cups my shoulder, runs his hand down my arm. 'You get hurt.'

'I'm fine.'

He hesitates, puts his hands on my legs. 'The longer I wait, the faster you run.'

'Wait for what?'

He groans as he kisses my mouth. 'You.'

My breathing all over the place, I find his hand and press my lips against his wrist. 'You don't have to wait.'

He strokes my cheek with a thumb. 'I don't want to lose you.'

The top two buttons of his shirt are undone. I slip my hand under his collar to find the skin of his throat, smooth and warm and dry. His pulse beats steadily against the tips of my fingers. Uncertainty. Longing. Desire.

'I don't want to hurt you.'

'Kiss me.' His mouth is centimetres away.

I lean forward, my breasts against his chest. The tips of our tongues meet sweetly. He exhales as he threads his fingers through my hair and deepens the kiss, takes over my mouth. His hands slide to my waist, they tug at my shirt. The doors rattle and creak in the wind.

When he takes a step back, I slide from the platform, my hands still resting on his chest.

'Has Nate gone?'

He takes my hand and pulls me towards the door. 'Yes.'

My footsteps are light as I whistle for Wickham. One of the doors closes easily enough, but the second one sticks on the threshold. When I struggle with the fastening and pick up a brick, Sinn takes it and hits the end of the bolt. The shaft slides into the barrel.

∪

Camelot, his mane sticking to his neck and his rug dark with rain, stands in his yard with his ears pricked. Mintie peers out of his open stable door.

I glance at Sinn as he turns off the engine. 'It wouldn't be fair not to settle them for the night.'

Lottie's palace stands proudly near the paperbark trees with its double stable door, steeply pitched roof and white picket fence.

Tugging Sinn's hand, I veer off the path. 'You've finished it already? It's beaut—'

He pulls me back. 'She goes there in the morning.'

By the time the horses are stabled, Sinn is almost as wet as I am. Lottie bleats plaintively as we walk up the steps. 'I'd better clean out her pen. And she needs—'

He kicks off his boots. 'I'll prepare her bottle and feed Wickham.'

Ten minutes later, Lottie is tugging determinedly on the teat as Sinn, crouching at my feet, pulls off my boots and socks. My toes are ghostly white. I'm cold and hungry and dirty. But …

I want to rip off my clothes and make love to him *right now*.

I stroke his hair. 'Sorry about this.'

He rubs my feet between his hands as Lottie drains the bottle. When she totters to her bed, he takes the bottle, pulls me upright and wraps his arms loosely around my waist.

'You like me, yes?'

'I like everything about you.'

'Phoebe?' He tips his head to the side and studies my face, his gaze sincere and possessive. 'I have more than like.'

We can't possibly have a future together, but …

I saved him.

I'm in love with him.

Those things must count for something.

CHAPTER

34

I've barely closed the bathroom door before Sinn tugs open his shirt buttons and peels off the fabric, throwing it to the floor. His body is muscled and lean. His eyes are heated and bright. His hand goes to the button at the waist of his jeans.

'Oh …'

He looks up. Stills.

I swallow and nod. 'It's fine.'

He shakes his head before pulling me in front of him. He wraps his arms around me as we face the mirror. My eyes are enormous. My skin is parchment pale. Tangles of hair stick to my neck.

Shutting my eyes, I spin around and flatten my hands on his chest. 'That's how I look, not how I feel.' When I stand on my toes to brush hair from his forehead, he widens his legs so our heights are more even. 'I want this.'

'You're sure?'

'Positive.'

He reaches over my shoulder and turns on the taps. We sit side by side on the edge of the bath and yank off our jeans. He releases my shirt buttons slowly and then rubs my back, unclasping my bra and sliding the straps down my arms. My face warms as he stares.

'What?'

'You're beautiful.' He kisses my shoulder and then pulls back. I follow his gaze to the bruises. 'I don't want to hurt you.'

'It doesn't hurt.'

Steam fills the bathroom as he shepherds me backwards into the shower. I wash his hair and rinse it. I sponge soap over his shoulders, collarbones and sternum. I lather his chest, smooth soap down his arms and trace his abdominal muscles before circling his navel with my thumb. I follow the line of hair.

He stops my hands. 'Later.'

'My nails are dirty.'

Water coursing down his back, Sinn finds the nailbrush in the caddy and swipes my fingertips one by one. And then we kiss, long slow sweeps of our tongues. He cups my breasts and strokes my nipples. When he dips his head and takes a nipple into his mouth, lightning bolts of heat shoot straight to my thighs. My breath comes in gasps. I hold his arms to stay upright as his erection presses and nudges.

'Sinn ... maybe we should go to bed now?'

'Can I kiss you?'

'You just did.'

He smiles through the watery streams on his face. 'More.'

Trailing kisses down my neck and over my breasts, he kneels at my feet. He caresses my stomach, thighs and calves. When he puts a hand between my legs, I open for him, weak and shaky as I clutch his shoulders. His fingers move softly, gently ... deeply.

'Sinn ...'

He looks up innocently, his lashes wet and spiked. 'Okay?'

'Yes.'

When he holds my bottom and kisses between my thighs, clouds of steam, gossamer mists, whirl and spiral around us. My legs wobble. I thread my fingers through his hair. He teases and strokes, fast and hard, slow and soft. He licks and plays.

'Sinn!'

'Come.'

A demand and a request, all mixed up.

After I climax, he kisses his way up my body, but when I tug at his arms he finally straightens. He cups my face and we share slow searching kisses. His fingers get tangled in my hair.

'Sinn ...' I press against his erection, throbbing between us. I run my hands over his chest and down his sides. 'Please.'

He turns off the taps. 'Seng.' He drapes a towel over my shoulders. 'Bed.'

He's confident and demonstrative. I'm self-conscious and tentative.

He's fearless to my fearful.

And as he sits on the end of the bed and rolls on a condom, I remind myself again—he's nothing like Robbie.

The lamp sits on a chair in the corner of the room near the window. 'Is it all right to have it on?'

He runs a finger down my nose. 'I like to see you.'

We lie in the shadows and face one another. I reach for him and he pushes inside me.

Do not clench up.

He stills. 'Phoebe?'

My eyes sting. 'I'm fine.'

He pulls back. Leans on an elbow and searches my face. 'What happened to you?'

'He didn't care that it hurt.' I push words through the lump in my throat.

'What? Who?'

'A boyfriend.' My voice wavers. 'It was a long time ago.'

At first he kisses my mouth, but then he kisses me in the same way he did in the shower: my neck, breasts and stomach. He crawls to the bottom of the bed and kisses his way up my thighs until I'm heated and warm all over again.

When I pull at his shoulders, he covers my body and I wrap my legs around his hips. I soften against him as, achingly slowly and tense with restraint, he inches inside me.

'I'm fine.'

'You always say that.' He closes his eyes as he speaks.

I run my hands over his body and grasp his hips more firmly. When our stomachs press together, he exhales in a groan.

I run my hands over his bottom and down his thighs. 'I want ...'

'What?' A gravelly whisper.

The fullness, the tightness. I want you close.

'You can move.'

The sounds he makes: growls and endearments. The touch of his hands. The salt of his skin, the scent of his hair, the texture and taste of his mouth. The craving and yearning and longing.

I don't trust.

But I trust him.

I don't fall in love.

But I love him.

The wind as it cartwheels in the gum trees. The rain as it dances on the roof. The faraway thunder as it tumbles through the clouds. Our bodies joined, our limbs entwined, we search for release in the storm.

I tremble and shatter and sob.

He tenses and shudders and shouts.

We cling together, senses entwined.

A minute? An hour?

He lifts his head from the pillow, tips up my face and possessively kisses my mouth.

CHAPTER
35

There's soil in my nails from under the house.

Dust in my eyes. Dirt in my throat.

My arms are caught. I can't get out. A high-pitched cry.

'Phoebe! Kjære! Wake up.'

My breathing rough and raspy, I roll over and sit, scrubbing my face with my hand.

Sinn, wearing black boxers, is kneeling on the bed next to me. His pillows are stacked against the bedhead and his open laptop lies drunkenly against his thigh. The screen dims to nothing and sleeps. There's scratching and whining at the door.

'I have to …'

Sinn searches my face. 'I'll let him in,' he says quietly. When he opens the door, Wickham shoots inside, sits by the bed and offers a paw. I gather the sheet over my breasts and lean over the side of the bed to stroke his head and gently pull his ears.

'It was only a dream,' I say to Wickham, then I sniff and point a shaky hand. 'Go back to bed.'

After one last glance at me, and a rub under the chin from Sinn, Wickham pitter patters down the hallway. I shut the laptop with a click and lay it on the floor.

'Sorry I disturbed you.'

Sinn pulls on a T-shirt and sits on the side of the bed. 'What did you dream of?' he asks as he takes my hands.

My nails have neat white crescents at the top. 'It was because you cleaned my nails.'

'What?'

'Prim kept her bike under the verandah at the back of the house. She'd lean it against the lattice. I went down to get it for her.'

My father's storage room, a roughly excavated space with a sloping floor, was also under the house. I didn't know he was in the storage room until he opened the door and asked me to carry files up to his study. I was wary because the further I moved from the lattice, the darker it became, but I agreed, reassuring myself that he had to stoop to fit under the verandah but I could stand upright, so that's why he'd asked. The lattice threw patterns on the hard-packed earth. I counted the diamond shapes as I stood outside the storage room and waited for Dad to pass me the box.

'Don't drop it,' Dad warned, as he handed it to me. He must have suspected that it would be too heavy.

I managed to get hold of it, but the cardboard was old and brittle. When I staggered under the weight, the load shifted and the box split, spilling reams of paper onto the floor, some at my feet and the rest at Dad's.

Before I could run, he grabbed my arm and pulled me inside the storage room.

'Clean it up!'

There must have been light—a naked bulb hung from the ceiling. But I was blinded by fear and unable to see it.

I don't know how long I was down there before Patience, head and shoulders smaller than me, dragged me, sobbing, through the gap in the lattice.

Soil in my nails. Dust in my eyes. Dirt in my throat.

Swallowing hard, I pull my hands free from Sinn's, wriggle further back on the bed and pull the sheet higher. 'Could you pass my pyjamas?' My throat aches.

'Hot chocolate?' he asks as I pull my pyjama top over my head.

'Yes, please.'

He's back within minutes, placing my mug and his glass on the side table before positioning the chair close to the bed. As he drinks his juice, I blow on the milky froth of the chocolate.

My phone is on the side table. When the screen lights up, I check the messages. No word from Patience. I told her she had until midday; it's only three thirty.

'What you're doing ... it brings back memories of my father.' I look past the light cast by the lamp to the window. The curtains are drawn back. 'It's still dark.'

He opens his mouth and closes it again. Then he says, 'Not for long.'

'Were you awake because the lamp was on?' I place my mug on the side table and push back the sheet. 'I'll sleep in the spare room.'

He puts his arm across my legs. 'Talk to me, Phoebe. Tell me what you're thinking.'

'You already know. I'm scared of the dark.'

'Sleeping with someone doesn't help?'

I swing my legs off the bed. 'It's happened both times I've been with you.'

'Before that?'

'I'd always go home. Or ask them to go. Could you get out of the way, please?'

His eyes narrow. 'I'm different.'

'I don't—'

He picks up my hand, opens my fingers and puts them against his throat. His skin is warm. His pulse thumps steadily.

'I'm different, Phoebe. Admit it.'

'I— Yes.'

'I want to stay with you.'

I stare at the window, the sheet of glass that keeps out the black. 'You don't know what it's like.'

'I've seen what happens.'

'Even if I have warning, I panic.'

'I don't care.'

'No?' I pull my hand free and wriggle back onto the bed. I lean against the bedhead and point to the lamp, my hand not quite steady. 'Turn it off.'

'You want me to frighten you?'

'I'm better on my own.'

'Is this a test?'

When my eyes burn, I squeeze them shut. 'If you like.'

His movements deliberate, he switches on the overhead light, unplugs the lamp, puts it on the side table and turns it on. He extinguishes the overhead light before climbing on the bed and reaching for me. 'Come here.'

When I sit in front of him, his legs bracket mine. I take his hand. 'Have I offended you?'

He holds me firmly. 'Look through the window.'

'The glass is wet from the rain. I won't see the stars.'

He rests his chin on my shoulder. 'You'll see the clouds.'

'After you turn off the lamp, how long will it take for my eyes to adjust?'

'Ten seconds, maybe longer.'

Tightness works its way up my throat. 'Can you count?'

'You don't have to do this.'

I'm not only afraid of the dark, I'm afraid of him. Loving him. Trusting him. Losing him.

'Turn it off.'

He flicks the switch and my breath catches.

Dark. Cold.

Black.

'Sinn! Count!'

When my knees shoot to my chest, he brings me even closer. 'The window, Phoebe.'

The shiny, slick blackness of the well. The deep dark soil of underground. 'There's nothing—'

'The moon is behind the clouds. Look for the light.'

Silvery ghosts in the darkness. 'Oh.'

'It's always there.'

Far too afraid to blink, I hang on to the shimmering light. The clouds take shape; light and shade. The creep of dawn. The trees. 'Yes.'

'Now close your eyes.'

I do as he asks.

'What do you see?'

'Don't you mean feel?'

'It's the same.'

The roughness of his bristles on my cheek. The warmth of his body, the strength in his arms. The scent of his skin. The thump of his heart as it echoes mine.

Touch, scent, sound.

Sight.

My senses belong to him. My eyes might be closed but I see it. I feel it.

He kisses my shoulder. 'Can I stay?'

An hour? A day? A week? A month?

He doesn't know me.

And I know nothing but him.

Cockatoos call out the morning. Rain drips from the downpipe and onto the path. The wind whistles quietly. I turn and wrap my arms around his neck. I talk against his lips. 'Yes.' I kiss him.

Taste.

He lifts my hair and nuzzles my throat. His hands slide under my top and, fingers wide, he rubs my back. He kisses my mouth slowly and carefully as if I might break.

How would I break?

Into a thousand little pieces that all belonged to him.

We cartwheel, dance and tumble. Heated bodies, gentle hands, racing hearts and whispered secrets.

The clouds scatter, the dawn breaks.

Finally, we sleep.

CHAPTER
36

The sun glows golden on Sinn's back. His breath is warm on my breast and his arm is heavy round my waist. The shades of his hair are darkest brown to cinnamon. His features, his cheekbones and mouth, are softer in sleep. I like him like this. I can watch over him. I can let him rest.

I run my fingers through his hair, brush it back from his forehead. I kiss his shoulder and take in his scent. I whisper against his skin. 'Yes, Sinn. You can stay.'

Wickham whines at the door.

Sinn frowns as I ease out of his arms, but then he rolls onto his side and settles again. I pull underwear, jeans and a shirt from the cupboard and dress in the hallway. In the bathroom, I put a strip of tape on the scar and wrap a bandage around my arm. Wickham, wagging a happy good morning tail, waits at the kitchen door.

I step onto the verandah and Lottie bleats a welcome. When I open the pen she darts to the steps and stumbles clumsily to the garden. I'm opening the living room curtains when tyres crunch on the gravel. I check the clock—barely seven. Nate is here already.

Sinn is still asleep when I return to my room. Lying with his back to me, he breathes deeply but silently. I'd like to leave him here in my bed. I'd like to climb in beside him and hold him again. He always says we should talk. This would be a good place.

Nate, in the back garden, whistles a marching song. I perch on the side of the bed and put my hand on Sinn's shoulder. 'Hey.'

He spins and sits all in one motion.

I jump. 'Oh!'

His body is tense, his eyes are bright. 'What—' He blinks. 'Phoebe?'

'Who else would it be?'

He runs his hands through his hair. 'Why are you dressed?'

'I had to let Wickham and Lottie out.'

'I scared you.' He takes my hand.

I trace around his fingers. 'Nate is here.'

He curses as he reaches for his watch on the side table. 'I sent him home early yesterday. We'll be a few hours.'

'I'll take Camelot out.'

'I don't—'

'I always ride on Sundays.'

'Where will you go?'

'The fire trails past Mr Riley's shed.'

Sinn's eyes search mine. 'Don't run away.'

I lift his hand and kiss his thumb. 'I won't.'

The shed's corrugated roof, wet from the storm, catches the light and sparkles. Beyond the shed, the grass is wildly green. Statuesque grey gums, trunks silver-white, stand in a queue near the dam.

Camelot, keen to reach softer ground, looks straight ahead as we continue along the laneway. I bend down and pat his neck. 'You don't have long to wait.'

Sinn said the more he waited, the further away I ran. He doesn't know me as well as he thinks he does, but—

My phone rings and, for the second time this morning, I jump. I loosen the reins as I fumble in my pocket.

'Patience!'

'I only got your message this morning. Are you okay? Brent grabbed you? What's going on?'

I pull Camelot back from a trot, adjust my ear pods and drop my phone in a pocket. 'I don't know what he'll do. He knows you were involved.'

'Why would he care? What did he do to you?'

I lean low to open the gate. 'It was nothing serious, but it scared me. I have to—'

'Have you told Tørrissen? Tell me you have!'

'I will, but—'

'You were waiting for me to call, weren't you? Phoebe! When will you stop doing this? You have to tell Tørrissen!'

'I will, I promise. I just wanted to warn you first.'

'Tørrissen's UN people look at serious crimes, international crimes. If Brent is involved in anything like that and Tørrissen is on to him, he could do anything.'

'Brent said he'd been indiscrete. That doesn't sound like a criminal mastermind to me and—'

'Phoebe! Tørrissen's been there for months. Why didn't he work this out earlier?'

'I don't think Brent would be capable of—'

'Where are you? Is anyone with you?'

'I'm riding near Mr Riley's farm.'

'In other words, you're alone.'

Camelot tosses his head and skitters as we approach the track where I usually give him his head. 'Sinn has been staying at the church. He's there with Nate now.'

'What good is that if you're out riding?'

I steady Camelot. 'A couple of men came to the church a few weeks ago. They frightened Camelot and he knocked me over. I wasn't hurt badly, but I think—'

'Phoebe! Why didn't you tell me about—'

'I'm telling you now! Can I finish?'

'I'm listening!'

'Brent might have been behind what happened. He said the locals were opposed to having someone like Tørrissen, an outsider, poking his nose in, and I should keep away from him. He also said I should keep my mouth shut about things I might have seen at Roxburgh Estate.'

'What did you see?'

'Nothing I can think of as relevant, which is part of the problem.'

'Tell Tørrissen everything you've told me, Phoebe. You have to.'

I push Camelot into a trot at the straight stretch of track. 'I will, but you have to promise you'll talk to your captain.'

'What?'

'Let him know that Dad did something wrong, but it had nothing to do with you. And nothing to do with you being assaulted or—'

'Phoebe! Shut up!' Patience takes a breath. 'Go home. Talk to Tørrissen. And while you're at it, tell him that I helped Dad. Because if you don't, I will.'

'I'll say as little as—'

'Tell him everything you know! You should have done it months ago.'

'I like him.'

Silence. Then, 'What?'

'He likes animals, and he knows about the weather and he builds things.' I slow Camelot back to a walk. 'He doesn't care that I'm scared of the dark.'

'He knows that?' Another silence. 'Are you sure you can trust him? Why did he stand back when Brent—'

'He doesn't know what happened!'

When an echidna waddles out of the trees, Camelot shies. I bend down to stroke his neck and my phone falls out of my pocket.

'Patience?' Kicking free of my stirrups, I drop to the ground, but by the time I rescue the phone from a ditch and wipe it dry on my jeans, the call has dropped out. I hold it up. Reception comes and goes. 'Damn.'

Camelot walks curiously behind me through the bush until I find a fallen tree and climb onto the trunk to remount, but as soon as we return to the track, he prances and champs at his bit. I don't have the heart to turn him home yet.

'Just to the crest of the hill.'

He gallops up the incline, hooves thundering dully on the rain-soaked track. The crisp morning air, the speed, the scent of eucalyptus. Clods of earth fly into the air behind us. Trees are a blur of browns and greens as we pass.

It's exhilarating, but it's not enough.

I have to get home to Sinn.

When we slow to a walk at the top of the rise, I stroke Camelot's neck, warm and damp with sweat. 'Time to cool down.' It seems to take forever to reach the gate and lane. A car, a black four-wheel drive, pulls up near the shed. Sinn, his shirt hanging out of his jeans and his phone to his ear, gets out but stops dead in the middle of the lane. He barks something into his phone before shoving it into his pocket.

'Sinn? What are you doing here?'

He looks up—eyes wild like storm clouds. 'Your sister called.'

The knot in my chest pulls tight. 'Which sister?'

'The one in the military.'

Long strips of cloud stretch across the sky. *Stratus.*

I slide from Camelot's back, retying my hair in a ponytail as we walk to the shade of the gums. Camelot lowers his head and crops the scrappy grass as I move to higher ground and stand on a tangle of tree roots. I'm taller than usual, but not as tall as Sinn.

I cross my arms then uncross them. 'I didn't give Patience your number.'

'She tracked me down.'

I swallow. 'Why did she call?'

Face grim, he holds out his hand. 'Show me your arm.'

A few hours ago, his touch was warm and passionate. Now, as he turns my arm, eases back the bandage and inspects the bruises, the small blue stains, his hold is cool and clinical.

'It was Brent Green, wasn't it? You lied.'

'I was going to tell you.'

'You told Nate you were going to Horseshoe Hill. Did you arrange to meet Green then?'

'Afterwards.'

'Here?'

'Yes.'

'Did you meet him today?'

'No!' I yank my arm free. 'Why would I do that?'

'Why meet him on Friday?'

'Why did Patience call?'

'She blames me for what happened. She said he threatened you.'

'He said I should keep away from you. Anything I'd seen at Roxburgh Estate, he said I had to forget about it.'

He turns on his heel and walks a few long strides before walking back. 'Explain that.'

'I can't.'

'Why should I believe you?'

'I'm telling the truth! I told you not to trust him.'

'I ordered you to stay away.'

'I don't take orders!'

He opens his mouth. Slams it shut. Then, 'Green might have a connection to the man we want, our target.'

'The arms dealer? You know who he is, don't you?'

His eyes narrow. 'I can't say.'

I take a step back and rest a hand against the tree. 'I wanted to warn Patience about Brent. I didn't know how you'd react, what the fallout would be. I gave her until lunchtime.'

Sinn looks over his shoulder, back towards the car. His phone buzzes and he takes it from his pocket. Lines of messages fill the screen. He puts the phone to his ear. 'Do it.'

I shorten Camelot's rein, ready to walk him to the sheep pens so I can climb on a railing and mount. 'I'll see you at home.'

'I'll follow.'

'Why?'

'I don't trust you.'

'I haven't lied about everything.'

'You lied about Robbie Roxburgh.'

'I hardly knew you when we went to Roxburgh Estate.'

His jaw clenches. 'We shared a bed when we were there.'

Camelot nudges my back. My horse is beautiful and kind-natured, uncomplicated. I can love him safely. 'I should have told you about Brent.'

'Look at me.'

My eyes sting, but I do as he asks. 'I'm sorry.'

He has a crease between his brows. 'Sex. It was Roxburgh who hurt you, wasn't it?'

I run the leather of the rein through my fingers. 'It doesn't matter who it was.'

'For fuck's—'

'Don't swear at me!' A large crow swoops into the tree, perches on a branch and settles his feathers.

Sinn glances at his phone again. 'I have to get back. We finish this then.'

CHAPTER
37

When I return to the house after settling Camelot in the paddock, Sinn and Nate are arguing quietly in the living room. I kick off my boots and go to the bathroom to wash my hands and splash my face. I'm afraid to look into the mirror in case I burst into tears.

A tap on the door. 'Phoebe?' Nate says. 'Ready when you are.'

In the living room, Sinn directs me to a chair. 'Sit down.'

'It's my house. Don't tell me what to do.'

He sits in the chair opposite, a piece of paper in front of him. When Nate pushes a glass of juice towards me, I pick it up with both hands and carefully sip. Wickham, lying in his bed, wags his tail.

'Nice to talk to your sister earlier.' Nate attempts a smile. 'Just want to clarify a few things.'

'How did Patience find you?'

Holding up a hand, he counts off on his fingers. 'She serves with Catriona Stevens, who knows Per Amundsen. Per got onto his brother Tor. When Tor couldn't get onto Sinn, he called me.'

'How did she sound?'

'Friendly enough to me.' He winces. 'Tore strips off Sinn.'

Sinn turns his mug of coffee three hundred and sixty degrees. 'She claims to have assisted your father. She wants you to give me the facts.'

I lay my forearms on the table and link my fingers. 'My father ...' *Squeeze. Release.* 'My father has resisted personal interactions for as long as I can remember. After Mum went away ...' *Squeeze. Release.* 'Patience and I both played our parts: shopping, paying bills, parent–teacher interviews. If I'd known he'd asked Patience to help him, I would have prevented it.' *Squeeze. Release.* 'I was doing my final exams for school and I didn't know she'd taken over. After my exams, things went back to how they were. I helped my father again.'

'Just need a little clarification on that,' Nate says, turning his monitor around so Sinn and I can see it. An image of one of Dad's spreadsheets with handwritten calculations in the margins is blown up on the screen.

I sit further back in my chair. 'Oh.'

Nate's brows lift. 'You told us your father dictated these numbers.'

'I— Yes.'

'Looking into data, that's our job, right?' Nate says. 'As part of that, we make assessments of people.'

'Criminals.'

'Witnesses. You left your devices, your phone and laptop, and your purse, lying around. You let us into your house. Not only that, everything you told us about your father checked out, and no one had a bad word to say about you. We figured you were mostly telling the truth.'

'I have nothing to hide.'

'You volunteered your father's documents—' he glances at the screen, '—including those spreadsheets, and when we asked you questions about the arithmetic, the calculations, it was clear you had no idea what they meant.'

'I didn't. I don't.'

Sinn drops his pen on the table. 'They weren't your numbers.'

'They were my father's.'

'We attributed your defensiveness,' Nate says, 'to your fear that you and your sisters might be blamed for your father's actions. Turns out that was a mistake.'

'I don't understand.'

'Doing your father's bidding, copying out numbers, would mean you didn't know there were, in essence, two sets of books for the syndicate.' A different image comes up on the screen. My handwriting, with Benjamin's commentary: *Wickham could do better than this.*

'When did you do this? You had no right!'

Nate looks towards the bookcase, with my folders stacked high. 'Something about your writing niggled, made me uneasy, but I was busy with other things. After we spoke with Patience, I had a better look. She slopes right, you go left.'

I lift my chin. 'What's the relevance of this?'

'Your sister, independently of your father, calculated payments and made deposits. She dealt, indirectly, with the person who infiltrated the syndicate.'

'She didn't know what she was dealing with.' My nails dig into my palms. 'It wouldn't matter so much if it were me. It's different for Patience.'

'She's a naval officer and a mathematician.' Sinn's eyes are icy cold. 'She's on a fucking war ship!'

'Sinn,' Nate warns, 'you said you'd leave this to me.'

'Patience remembers all kinds of things, especially numbers. She'll help if you want that.'

Hands in his pockets, Sinn strides to the stained glass window. 'She'll have no choice.'

Nate puffs out his cheeks and slowly exhales. 'Professor Cartwright wouldn't be medically fit or legally competent to give evidence. Patience is different. Knowing this earlier could have made our job a whole lot easier.'

'Now you do know.' I focus on Nate, almost as serious as Sinn. 'Now you can talk to her.'

'And trust her?' Sinn says. 'Like we trusted you?'

'I tried to help.'

'You hoped I'd protect her, didn't you?' Sinn says. 'Is that what last night was about?'

Tears threaten. I blink them back. 'How can you say that?'

'How could you let me ...' His jaw locks and unlocks.

Nate whistles quietly. He leans back in his chair. 'Patience is a math freak like your father, right?'

'No!' Wickham startles, jumping from his bed and trotting to my side. He rests his head in my lap and I stroke his ears. I lower my voice. 'Patience is clever like my mother.'

'And Green knows that?'

'Brent said my father had sent Martin a document by mistake—a spreadsheet to do with the syndicate—and my father was really upset about it. He called Brent to make sure he'd deleted it, and he had. But Brent now believes the document had something to do with the syndicate after the extra member joined. He thinks if Dad knew what was going on, Patience would have too. Brent knew she'd helped my father.'

'Brent was always a loose cannon,' Nate says. 'But we're still not sure how much he knows. We've been wary of moving too early—if he does know who the target is, he could warn him.'

Sinn mutters as his thumbs fly over his phone. 'Now we have no choice. Brent will be arrested.' He looks up and addresses Nate. 'My flight leaves at four. I'll book a car. You stay here.'

'Phoebe?' Nate pushes my juice across the table. 'Drink up. You don't look too chipper.'

Condensation wets my fingers. 'I'm fine.'

'*Fine*,' Sinn mimics, then curses under his breath.

I can't look at him, and my hands are too unsteady to risk lifting the glass.

'Her bedroom, the stables, the bathroom,' Sinn snaps at Nate. 'Wherever she goes, you follow. Don't let her out of your sight.'

'We're picking Brent up. He'll no longer be a threat.'

Sinn walks to his chair and grips the backrest. 'The target could be.'

'The guy who has billions of bucks to fight us in the courts? He's so clean he squeaks. There's no way he'll risk that reputation to go after the daughter of a crackpot—'

'Do it!'

Smiling stiffly, Nate turns to his screen. 'It wasn't me who took my eyes off the ball,' he says conversationally.

'You know what I want.'

'Keep her safe,' Nate says. 'Reckon you've made that pretty darned clear.'

U

The sun disappeared this morning and hasn't come back. Sinn, his bag at his feet, stands next to the taxi with Nate and the driver. I back away from the window and whistle for Wickham.

Sitting on a milk crate just inside the door of Camelot's stable, I open my laptop to call Mum. Camelot grazes in the distance but

Mintie stands in the yard and peers inside, looking hopefully at the trough for a midday feed. 'There's plenty of grass in the paddock,' I tell him.

Wickham jumps over a puddle in the yard and skirts around Mintie before joining me in the stable. He drops to the straw and rolls onto his side.

Debra appears on the screen. 'There you are, Phoebe. Sorry we're late, love. Your mum was sowing tomato seeds ready for summer. Isn't that right, Barbara?'

When Debra repositions the laptop, I see Mum, cheeks flushed and hair pulled back.

'Hey, Mum. It's Phoebe.'

'Hello, my darling. How lovely to see you. How are you? How are all my girls?'

'Prim is still in the Northern Territory. And Patience is …' When my voice fades, I clear my throat. 'Patience is safe and well on her ship, and I'm fine at home.'

'I think about you all the time.' When Mum looks at Debra, I see her in profile. 'I do, don't I? I love my girls.'

'Yes you do, Barbara, of course you do.'

'We love you too, Mum.'

'Phoebe?' Sinn stands stiffly at the door.

'I thought you'd gone.' My voice wavers.

'No, no, Phoebe.' Debra laughs. 'We're still here!'

I turn back to the screen and force a smile. 'Can I put us on mute, Debra, just for a minute? Tell Mum I won't be long. You'll wait for me to come back, won't you?'

Wickham gazes lovingly at Sinn, tail wagging in welcome. Leaving my laptop open on the crate, I stand.

'I'm going,' he says.

'Yes.'

When Mintie appears at the door again, looking at me as if afraid of missing out on something, Sinn absently strokes his neck.

I link my hands. 'You'll talk to Patience?'

'I've booked a call for tomorrow. You'll do what Nate tells you?'

'Do I have a choice?'

'I'll be a week, maybe two. I'll call and—'

'No!' I can't hear Mum and Debra, but I focus on their mouths as they chat. Grief, a tonne of it, is lodged in my throat. 'It didn't work out. I'm sorry.'

He stills. 'What do you mean?'

'It's over.'

Pointing and gesturing, Debra, for the hundredth time, maybe the thousandth, explains how to use the computer. Even though Mum has a first class degree in mathematics and a PhD in computer science. Even though she was respected and admired and won scholarships and awards and …

I hide my sob in a cough.

When Sinn steps closer, our eyes meet again. 'Over?' he says. 'What does that mean?'

He was a yearning.

A longing.

A hope.

I should never have dreamt there could be more.

I take a rapid step back and trip on the crate. The laptop tilts and I steady it. Mum peers into the screen.

'I have to go.'

'Answer me, Phoebe.'

He's wearing tailored pants. Clean leather shoes. A white linen shirt with the sleeves rolled up. His arms are tanned and muscular. I know those arms, the strength of them, the tenderness.

'You were angry that I didn't trust you. That's because …' An icy clamp takes hold of my heart. 'I can't.'

The light is behind him; his eyes are impenetrable. 'You've given up. Is that what you're saying?'

'You'll go back to the navy or wherever you belong.' I look beyond him—to the church, the gum trees, the threatening band of cloud. 'My life is here.'

'Alone?'

'I'm better alone.'

He doesn't respond. And he doesn't look back as he strides through the yards and garden to the graveyard. Shoulders tense, he holds onto the spikes as he stares at the graves. Was it only three days ago I was pulling out weeds?

I sniff and swallow, forcing back tears. I sit on the crate and put my hands on the keys. Unmute.

Debra beams. 'She's back, Barbara, just like I told you she would be. There she is!'

Alone.

CHAPTER

38

On Friday morning, for the fifth day in a row, Nate is at my table, a mug of coffee by his elbow and his phone against his ear. 'Hey, Sinn. Yeah, all good here.'

When I point in the direction of the stables, Nate lifts a thumb in acknowledgement.

It's only six o'clock, but the sun peeps over the tree line and the skies are a washed-out blue. As I pull on boots, Mintie peers between the railings. Camelot, standing next to him, nickers a greeting and stamps a foot.

'Won't be long!' I call to him as I jog to Lottie's palace. When I open the door, she steps delicately over the threshold and peers into the light before skipping through her picket-fenced garden and lowering her head to the grass. 'You're hungry too, aren't you?'

Leaning over her little body, I run my fingers through her fleece. She might be small for her age, but a layer of fat now covers her ribs.

Mike and I will take her to Gus's farm next week. I have to give her the chance to go back to her family.

I'm loading manure into a wheelbarrow when a police car parks behind Nate's four-wheel drive. Jeremiah walks around the car and stands with his hands on his hips.

'Want a break from shovelling shit?' he shouts. 'Time for a coffee?'

'Hot chocolate, please.'

By the time Jeremiah, keys and other paraphernalia jiggling from his belt, walks from the back verandah into the garden, the horses are in the paddock. We sit on the bench and he passes me a mug.

'Wanted to catch you before your clients turned up.'

'It's about Brent, isn't it?'

'He's scared shitless, but no one can get a word out of him. Which, according to Sinn, isn't too bad. He's not tipping off the target either.'

'Nate thinks he passed Martin's details, his email and passwords and things, to somebody.'

'Trouble is,' Jeremiah says, 'who is that somebody?'

'I feel bad about Brent losing his job.' When Jeremiah shoulder bumps me, I yelp and hold my mug over the grass.

'He set out to scare you, Phoebe. Doesn't that piss you off?'

'I still don't understand how I was a threat—what he wanted me to keep quiet about.'

'Like I said, he's not talking.'

'At least he's admitted to assaulting me, so I won't have to go to court.'

Lottie, grazing near the yards, looks up when the back door slams.

'Hey again, Phoebe. Morning, Jeremiah.' Nate strolls over the grass, sitting beside me and crossing his ankles. 'I'm outta here tomorrow. You going to miss me when I'm gone?'

Lottie trots straight past Jeremiah and butts Nate's leg. Her palace has full sun early in the mornings, but later in the day there's shade from the paperbark trees, just as Sinn predicted.

'Lottie will miss you a lot.'

He scratches between the lamb's ears. 'Our colleagues are watching our target, not that he's going anywhere or doing anything to draw attention to himself.'

'Brent is definitely out of the picture?'

'He knows more than he's letting on, so we'll keep an eye on him, but he's no threat to you.'

'Why didn't the target set up his own syndicate? Why infiltrate Martin's?'

'If the regulatory authorities ever looked into it, the target's involvement would, like the other five members, appear to be legitimate. Investors pooling resources and betting on overseas races. Happens all the time.'

Jeremiah tips the dregs from his mug. 'The target never came here?'

'He didn't need to—he's got associates on every continent in the world, and access to a network of companies and trusts. We follow one strand of his web, only to get caught in another.'

Lottie plucks grass near my feet. 'Patience wasn't much help, was she?'

'She didn't know where the money came from, or where it ended up.' He grins. 'But you've got to admire a woman who can recollect, to the hundredth decimal point, how the distributions were calculated.'

I nod stiffly. 'Yes.'

He nudges my foot. 'You withheld information and Sinn was pissed, no mistake about that. But he'll get over it.'

I curl my fingers and hide my dirty nails. 'Is he coming back?'

'He'll be a couple more weeks.'

U

On Wednesday evening, I herd Lottie through the garden to the driveway, wedging her between my knees to keep her still.

Supporting his dodgy hip, Mike steps carefully from the cab of his ute. His thick white hair needs a cut. He scratches his ear. 'G'day, Phoebe.'

Wickham, leaping like a puppy, runs circles around Mike before sitting at his feet and licking his hand.

'Thanks for picking me and Lottie up.'

'I feel like a dentist, you and Lottie looking at me all wary like that.'

'Gus and I agreed we'd let Lottie decide where to live.'

'He don't care whether he gets her back or not, seeing as she only survived through your ministrations.'

When I take a carrot from my pocket, Lottie's tail wiggles back and forth. 'It would be unfair to make her a pet if she'd prefer to be with her family. Even though it might take time for her to settle in.'

'Family?' He harrumphs. 'I reckon she's got a nice comfy home with you. Even better, she won't end her days hanging from a hook in a butcher's shop.'

'Mike!' I open the door and pick Lottie up, standing her in the foot well in front of the seats. 'She's bred for wool, not meat.'

'She'll end up mutton whatever her breeding.'

When I whistle, Wickham jumps onto the seat behind Lottie. 'Stay.'

'This is a waste of time, I reckon,' Mike says, his hand supporting his hip as he climbs awkwardly into the driver's seat. 'When we'll be bringing her back next week.'

U

Gus's home paddock slopes towards his tiny timber house. His late wife Maggie's roses, now meticulously tended by Gus, create a riot of colour in the garden. A yellow banksia rose climbs up the verandah posts and trails over the porch. Banjo and Patterson, Gus's kelpies, wait for instructions as they watch over a small flock of sheep. Most are four or five months old like Lottie, but there are a number of ewes and newborn lambs. Lottie was born here, and this is a gentle introduction to farm life. She doesn't seem to be afraid of the other sheep. But when she's not at the fence peering at me and baaing pathetically, she's following Banjo around the paddock, confused when, instead of tolerating her like Wickham does, he chases her back to the herd.

Gus, his bushy eyebrows drawn, puts an awkward arm around my shoulders. 'Sheep are social animals, but what social means to Lottie is humans, horses and dogs. It'll take her a while to assimilate. You doing all right?'

'I'll be fine.'

'Saying goodbye at the school gate was the worst of it, that's what my Maggie always said.'

I attempt a smile. 'Thank you for looking after her. You will call though, won't you, if she's—'

'If Lottie doesn't settle, she'll come back to you, don't you worry about that. In the meantime, I'll vaccinate and worm her.'

I'm about to step into Mike's ute when my phone rings. *Sinn Tørrissen*. It's not like I can leave the room like I do when he calls Nate. I could ignore the call, but both Gus and Mike are nodding encouragingly.

I put the phone to my ear, but can't think what to say.

'Phoebe?'

I haven't allowed myself to cry since he went away. But my throat is so thick with tears that I can't hold them back. One escapes. And another. Then streams of tears trickle down my face. Buckets of them. A tipping bucket rain gauge. I squeeze my eyes shut. Wipe my face with my sleeve. Shudder and swallow.

Smothered tears. Soundless. Silent. Shhh.

After Mum went away, I'd cry when I had nightmares. But I'd muffle the sounds as soon as I woke up. It was too dark under the bedclothes but if I buried my face in the pillow, it quietened the sounds. Sometimes not enough.

My father would open the door and shove Patience out of the way. He'd turn off the light. 'Go to sleep!'

We knew he waited outside, listening for the sound of the light switch. I'd curl up in a ball and Prim would cuddle close, her voice low and tremulous.

Baa, baa, black sheep, have you any wool,

Yes, sir, yes, sir, three bags full.

One for the master, one for the dame,

And one for the little girl who lives down the lane.

Gus, clearly alarmed, finds me a neatly pressed handkerchief deep in one of his pockets. 'Now, now, Phoebe, you know I'll take good care of Lottie.' He pulls the phone from my hand and tucks it through his belt as I scrub at my face with the hanky.

'I'm fine, really, it was just—'

'Let's take the lamb home now,' Mike grumbles. 'It'll save us the trouble of driving all the way back.'

'Good idea.' Gus, patting my shoulder, nods in agreement. 'Take Lottie home, Phoebe, right this minute.'

'No, Gus. I have to give her a chance.' I sniff and hold out my hand. 'Can you give me the phone, please?' Wickham jumps into the back seat as I put the phone to my ear. 'Sorry about—'

'What the fuck is going on?'

I've missed your touch.

I lean against the ute as the men, Gus shortening his stride to accommodate Mike's limp, walk towards the shed. 'I'm here with Gus and Mike.'

'What's happened to Lottie?'

'She's back at Gus's farm.'

'Why?'

'She has more room to run around here. She's with other sheep.'

Silence. I imagine him running a hand through his hair. 'I had a call from Elizabeth. She said she'd invited you to Beatrice's party.'

I shade my eyes from the low-slung sun. 'That's right.'

'I don't want you to go, Phoebe.'

'Nate said, so long as I keep quiet about what I know, it would be okay.'

High-pitched beeping, the rumble of traffic, comes through the phone. 'I'd prefer you stayed away.'

'Elizabeth was a member of the syndicate. If she and Beatrice don't blame my sisters or me for what my father did, others shouldn't either. Anyway, it was kind of Elizabeth to invite me. I knew you wouldn't be there. That's why I thought it'd be all right.'

'Why does it matter whether I'm there or not?'

'It shouldn't.' I swipe at my eyes again. 'It doesn't.'

By the time the call ends, Gus and Mike, deep in conversation, are on their way back to the ute. The other sheep have moved to one side of the paddock and Lottie is standing alone. Looking up, she sets off at a trot towards me, stumbling as she reaches the fence.

CHAPTER
39

Benjamin, dressed in his AFL kit, sprints across the grass before skidding to a stop at the edge of the playing field adjacent to the park and community centre. He plants his foot on a ball and his hands on his hips.

'Hey, Phoebe! You here to watch the last quarter?'

'I promised I'd help Mandy in the hall. We're doing the Christmas fete planning.'

His smile fades. 'It's the grand final. Can't you do that later?'

I glance at my watch. 'I'll see what I can do.'

He grins over his shoulder as he runs towards his teammates. 'I'm way better at footy than I am at stupid pegs.'

Mandy, wearing her customary jodhpurs and long black boots, is happy to take a break, but rolls her eyes when I tell her I want to watch Benjamin's game.

'You've been coming and going all day,' she says. 'How many clients do you see on Saturdays?'

'I offered to mind Saxon while Kelly had a coffee with her girl-friends. And I had lunch with Jane and Matilda because Jane and I are friends. She's desperate to find a role for Matilda in the nativity play.'

'Poor little mite. I heard her screaming her head off when her hair got tangled in the tinsel.'

'There's no way she'll tolerate angel wings or any other costume, so Jane and I are trying to think of another way to involve her.'

'Is Mintie in Jesus's stable? Put Matilda in charge.'

'What?'

'I'm not keen on anthropomorphism, but you could let Mintie do the dressing up for Matilda.'

'You mean—' I laugh. 'He could be an angel. I'll thread tinsel through his mane and tail, and put a halo on his halter. Matilda could wear a white dress. What a great idea.'

'The other kids will love it.'

'It's something Matilda and I can work on, practising holding the rope. I think she'll be able to do it.'

As the whistle signals three-quarter time for the game, Mandy and I sit on one of the long timber benches cut into the slope of the hill. The small crowd—mostly parents, siblings and play-ers from other age divisions—gather in groups either side of the field. Benjamin, one of the tallest on his team, leads them into the middle.

'Go team! Go the Magpies!' Mandy shouts. But after the kick-off, she turns away from the game and taps the toe of my boot with hers. 'Mike came over last week. He trimmed Captain Went-worth's and the broodmares' feet.'

'I saw him too.'

'How's Lottie getting on at Gus's farm?'

'She's started eating grass again, so that's progress.'

Mandy prises the lid from her coffee. 'Mike said you were upset. And he suspects Lottie was only part of the problem.'

I wince. 'I had a bit of a meltdown.'

'You've had a busy few weeks.'

'Mandy, I—'

'All you do is work—paid and unpaid. This is the first time you've made it to the community centre. And we haven't seen you at the pub or anywhere else.'

'I'm going to Denman the week after next for Beatrice Oldfield's birthday.'

'Will Sinn be there?'

'No.'

'He's no longer on the scene?'

'Him being here was tied up with other things.' Benjamin jumps and catches the ball before setting it on the ground and kicking it through the posts. 'I stuck up for Patience over something our father had done wrong. That had consequences.'

Her brows lift. 'Want some advice?'

I sigh. 'Go for it.'

'Your father's abuse,' she says, 'has shaped your self-worth, the woman you've become. You take responsibility for others.'

'I like to look after my family.'

'Patience and Prim are adults now. Thanks to you, they're able to look after themselves.'

'They cared for me, too.'

'To an extent, I agree. But Prim was young and Patience ...' Mandy gives a low whistle. 'You recall I worked at the school? Patience was anti-authoritarian, headstrong and argumentative. If she hadn't been so clever—and if not for your guidance and intervention—she would have been suspended or expelled three terms out of four.'

'Are you saying I'm overprotective?'

'Your care for your sisters could be detrimental to you, particularly as you take responsibility for your parents as well.'

I stare through my water bottle. 'My aunts look after Mum.'

'Every Sunday at midday—not a particularly convenient time for you—you call for an hour. You send gifts and visit when you can. You worry about her.'

'I want her to be happy.'

'You hid years of abuse because of your fear that you'd lose your sisters.' Mandy touches my arm. 'What about now? Do you tell your New Zealand family about the difficult times?'

I shake my head. 'They'd worry, get upset.'

'As would your sisters. Which brings us back to the start. As the eldest child, you developed an acute sense of duty and obligation. Despite your fears and vulnerabilities, you were the responsible child. It's past time that you and your sisters relied on others.'

'Others can let you down too.'

'Did Sinn?'

Every morning, I imagine he's with me. I turn off the lamp, lean against the headboard and count to ten. I look for pinprick stars and the hint of dawn as the sun pushes rays through the clouds. I search for the light like he taught me.

'He didn't let me down.'

She drains her cup. 'Are you still at your father's beck and call?'

'I see him once or twice a week.'

'You shop for him and clean his house. You coordinate his care.'

Benjamin takes a mark, makes a fist and punches the air. 'He had a fall last week.'

'Good news at last,' she says. 'Did it kill him?'

I nudge her with my elbow. 'He wasn't hurt badly, but his neighbour called an ambulance and they took him to the hospital. The social worker assessed him and offered more support, but—' I shake my head. 'He'll hate it. They'll have to force their way in.'

'If not for you, he'd have been taken into care years ago.'

I bring my feet onto the bench, bend my knees and wrap my arms around them. 'I don't want to lock him up because he's not wanted. I don't want to be like him.'

'That man hates everything and everyone, Phoebe, including you.'

'The last few months … I'm more aware of the damage than I was. I'll consider additional help.'

'Grab it with both hands!'

The final whistle blows: 48–36 to the Magpies. Benjamin catches my eye, laughing as he lifts his arms above his head and opens and shuts his hands.

'Man of the match!' Mandy shouts.

As we walk across the field, Mandy loops her arm through mine. 'Sinn is a fine-looking man, according to all and sundry. How was the sex?'

'Mandy!' I smile. 'I'm not going to answer that.'

'Nothing worth sharing?'

The grass is green, but the flowers on the bottlebrush trees have faded. 'I didn't trust him. He hated that.'

'You've got emotional armour six inches thick.'

'I didn't know what he wanted.'

'You didn't understand his motivations? Ask him about them when he comes back.'

'I doubt he'll want to talk to me.'

'An attractive man has a civic duty to make conversation. Do you think he'll abandon you?'

I stand back when a boy on a scooter whistles past. 'I wanted to tell him things, but then he found out I'd lied. I don't know whether I was pre-empting him or not when I told him it was over.'

'We've talked about the flight or fight response, haven't we?'

I look through the branches to the clouds. 'I've run away again, haven't I?'

'You fight for your family, your friends and your clients. You haven't had a partner for years, but permitted Sinn to get close. That's progress.'

A tiny blue wren hops and skips as she forages for crumbs on a picnic table. My chest tightens. My eyes sting. 'I told him I was better alone. That wasn't true.'

'If you want the conventional things—a husband, children and security—you're bound to find somebody else.'

'My problem is ...' As I search for the clouds again, my eyes fill with tears. The cotton balls blur, scatter and fade. 'I only want him.'

CHAPTER

40

It's midday on Thursday when I pull up at the kerb outside my father's house. He won't tolerate the sound of a mower, so the grass is long and straggly. Dandelion and onion weeds shoot through cracks in the concrete. I place the shopping at my feet and ring the doorbell. When he doesn't respond, I turn the key in the lock and open the door.

'Dad? It's Phoebe.'

He fell asleep in his chair last weekend. I opened the windows and doors, stripped his bed and soaked the bedding. I bleached the bathroom and scrubbed the kitchen. Only a few days have passed, but it already smells as bad as it did. He dresses in the same clothes, day after day after day. I leave the door open so the breeze drifts inside.

Sitting in his study at the back of the house, ramrod straight in his chair, he watches silently as I store meals in the fridge.

'Is there anything you'd like me to tell the nurse?'

Even through his hair, his scars are fiery red. 'Why are you here?'

'I called this morning to explain. I've spoken to the nurse on the phone, but today we're meeting in person.'

'I forbid you to let her in.'

'Her name is Joan, and she's a very well qualified aged care nurse. We were lucky she agreed to help. She's—'

'Send her away!'

I kneel at the fridge to clean out the slot where he stores the milk. 'She'll be here every morning and evening for the next few weeks and if that doesn't work out, then—'

He grips the desk, pulls himself to his feet and finds his balance. He walks, unsteadily but determined, towards me. As I stand, his hand snakes out. He grasps my arm and twists it. His nails dig into my skin. 'Get rid of her!'

'It's not fair to make me—'

'I won't see her! I won't!'

'You're hurting me.'

'You told your mother you'd stay!'

'Let me go.'

'You gave your word!'

'I was twelve years old!'

The bell rings. A tap on the door. 'Hello, there?' Footsteps in the hallway. 'It's Joan from community services. I hope you don't mind that I let myself in.'

Joan's navy blue skirt falls just below her knees and her smart white shirt is crisp. She's in her sixties with silvery hair secured in an elaborate bun. She looks from Dad to me.

'Hello,' I manage.

'What is going on, Professor Cartwright?'

'Get out!'

She steps between me and Dad, using both of her hands to prise open his fingers. 'Let your daughter go,' she says sternly.

When I'm free, I bend my arm. 'He doesn't usually ...' I open and shut my hand. 'He doesn't always do this.'

'Get out of my house!' Dad shouts in Joan's face.

She meets his gaze calmly. 'I'm not quite ready for retirement.' When he loses his balance, she grasps his arms to steady him.

'Get out!'

'Once you're settled, I'll make a pot of tea. Phoebe has told me how you like it. A nice strong brew with milk and no sugar.'

He pulls his hand free and points at me. 'She can do it! She has to do it!'

Slowly but firmly, Joan propels him back to his chair. 'Once you've had your tea, I shall see to the dressing on your leg. When the carer arrives—' she checks her watch, '—in half an hour, we can assist you in the shower. After that, I'll make your lunch and leave you in peace until this evening.'

Joan puts cushions behind Dad's back, ignoring his complaints, and makes a call. I'm washing the dishes when she returns to the kitchen.

'Thank you, Joan.'

'There's no reason to thank me.' She unfolds a tea towel. 'This is my job, dear.'

'Thank you, anyway.'

'What a gorgeous jacaranda tree.'

Bright purple flowers dance in the breeze and carpet the ground. 'On windy days, my sisters would hold out their dresses to see how many flowers they could catch.'

Joan rests a hand on my arm. 'And you, dear? What did you do?'

I turn to her. 'What do you mean?'

'You were also a child.'

I look through the window again. 'I watched over them.'

She pushes the tea towel into my hands. 'Dry your hands and go back to work,' she says. 'I'll call you tonight and we'll have a chat.'

♘

After my last client leaves on Friday afternoon, I sit at the table in the living room and re-read Patience's email.

> *Hey Phoebe,*
>
> *Sinn has given me the all clear, so I won't have to plead our messed-up childhood and subsequent counselling as an excuse for what happened with the syndicate (this also means the navy is less likely to find out about it). Consistent with the past sixteen years, sticking up for me has made life more difficult for you (just ask Sinn). I'm sorry I've put you through this on top of everything else.*
>
> *I'll be grounded when we get back to Sydney (pending the hearing of Grantham's allegations of insubordination).*
>
> *What a shit year.*
>
> *Love, Patience*

Wickham jumps to his feet and follows me into the kitchen, but goes back to his bed when I top up my hot chocolate and return to my laptop.

> *Hi Patience and Prim,*
>
> *I can't wait to see you both at Christmas.*
>
> *In the meantime ... the nurse who's taken over Dad's care is, no exaggeration, a reincarnated Florence Nightingale. In less than a week, she's sorted out his medical care, meals and cleaning. He's very unhappy, but Joan thinks it's better I stay away for the next few weeks*

to see whether he can settle in to the new routine. If he can't, and his
health gets worse, he'll have to go into a nursing home.

I feel guilty, but I don't think there's another way to handle it.
Mike has just pulled up! Lottie is back!
Love Phoebe

When I open the picket gate, Lottie skips into her garden as if she's never been away. Her wool has grown, but she's still very small and far thinner than she was.

'Thanks for bringing her home, Mike.'

'Gus's dogs couldn't wait to get rid of her, and neither could Gus. He says you can supplement her grazing with a handful of grain pellets until she puts on weight.'

'I will. And when Lottie has a proper fleece, I'll knit you and Gus a pair of socks.'

'We'll hold you to that.' Taking off his hat, he peers at me closely. 'You okay, Phoebe?'

I sigh. 'Have you been talking to Mandy again?'

'She said it's something to do with that Norway bloke. Where's he been the past few weeks? Gus reckons he's broke your heart.'

'We're not all like Gus and his Maggie.'

'Some things we can change, others we can't.' He pats his chest and Wickham jumps up. 'Wickham here—' he ruffles the fur around the dog's neck, '—with no herding gene, he couldn't do the job he was bred for. Lottie's the same. She had a bad start to life, and she's a bit on the stunted side. She don't fit in neither.'

'Are you saying I don't fit in?'

'I'm saying you're different from Wickham and Lottie.' He scratches behind Wickham's ear. 'I've been a blacksmith ever since I were a lad. If a horse gets a stone stuck in its hoof, fix the problem and it'll be sound.'

'My problem is fixable?'

'If your problem's from Norway, I reckon it might be. Jeremiah's a good judge of people and he thinks a lot of him.' He gestures to Lottie's palace. 'Any fool can see he knows a hammer from a wrench. If you're willing, he could be worth a second look.'

The sun is low in the sky by the time Mike drives away. Beyond the palest of moons, there are translucent clouds and a sprinkling of stars.

Sinn will be back next Saturday. Do I want to see him?

Will he want to see me?

CHAPTER

41

In heels and a fitted blue dress, I walk past the crowded bar at the Denman Hotel to the stairs that lead to the function room. The photographs on the landing are just as I remember them. Camelot as a newborn foal. His nose in front in a photo finish. Ears pricked, eyes bright, galloping through the rain in a storm.

'Phoebe! Wait up!'

I turn and face Martin, my smile a little uncertain. 'I wasn't sure whether you'd be here or not.'

He takes the stairs two at a time. 'Who'd dare turn down an invitation from the Oldfield sisters without a jolly good reason? Why are you hovering? Not waiting for Tørrissen, I trust? Elizabeth tells me that's well and truly over.'

When I look away he puts a hand on my arm. 'Have I put my foot in it? My sincerest apologies.'

'No, it's … It was never serious.'

He nods sympathetically. 'Your father dragged you into this syndicate palaver through no fault of your own. I imagine it's not only Tørrissen you'll be glad to see the back of.'

'The palaver isn't over yet, but yes, I'll be happy when it is.'

'I've been meaning to get in touch about Brent Green. I was horrified when I heard he'd assaulted you. Horrified.'

I nod stiffly. 'He didn't do you any favours, either.'

'I know we're not supposed to talk about it,' he says quietly, 'but have you heard what they're saying? That Brent gave my details to all and sundry? Let some stranger splash my name around in emails. Mind you, since Brent won't talk, they can't prove any of it.'

'Sinn told you this?'

'I must admit he was fair about it. He's cleared me and the rest of the genuine members.'

'You didn't do anything wrong.'

'True enough.' Martin grimaces. 'Bit of a shame though, given Brent was a damned fine stud manager.' He glances at the photos. 'Ah! I should have known you'd be looking at these.'

'I had no idea they were here until I came to Elizabeth's party.'

'We could hardly display them at Roxburgh Estate.'

'Did you run out of wall space in the pool room?'

'Not quite.' He grimaces. 'Robbie had them done for your twenty-third birthday.'

'What?'

'You broke up after he'd ordered them. He thought it was bad enough giving you the horse; hanging the pictures at home would just rub salt into the wound.'

'I paid for Camelot.'

'Well, yes, but …' He fidgets with his tie.

'What, Martin?'

'Robbie didn't tell you?' He smiles. 'In that case, my son might be more of a gentleman than I've given him credit for.'

'I appreciate the owner sold him for far less than he was worth, but—'

'How much did you pay? Two thousand?' He laughs. 'We knew he lacked a winning temperament the minute we put a saddle on him, but a career in Division Two was more than feasible.'

'The owner wanted a good home.'

'As an untested show horse he was worth at least twenty, twenty-five thousand. As a racehorse, he was worth far more. And he would have been sold for it, if not for Robbie's intervention.'

I'm suddenly uneasy. 'Brent hinted at something like that.'

Martin leans in closer. 'Robbie had a pal, Amir. Did you ever meet him? He and Robbie played polo together. He wasn't particularly talented on horseback, but with money no object, he had the best ponies money could buy. Represented his country I think.'

'He was tall and thin, wasn't he? Longish dark hair. We met a couple of times at Roxburgh Estate.'

'He fancied himself as the Middle Eastern version of a young Hugh Grant.' Martin winks. 'Charm in spades, deep pockets and good with the ladies.'

I'm suddenly light-headed. 'What did he have to do with Camelot?'

'Are you sure you want to hear this?'

'Yes!' I lower my voice. 'Yes, please.'

'Camelot's owner was a company, but one of the chaps behind it, Sheikh something or other, was the head of a wealthy family. Robbie's pal Amir was a distant relative of the sheik—second or third cousin, once or twice removed.' He looks more closely at the racing photo. 'Amir prided himself on being some kind of agent for his cousin, but Robbie always laughed about that, claimed Amir had no idea what a day of work looked like.'

'You haven't explained, Martin. How does Camelot fit in?'

He takes his glasses from his pocket and peers at the photo more closely. 'That's at Rosehill, I think. The spring racing carnival around seven years ago. They'd resurfaced the track a few months earlier, but the drainage wasn't right. Night before the race, it rained cats and dogs. That race was about the only time that horse of yours picked up his feet.'

'Martin? Are you saying Robbie paid something for Camelot too? I would never have taken him if I'd known.'

'I'm saying no such thing—Robbie never had that sort of money. It was Amir. He said if you paid the two grand you had, he'd chip in the balance.'

'How much?'

'Forty-eight thousand.'

'What?'

'Amir was well paid by that cousin of his. Never met the man, but he was apparently rich as Croesus.'

'I barely knew Amir.' My voice is high and thin. 'Why would he do that?'

'Middle Eastern men, Phoebe—' Martin looks around as if someone might be listening, '—they don't like to lose face. The sheikh had paid a fortune for Camelot. On the one hand, he wanted to put that behind him. On the other, he was adamant he be paid a fair price—what the horse was currently worth. Amir, by topping up the amount you could pay, not only gave the sheikh his market price, but helped Robbie out. Amir thought a lot of Robbie; they were pals for years.'

I stare at the images without really seeing them. 'Brent knew about the arrangement, didn't he? That's why he told me how lucky I'd been.'

'When Brent brought Camelot back to Denman, he was negotiating with a number of potential buyers. As it happened, the buyer turned out to be you. Brent ran the office, as you know. He would likely have had something to do with the money side of things.'

The first time I saw Camelot at Roxburgh Estate, I asked Robbie why he was there with the broodmares, colts, fillies and other young horses newly broken in. When he asked whether I'd like him, I laughed. 'As if I'd ever have that sort of money?'

Within a few weeks, he was mine.

'Why didn't Robbie tell me?'

'You wouldn't have taken him, would you?'

'Of course not!'

He smiles. 'Robbie knew that. Though, as I said before, I'm amazed he didn't throw it in your face after you left him. Then again …' He shuffles his feet. 'Robbie always had a soft spot for you. I suspect he still does.'

'I should have known.'

'But you didn't. And frankly, as Robbie's never raised it, I shouldn't have said anything myself.'

I dredge up a smile. 'We can't do much about that now, Martin. Don't worry about it.'

'You're right.' He slaps his hands together. 'The owner was happy, you were happy, Robbie was happy. And it was all done and dusted years ago.'

A couple walks past, Beatrice's neighbours. When they open the door to the function room, laughter, chatter and the sound of clinking glasses filters down the stairs. Martin holds out a hand for me to precede him.

'About time we went up.' He winks. 'You look lovely, by the way.'

Feeling sick and jittery, I glance at the photos again. Brent denied he knew about them, even though he would have. He made digs about Camelot's price. On the day he grabbed my arm, he said I should forget what I'd seen at Roxburgh Estate. I feel for my phone in my bag. It might be nothing, but … does Sinn know about Amir and this second or third cousin, once or twice removed? He's back tomorrow. Even if he weren't, I'd have to tell—

'Phoebe, my dear.' Beatrice appears and kisses both my cheeks. 'I'm told you can't stay, but Elizabeth and I were delighted you could come at all.' Her dress is layered and floaty and she smells of expensive perfume.

I scrabble in my bag for her gift. 'Happy birthday.'

'You shouldn't have.'

'It's only something small.'

She links her arm through mine as we walk across the room. 'There's someone else who'll be delighted to see you. You recall William from our weekend away at Roxburgh Estate? He's been waiting patiently for you to arrive …'

♘

As other guests drink, eat canapés and talk about racing and politics, I glance regularly at my watch and count down the hour until, finally, after thanking Beatrice and Elizabeth, I'm given their blessing to leave. I dart down the stairs, barely glancing at the pictures of Camelot. The crowd at the bar has spilled onto the footpath, so it's only after I weave through them that I see him, leaning against my car and looking down at his phone, typing with his thumbs. I can't see his face but I know it by heart. Clever eyes, high cheekbones, a serious sensual mouth.

'Sinn.'

He pockets the phone and looks up. 'I said you shouldn't come,' he says.

'I'm glad I did.' I lift my chin. 'It's probably irrelevant, but there's something you should know.'

'What?'

'I spoke to Martin. He said Camelot's original owner had connections to someone from the Middle East and—'

'I told Roxburgh to keep his mouth shut.'

'He was aware of that.'

'Did you talk about Green?'

'Only briefly, but—'

'Why?'

'Will you let me finish a sentence?'

'Let me finish this fucking assignment!'

I take a step back. 'You want to move on. To get back to Norway.'

'Yes.'

'Can I tell you what I found out?'

'Can I believe you?'

The tension in his jaw, the darkness of his eyes. He's angry, but this anger, his anger, is nothing like my father's. It saddens me, but it doesn't scare me.

I'm not sure who is more surprised when my hand goes to his cheek. My little finger lies on his pulse. Beneath my palm, his jaw is cleanly shaven.

His eyes close briefly. 'Phoebe.'

'When did you get in?' My voice is high and shaky. 'Did you have a shower in Sydney again? Before you flew to Dubbo? Did you come here from the airport? You must be tired.'

'I had to come.'

My heart is flipping somersaults. 'Brent's name came up because I was looking at the photos of Camelot. Martin said something about his sale and that led to other things.'

Sinn shakes his head. 'I can't do this.' His hand goes to my waist.

Desire, a wild thing, burns through my veins. 'What?'

'My assignment.' His hand slides to my hip. 'And you.'

I sway, leaning into him. My breasts touch his chest. 'Nate said you took your eyes off the ball. You didn't like that, did you?'

His head dips. He presses his cheek against mine. 'No.'

I shut my eyes. 'You don't trust me.'

He stills for a moment. 'No.'

My hand drops to my side. I take a step back. 'You've never wanted my help.'

'You pulled me into your life. Then you forced me out of it.'

My throat is dry, my brain is mush. My words are all caught up.

I'm sorry.

I love you.

Stay with me forever.

A breeze shoots through the night. A raindrop falls. After Sinn walks away, I slip behind the wheel of my car. His back is straight, his stride is long, his hands are deep in his pockets.

The windscreen wipers scrape on the glass, blurring the drizzle and dust. He's hurt. He's cranky. He doesn't trust me. And he didn't give me the chance to tell him about Amir.

But I'll try to help him anyway.

CHAPTER

42

It's only four in the morning, but I open the curtains, lean against the bedhead and turn off the lamp. Lottie's picket fence. The buckles on Camelot's rug. Mintie's silver tail. The trunk of the grey gum and the pale creamy glow of the clouds. I've learnt how to search for the light.

Once the sun comes up, I ride Camelot to the fire trails, clean up the yards, hang out a basket of washing and write two reports, but it's still only nine when I pass through Denman and turn off the highway. The entrance pillars at Roxburgh Estate are wide and tall and the car thumps over the cattle grate. Occasional raindrops spot my windscreen as I drive slowly past the broodmares, many with foals by their sides. At the fork to Robbie's land, the driveway dips to the river.

The house—glass, concrete, steel and painted render—is built into a slope and screened by shrubs and trees. At the end of the long driveway two four-wheel drives are parked in front of the closed garage doors. One of the cars looks identical to the car Nate had when he stayed at the church. It could be another hire car.

I pull over next to the shrubs at the top of the driveway and take out my phone.

Nate answers straight away. 'Hey, Phoebe. How're you doing?'

'Fine, thanks. You don't happen to be at Roxburgh Estate, do you? At Robbie's house?'

'Whoa, there. Robbie's house?'

'I thought it might be your car. I didn't want to interrupt.'

'Interrupt what?'

Two men walk around the side of the house. Another one follows. They're in their late twenties or early thirties, big and muscly.

'If it's not you, there's nothing to worry about. I'll see you—'

'Wait! Stay on the line, Phoebe.' Papers rustle. A door slams. 'How about you tell me why you're there?'

One of the big men talks into a phone. The second man points to my car, then he and the third man walk up the driveway towards me. All the men are dressed in pants and identical black polo shirts. They look like nightclub bouncers.

'I was going to tell Sinn about this, but he was a bit …' I unbuckle my belt. 'He had other things to think about. Last night, Martin said something about Camelot. I don't know that it'll be anything relevant to you, but it's important to me and I want to confirm things with Robbie.'

Muffled voices. Then, 'You're on speaker, aren't you? You're still in your car?'

'Yes.'

'That's good, Phoebe, real good. Because I want you to turn around.'

One of the men walks to the back of my car. The second one approaches from the front. He stares through the window as he opens my door.

'I have to go, Nate. Talk to you soon.'

I switch my phone to silent and put it in my pocket before stepping out of the car.

The man who opened the door has a piercing—a gold ring through his eyebrow. When he crosses his arms, his biceps bulge. 'This is private property.'

'I'm a friend of Robbie's. Is he at home? I'm Phoebe Cartwright.'

The man puts his phone to his ear and grunts my name and yes and no into it before leading me along a paved path that runs down one side of the house.

Robbie sits at a round table in a spacious courtyard surrounded by earthenware pots. Giant cycads with long strappy leaves burst from the pots like fountains. He doesn't look up from a thick wad of documents until I get close. His smile is reserved as he stands and kisses my cheek.

'It's great to see you.' He glances at his watch. 'But I'm about to leave for Sydney.'

'The house looks fantastic. You must be really pleased with it.'

A fourth man, taller than the others but also bulky and dressed in the same outfit, comes to the table with a jug of water and glasses, setting them out before returning to the house.

Robbie waves a hand, gesturing that I sit. 'Sorry I don't have time to show you around.'

'Martin said you were here for the week.'

The man with the brow ring sits on a chair close by and rests his feet on a pot. The other two sit at a large table near a stainless steel barbecue.

'Are you running a nightclub here?' I ask. When Robbie raises his brows, I lower my voice. 'Why do you have bouncers?'

He barks a laugh. 'I wish. They're security, top notch. Cost me a fortune.'

I fill our glasses. 'Can I ask why?'

'Sinn Tørrissen.'

'Martin doesn't need bouncers. Why do you?'

'Good question.' When he leans back, the front legs of his chair lift off the ground. 'And here's another one. What brings you back?'

'I heard something last night, at Beatrice Oldfield's party in Denman. I wanted to find out whether it was true. It's about Camelot.'

When he sits forward, his chair lands hard, scraping the pavers.

The security man takes his feet from the pot. 'All okay, boss?'

Robbie nods brusquely. He turns back to me. 'What about him?'

'How much was he sold for?'

He smiles stiffly. 'Exactly what you paid for him.'

'I heard you had a friend who did a deal with the owner.'

'You got that from Dad, didn't you?' Robbie stands so quickly that his thigh hits the table. 'He has no idea what he's talking about.'

I steady the water jug. 'Why so defensive?'

He stretches out his fingers. 'You'd be on edge too, Phoebe, having Tørrissen sniffing around, asking questions.'

'Brent said something similar. He was afraid.'

'I might be cautious—' he glances towards the bouncers, '—but I have nothing to hide.'

'And nothing to tell me about Camelot?'

'You got it.'

The security man with the pierced brow gets up and stands, legs apart, with his hands behind his back. His gaze goes from Robbie to me.

'Do I get escorted to my car?' I say, pushing back my chair and getting to my feet. 'You said you needed security because of Sinn, but you didn't explain why.'

'I thought you and Tørrissen were over.' Robbie crosses his arms. 'Did he send you?'

'He doesn't even know that I'm here.'

We both startle at the sound of a high-pitched whistle coming from the front of the house. There's an answering whistle from the barbecue area. The man with the piercing picks up his phone. When he jerks a thumb, the other two sprint down the path, shoes thumping loudly on the pavers.

'Robbie?' I say. 'What's going on?'

'Boss?' The man still has his phone to his ear. 'You expecting visitors?'

'No. Who is it?'

'No dramas. We can handle them.'

'I've got to get going,' Robbie says, as he stacks his documents. He checks his phone before looking impatiently across the table. 'Phoebe?'

I was his ice princess, reserved and self-contained. He liked to have sex with me. He didn't care that it hurt. Maybe he liked that part of it best? How could I have believed that I was in love with him? How could I have believed that he was in love with me?

'I get the message,' I say. 'But if you do remember anything about Camelot—'

The back doors fly open. A string of expletives. Sinn, a bouncer hanging from each arm, crashes into the courtyard. One of the bouncers, the tall man, drags a leg and the other man is bleeding from a cut on his mouth. Sinn looks left and right. Our eyes lock.

'Get inside,' he orders.

The man with the bleeding mouth swings an arm, catching Sinn on the side of the face. Sinn kicks out, striking the man's hip and propelling him across the pavers. The tall man, so large that he blocks my view, turns to attack Sinn. I hear a curse and the thud of a fist.

'Phoebe!' Sinn says, louder this time. 'Go!'

Robbie backs away as the man with the piercing runs across the courtyard. He roars like a lion as he approaches Sinn, hitting him hard in the stomach. Sinn bends double and holds his side.

I pick up a chair, holding it in front of me. 'Leave him alone!'

When the tall man leans over Sinn, Sinn jerks upwards, striking him with the back of his head. With a groan, the man grabs his jaw and drops to the ground, rolling clear before crawling away.

Rubbing his head, Sinn faces the man with the piercing, hands bunched in front of his face.

I tighten my grip on the chair. 'Get away from him!'

'Phoebe!' Sinn shouts. 'Get back!'

I run across the courtyard holding the chair seat to my chest but the man with the piercing grabs the legs and jerks it forward and back.

'Fuck off!' he screams as he lifts the chair higher and swings it and me in an arc; the cycads pass in a nauseating blur.

'Phoebe!' Sinn's voice from somewhere behind me. 'Let go!'

When the man lifts the chair again, jerking it free of my grasp, I shoot across the courtyard towards Sinn. He grabs me around my middle and pulls me against his chest.

The man throws the chair across the courtyard and raises his fists. His lip is puffy.

My breaths are loud and frantic. 'Robbie! Tell them to stop!'

Robbie is only metres away, standing with the barbecue at his back. His lips form a word: *Enough*. But nobody hears it.

Sinn steps in front of me. 'Stay!'

The bodyguard dodges and weaves around Sinn, but falters when Sinn kicks him in the thigh. Sinn grabs him by the throat, lifts a knee to his stomach and, as the man crumples, hits him in the side of the head. Groaning and cursing, the man rolls onto his side.

'Nate!' Sinn shouts. 'Get out here!'

A few seconds later, Nate pushes a man with shoulders even broader than his into the courtyard. The man's arm is twisted behind his back and his eye is swollen. When Nate trips him up, he falls heavily to the ground.

'No more, mate,' the man says, as he puts his hands above his head.

Nate positions a foot between the man's shoulder blades. 'Move a muscle, *mate*, and I'll break your neck.'

'Nate?' My voice is a squeak.

He grins. 'Hey, Phoebe.' His shirt is hanging out. His hair is messed up. 'Didn't I tell you to turn your car around?'

Sinn puts his hand on my arm. 'Are you all right?' He has blood on his knuckles, a graze on his cheek.

'I didn't—' I lift a hand and drop it. 'I didn't expect that.'

His eyes are unreadable. He takes my hands and opens them. Head bowed, he runs his thumbs over the lines the chair left on my palms.

The tall man leans against a pot, opening and shutting his mouth with a hand on the side of his face. The man with the piercing has his knees to his chest and is rocking back and forth. The man with the bleeding mouth rubs his hip. Nate's man is prostrate at his feet.

'I'll round up the posse,' Nate says cheerfully to Robbie, still standing at the barbecue. 'And then we'll have a chat.'

Nate follows me into the kitchen where I search the cupboards and fridge, finding four bottles of water for the bouncers and a few clean tea towels. When I add two icepacks to the supplies, he rolls his eyes.

'We didn't do permanent damage.'

'I had no idea you could fight.'

He grins. 'I had no idea Sinn could fight so *good*.'

'Why did you come?'

He indicates Sinn who, now he's washed his hands, is studying his phone. 'Reckon he can't keep away.'

My hands are flat on the bench. My nails are brushed clean. Sinn brushed them once, a lifetime ago. 'He wants to finish his assignment,' I say.

Nate opens the door and stands back. 'You reckon Robbie knows anything?'

'Like Brent, I think he might be scared of something.'

He taps his nose with a finger. 'Let's have a bit of fun with him.'

Robbie sits at the table nursing his glass. Sinn and I sit opposite. After Nate hands the supplies to the bouncers, lined up in a row between two pots, he sits next to Robbie and stretches out his legs.

'What happened back there,' he drawls, 'that wasn't real welcoming.'

'You were asked to go and you refused,' Robbie says. 'You not only trespassed, you assaulted my employees.'

I bang my glass on the table. 'You said I could come in.'

He nods stiffly. 'They didn't go after you.'

'Phoebe?' Sinn touches the bruise on his cheek. 'You told Nate you had to find out about Camelot. What did you mean?'

'I'm not sure that it's relevant to you, but Robbie had a friend called Amir—I don't know his last name. He was a few years older than Robbie, and I met him a couple of times at Roxburgh Estate.'

'He was an acquaintance,' Robbie says.

'You'd known him for years. When I saw Martin last night, he—'

'Dad drinks too much,' Robbie says. 'He gets confused.'

I push my glass away before bringing it closer again. 'Martin told me that buying Camelot wasn't the straightforward purchase I'd imagined. Brent hinted at that too.' I wrap my hands around the glass. 'Camelot was owned by a company, but Martin said a sheikh, a wealthy man from the Middle East, was behind that company. I knew Camelot was worth far more than I'd paid, but I was told the owner's primary concern was finding him a good home. It was only last night I found out that, while I paid two thousand dollars to the owner, Amir paid forty-eight.'

Nate whistles. 'Some acquaintance you got there, Robbie.'

'Amir had money to burn.'

Nate takes out his phone and his thumbs fly over the screen. 'Must've got something back for it.'

Robbie slaps the table. 'Not from me!'

'Phoebe,' Sinn says. 'Go on.'

'Martin said Amir was a relative of the sheikh, a cousin a few times removed. He said Amir worked for this man as some sort of agent. He was doing the sheikh a favour by buying his horse at market price and he was doing Robbie a favour because he wanted Camelot for me.'

After Nate shows Sinn something on his screen, he turns to Robbie. 'Amir Ashraf al-Sharif is related to Sheikh Mohammed bin Said. Is this the man we're talking about?' He pushes his phone across the table. 'He played polo for Saudi Arabia.'

Robbie glances at an image. 'That's him,' he says, 'but I never met the sheikh.'

'A Saudi racehorse owner. Amir. And you.' Nate rolls his shoulders. 'Links between our target and the Roxburgh syndicate are multiplying.'

Robbie fills his glass from the jug. 'Is the sheikh your target?'

'No comment,' Nate says.

'Yeah,' Robbie says. 'And the same goes for me. I had nothing to do with the syndicate.'

'Let's backtrack a little.' Nate leans back in his chair. 'At the time Martin set up the syndicate, Brent Green was newly divorced and had lost his property. He was also in debt, which is how he ended up working for Martin. Professor Cartwright was appointed to set up the syndicate, manage it and do the books. The syndicate was all above board—Martin, Elizabeth and the others were out and proud about it.'

'When Amir got involved,' Sinn says, speaking so quietly that I barely hear him, 'everything changed.'

'Brent won't admit to giving Martin's personal details away,' Nate says, 'but we're certain that he did. We also know Cartwright allowed someone else to join the syndicate. Factor in Amir and all the ducks would line up.'

'Would my father have known what was going on?'

'We think he was engaged by a third person, identity untraceable, and didn't look beyond what he was asked to do. It was one of the benefits of having him on board. He didn't ask questions. He was never going to talk.'

'Robbie.' Sinn leans forward, his elbows on the table. 'Tell us what happened with Camelot.'

'Phoebe bought him after the syndicate was wound up.'

Nate and Sinn exchange glasses. 'That'd fit,' Nate says.

'Fit what?' Robbie says. 'How is Camelot relevant?'

'After the syndicate folded,' Sinn says, 'our target, through Amir, would've wanted ...' He rubs his temple. He turns to Nate. 'What is the expression?'

'Amir would've been told to get insurance,' Nate says, 'a guarantee that, if questions were ever asked about the infiltrated syndicate, you and Martin wouldn't talk.'

'If you did talk,' Sinn says, 'Amir's contribution to Camelot's price could be framed to look like a kickback, or hush money.'

'That's how—' Nate nods towards Robbie, '—you got a forty-eight thousand buck favour.'

'Bullshit!' Robbie says. 'I don't know anything about this! Phoebe is Cartwright's daughter and she got the horse. I'm no more a crook than she is.'

Sinn's hand is close to mine on the table. He turns it palm up. 'Phoebe had nothing to do with her father's work. She didn't know about Amir's payment for the horse.'

'What about Amir?' Robbie says. 'Why don't you go after him?'

'When did you last see him?' Sinn asks.

'Years ago,' Robbie says.

'That figures,' Nate says, glancing at his phone again. 'According to official records, he's disappeared.'

'What do you mean? What are you getting at?'

'Money laundering is a dirty business. Is "disappeared" a euphemism for "murdered"?' Nate lifts his hands. 'Who am I to say?'

Robbie flushes. He looks from Sinn to Nate. 'According to you, Amir was a link between the syndicate and your target. What does his death do to your case?'

'What it does,' Nate says, 'is to make us real curious. If Amir isn't keeping you up at night, who is?'

Robbie stands but when Nate stands too, towering over him, Robbie slumps into his chair again. 'All right,' he says. He drinks from his glass, swishing the water around in his mouth. 'I suspected Brent knew something.'

'What?' Nate says, sitting again.

'From the moment you two turned up, he was as jumpy as hell. He blamed me for bringing Amir to Roxburgh Estate, he ranted about it. It wasn't too hard to guess he had something to hide.'

'Be more specific,' Nate says.

Robbie glances at the bouncers. 'Brent had it in his head that the guy you were after, your sheikh or target or whatever you want to call him, was dangerous. He also said you two could be trouble, big trouble, for him and for me. But that added up, didn't it? When you went to parties and made small talk about arms deals.'

'We want your cooperation, and Brent's,' Sinn says. 'Like you said before, we need to link our target, via Amir, to the Roxburgh syndicate.'

'Get fucked.'

'The target has been on INTERPOL's radar for years,' Nate says. 'They needed hard evidence and, over the past six months, we've given it to them—enough to put him away.'

'So why harp on about the Roxburgh syndicate?'

'We want as many nails in his coffin as we can get. The syndicate not only goes back ten years, it gives us documentation. The target didn't hide his tracks as well as he could have.'

Robbie shakes his head. 'Why would I take some Saudi prick on?'

'We can protect you until we have him.'

'I won't take that chance, not when I'm innocent. So far as I knew, Amir paid for Camelot because we were friends.' He looks past the others to me. 'To make Phoebe happy, I accepted.'

'You know I wouldn't have wanted that!'

'I was in love with you.'

'Stop it!'

'Tørrissen knows what happens.'

Sinn's eyes narrow. 'Shut up.'

'She burrows under your skin, doesn't she, mate?' Robbie lifts his glass and, with a finger, draws a heart shape in the condensation. 'I wanted to be different from the others—I would've done anything for her.'

I grip the table. 'Be quiet!'

'And d'you know what hurts most?' He wipes through the heart, obliterating it. 'I was wasting my time. She doesn't have it in her to love a man back.'

I suck in a breath. I swallow.

Silence.

'Robbie, Robbie, Robbie ...' Nate says as he picks up his chair and turns it around. He sits and straddles the chair. 'How about we backtrack again?'

Robbie swears under his breath. 'What now?'

'Tell us more about Amir.'

'When I was twenty-one, I met him in New York. He came to Australia a few times, we played polo together. He was a guest at Roxburgh Estate.'

'You never met his cousin, the sheikh?'

'I've already said no to that.'

'You agree that Amir paid forty-eight thousand for Camelot? The money was transferred to the owner, a company controlled by the sheikh?'

'So far as I know.'

'Oh!' I'm barely aware of making the sound until the men turn towards me. I pull out my phone before holding it in my lap.

'I paid for Camelot too.'

Nate steeples his hands. 'We know that, Phoebe.'

'But …' I take a few deep breaths as I order my thoughts. 'Nate? You said the target didn't cover their tracks as well as they could have.'

'True.'

'I was at uni when I bought Camelot. Robbie? Do you remember how I moved Camelot to Armidale for my final prac? Brent arranged to float him for me.'

'So?'

'I was worried about taking him away, because I hadn't paid for him yet. Do you remember that too?'

He hesitates. 'Sounds like the type of thing you'd fret about.'

'Martin was selling on the owner's behalf, but Brent was in charge of Martin's office. I asked him for the owner's bank account details so I could transfer the money. When I didn't hear from Brent, I asked you to chase him up.'

'Maybe.'

'I remember …' I put my phone on the table and then back on my lap. 'I did the transfer and it seemed to be fine, but then I got a call from my bank. They said it was a valid account, but for some reason, the money had come back.'

Nate nods. 'Go on.'

'I chased Brent myself this time. He apologised for it taking so long, but he'd had trouble getting onto the owner's assistant. In the end though, she gave Brent another account. I did the transfer and didn't think any more about it.'

'Okay …'

'Right from the start, you and Sinn have been talking about bank accounts, and that's why I suddenly thought of—'

Sinn puts a hand on my arm. He glances at Nate. 'Stay with him.'

'What?' Robbie says. 'What's this all about?'

Sinn and I stand next to a pot at the rear of the courtyard, far from the security men, as we look at my phone. I don't have records of the transactions, but Sinn pretends that I do, barking fake instructions as I scroll through irrelevant messages.

'Sinn?' I keep my eyes on my phone. 'What's going on?'

He continues to study the screen before getting out his phone and sending a message. 'Ideally, we link your money to our target. If we can't, we want Robbie to think that we can.'

'Why?'

'He's a connection to Amir.'

'You didn't know about Amir, did you? I was helpful, wasn't I?'

His lip lifts. 'Yes.'

'Is the sheikh your target?'

'I can't answer that.'

'Was Amir murdered?'

He looks at his phone. 'According to Nate, his death had nothing to do with the syndicate. He had an affair with the wrong man's wife.'

'You want to scare Robbie, don't you?'

'Without Robbie and Brent, Amir's involvement is tenuous. If we can convince Robbie to cooperate, it's likely Brent will come on board. As Nate said, another nail in the coffin.' He looks towards the bouncer pressing a tea towel against his mouth. 'I saw that man in June. He drove me to Warrandale at midnight.'

'What? On the night I found you?'

His eyes slip to my mouth. 'Nate and I were at a hotel in Denman. So was Brent.'

'What happened?' When he hesitates, I touch his arm. 'You have to tell me.'

He frowns, but not for long. 'Brent was on his third bottle of wine and boasting about running Roxburgh Estate single-handed.

When he claimed he'd set up the syndicate that'd made thousands for Martin Roxburgh and Elizabeth Oldfield, I became interested. His friends had a van. I followed them out of the hotel and hid in the back.'

My breath catches. 'They discovered you were there?'

'The driver braked suddenly and I was thrown against the cab. When they slowed to investigate, I jumped.' He touches his forehead, the place where it bled. 'I rolled into a ditch and waited until they'd gone.'

'You were kilometres from the road when I found you.'

'I don't remember much.' His lip lifts. 'Except for you.'

'Sinn!' Nate calls, looking at his phone and raising his thumb. 'Great result, I got it. Are you done over there?'

As Sinn and I sit opposite Robbie and Nate at the table, Nate counts points off on his fingers. He tells Robbie his security men won't be up to the task if the target decides—as likely happened with Amir—that he should disappear. He informs him he's confident my transactions will be linked to one of the hundreds of bank accounts Sinn and he have already unearthed—which won't look good for Robbie because he not only introduced Amir to Martin, but personally negotiated Camelot's purchase from a company associated with the sheikh. Finally, he tells Robbie he had a responsibility to report his concerns about Brent.

Half an hour later, Robbie's lawyer joins him on a Zoom call and they agree that full cooperation with the UN is the best way to protect Robbie's safety and reputation. As Nate winds up the call, Sinn stands. He gingerly touches the back of his head.

'Are you okay?' I whisper.

He glances at his watch. 'You call your mother today, yes?'

I check my phone. 'Oh! It's eleven.'

He holds out his hand. 'Come.'

We're halfway to the car before I can think of anything to say. 'Martin didn't do anything wrong, did he?'

'No.'

'And, besides not telling you about Brent, Robbie didn't do anything either.'

He frowns. 'I don't like him.'

I touch his arm. 'When Brent told me to forget what I might have seen or heard at Roxburgh Estate, he could've been referring to Amir.' When I stop, Sinn does too. 'You have to go back to Saudi Arabia, don't you?'

He takes my hand and sandwiches it between his. 'I have to finish, Phoebe. After this, no more.'

'You don't like being an investigator?'

'I want something else.'

I take a deep breath. And then we walk again. 'Thank you for talking to Patience, for explaining everything.'

'Does she always shout?'

'Only when she's upset.'

'She doesn't trust men either.' He's so very serious. 'Who is Hugo?'

'They were friends years ago. But why—'

'She won't like what happened today.' He hesitates. 'I didn't either.'

'I worry too.' We reach the car and I put my hand on his arm. 'That's why I saved you.'

'With the chair?'

Another deep breath. 'I think I did better in Mr Riley's shed.'

'You will do this always?'

I'm hot and cold, a jumble of uncertainty. 'When will you be back?' I lift my hand and his jaw clenches. Does he want me to touch him or not? 'Sinn?'

He captures my hand and threads our fingers together. He kisses my knuckles one by one. I lay my other hand against the side of his face. When he turns his head, the bruise on his cheek presses on my palm. His heartbeats crash against my breast.

A flock of cockatoos flies overhead. I smooth the collar of his crinkled linen shirt. I find his pulse.

'You'd better get back to Nate.'

'Yes.'

His eyes are grey, the dusky skies of winter. I stand on my toes and press my mouth against his. A touch. A promise.

'I'll wait for you to come back.'

CHAPTER

43

When Nate's call comes through late on Tuesday afternoon, I pause
at the graveyard's wrought iron gate. Delicate alyssum flowers, purple, white and sweetly scented, dance around Anna Amelia's cross.

'Hi, Nate.'

'Hey, Phoebe Cartwright.'

'How are you?'

'Pretty flat out.'

'Where are you?'

'Thirty thousand feet in the air, but I'll be in Geneva for breakfast. How's Lottie?'

'Eating like a horse. You're in a plane?'

'Satellite call.' He yawns. 'Have you noticed a car parked out the
front of the church?'

'With tinted windows? Two men? There've been a procession of
cars since I got back on Sunday.'

'I should've warned you earlier.'

'Jeremiah checked them out for me.'

'Good thinking. What'd they tell him?'

'That they'd been sent by you and they were the good guys.'
Wickham doubles back from the end of the path and sits at my feet.
'I offer them sustenance, but they always say no.'

'I warned them about your coffee.'

I laugh. 'How much longer will they be here?'

'It was a precaution. I'll pull them out tomorrow.'

'When will you arrest the target?'

'INTERPOL and the local authorities picked him up yesterday.
He's out of circulation, hopefully for good.'

'Was your target the sheikh? Amir's second cousin once or twice
removed?'

'Check out the media in a week or two. You'll get the gist of it
then.'

I brush cobwebs from Anna Amelia's cross. 'Are you happy with
how everything's turned out?'

'We got a statement from Robbie, confirming Brent was scared
about Amir and us. Robbie also remembered answering Amir's
questions about the syndicate. He told Amir it was your father who
managed it. Amir would've passed that on.'

'You said a third party got in touch with Dad.'

'It's ancient history, Phoebe. Your father is beyond punishment
and we've got what we want.'

I clear leaves from Mary's grave. 'What about Patience?'

'The authorities have zero interest.'

I close my eyes, release a breath. 'Did Brent give you a statement?'

'After we'd told him about Robbie's evidence, he sang like a
canary. Told us he sold Martin's details for ten thousand bucks, but
denied knowing why Amir wanted the information.'

'He must have known it had value.'

'Amir gave him a cock and bull story about using Martin as a referee and not wanting to trouble him, but Brent's professed ignorance rings true. He didn't want to know.'

I crouch by Reverend Brockman's grave. 'He knew enough to be rattled when you and Sinn turned up.'

'In one of our early chats with Martin, we hinted that we were looking into possible links between wealthy racehorse owners—some of them his clients—and the syndicate. When Brent got wind of it, he connected the dots. He feared the information he'd sold to Amir might come back to bite him.'

'He called it an indiscretion.' I trace the reverend's birthdate, inscribed in the granite. 'Will he get into trouble for it?'

'He's small fry to us, and your police have got better things to do. The assault conviction will teach him a lesson and karma will get him for the rest.'

Camelot, head up and long black tail held high, trots to the fence on the boundary. 'The money Amir paid for Camelot. I don't like the thought of it.'

'It might never have been paid, and even if it was, it was done to hold something over Robbie and Martin. Don't give it another thought.'

I'm suddenly teary. 'I'll miss you, Nate.'

'Tor and Golden will need a babysitter—I've told them I've been practising on Lottie.' There's a smile in his voice. 'I'll see you and Lottie in February.'

'The morning we met ...' I hold tightly to the phone. 'The lieutenant said I could trust Sinn. That's right, isn't it?'

The plane's intercom hums in the background. 'We'll be crazy busy for another week or two, finishing this thing off.'

'Is he still in Saudi Arabia?'

'A few more days, then he flies to Geneva. He'll be in touch.'

CHAPTER
44

In the ten days since I spoke to Nate, I've received four texts from Sinn. My responses to his texts have contained a few more words, but little more meaning.

You okay? Did Nate explain?
Nate explained, and yes, I'm fine. I hope you're well too.

Arrived in Geneva this morning. You okay?
Nate said you'd go there. All well here. Please be careful.

Lottie okay?
She's very well, thank you. It's raining again.

I got a follow-up text to that one.

La Niña.

Saxon undoes his own seatbelt and bolts from Kelly's car, running across the garden and lying on his stomach in the long wet grass. As Kelly struggles to lift him, Lottie, grazing outside her palace, raises her head.

I crouch next to Saxon. 'Hello, sweetheart. You love the rain, don't you? Just like Camelot. But we have a lot to do inside, and Wickham is waiting for you. Look—' I point, '—there he is.'

Saxon laughs as he scrambles to his feet. 'Wickham!'

Kelly takes Saxon's hand as he skips along between us. When I pass her a towel, she wraps it around her son and he laughs again, pressing his head against her stomach before charging into the house and throwing himself on the couch, burrowing into the cushions.

She burrows under your skin, doesn't she, mate?

I was never in love with Robbie. I am in love with Sinn. But what good is that if he doesn't come back?

'Saxon!' Kelly sits next to her son and pulls off his shoes. 'You're too wet to play on the furniture.'

I kneel by the couch. 'His neuropsychologist called yesterday, and I spoke to his psychiatrist this morning. Are you comfortable with their diagnosis?'

'Autism, ADHD and associated sensory processing difficulties.' She rubs Saxon's back. 'They said you're still stuck with us.'

'Never stuck, Kelly. And there's a lot more we can do.'

She sighs as Saxon buries himself more deeply into the cushions. 'You know what I want.'

'To make Saxon comfortable and safe.'

'Annabelle, too. He's still swinging from her plaits.'

'I could talk to Marion, Annabelle's mum. Would you mind? A different hairstyle might help.' I smile encouragingly as I twist my ponytail into a bun.

Kelly groans. 'Go for it.' When she wipes her phone on her jeans, it comes away wet. Saxon spins around, accidentally kicking her hip. Her eyes water as she rubs it.

'Saxon?' I take his hands, pulling him to a sitting position and holding on gently but firmly until I have his attention. 'It's time to do our activities now.'

'I'd better stay,' Kelly says.

'Why don't you go into the kitchen, and I'll call out if I need you? You know where the tea and biscuits are kept. After the session, I'll take Saxon outside. He can gambol around with Lottie before you take him home.'

'You sure?'

'Lottie's in training as a therapy sheep.' I smile. 'You and Saxon will be doing me a favour.'

U

A few hours later, I answer the door to Matilda, my last client of the day. She holds out a pink paper bag, smiling as I try to look inside.

'What do you have in there, Matilda?'

'It's a present!'

As the rain falls in drifts behind her, Jane opens and shuts her umbrella to shake off the moisture. 'Matilda can't wait to show you what she has.'

'Is it for me?' I ask Matilda.

She laughs. 'It's not for a girl!'

I glance over my shoulder. Wickham, his fur sticking up more than usual because he romped in the garden at lunchtime, is curled up in his bed. 'Is it a present for Wickham?'

'It's for Mintie!' Matilda places the bag on the ground before pulling out a bright red lead rope. She proudly pushes her fingers through the handle and grips it. 'I can hold it!'

I smile. 'You must have been practising very hard. I'm so proud of you. And next week when you visit, the sun might be shining. We can go outside and show Mintie the rope. I can clip it onto his halter and you can hold the end. You can be angels together.'

'If she doesn't have to actually touch Mintie,' Jane whispers, 'she'll do well in the nativity play.'

'Wickham wants to see the present,' Matilda says. The rope bumps along the floor as she runs towards Wickham, stopping a metre away. 'Look what I've got for Mintie!'

He sits up with interest, lifting a paw.

'Wickham! Stay.'

Jane laughs. 'Poor dog. He thought he was getting a walk.'

I lower my hand. 'Down.' A little shamefaced, Wickham curls up again. 'We'll go to the horses later.'

'And then to the pub?' Jane asks. 'I haven't seen you there in weeks.'

'I haven't had the time.'

'Or the inclination. Is it because of Sinn?'

A colourful activity mat—corduroy, velvet and satin—is laid over a chair. I run my hand over the textures. When we were at his house, Robbie ran his hand through the heart shape he drew on the table.

She doesn't have it in her to love a man back.

Sinn said he had to finish his investigation, and then, 'No more.' He said he wanted something else—but didn't say what. I talk through the discomfort in my throat.

'A while ago, I told Sinn I was better on my own. And I thought I was, but then ...' The rain twists a path down the stained glass window. 'If I don't hear from him over the weekend, I'll call. I can't go on like this.'

She tips her head to the side. 'In the meantime, it's Friday. Why don't we meet at the pub? Take a break from this miserable weather?'

'We're meant to see the sun this afternoon.'

'Before or after the thunderstorm?'

U

Once the rain eases, I pull on my waterproof jacket and trudge through the garden. Lottie's head pokes out of the door of her palace as I walk to her picket fence. When she nudges my leg, I rub beneath her fleece.

'Good afternoon, Lottie.' Her skin is warm and she's gaining weight, but she's still very small. 'Are you a horse or a dog this afternoon?'

Mintie, head bowed to the grass, grazes on the far side of the paddock near the fence. Camelot, his hooves caked with mud, is in the yard with his head hanging over the railing. When I stroke under his mane, he turns his head and nudges my side.

'Are you serious?' I look suspiciously at the sky, thick and dull with cloud. 'I suppose you could stretch your legs in Mr Riley's paddock. Thirty minutes, tops.'

Camelot, playful in the wind, prances as we walk along the road, but settles after we pass through the gate. We trot over the soggy grass to the track that leads to the dam. When a gust of wind scatters drops from the trees, I fasten the press studs at my throat. As I look up, a jagged bolt of lightning bursts through the clouds. 'Oh!'

Thunder rumbles overhead as I guide Camelot away from the gums. I can't keep away from the trees if I ride home, but the path to the shed is clear. When I push Camelot into a canter, he covers the ground in long easy strides. Gusts of wind push back my hood. Drizzle turns to rain. A white four-wheel drive is parked at the gate near the sheep pens, but there's no sign of the driver and the doors to the shed are shut. I haven't seen Mr Riley or anyone else up here since he put the farm up for sale. I slip from Camelot's back and take the reins over his head. In the back of the car, there's an overnight bag, a double-sided toolbox and a few larger items like a crowbar and shovel. As I walk to the shed, I pull up my hood. A puddle of rain runs down the back of my shirt as I reach for the …

I rub my eyes in case I'm seeing things. The bolt is shiny stainless steel. With a clunk, it slides free of the barrel. Both doors hang perfectly straight and swing on double hinges, also brand new. I anchor the doors to the outer walls with hook and eye latches that keep them securely in place.

Inside the shed, the rafters, shearing platform and rust-pitted roof look just the same. Camelot stands quietly as I tie him to the railing of the sheep pen at the back of the shed, take off his saddle and rub him over with the saddle blanket. A crack of thunder shakes the roof. When Camelot skitters, I scratch under his forelock. 'We're safe in here.'

I've almost reached the hay bales when I see the slender leather wallet, key and phone. As I pick up the wallet, it opens. Crisp banknotes. One card.

United Nations First Committee
(Disarmament and International Security)
Sindre Tørrissen

My heart skips a beat.

Skips several beats.

Slipping through the mud and weeds, I circumnavigate the shed. Nothing. And there's no sign of him on the road or in the paddocks.

By the time I run to the lane that leads to the trails, I have a stitch in my side and my breath comes in gasps.

'Phoebe!'

Sinn rolls up his sleeves and pushes back his hair as he walks purposefully towards me. His T-shirt is blue. His mouth is wet. Hair drips into his eyes.

There's an ache in my chest. A lump in my throat. Tears spring out of nowhere, flowing down my cheeks in a hot and salty mess. I swipe them away, wipe my hands down my jeans. Rivers of water gush around my boots.

He holds out a hand. 'What—'

I bunch my hands into fists and push against his chest. 'Why are you here?'

'I was working.'

'Doing what?' I push again. 'What?'

Rain spikes his lashes. He grabs my hands. 'It's okay.'

'No, it's not!' I yank my hands free and wipe a sleeve across my eyes. 'I thought … I thought …' I look behind him to the trail. 'Where did you go?'

'I didn't know you were here.'

'You drove past my house!'

We both look down when he reaches for my hands again. And I'm not sure who moves first, but our fingertips touch, and then our palms. He rubs the back of my hand with his thumb.

'I was checking the fences.'

He's safe. He's here.

I want to trust him.

Camelot, almost hidden by the shadows, nickers as we walk into the shed. I pull off my coat and shake it before throwing it over his rump and smoothing out the creases. Sinn stands at the hay bales, patiently waiting.

Finally, I turn to him. 'Why didn't you call?'

He holds out a hand and as soon as I get close, he pulls me closer. He trails kisses across my cheeks. 'Why did you cry?'

When I don't respond, he kisses my mouth, warm and wet and achingly slowly. I grasp his T-shirt and feel the contours of his chest as his hands slide over my shoulders and down my back to my bottom. He lifts my shirt and runs his hands over my skin and—

He growls as he buries his face in my neck. 'You're cold.'

'No, I'm not.' I stroke his hair, sleek and dark like a seal. 'You're wet.'

His erection is long and hard, pressed against my stomach. He eases away. 'There's something I should say.'

'Why did you take so long to come back? When did you get here?'

He pushes his wallet, key and phone aside and I sit on the bales. The rain beats a rhythm on the roof. Sitting next to me, he stares at my profile and then looks away. He leans forward and rests his forearms on his thighs.

'Sinn? When did you come back?'

'Three days ago. I didn't want to talk to you over the phone.'

A chill passes through me. I force out words: 'What did you want to say?'

He straightens and takes my hand. Pulls back the cuff of my shirt and kisses the inside of my wrist.

'Sinn?'

Bringing one of his legs onto the bales, he loops it around me, drawing me closer. He strokes my neck. Our foreheads touch.

'You said you'd wait for me,' he says. 'I can wait too.'

'What for?'

'I thought it was right. Now ... I don't want to trap you.'

His hair has grown longer. I draw away and push back his fringe. 'I don't know what you're talking about.'

'I know what I want.' He picks up my hand and draws a line across my palm. 'I can wait until you're ready.'

'For what?'

'I want to stay.'

I touch his face, the solemn seriousness of it. 'You don't know how long you can stay? Is that what you're trying to say? That worries me too, but—'

'I know how long.'

'Well?'

'I don't want to rush you.'

'Sinn.' I press shaking fingers to his cheek. 'I don't understand.'

He takes both my hands and studies them intently. As if they're new to him. As if he's never seen them before. 'When you took Lottie to Gus's farm,' he says, 'you said she'd have more room. You said it would be better for her.'

I nod slowly. 'Yes.'

'She could live at this farm.'

When he glances over my shoulder, I follow his gaze to the doors. 'Why would she—'

After I found Sinn on the track, I brought him to the shed. I used a brick to hammer the bolt and free it from the barrel. I wedged the brick between the ground and the door, afraid that it would close again. I was afraid of the dark.

The wind whistles and sings outside, but the doors stay open. 'Sinn?' I curl my legs to one side and rest my hands on his chest, feel the fast steady beats of his heart. 'You changed the fittings, didn't you?'

He nods. 'It's my door. I own it.'

'Did you buy the shed from Mr Riley?'

'You saved me here.'

Warmth, achingly sweet, threads through my veins to my heart. 'I don't think Mr Riley would have sold the shed on its own. Did you buy the land as well?'

He runs a finger down my nose. 'Yes.'

'A few hundred hectares? For Lottie?'

'I want to stay.' He traces a line around my lips. He tips up my chin. 'If that is what you want.'

The sound of his voice.

Taste of his mouth.

Scent of his skin.

Touch of his hand.

Truth in his gaze.

I wrap my arms around his neck and mumble words against his lips. 'I want you.'

CHAPTER
45

A watery sunset filters through the window as Sinn, naked and damp from the shower, walks me backwards around my bed. He nuzzles my neck. 'Why did you dress?'

I hold his shoulders to steady myself. 'It's only a nightie.'

He loops his leg through mine to trip me, then catches me as we tumble to the bed. He sprawls on top of me, pinning me down, and smothers my complaints with a kiss.

When he lifts his head, I wrap a leg around his back. 'Thank you for feeding Wickham and Lottie.'

'I love you, Phoebe.'

When I open my mouth, nothing comes out.

He rolls onto his side and traces the piping at the neck of my nightie to the V at my throat. 'I want you to trust me.'

Pushing him onto his back, I straddle him and touch his lips with a fingertip. 'I do trust you.' I run my hands possessively over his chest and brush his nipples with the backs of my hands. When I wrap my fingers around his wrists and pin his arms to the pillows, he smiles.

'Where are your tattoos, Commander Tørrissen?'

'Do you want me to get some?' he asks.

A lump forms in my throat. 'I wouldn't change anything.'

When I let go of his hands, he draws a line between my brows. He rubs with two fingers. 'What is it, Phoebe?'

I look towards the window, the emerald green grass and the soft silver sky. 'It's not usually like this, and you haven't even seen summer yet. We have droughts and dust storms and fires and …' I pull my nightie down over my legs. 'I want to spend time with you, that's what's important. I can travel too. I can—'

'I want to be here.' He runs his hands up my legs, pushing my nightie back to where it was. 'With you.'

'Your family will miss you.'

'They're twenty-four hours away. My cousins are here.'

'What will you do for work?'

'What I'm qualified for.'

'Satellites and weather and ships? Tracing bank accounts?' I touch his cheek where he was punched. 'Fighting?'

His eyes narrow. 'I'm a maritime geospatial officer in meteorology and oceanography.'

'The sea is hours away.'

'I specialise in climate. I have transferable skills.'

'They don't sound trans—'

He mutters under his breath as he lifts me and sits, leaning against the headboard. He trails kisses down my cleavage.

'I can work remotely. And on the land.'

'But—'

'We can go to Norway and see my family. I'll resign my commission. After that, we can live here.'

'Maybe you should go to sea first, to make sure—'

'Phoebe.' He pulls me against him, my back against his front, and crosses his arms over my breasts. 'I know what I want.' He kisses along my shoulder but when I try to turn, he lifts the sheet higher. 'Don't distract me.'

'I *want* to distract you. Why—'

'Look out of the window.' He rests his chin on my shoulder. 'What do you see?'

The rain is clearing; there are patches of blue among the clouds. A rainbow, ribbons long and bright, makes a bridge across the sky.

'It's beautiful.'

'Tell me the colours.'

'Are you sure we have to do this now?'

'I need to explain.' He lifts my hair and gently bites my nape. 'The colours.'

I slump against him. 'Red, orange, yellow, green, blue, indigo, violet.' He tips up my chin and kisses me. My thighs tingle, my breasts ache. 'Sinn. Please …'

His breaths are unsteady like mine. 'A rainbow is an optical illusion,' he says. 'This is a primary rainbow—'

'There's more than one kind?'

'Rainbows appear opposite the sun. When the light strikes rain, it slows. It bends and reflects in the raindrop. It's an electromagnetic spectrum, made up of light of different wavelengths refracted at different angles. Red light, the outer arch, has the longest wavelength.'

'And violet has the shortest.' I trace between his fingers, hesitating on the fourth. He loves me. He wants to stay. Does that mean—

He nuzzles my shoulder, picks up my strap with his teeth. 'Are you listening?'

I admire his neat, clean nails. I lift his hand and kiss his thumb. 'Wavelengths.'

'The antisolar point is abstract, but it connects the observer, the sun and the sky. An observer at another location will see a different rainbow. The light will be reflected off other raindrops. The angle of the rainbow will differ.'

'That's very interesting, Sinn, but—'

'To see the same rainbow, we have to be together.' He kisses my temple. 'This is why we marry.'

I hid my tears when I had nightmares. I refused to cry when Dad was cruel, when my sisters were in trouble, or when Robbie was unfaithful. But in the past few weeks ...

Sinn shoots over the sheets to sit in front of me. 'What the fuck?'

I reach for the tissues on my bedside table. 'The rainbow—' I swallow. 'I liked it.'

He runs his lips over my eyes and cheeks. His kiss on my mouth is salty and wet. I climb onto his lap and we consider the rainbow together.

'When you fed Lottie at the fete,' he says, 'I knew we belonged here.'

'What? We hadn't even kissed yet.'

'I wanted to.'

His gaze sweeps my body. He fingers the strap of my nightie and I pull it over my head. He touches my breasts with wonder. When he kisses my mouth, the strokes of his tongue are familiar and deep. Our bodies heat, our breaths tangle.

Sunset falls on his shoulders as he comes inside me. When I grasp his arms and wrap my legs around his hips, he groans. My body softens as he moves. His hands sweep down my sides and over my bottom. He touches where we're joined. Our breaths are harsh, our bodies slick. The pressure builds, the wanting and needing and craving. A mist, a shower, a downpour, a deluge. A torrent, a lashing, a tumultuous storm.

Closing my eyes, I see the colours of the rainbow.

I call his name and he calls mine.

The brightness shatters around us.

♘

He lies safely in my arms and I stroke his back. 'Are you awake?'

He yawns. 'Hmm.'

'I can see the moon through the clouds.'

'Do you want the light on?' he whispers against my breast.

'I turn it off sometimes, early in the mornings.'

'You don't have to change, Phoebe. Not for me.'

'I'm not scared like I was. And my sisters …' I trail my fingers over his shoulders. 'They've grown up. I have to accept they don't need me like they did.'

'You'll always protect them. You love them.'

The wind blows softly through the gum trees and the rain falls gently on the roof. I run my fingers through his hair. I find the pulse at his jaw. I feel the strong, steady beats of his heart.

'I love you, Sinn.'

He comes up on his elbow and searches my face. 'Always?'

Thunderstorms, rainbows, white picket fences.

Small busy children with smoky grey eyes.

Cumulus clouds, nimbus and stratus. Blue winter skies, autumnal showers. Windy spring days and warm summer nights.

'Always.'

ACKNOWLEDGEMENTS

Clouds on the Horizon is my fifth novel published by Harlequin, so once again I'd like to thank my publisher Jo Mackay and senior editor Annabel Blay. It's a privilege to work with both of you. Thank you also to my editor Kylie Mason for your thoughtful suggestions and attention to detail. To the HarperCollins team who work so hard behind the scenes in editorial, sales and marketing, in particular, Sarana Behan and Johanna Baker, many thanks for all that you do.

Thank you to writer and speech pathologist Vani Gupta, for your advice and guidance regarding the treatment of Phoebe's children. Your friendship, generosity and expertise know no bounds. Thank you also to occupational therapist and fellow writer Carrie Molachino, for your valuable feedback. To doctors Margaret and Norman Janu, thank you for answering my medical questions with your customary generosity (and good humour!). Grateful thanks also to Stine Hagen, for your assistance with Norwegian language references. Any inaccuracies or omissions in this novel are very much mine—and creative licence.

The Harlequin cover design team always do a wonderful job, but I have a particular fondness for the cover of *Clouds on the Horizon*. The photograph of the cover model was taken by the very talented Jared Lyons, and the cover model is the clever and talented actress and model Hayley Watkins. Hayley's mother Kathryn, me, and our dear friend Anne, spent many years weighed down by pregnancy, toddlers and cake, but we must have done some things right. Thank you, Hayley, for being on the cover!

Many thanks also to Karly Lane for the cover quote, and for sharing my view that attractive Norwegian naval officers should be found in thunderstorms more often. And to another fabulous author, Joanna Nell, thank you so much for your cover words. I am blessed to be supported by wonderful writers in my writing community, including Sandie Docker's Friday group, *Not So Solitary Scribes*, and my many friends in Romance Writers of Australia.

Warrandale and Horseshoe Hill are fictional, but are based on farming districts and towns in the central west of NSW. It's been a privilege to revisit the landscapes and people of this region over the past twelve months—if only in my mind. Many thanks to Dr Dominique Van der Saag for your knowledge and insights on rural veterinary matters, particularly in respect to the rearing of orphaned lambs. Thanks also to fellow writer and friend Léonie Kelsall for the perfect images of Lottie.

To my writing group, the Ink Well—Pamela Cook, Terri Green, Michelle Barraclough, Rae Cairns, Laura Boon, Angela Whitton and Joanna Nell—thank you from the bottom of my heart for your generous and invaluable writing and personal support. And particular thanks to Pam who read early chapters of this novel in our Pen2Pam sessions. While I've missed seeing all of you in person, our group chats, writing sessions and Friday Inkies Drinkies have kept the words flowing, made the difficult times less difficult, and allowed us to celebrate many milestones and achievements. I can't wait to do it all over again (in person) in 2022.

As always, thank you to Peter and our children, Philippa, Tamsin, Ben, Max, Michaela and Gabriella, for your encouragement and support. Benjamin, thank you for inspiring me to write the character Benjamin (you'll remember the pegs). Michaela and Max, while working from home you've been forced to experience more of my writing life than you might have found optimal, but I've loved having the extra time with you both and will always treasure it. Thank you to my mother Ann for her ongoing support (and for ensuring my books are stocked in her local bookshops). To my father Philip, a navigator in the air force many years ago, thank you for sharing your knowledge of cloud formations and other meteorological matters. (Any errors and omissions are definitely mine!)

Last but never least, thank you to my readers for giving me the opportunity to create the characters, settings and stories that I love to write.

Don't miss ...

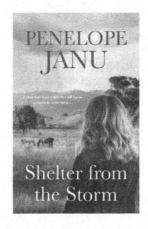

Shelter from the Storm

by

PENELOPE JANU

Available January 2023

talk about it

Let's talk about books.

Join the conversation:

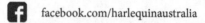 facebook.com/harlequinaustralia

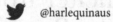 @harlequinaus

 @harlequinaus

harpercollins.com.au/hq

If you love reading and want to know about our
authors and titles, then let's talk about it.